His Death of Cold

☐

Trudi didn't answer but went across to the freezer, pressed down the handle, and pulled. The door didn't budge.

"He really was security conscious," said Janet. "Even protected his fish fingers. Come on, girl, let's go."

Obstinately, Trudi ignored her. She examined the bunch of keys she was carrying. There was a small flat one. She inserted it into the freezer lock and turned it.

"There," she said triumphantly. "I've done it."

And pressed the handle and opened the door.

Who shrieked first was hard to say.

DEATH OF A DORMOUSE

ALSO BY PATRICK RUELL

Red Christmas*
Death Takes the Low Road*
The Castle of the Demon
Urn Burial
The Long Kill

***Published by
THE MYSTERIOUS PRESS**

DEATH OF A DORMOUSE

PATRICK RUELL

THE MYSTERIOUS PRESS

New York • London • Tokyo

MYSTERIOUS PRESS EDITION

Copyright © 1987 by Reginald Hill

Cover design by Jackie Merri Meyer
Cover illustration by M. Christopher Zacharow

Mysterious Press books are published in association with
Warner Books, Inc.
666 Fifth Avenue
New York, N.Y. 10103
A Warner Communications Company

Printed in the United States of America

Originally published in hardcover by The Mysterious Press.
First Mysterious Press Paperback Printing: August, 1988

10 9 8 7 6 5 4 3 2 1

This one for Billy and Choc—
who else?

When one subtracts from life infancy (which is vegetation),—sleep, eating, and swilling—buttoning and unbuttoning—how much remains of downright existence?
The summer of a dormouse . . .

BYRON: *Journal* (December 7, 1813)

She was lying on a bare mattress in a darkened room. Her wrists and ankles were bound, but this was an unnecessary refinement. In her mind she had been here many times before and knew there was no escape. One strip of light there was which could not be blinked away. It lay on the floor, seeping in beneath the door, and beyond that door on bare stone flags she could hear the sound of footsteps getting nearer.

She lay as still as the mouse which huddles in its cornfield nest, and hears the approach of the coulter, and knows what it means, but does not know how to fly.

Nothing remained in her life, no spur to action, no prick of hope. Nothing of past, present or future touched her life, only that crack of light beneath the door and the footsteps which were approaching it.

She had been waiting for them all her life. They belonged to the secret police who strike with the dawn; to the cruel rapist who lurks in the shadows; to the man she loved, come here to kill her.

Now they were close. Now the line of light beneath the door was broken by a growing shadow.

Now the footsteps halted.

Slowly the door handle began to turn. Slowly the door swung open. In the threshold loomed a figure, bulky, still menacing.

Now it was in the room and advancing.

Her mouth gaped wide as her desperate lungs drew in one last, long, ragged breath . . .

1

PART ONE

Wee, sleeket, cowrin, tim'rous beastie,
O, what a panic's in thy breastie! . . .

BURNS: "To a Mouse"

CHAPTER
1

"Trudi? Trudi Adamson? My God! Trudi, is that really you?"

"Well, it's me anyway," said Trudi.

"Where're you ringing from? Vienna? You're so clear."

"No. Not Vienna. Sheffield."

"*Sheffield*. You mean Sheffield, *Yorkshire?*"

The note of Celtic incredulity made Trudi laugh. Perhaps this had been a good idea after all.

"If there's another, please tell me. I'd probably prefer it."

"But what are you doing in *Sheffield?*"

"Living here, Jan. I've been living here for three whole days."

A silence at the other end as though this were too much to take in; then in a perceptibly casual tone, "And Trent?"

Trudi laughed. The second time in a minute. Perhaps in a decade?

She said, "No, I've not run away or anything. Trent's here too of course. That's why I'm here. He's been moved again. I thought when we got to the center of things three years back, that would be the end of it. But evidently not. And this time, I got two days' notice, would you believe it?"

"From what I know of Trent, yes. But at least this time, he's brought you back to England."

"That's right. And naturally I thought, now I'm here and

4

so close, first thing I've got to do is ring Jan and fix to see her."

It was a lie.

The last time the two had talked had felt like the last time ever. Friends since school, they had seen little of each other over the past quarter-century as Trudi drifted across the face of Europe in her husband's wake. But they'd kept in touch with fairly regular letters and cards. Then a year ago Janet's husband, Alan Cummings, had died. They should have returned to the U.K. for the funeral, but Trent had pleaded a vital business trip. Trudi had fully intended to travel alone, but night after night she had started waking full of terror at the thought of going all that distance without Trent. Agoraphobia was what they had called it all those years ago when she'd refused to leave the house after her father's death. Twice in her marriage the terror had returned. Drugs and psychotherapy had got it under control. But here it was again and Trent had seemed callously indifferent both to her fears and Janet's grief.

"Don't go then. Ring Jan. Tell her you're sick. She'll understand."

She hadn't. Grief, tension, drink perhaps, had combined explosively.

"Neither of you coming, is it? Trent was one of his oldest friends! And *you*, you cow! Who looked after you at school? *Me!* Who got you your job? *Me!* Who got you your sodding husband? *Me!* And now you can't stir yourself when I need you! Useless sodding bitch!"

The phone had gone down hard. Trudi had written an apologetic letter. There was no reply, nor had her Christmas card been reciprocated that year.

Trudi had resigned herself to feeling this chill on her one old friendship thicken into permafrost. She regretted it, but lacked the energy or the will to resist it. Had Trent urged her to action she might have made a move. But he hadn't, becoming more and more distant and self-absorbed in the past twelve months.

But it had been Trent who in the three days since their return to England had become a passionate advocate of reconciliation. *Ring Jan*, he urged. *You don't make new friends so easily you can afford to dump old ones.*

This was cruel, but he had compensated by adding with a rare smile, *Fix up to meet her one day soon. Tomorrow if she's free. I'll drive you over. It's only thirty miles over the hills. Then I'll come and pick you up at night.*

And again as he had left, he had said, *Ring Jan. Arrange to meet. It'll do you good, you'll see.*

Then he had driven away in his rented car, leaving her in their rented house. What had made Trent pick this place she didn't know, but she admitted she was biased against it from the start. The move had been so rapid that her own furniture was still in store in Vienna, and the lack of the familiar sights and smells of her comfortable apartment there was a constant irritation, keeping her from that pleasant supinity which was her normal waking state.

In the end, untypically restless, she had gone to the phone and dialed Jan's number.

And it *had* been worthwhile! Trent as usual had been right.

But now her naturally fearful view of life, her sense that cups are generally raised only to be dashed, set out to prove that it was as right as Trent.

Janet was speaking again. Putting her off.

"Trudi, I'm sorry. But I can't talk now. I'm sorry, but oh, crazy it is, and I should maybe have written, but it's all happened pretty quickly, like your move—well, not so quickly as that, but quick enough!"

Janet's Welshness still broke loose at moments of high excitement and hearing it now took Trudi back thirty years.

"Calm down and tell me what you're talking about," she said.

"Well, I'm getting married again, aren't I? Yes, today! Now! This very minute almost. It's just a registry-office job this time, of course. When I heard the phone ring I thought it's Frank (that's the unlucky fellow), the bastard's ringing up to call it off. But if I don't rush, we'll lose our place in the queue and then it'll be off whether I like it or not. Oh Trudi, I'm sorry. No guests you see, but if I'd known you were going to be so handy, you could've been matron-of-honor or something!"

Here was a reasonable explanation for any oddity of reaction. A year ago she had been abusing her friend on the phone for not attending her first husband's funeral; now she was having to apologize for not inviting her to her second wedding!

"Jan, that's marvelous," said Trudi, straining for conviction. "Many congratulations."

"Thanks. Look, I really must go. Then straight after the ceremony we're off to the Costa del somewhere for a week. Ring me then, promise. Oh shit. I won't be here, we're moving into Frank's house in Oldham and I can't recall the number. Here, give me your address and number. I'll ring you."

"Hope House, Linden Lane," said Trudi, adding the telephone number.

"That sounds posh."

"It might have been fifty years ago. Now it's an ancient monument. Thank heaven it's just on a short lease," said Trudi.

"Oh, we *have* become choosy in our old age," said Janet. "Look, I really must go, girl. I'll be in touch, I promise."

After she had replaced the receiver, Trudi stood in a confusion of feeling. Trent had been right. It really had felt good to talk to Janet again. But counterbalancing this was a feeling of illogical resentment at her remarriage. All that hysteria a year ago, and here she was getting married again! No, it wasn't some awful moral self-righteousness which was bothering her, Trudi assured herself. It was more like a simple jealousy. She could hardly expect to get her friend back when she was just starting to share her life with a new husband.

She made a resentful face in the old pier glass hanging behind the phone. Its chipped and peeling gilt frame was characteristic of this dark suburban villa Trent had brought her to, but perhaps it was too well suited to the picture it now contained. Viennese cooking had turned her dumpy, forty-five years had turned her gray. Only her eyes, clear and brown, belonged to the girl who'd married Trent Adamson a quarter of a century ago. She almost wished they too had turned dull and old and could no longer see so clearly.

The doorbell rang, distracting her from the displeasing image.

The door opened into a glass-sided storm porch. Through the rippled glass she could see a man, flanked by the two ghastly stone gnomes who guarded the main door of Hope House. The man seemed to be in uniform. She opened the outer door and saw he was a young policeman, with his cap in his hand.

That should have warned her. When policemen remove their hats, they don't bring good news. But his accent was so broad and his face so unrearrangeably jolly that it took a little time to realize he wasn't simply collecting for something.

Slowly she made sense of him.

There had been an accident.

She knew at once that Trent was dead.

She knew it as she sat in the police car on their way to the hospital.

She knew it as she listened to a staff nurse explain that someone would be along shortly.

She knew it when a soft-spoken man in a blue suit showed her Trent's tempered-steel identification bracelet.

At last, as if worn down by her silent certainty, they too admitted it.

"I'm sorry, Mrs. Adamson. I'm afraid that your husband is dead."

CHAPTER
2

A week in Sheffield had been long enough for Trudi to take a strong dislike to the place.

She found it cold, drab and ugly, and the people weren't much better. The North of England was almost more foreign to her than anywhere else in Europe. She disliked in particular the way everyone addressed her as "*love*" or rather "*luv*." It felt like an invasion of privacy.

It was only now that she began to realize just how little, in truth, her privacy was likely to be invaded.

She knew no one. No one knew her. She went home and sat and waited for tears to come. When they didn't she tried to induce them by going back over her life with Trent, like a video run in reverse. But nothing happened till she went beyond their wedding day and found herself suddenly three months earlier at her father's deathbed.

Now the tears came close. Then the moment was past and her cheeks were still dry.

She took a strong sleeping pill and went to bed.

She awoke to instant remembrance but when she cautiously explored her feelings, she discovered a barrier, thin as cellophane round a packet of biscuits, but irremovable without the risk of damage.

So she turned away from feelings and concentrated her thoughts on the bureaucracy of death.

Another policeman came, a sergeant, older, more solemn.

"Just a formality, luv," he said. "Just a few details."

He noted Trent's full name, his age, his business.

"This firm he works for. Silver Rider . . ."

"*Schiller-Reise* of Vienna." Trudi spelt it out. "It's a travel company. *Reise* means 'journey.' And Schiller is the name of the man who runs it."

"Oh aye? German, is it?"

"Austrian."

"And they've got an office here."

"Well, no, I don't think so," said Trudi hesitantly. She felt the officer regarding her dubiously and she pressed on. "They're in most big European cities, of course. But I'm not sure about the U.K. Probably that's what my husband was doing, setting something up. He traveled a lot in his work, looking at hotels, locations, amenities. He used to be an airline pilot himself."

She produced this last statement as if somehow it justified the preceding vagueness about Trent's work. The sergeant looked unimpressed.

"Is that right?" he said. "Well, I reckon Sheffield'd be as good a center as anywhere."

He didn't say for what.

There would, he told her, be a postmortem; it was routine after any sudden death.

The facts of the accident were tragically simple.

It had happened a few miles south of the city in the Derbyshire Peak district. The car had been parked at the side of a narrow undulating country road. A fertilizer truck moving at speed had come over a rise some fifty yards behind it. It had been raining earlier in the day. There was muck on the road surface, which was long overdue for repair after the previous bitter winter. The driver had braked, the truck had skidded, caught the parked car from behind, and driven it a hundred yards before slamming it into a telegraph pole. The truck driver had been flung out of his cab.

"Lucky for him," said the sergeant, perhaps in search of some consoling circumstance. "Old farmer working in the fields saw it all. Said the car went up like a bomb. Fractured the tank, likely. And he seems to have been carrying some spare fuel in a jerry can in the boot. Probably for his scooter."

"Scooter?"

"Aye. We found the remains of one of them foldaway motor scooters in the boot. Didn't you know he had one?"

"No," said Trudi. "I didn't know. Perhaps he hired it with the car."

"Aye. Mebbe. Well, one thing, Mrs. Adamson, it must've been quick."

In support of this assertion he educed the fact that identification had only been effectible through the number of the hired car and the name on the fireproof bracelet.

Realizing too late that these considerations were as likely to aggravate as to ease pain, the well-meaning sergeant hopped from the past to the future, pointing out that the police would be swift to establish the extent of the truck driver's responsibility, as soon as the man came out of hospital.

"Shock; broke his collarbone and a few ribs falling out of his cab; and he got pretty badly scorched too. Well he would. Like an inferno. Burnt the telegraph pole like a Yule log, brought all the wires down, you know. Sorry, luv. All I mean is, you'll want to get your insurance company working on this. And your solicitor too, I shouldn't wonder. You've got someone to help you with all this, haven't you? Someone to talk to? Friends?"

"Oh yes," said Trudi, with dismissive certainty.

She thought of Janet in distant Spain. There was no one else to think of, but there was no way of reaching her even if she wanted to. It was bad enough working out who to call in Vienna. Friends? She couldn't think of anyone close enough to require a personal notification. Shyness, agoraphobia, call it what you will, but a woman who gives the impression that the end of any social occasion can't come soon enough doesn't attract friendship. Consciously or unconsciously, Trent had encouraged her isolation, rarely bringing people home, rarely involving her even in business entertainment. Herr Schiller, the head of the firm, was the only one of Trent's senior colleagues she'd met more than a couple of times socially. She'd not much liked the old man, but he had seemed to take a benevolent interest in Trent's career, and for the sake of her husband she'd put on her best social face. It seemed to have worked, for Trent had risen close to the top. But Schiller was old now, semi-retired and invalid, and it would be no kindness to contact him direct. In the end, she sent a telegram to Schiller-Reise's head office and left it to them to pass on the news where and how they saw fit.

By the day of the funeral there had been no response, and the vicar in the cemetery chapel was clearly disturbed to be faced by a congregation which, bearers apart, was divided evenly between the quick and the dead.

Before the service started, the door opened and a man came in. He had a narrow intelligent face which was hard to put an age on (probably mid-thirties) particularly as the eye was diverted by his hair, which in a woman would have been called beautiful, worn rather longer than was fashionable, and swept back in powerful waves of rich black tinged becomingly with gray. His elegance was underlined by his clothes, of such immaculate manufacture that the professional bearers shifted uneasily in their shabby mourning.

He came straight to Trudi, stooped over, took her hand and said in German, "My dear Mrs. Adamson, what a tragedy! What a loss! Believe me, I am truly devastated."

At this point Trudi recognized Franz Werner, her husband's Viennese doctor. She hardly knew the man, certainly did not know his relationship with Trent went beyond the professional to the extent of flying eight hundred miles to catch his funeral.

This was explained to some extent as they followed the coffin out of the chapel. Perhaps aiming at a therapeutic distraction, he told her in a reverential whisper that he had been on the point of departing from Vienna to attend a conference in London when he'd heard the news.

"I admired your husband greatly. I am proud to think I was his friend as well as his physician. So I rearranged my schedule in order to be here."

"That was kind," said Trudi.

They were approaching the open grave.

"We will talk later," said Werner.

What about? wondered Trudi, who was finding it very hard to believe that this brass-handled box contained her husband. Her *husband*. Who was he? What had he been? She concentrated hard upon his image but found that somehow her knowledge seemed to stop round about their wedding day. Up till then, there were plenty of people willing to fill in on Trent's origins. An East-End boy, brought up in an orphanage, who had grabbed with both hands the opportunity offered by the war to advance himself. He'd made *per ardua ad astra* his personal motto, his best man, an old RAF chum, had said at the reception. And he'd finished his drunkenly risqué speech by saying, "One thing the boys always said about Trent, you might not trust him with your wallet or your wife, but by Christ, old Trent was the chap you wanted to fly with. He always came back!"

Well, old Trent wasn't coming back this time.

As though in confirmation of her irreverent thought, the vicar was scattering earth on the coffin. She wasn't listening to his words and it took a slight pressure from Werner's hand to tell her it was all over.

But not quite. As she turned away, she saw a bright red Fiat Panda come rocketing through the cemetery gates, a long pennant bearing the name of a hire firm streaming from its aerial. It halted on the narrow driveway and a long, slim, blond woman in her thirties got out and came running towards Trudi.

She reached her, embraced her.

There were tears streaming down her face.

"*Oh Trudi, mein' liebe Trudi! Es ist schrecklich, ganz schrecklich.*"

"Hello, Astrid," said Trudi Adamson.

CHAPTER
3

Astrid Fischer had been Trent's personal assistant during the whole of his time in Vienna. She was a striking woman, full of nervous energy. Her bright blond hair was matched with smokey-blue eyes and the kind of skin which would stick at twenty-nine for at least another decade.

She was the only one of Trent's colleagues Trudi knew at all well, apart from Manfred Schiller, the head of the firm, and even this closeness was only relative. A couple of years earlier, perhaps in an attempt to rekindle her own almost extinct emotional fires, Trudi had gone through a period of intense jealousy of Astrid. There'd been no material cause of it, she'd never said anything to Trent, and the flame had died as rapidly as it ignited; doused by trust, indifference, or fear, she didn't care to find out which. But jealousy's the next best thing to friendship and for a moment she felt genuinely moved by the woman's appearance.

Werner was shaking her hand.

"I must go. Already I'm late," he said. "Again, my deepest sympathy."

Astrid whispered, "Who's he?"

"Trent's doctor. It was nice of him to come. I thought he would stay longer though."

Astrid seemed to take this as an invitation and accompanied Trudi back to Hope House. Trudi didn't mind. In fact she found herself almost pleased at last to have a partner in mourning.

They sat in the kitchen, its gaudy surfaces reflecting the brittle blank of Trudi's feelings, and drank whiskey.

"I wasn't really awake when he left that morning, you know. He kissed me goodbye. He didn't always, sometimes but not always. He said he'd try not to be late. Then he was gone. I heard the car. I didn't go out to wave or anything. We were past all that. And that was the last I saw of him, alive or dead."

"Alive or . . ." Astrid hesitated delicately.

"I never saw him. He was burnt . . ."

She felt her voice tremble like a rail at the approach of a train. But it was a long way away. She took a deep breath and described the accident as it had been described to her.

"I don't even know what he was doing there!" she concluded.

"Why he stopped, you mean?"

"Presumably he stopped to read his map, stretch his legs, something. No, I mean I don't know why he was driving around Derbyshire. I don't even know what we were doing in Sheffield. Why did Schiller-Reise send him here, Astrid?"

The girl was regarding her uneasily and Trudi, guessing at the cause of her unease, said, "It's all right. I can talk about him. Really."

"It's not that. No. Trudi, you clearly do not know, but Schiller-Reise did not send Trent here. No. He had handed in his resignation only a week before he left the country. Trudi, he was no longer working for the company!"

Trudi was dumbfounded.

Astrid said, "You knew nothing of this?"

She shook her head slowly and the movement brought back her voice.

"No. We rarely talked about his job. He didn't want to . . . or perhaps I didn't want . . . but we didn't talk . . . The move was sudden, but then we'd made sudden moves before. When we came to Vienna from Milan, three years ago, that was quick. Well, this was even quicker, but not so quick that . . . though it's true when I saw where he'd brought me, I thought of the other places we'd lived, the apartments, the cities, and compared them with *this* . . ."

Her gesture took in the room, the house, the suburb, the city.

Oh God! she suddenly thought. *I'm a widow and I'm complaining about the domestic arrangements.*

She said quite sharply, "Astrid, if Trent had left Schiller-Reise, what are *you* doing here?"

Astrid said, "I was on holiday in London. I had to ring the firm on a personal matter. When I heard of Trent's death, I was dumbstruck! I asked about the funeral. They knew when it was, but didn't seem to know if anybody was going from the company. This made me very angry. It was not a proper way to act. If Herr Schiller had still been in charge . . . But I'm sure you must have worked out that if Herr Schiller had still been in charge, probably Trent would not have left."

Trudi shook her head.

"I didn't realize Herr Schiller was no longer in charge," she said.

"It's not official. Technically while he's still alive, but he's a very sick man, you knew that?"

"I know he had a stroke just after we came to Vienna and spent a lot of time at his house in the Wachau. The last time I saw him was there, about six months ago. He looked ill, yes, but still alert."

"He's deteriorated greatly in the last couple of months," said Astrid. "A second stroke. You didn't know?"

"No," said Trudi with an indifference not caused solely by her circumstances. Even if her own troubles didn't exist, she would probably have felt little sympathy for the old man. She'd never liked him, despite the many kindnesses he showered on her as Trent's wife. Something about the dry voice, the coldness of his skin when he took her hand, the way the rarely blinking pale blue eyes never left her face, as though searching for something there that she did not have to give. A sense of cruelty mingled with his kindness had always repelled her, and she sometimes thought he sensed it though she did her best to keep it hidden.

"No. I did not know. Trent and I agreed that it was best if he could relax at home and not talk of office matters."

That was one way of explaining one area of noncommunication.

"Yes. I see," said Astrid unconvincingly. "Well, it's none of my business, so forgive me for asking, but have you any idea how you stand financially?"

Trudi said in surprise, "I don't know. I've not thought. I've no idea how much or little there may be."

"What I mean is, well, since you do not know about Trent leaving his job, you may be relying on a pension from Schiller-Reise. If Herr Schiller had still been in charge . . . well, he always seemed very fond of you, Trudi, and I'm sure he wouldn't have . . . but it's the accountants in control now, and I don't think there will be anything coming . . ."

She tailed away, embarrassed.

Trudi said brightly, "I'm sure Trent made other arrangements. I haven't looked through his papers yet. Everything will be sorted out eventually, you'll see. Have some more whiskey. You'll stay the night, of course."

She tried to make it sound like a casual invitation rather than a plea. This talk of money, or the lack of it, had sent a chill of unease through her which she hadn't felt before.

"Of course. You mustn't be alone . . ."

"Don't let that bother you," said Trudi coldly. "Please yourself whether you go or stay. It's not as if we were ever friends or anything . . . you needn't feel . . ."

To her horror she realized she was weeping unrestrainedly, and there were tears too on the perfect skin of Astrid's cheeks. Now the younger woman took the older in her arms and they wept together. Then they drank some more whiskey and wept some more.

When Trudi at last went to bed, she was slightly drunk and the springs of grief felt dried up. She felt as if she'd undergone some cleansing, cathartic experience and she would wake up in the morning light calm and resolved and able to cope boldly with the new life that stretched before her.

Instead she woke into a drowning darkness. Gasping for breath, she scrabbled for the bedside lamp, missed it, caught it, knocked it to the floor. Sobbing in panic, she half fell, half crawled out of bed and staggered across the suddenly alien room, crashing into pieces of furniture she could not identify, towards the thick-draped window.

Light! She had to have light! She reached the curtains, flung them apart. Light filtered in, turgid, gray, scarcely able to put an edge on the luxuriant foliage of the neglected garden, but for a moment refreshing and soothing to her desperate soul.

Then she saw him, halfway down the garden, concealed at first by stillness but, once spotted, unmistakable. A solid living presence amidst this rampant vegetation, his face raised toward her window, pale, death pale in the cloud-strained luminescence from a wild night sky.

She screamed. "Trent!"

She tried to raise the window. It was locked. Her strengthless fingers wrestled with the catch. All the time she could hear her voice as though emanating from some separate electronic source in the ceiling screaming, "Trent! Trent! Trent!"

The catch moved. But suddenly there was light in the room, bouncing back off the glass and turning the light beyond the window into perfect darkness.

She turned. Astrid stood in the doorway, her hand on the light switch, her face amazed.

"Trudi, *was gibt's?* What are you doing?"

"It's Trent: He's there in the garden. I can see him! I can see him!"

The other woman moved swiftly across the room. Even now her slim athleticism seemed a reproach to Trudi's neglected dumpiness. Grasping the window frame, she thrust it upwards and leaned out into the dark night air.

"See Trudi, there is nothing. There is nobody. See!"

Trudi looked. The trees moved in a gusty breeze, the shrubbery rustled and the long grass on the uncut lawn rippled like the sea. But of any human figure there was no sign.

"I saw him!" she insisted. "I saw him!"

"Keep looking, Trudi," said Astrid peremptorily. "Strain your eyes. Soon you will see anything your mind wants you to see!"

It was true. As she looked, the shifting trees and shrubs began to takes strange shapes, living, threatening, but none of them human.

Shaken, she turned away from the window.

"Oh, Astrid," she said. "I was so certain. I was so certain."

"Yes, I know, I know," said the Austrian gently. "Now you must sleep. Come to bed, come to bed. No, *liebchen*, do not be afraid. I will not leave you."

She helped Trudi into bed then started to slip off her own clothes.

"I too have been restless, not able to sleep," she said. "I sat downstairs, listening to the radio. Perhaps it is I who disturbed you. I'm sorry, but now you will sleep. Now you will be safe."

Stripped to bra and pants, she switched off the light and got into bed beside Trudi, whose body tensed at the thought of contact. But Astrid lay quietly on her own side of the bed with a safe space between them. And eventually Trudi fell asleep.

CHAPTER
4

Trudi woke the next day into broad daylight and the certainty that something inside her was dead. She must have given an impression of normalcy, for she observed Astrid slowly relax as the morning wore on. The Austrian woman said she would have to go that evening, but meanwhile she offered her services in getting things sorted out. Trudi agreed. It was easier than not agreeing.

Swiftly and efficiently, Astrid went through Trent's papers, discovered the name of the solicitor who'd arranged the lease on the house, rang him up, made an appointment for that afternoon. Trudi gave thanks, but felt no gratitude. It all seemed to her mere charade, shadow activities in a shadow world.

The solicitor, who was called Ashburton, was almost a parody of his profession. Small, sharp-nosed, birdlike of movement and voice, he wore a disproportionately large pair of spectacles whose round blanks reflected light like Perseus's shield. He looked to be close to retiring age, but he seemed efficient enough, taking charge of the papers Astrid gave him and assuring Trudi he would put everything into motion instantly.

Trudi thanked him indifferently, shook his hand indifferently, and later kissed and thanked Astrid with the same massive indifference. Only for a brief moment as the little red car turned out of the drive and Astrid raised her arm beside the fluttering pennant in a gesture of farewell did Trudi feel something stir in that vast ocean of indifference. Then it was still again.

She went back into the house, sat unmoving for four hours, then rose and went to bed.

Up to the funeral, her nights had been dreamless. At least when she woke up from her unrefreshing sleep she could remember no dreams.

Now instantly she was in the living room of their luxurious flat in Vienna. Trent was standing by the window, gazing out towards the distant view of the great plant-house in the Schönbrunn gardens. She knew he was dead. He slowly turned and reached out his hands to her and she knew if she took them they would be chill and stiff and clammy. He began to move forward with slow dragging steps and she fled to their bedroom, slamming the heavy oak door and turning the key. But she knew it could be no barrier to that relentless pursuer, and she crouched helpless on the bed as the slow footsteps approached and the handle began to turn.

She awoke in terror, lay in a straining silence, then slowly wrapped the pain-dulling gauze of her waking indifference around her once more.

This rapidly became the pattern of her existence. Waking,

she was safe, but dead. She stayed in or went out as the fancy took her. Outside she felt invisible, anonymous. Inside she sat and watched flickering images on the television screen, drank whiskey, ate next to nothing, then went to bed to the only real experience left to her.

One day, Mr. Ashburton's secretary rang and asked her if she could come to see him that afternoon at three o'clock. She said yes, but didn't go. Ashburton himself rang. She listened to him twittering about wills, pensions, insurance policies—or rather the lack of these things. ". . . just over four thousand in your husband's current account . . . nine months lease on the house but when this runs out . . . case for compensation . . ."

She said thank you and put the phone down.

She could have told him Trent was rich, had always been rich, wasn't the kind of man to be anything but rich. Everything she had wanted she had had, except that there wasn't really anything she wanted, except to be safe . . .

The next day a letter came with the firm's name on its envelope. She let it lie unopened with all the other mail, mainly junk, which had dropped through the letter box. That day the phone rang at regular intervals from morning to night. In the end, she picked it up and let it dangle over the edge of the table without putting it anywhere near her ear.

That night the dream came as usual. Trent turned, she fled, he followed. She crouched on the bed and watched the door handle slowly turn.

She awoke, and lay bathed in sweat, waiting for the terror to recede and the dull, deadening silence to rise around her.

But this time there was a noise, a real noise. Like a door opening below. Still savoring the relief of escape from her dream, her first reaction was to treat it like all the noises of this so-called real world—people talking, cars passing, wind and weather—which to her were an empty buzz.

But now there was another sound, a sound all too familiar to her straining ears, the sound of the slow tread of feet coming nearer and nearer. She knew in that instant that the ultimate horror had been born and the walking corpse of her husband had at last broken through from her sleeping world to her waking.

She lay quite still, not unable to move, but unable to think of anywhere to move to. There was only the window, and what help lay there? Her cries into the night air would only reach the ears of her unknown neighbors like the high wail of some restless night creature. And in any case she knew with a certainty beyond faith that when she opened the window, Trent would be there already, standing on the unkempt lawn, his pale face raised towards her.

Now the footsteps were at her door. The handle moved fractionally. She put her hands to her ears and closed her eyes and opened her mouth in a silent cry of terror.

When she opened her eyes, it was broad daylight. She had no recollection of fainting, less of falling asleep, but did anyone ever have such recollections? Anyway, it meant nothing. The crisis had come as she had known it must. Her defenses had been breached, the barrier of her indifference lay in ruins. Trent had broken through into her waking life, and the consequences were unthinkable. She was not yet mad, but she could go mad. Grief, terror, guilt, she did not know how to itemize her emotions; all she knew was that she was ready now to give anything for peace. Including her own life.

She sat in the lounge and, like a little girl with her birthday sweets, she considered her tablets. So she had sat at her father's feet with a tea-tray before her on which she counted and classified dollie-mixtures, jelly-babies and chocolate buttons.

The supply of sleeping pills she had brought from Vienna was sadly depleted, but there was a good number of Valium and an assortment of other tranquilizers from her old agoraphobia treatments. A mixture of these washed down with whiskey, which she'd heard intensified the effect, must surely do the trick.

She started off very slowly, thinking for some reason that she ought to savor the experience. Then a sudden fear struck her that this leisurely approach would give the tablets time to put her to sleep long before she had taken a fatal dose. Panic-stricken, she began to take them in twos and threes, gulping them down with mouthfuls of raw whiskey. Eventually, with most of the tablets gone, she found she could manage no more. Surely she'd done enough. Now there would come that delicious, easy drifting off into oblivion she longed for.

Time passed, perhaps a little, perhaps a lot, she couldn't tell. Where she was, it was timeless. Something was definitely happening, some great change was about to take place. But it was not going to be easy, it was not going to be delicious! Her body felt as if it was being racked apart. She was leaving not in peace and quiet but in turbulence and agony. But she had to go. She could hear somewhere last night's noises again: the door opening, the footsteps approaching, a voice calling her name. She looked up and saw the door handle turning and she willed herself to die.

The door opened; a last spasm convulsed her body. In the doorway stood a woman, middle aged, strikingly good-looking, with a full, sensuous figure and shoulder-length black hair framing a heart-shaped face which wore an expression of incredulous horror.

"Trudi?" she said. "Trudi! For God's sake."

"Janet?" gasped Trudi. The word brought relief. She doubled up and vomited over the carpet. Her stomach, which had received practically no food for days, gladly gave up its mixture of bile and whiskey in which lay scattered like daisies on a summer lawn a myriad of little white pills and tablets.

PART TWO

Thy wee bit housie, too, in ruin!
It's silly wa's the win's are strewin'!
An' naething, now, to big a new ane,
O' foggage green!
An' bleak December's winds ensuin',
Baith snell an' keen! . . .

BURNS: "To a Mouse"

CHAPTER
1

Frank Carter was a reasonable man; reasonably tall, reasonably tempered, reasonably good at his work in a Manchester estate agency.

He tiptoed out of the spare bedroom in which Trudi was lying with her eyes screwed up tight as if to keep out more than just the light. And he asked the reasonable question.

"How long's she staying?"

"I don't know," said Janet. "Frank, I'm sorry. I know we didn't plan starting married life with a nonpaying guest, but she's nowhere else to go."

"Hospital; nursing homes," said Carter, moistening his lips as though at the start of a long list.

"No good. Look, she needs someone she *knows*, that one. Always has done, though she's come on a bit since I first met her, I reckon. God, Frank, you should have seen her at school, little Trudi Shoesmith! She never went out at playtime, special medical permission. If it hadn't been for her funny name, she'd have been completely invisible. It was her name first made me take notice of her. *Janet Evans* was so ordinary, I thought! I really envied her being called Trudi, especially when I found out it should really have been Trudi Schumacher!"

"Schumacher? That's German, isn't it?"

"Austrian. Her father was a Jew, nonpracticing, but that

didn't matter evidently in 1938. He got out, came to England. I gather her mother died giving birth, so her dad brought her up more or less single-handed. That was half the bother, I reckon. Lots of substitute mums, lots of moving about, and a father who never got over his suspicion that everything in uniform was a storm trooper and every knock at the door was the Gestapo! It's no wonder she was such a timorous little thing. Her father changed their name to Shoesmith when he was naturalized, but I reckon he never stopped thinking of himself as a refugee. Anyway, I took little Trudi in hand, didn't I? Looked out for her at school, got her a job later on, even introduced her to Trent Adamson, though that turned out a mistake!"

"How do you mean?" asked Carter, puzzled.

"Well, just that if she'd not met and married Trent, she wouldn't be here now," said Janet, not altogether convincingly.

Trudi, half hearing but totally unresponding to this conversation drifting through the open door, could have told Frank Carter exactly what Janet meant.

Most of what her friend said was true. Before the Evanses moved to Surrey from Cardiff, no one had paid any attention to the slight, pale, self-effacing child with the funny name. Janet Evans on the other hand was instantly the center of interest. Voluble, impassioned, darkly attractive, she was admired or resented but never ignored. There was no shortage of applicants for the position of "best friend" but to the amazement of everyone she plucked Trudi out of obscurity and gave her the job. Trudi was more taken aback than anyone. Nor was she much assured by overhearing a spiteful peer declare, "It didn't surprise *me*. What else would a cat look to play with but a dormouse?"

Janet had exaggerated when she said she got Trudi her job. School over, Trudi had found employment as a copy typist in a council office at Staines. Janet had sought the lusher pastures of the West End, but after a couple of years, she had returned to Staines to train as an air hostess at nearby Heathrow. And it was then that, hearing of a well-paid secretarial opening in her company's airport office, she urged Trudi to apply. How much the full beam of Janet's charm influenced the office manager was hard to say, but Trudi got the job.

A few weeks later, Janet came into the office just as she was preparing to leave.

"All right, girl," she said. "Glad rags on, color in your cheeks, I'll pick you up at eight. Be ready."

"What? Jan, no, I mean, what—"

"Don't play hard to get! I've got two lovely men lined up, but my other lovely girl's gone down with flu, silly cow. I need you, lovey, so don't say no."

"But I can't—" said Trudi, panic-stricken.

"Can't what? You can drink orange juice, eat a chop, and laugh politely when I kick you under the table, can't you? Trudi, I don't ask much, do I? So, *please!*"

Trudi had given in. The men had been Trent Adamson and Alan Cummings. Cummings, who worked for Customs and Excise, was the younger and livelier of the two, but it was Trent that Janet had in her sights. An airline captain with the wit and the will to move profitably from air to chair when the time came, he was, in Heathrow terms, a great catch. It was only to be expected that he would take Jan home.

"But all he wanted to do was talk about you!" said Janet the next day in mock pique. "Perhaps he's a secret mouse-fancier!"

"Don't be silly," said Trudi, flustered. She had no desire to be fancied by Trent or any man. The previous night Alan Cummings had made a token pass and she'd literally run away from him. It had not been her father's intention that his distrust of authority and uniform should have been communicated so strongly to and extended so comprehensively by his daughter, but bringing her up single-handed had made his influence paramount and had given his overanxious warnings, both political and sexual, the force of divine law.

A week later Trudi was dumbfounded when Trent came into the office and gravely asked her for a date. She refused. He wasn't put off. Janet's pique soon ceased to be moc ., but her sense of realism eventually prevailed and she started urging her friend to grab her chance with both hands.

Trudi was simply bewildered. She did not feel she had anything to offer a man like Trent. More important, he had nothing to offer her. She was happy to contemplate a life living at home, looking after her father.

And then one evening everything changed. Walking home from school in the November fog, her father was knocked down by a hit-and-run driver. She sat at his bedside for twenty-four hours and would not believe them when they told her he was dead. She'd refused to leave the house after that, even to attend the funeral. There was talk of forcible removal to hospital, but Janet squashed that, moving in with her friend. Then Trent started calling round, and it was in his company that Trudi first stepped into the open once more. Few people thought of this as courtship, attributing it to some hitherto unsuspected vein of human kindness in Trent. The question, which only Janet dared put to him direct, was, what would happen if and when he withdrew his protective shadow from the little dormouse? Trent's only reply was a faint smile.

Two months later, he and Trudi got married.

And three months after that, to further amazement, Trent gave up his prestigious job and secure future and went to work for a Swiss-based charter company trading out of Zürich. The Adamsons moved to Switzerland, the first step in a twenty-five-year separation from England which was to see them living in some of the most glamorous cities in Europe. Not that it mattered to Trudi, not in those early years anyway. Home was where Trent said it was. That was all that mattered.

Janet, meanwhile—lovely, lively Janet for whom the sky always seemed the limit—married Alan Cummings, had a couple of quick kids, and when promotion took her husband up to Manchester's fast-developing international airport, she'd settled down stoically to a life of middle-class obscurity in the depths of Cheadle Hume.

"I think it's time I moved out," said Trudi.

"Good Lord. Why?"

A month had passed. Slowly Trudi had returned to normalcy. The bad dreams persisted, but she had begun to feel perfectly safe in the day. Then that same morning, lying in bed enjoying the pale gold of the autumn sunlight on her window, she had suddenly recalled entirely that overheard conversation of her first day here. Resentment of Janet's condescending interference had rapidly cooled to a general embarrassment that required instant action.

"I've been here ages. I can't impose on you forever."

"Impose! We love having you, really."

She sounded persuasively sincere.

"You've both been marvelous," said Trudi. "But when Frank married you, he didn't expect to get landed with another fat old widow."

"Another?"

"Oh God, Jan, I'm sorry, I didn't mean . . ."

But Janet was laughing with the confidence of one who knows that all a few extra pounds have done to her figure is add a certain sensuous roundness to its attractive contours.

"Forget *old*, girl!" she commanded. "We're in our prime, you'd better believe it. As for fat, well, I can tell what you mean by the sizes of those clothes of yours. But have you taken a look at yourself lately? You haven't been eating enough to keep a dormouse healthy! Take that blouse off. It's like a surplus parachute anyway. Now take a good look in that mirror. Not much fat there, is there?"

Trudi didn't reply. She was regarding with fascinated horror what she must surely have seen but somehow not managed to register. Her shoulder bones stood out like a fashion model's, and against her löuvered ribs hung tiny breasts like deflated balloons left over from some long-forgotten party. This was how she'd looked at nineteen. A quarter of a century of *crême patisserie* had been stripped off her in a month.

"Oh God, Jan, what a mess I look!"

"That's the first sensible thing I've heard you say. Right, here's what we do. You want to leave? O.K. As soon as we get you looking like a human being again, you can go. That includes getting you back on a decent diet. We don't want you putting up two stone overweight again, but we don't want you anorexic either! Deal?"

"Deal," said Trudi, still staring at herself. For some unfathómable reason, it occurred to her she was now as slim as Astrid Fischer.

* * *

It took another three weeks. Frank, with an end in view and perhaps some guilt in mind, was kindness itself, and when the time came Trudi hugged him tearfully in farewell.

"It's high time you were going," said Janet grimly as they drove away in her Ford Escort. "Another week and you'd have been giving the randy old devil ideas."

Trudi looked down with undiminished surprise and pleasure at her new slim body, clad now in tight-fitting cords and sweater.

"All right," she said. "You've been right so far, Jan. I'm not fat, and I'm not old—well, not so very—but . . ."

She felt her brief mood of happiness already slipping from her and when Janet prompted her with a "But what?" she burst out, "Yes, that's it. But what? But what *am* I? I need a new me inside as well as outside. Inside, I'm just lost. Bewildered. I feel *useless*, Jan. Help me to stop feeling useless, then you'll really have done me some good!"

Janet slammed on the brakes as she changed her mind about jumping some lights on amber. An old blue pick-up with a long double radio aerial almost ran into her, but the driver, with surprising restraint, refrained from blowing his horn.

"For God's sake!" Janet exploded. "If you're useless, then what does that make the rest of us? I mean, what's the difference between your contribution to the big mad world and mine?"

Trudi said with quiet vehemence, "You've had a real life, I've just lived in a kind of cocoon. You've brought up children, worked for a living, and I bet you didn't need to look back twenty-five years for a friend when Alan died. You had a real life to put back together, family and friends to give it a framework. Me, I've been like a dormouse in an old teapot that Trent made comfortable for me. He's gone, the teapot's shattered, and there's no way I can put it together again. That's what I mean by useless. *Kaput!*"

Janet did not reply for a while, concentrating on her driving. But when the houses began to fall behind them and they were properly out in the country, she said quietly, "Trudi, I don't want to get into any scar-trading competition with you, but just to set the record straight. All right, I had the kids, but where are they now? Eileen's settled down in Australia, Tim's in the Merchant Navy, sailing God knows where. They came back for the funeral. First time I'd seen them in ages. And I've not seen them since. Me and Alan before he died, we were just coasting along, just about tolerating each other. This great useful life you talk about all seemed pretty much a waste of time, I assure you! Then Alan died. I had friends, O.K. And they were kind. But what were they? Couples, mainly. Now I was half a couple. Let me tell you something. Six months go by. After that, if you show any sign of still hurting, you're a misery-guts and ought to pull yourself together. But if you go around smiling, then you're the merry widow and a menace to all good Christian marriages! So don't talk to me about a real life. It doesn't matter what you were before. For most of us, I reckon, being widowed means going right back to GO!"

Trudi considered this.

"But it *was* different for you," she said obstinately. "You *did* know people, you *did* have friends, you *did* have a social life to build on. I mean, you were able to get around and meet people, weren't you? You met Frank! It wasn't as if you had to advertise for him, was it?"

Janet glanced assessingly at her friend and then began to laugh.

"I thought for a second you were being nasty there, but it's not your style," she said. "Listen, want to know a secret? Something I've not even hinted at to all these so-called friends you're so envious of? Here goes, then. You're right, I didn't have to advertise for Frank exactly. But I did the next best thing. I met him through a dating agency, that's how!"

Trudi regarded her incredulously.

"What's up, girl? Cat got your tongue?" mocked Janet. "Let me spell it out. Me with my hectic social life you so envy, I went along and filled in a form, and I paid my money, and I waited!"

"Oh, Jan."

"What's that mean, disapproval? Pity? I don't accept either. It was the best move I ever made. I got just what I needed out of it. Frank. We're going to be very happy."

"Yes," said Trudi. "I can see that."

She tried to speak brightly, approvingly, but didn't feel that she succeeded. Janet glanced at her doubtfully, as if already regretting making the confidence.

They drove on in silence. The car was now beginning the winding uphill climb which would take them over the Snake Pass and down into Sheffield.

Behind them, the old blue pick-up drove in silence too.

The house was cold and unwelcoming and smelled of damp. There was a scattering of mail on the hall floor, mostly junk. Trudi went through it as Janet busied herself lighting the central-heating boiler and making a cup of tea.

There were two letters from Austria, one from Astrid Fischer saying she had contacted Trent's Viennese lawyers, but there was no record of a will, nor of any unrealized assets. She ended with affectionate good wishes and an offer to do anything else she could to help Trudi. The second letter was from the head office of Schiller-Reise. It expressed formal regret at the news of Trent's death, so soon after the termination of his long and highly valued connection with Schiller-Reise. It made no mention of money, or the lack of it. And it was signed on behalf of Manfred Schiller, the firm's founder and head.

Janet read it and said, "Bastards! I thought you said this fellow Schiller liked Trent and made a fuss of you both."

"That's right," said Trudi. "But he's ill. He probably doesn't know anything about all this. Anyway, I never liked him and I don't want favors."

"Pride, is it?" murmured Janet. "You'll learn."

There was also a letter from Mr. Ashburton, the solicitor. Despairing of ever getting Trudi to his office, he had set out the state of her affairs as he saw them. They were not good. In Trent's current account, there were about four thousand pounds, which, unless there were insurances, bank accounts, or realty so far undisclosed, was the sum total of her inheritance. Hope House was rented on a nine-month lease, he pointed out. At the end of that time, she would have to find and pay for alternative accommodation. He ended by suggesting that her main hope of improving her situation probably lay in a compensation claim against the fertilizer company whose truck was involved in the accident. He looked forward to hearing from her.

"I bet he does!" said Janet. "Leech! *Are* there any insurances or other accounts?"

"I don't think so," said Trudi. "Astrid looked through his papers."

Janet snorted her Celtic opinion of Teutonic interference and set about examining the contents of Trent's personal files herself. She soon had to admit that either Astrid or Trent himself had left everything in perfect order, except that *everything* meant *nothing*.

"This is your life, girl," she joked finally, pointing at the papers neatly arranged on the dining-room table.

It was an unintentioned cruelty, but Trudi's eyes filled with tears as she looked at the papers. Here was her life, traced in bank accounts. The Midland in Staines where they'd lived after their marriage; Neue Bank Schmidt-Immermann of Zürich where they'd moved after Trent left his job at Heathrow; Societé Generale de Banque in Brussels where they'd gone when he stopped flying and started working full time for Schiller-Reise, and the Banco di Sancto Spirito in Milan where they'd been when Herr Schiller summoned Trent back to be one of his close aides in Vienna.

Janet hadn't noticed Trudi's tears, and she brushed them away furtively as her friend went on, "Everything's in such perfect order there's not a crack anywhere for a handful of loose change to slip into! See, account closed in Zürich, balance transferred to Brussels, and so on right through to Sheffield. Always about the same, taking inflation into account. Wasn't much of a saver, your Trent, was he? Long as he had a few bob behind him, he clearly liked to spend the rest!"

"Four thousand's more than a few bob," said Trudi defensively.

"Try telling that to the butcher when you can't pay his bills in six months' time, my girl!" said Janet derisively. "You'd better go and see this lawyer fellow, Mr. Bloodsucker or whatever his name is. Ring him now. No, I'll ring him and make sure he fits you in tomorrow morning, then I can go with you."

"You're staying?" said Trudi. She hadn't dared mention it earlier.

"Just tonight, girl. After that, you're on your own," said Janet severely.

They dined that night on tinned ham and half a bottle of Riesling which Janet had brought with her. Afterwards, though it was still early, Trudi announced, "I'm going to bed."

As she started up the stairs the phone rang. She turned and looked at it. Janet came out of the lounge but halted when she saw Trudi was still there. The phone rang on.

"Aren't you going to answer it?"

With a sigh, Trudi stepped back down and picked up the receiver. Her reflection looked back at her from the gilded pier glass. The peeling frame no longer seemed to fit so well. This was a stranger setting out on a long and difficult journey.

"Hello?" she said, and listened.

After a few moments she put the phone down.

"Well?" said Janet.

"Nothing. Must have been a wrong number."

With great control, Trudi walked past her friend and began once more to climb the stairs.

To say anything more, to show her inward agitation to Janet, was impossible. Her reaction, whether of doubt or belief, would certainly be that her friend was not fit to be left alone. Eventually her irritated anxiety might even make her insist that Trudi should extend her stay in Oldham.

That was really what was impossible, the shame and embarrassment of being carried back like a sick child to spoil Frank's sense of relief and release.

Only time would show whether it was more impossible than remaining here where the phone could ring and out of a great hollow silence like the space behind the stars a voice, faint as false dawn yet in accents as familiar as day, could breathe, "Trudi . . . I'm watching you . . ."

CHAPTER
2

"What about personal property, Mrs. Adamson?" said Ashburton. "Apart from the usual things like watches, cufflinks, I mean. Did your husband collect stamps, for instance? Rare coins? Old china?"

"No way!" said Janet confidently. "But I'll be going through everything with Mrs. Adamson before I go back this afternoon."

Janet had done most of the answering, but Ashburton had courteously persisted in directing his questions at Trudi.

She felt stupid to be letting her friend answer for her, but her thoughts kept on drifting elsewhere. The truth was that it wasn't till here and now, listening to the little solicitor drily outlining her puny resources as he saw them, that she had really begun to understand the truth of her position. She'd never thought of Trent and herself as wealthy, but she realized now this was because she'd never had to think about such things at all. Not once from the start of their marriage had he ever denied her anything she wanted on the grounds of expense. Not that she'd been extravagant, but as even the gentlest of streams will over time carve itself out a wide and wider bed, so her expenditure over the years had spread and never found a limit.

Now it sounded as if she was going to be penniless. This was a dawn knock she'd never even imagined in her most fearful wakings. She felt panic fingering her throat and, desperate to deny it, she cut right across Mr. Ashburton's next sentence, saying, "He collected books."

"Books?" echoed the solicitor.

"Trent?" exclaimed Janet.

"Yes. Well, not books generally. George Orwell's books."

"Orwell? What did Trent have to do with Orwell? I never saw him reading anything thicker than a newspaper, and then he was usually doing the crossword!"

Her friend's incredulity was easy to understand. Trent was not a bookish kind of man in any sense, but at some point during his RAF career when he'd run out of crosswords to while away pre-sortie longueurs, he'd picked up something of Orwell's and been hooked.

"I asked him once why he liked Orwell," said Trudi. "He said he was a man who understood the rottenness of things. I'm not sure what he meant."

Janet shook her head in disbelief, but Ashburton was not to be diverted from the point.

"You say, *collected?* First editions, you mean?"

"Yes. I don't know. I expect so."

"They should be worth a little," said the solicitor, making a note. "Now, is there anything belonging to you still in Vienna?"

"Only our furniture," said Trudi. "The move happened so quickly, we just put it in store."

"Aha. Valuable, would you say? Antique, perhaps?"

"There are some nice pieces. I like to buy nice things and Trent . . ."

Her voice broke. Janet looked indignantly at Ashburton. He went smoothly on. "Then it seems that we must look to the courts for any substantial increment to your income. On the surface we have a good case. Stationary car, speeding truck, an independent witness. Unfortunately there has been a development. The witness, Mr. Harold Brightshaw of Six Mile Farm near Grindleford, Derbyshire, has had a stroke. He is an old man, almost eighty, and it is possible he will not recover. He made a statement of course, but there is a vast difference between a statement in the hand and a witness in the box."

"What about the truck driver?" demanded Janet.

"Still in the hospital. The police have not yet decided what to charge him with. In any case, he will certainly not be keen to give evidence against himself, and his firm can afford excellent legal advice."

"They can afford excellent damages too, then!" exploded Janet.

"No doubt. But litigation is costly, Mrs. Adamson. As things stand, I would recommend looking for an out-of-court settlement."

"Would you?" said Janet. "Mrs. Adamson doesn't actually need to instruct you in this matter, does she?"

"No, of course not," said the solicitor, unoffended. "Mrs. Adamson?"

He regarded her with the alertness of a sparrow waiting for a crumb. He was a slightly ridiculous figure, but she sensed in him a sparrow's strength and tenacity too.

"How did you come to act for my husband?" she asked.

"I was recommended, I believe."

That decided Trudi. No one made recommendations lightly to Trent.

On the way back, Janet said, "Are you sure about that little creep, girl? He looks as if a good belch would blow him away."

"I like him," said Trudi. She felt quite proud of her decision, but her pretensions to self-reliance quickly evaporated as they started going through Trent's things and she recognized there was no way she could have done this without Janet.

Janet knew someone who ran a nearly-new shop in Manchester and she offered to take Trent's clothes and also a large proportion of Trudi's which were untake-inable.

"Pity he didn't spend more on the insurance and less on the mohair," observed Janet as they sorted out the suits. "Hello, this is a bit out of character, though. Gardening clothes, is it?"

She held up an anonymous brown Terylene suit which bore the label of a down-market chain store. She went through the pockets swiftly and efficiently.

"Keys," she said, producing a ring. "Spares, by the look of 'em. Bright and shiny. Small change. Two pounds sixty p. But hello! This is better."

This was a wallet.

"Fifty quid in notes. Handy. And a couple of credit cards. Better chop those up when you've a moment."

She laid the money on the dressing table and tossed the keys and wallet into the shoebox which contained watches, cufflinks, etcetera.

"Now. What else? Shoes. Plenty of those. We'll give 'em to Oxfam. Hand-made by the look of them. Strange to think some poor sod out in the bush will probably end up with more than a year's income on his feet. Now, what's that leave?"

"There's the books," said Trudi.

She led the way downstairs into the lounge. The Orwell volumes were in a glass-fronted cabinet. Janet peered at them dubiously.

"Can't imagine that lot being worth much."

"I don't know," said Trudi. "That last night he was talking about having them valued. He said there was a dealer in Manchester he'd heard about and he might take them across when he drove me over to see you. He was very keen for me to see you again."

"Was he now?" said Janet neutrally. "At least it shows he really was hard-up if he was thinking of selling. Shall we take a look?"

She tried the door. It was locked.

Trudi went on as though her friend had not spoken. "And later that night, or rather early in the morning, I came downstairs. Trent had been sleeping badly since we came here. He often got up during the night and usually I pretended to be asleep. This time I came downstairs myself after a while and he was sitting with one of his books on his lap. Perhaps he was worried about money and thinking of selling. All he said was that he couldn't sleep."

"Are you going to unlock this thing or not?" said Janet brusquely, attempting to interrupt the growing melancholy of the mood.

"No!" said Trudi with sudden spirit. "I'm not. I've got nothing of Trent's that's really personal except these books. I haven't even got a photograph. He hated having his picture taken. So I'm not going to part with the books unless I have to."

Her spurt of independence was short-lived, and when the time came for Janet to leave, she was hard put to conceal the depth of her panic.

"Chin up, girl," said Janet, trying to be businesslike. "I'm just at the end of the phone. And we'll meet every week on Wednesday, like we arranged. I'll drive over in the morning, it's only a step."

Trudi clasped her tearfully and said, "Oh Jan, thank you, thanks for everything."

Alone in the house, she waited for the tears to flow freely. To her surprise they didn't. Now she realized how excellent Janet's psychology was in arranging a regular meeting. Wednesday was already feeling like an oasis, distant but reachable. Anything vaguer and she would have felt totally adrift.

Curiously, the first week ran by quickly and easily. She spoke with Janet on the phone nearly every night, going over her progress through the timetable which she and her friend had worked out. Interviews at the Department of Health and at a job center were large single features, brisk morning walks and the pursuit of a diet which would build her up without fattening her up were part of the regular pattern aimed at holding her life together. The officials at the DHSS made it quite clear she was entitled to nothing until she became destitute; her interviewer at the job center was not optimistic at the prospect of finding work for a middle-aged typist who had not been employed for twenty-five years. Not even Trudi's claim to have fluent German and French and passable Dutch and Italian impressed him. "Not much call up here," he said dismissively.

Time passed. So did her money, and there was still no sign of a job. Soon it was November. But it wasn't till the tinsel glitter of Christmas began to brighten the shops that she realized how quickly the weeks had gone. It had been high summer when Trent was killed. She'd been a widow for nearly four months.

This awareness of the passing of time wasn't sudden, but it was significant. It brought new pain which made her realize how much she had been flying, to use Trent's phrase, on automatic pilot. It also brought her new life into sharper focus in all kinds of ways.

Not the least significant of these was the certainty that she was being watched.

She glimpsed him twice, once reflected in a shop window, and the second, confirming, time when she suddenly turned in mid-stride and retraced her steps and saw him plunge into a shop doorway.

He was youngish, balding slightly, with a blond moustache. After that she didn't see him again. Her previous indifference to her surroundings must have made him careless till he learnt his lesson.

But she knew he was still there.

She told Janet about him at their next Wednesday meeting, and immediately wished she hadn't.

"You don't believe me!" she said.

"Yes, of course I do. I mean, I believe *you* believe you. But listen, in your state you'll get ideas . . . I mean, well, take me, good old solid-state-nerve-circuit me. After Alan's death, the police asked a lot of questions and some guys from his department came round, and I began to feel pretty persecuted I tell you! So I went down there and gave them a row. Christ, they must have wondered what had hit them! Anyway, I must have got a lot of tension out of my system 'cos I went away feeling really good. Only thing was, as time went by, I stopped feeling good and started feeling really stupid! Now the very memory of it makes me blush. What I mean is, if insensitive old me can get neurotic . . ."

"Then it's not surprising that little me, who's halfway there to start with, should be positively paranoiac, is that what you mean?"

Janet was taken aback by the vehemence of the response.

"No, I'm sorry, Trudi, that's not what I mean . . ."

Trudi, suddenly enjoying her insurgency, said briskly, "By the way, I may have got a job."

"What?"

"Mr. Ashburton rang this morning. Despite what you said about him, he's really been most helpful. He wants to see me. Something about the case. But he also said he had a client who might be able to use a typist with good linguistic skills."

"Well done, girl. But you be careful. Don't be taken advantage of. Top rates, luncheon vouchers, ask for the lot."

Janet was seeking to reestablish her ascendancy and Trudi found she didn't mind too much. Like many a colonial state in the past, she suspected she was in danger of making emotional demands for an independence she did not yet have the resources to support.

"We'll see," she said, gathering her things together.

"Hold on, it's early yet!" protested Janet in alarm. "I'll give you a lift home, shall I?"

Trudi laughed and said, "I'm not walking out in a huff, Jan. It's just that I've got this appointment with Mr. Ashburton, remember? I'll tell you all about it next week."

She rose and left swiftly. Her appointment wasn't, in fact, for another hour, but she felt an irresistible urge to get out of the restaurant and be by herself.

As she left, she had a sense of eyes focused upon her. She didn't think they were just Janet's.

CHAPTER 3

"First the bad news," said Mr. Ashburton. "Harold Brightshaw is dead."

"Who?"

"Mr. Brightshaw of Six Mile Farm, Grindleford, the witness in the accident case. I told you he had a stroke shortly afterwards. He never recovered, poor chap."

"I'm sorry. Does it make a difference?" asked Trudi.

"Oh yes. He made a statement but now he can't be cross-examined on it. It's my information that the police will be charging the tanker driver with one of the lesser offenses, driving without due care and attention perhaps. That won't help us, even if he's found guilty."

"*Even if?*" exclaimed Trudi. "Surely there's no defense!"

"There's always a defense," said Ashburton drily. "Mud

on the road left by Mr. Brightshaw's tractor—a hint there that
Mr. Brightshaw's statement might be a little biased. And
they'll use the post-mortem findings too, I've no doubt."

"What findings? And I thought that the fire . . ."

She didn't finish.

Ashburton said gently, "Yes, I know. Beyond recognition;
but an internal examination was still possible. Would you like
some more coffee, Mrs. Adamson?"

"No, thanks. Go on," said Trudi.

"Two things, then. There was a fairly high alcohol level in
the bloodstream, just about on the legal limit. And there were
present in the coronary arteries, let me see, *atheromas*,
lesions in the arterial wall. In a phrase, *coronary arterioscle-
rosis*, which eventually could lead to your husband having a
heart attack."

"But Trent died of his injuries, not a heart attack!"
protested Trudi indignantly.

"No one will contest that. What the defense will be
looking for is some way of suggesting that there was a
contributory negligence on your husband's part. If for
instance a sudden spasm of pain caused him to stop
unexpectedly or a sudden dizziness, say, leaving his car not
parked safely on the verge, but *slewed* across the road . . ."

"Because he was drunk, you mean, or sick? I never saw
Trent drunk in his life! As for being ill, he was always in the
best of health. Surely Mr. Brightshaw's statement doesn't say
his car was slewed across the road?"

"No, but it doesn't say it wasn't."

"But the truck driver . . ."

"Hitherto, I gather, his memory of things has been vague.
It would not surprise me, however, if now it began to sharpen
up," said Mr. Ashburton. "I fear that our hopes of a good
out-of-court settlement are fading, Mrs. Adamson. I'm
sorry."

"It's not right, Mr. Ashburton," said Trudi angrily. "It's
not just the money, though I could do with it, but it's just not
right that people should be able to get away with this sort of
thing. What can we do to stop them?"

"Not much, I'm afraid. Evidence of your husband's
excellent state of health could be useful. Perhaps his last

doctor could help there. Why don't you contact him and get a certificate of some kind? Now, on a happier note, as I told you on the phone, one of my clients, Mr. Stanley Usher, a man of many interests, mentioned to me the other day that he'd taken over a small export business and felt in need of some bilingual secretarial help. I mentioned your name to him. It would be part-time and it wouldn't make your fortune, but if you're interested . . ."

"Yes, I am," said Trudi firmly.

"Good. Here's the address. Mr. Usher will be there now. It's just a short walk. Down past the cathedral, turn left down the hill, then left again and there you are."

He handed Trudi a business card. On it was printed in bright red letters CLASS-GLASS with the address underneath in blue and *Stanley Usher: Director* at the bottom in a flowing black script.

The building she arrived at was under multi-commercial occupancy. Class-Glass was on the first floor. She knocked at the door. A voice called, "Enter." She turned the handle, stepped inside and stopped dead.

It was like being in a funhouse Hall of Mirrors except that here there was no distortion. There was, however, a fragmentation almost as disturbing from the mirrors that covered every inch of the walls. They came in all shapes and sizes and they all had pictures and words printed on them, some advertising old drinks which had disappeared years ago, others referring to new and up-to-date products.

"Mrs. Adamson? Come in, have a seat. Don't worry, you'll soon get used to the mirrors, unless you hate the sight of yourself!"

Stanley Usher was a tall dark man with a spare frame and a rather cadaverous face. She put his age at about forty. He was expensively suited in traditional charcoal gray worsted and the only touch of color about him came from the two rings he wore on his left hand, one a ruby, the other an emerald. His voice had a slight under-accent which might have been Australian.

Trudi sat on a hard office chair on one side of a typist's desk that carried a gleaming new electronic typewriter, the sight of which filled her with dismay. She was definitely pre-microchip. Usher sat on the typist's swivel chair opposite her. The only other furniture in the room was a filing cabinet.

"Let me explain the setup, Mrs. Adamson," said Usher. "This job might be *owt or nowt*, as they say in these parts. Probably the latter. These are hard times. Little businesses are going down like ninepins. What I do is buy them as they tumble and their prices tumble too, of course! Then I use my own cash and know-how to see if anything can be retrieved from the wreck. If it can't, tough. I usually make as much as I put in. You follow me?"

"I think so," said Trudi.

"Great. Class-Glass exports mirrors, these kind of mirrors, ornamental advertising. Only it didn't. Export many, I mean. So it failed, I bought it. Now I'm using my know-how and Continental contacts to see if there's any life in the corpse, right? What I need is someone who can deal with the mail, in and out. I've a smattering of Frog and I can buy a drink in Kraut, but that's it. So what I want is this. You come in on Mondays and Thursdays. Open the mail. Translate it. Deal with anything you can deal with. Leave a note and translation with anything you can't. I'll be in from time to time. You'll find letters from me to be translated into the appropriate language, typed, dispatched. O.K.?"

"O.K. But—"

"Let's say forty pounds for the two days, see how we go from there? I'll get Ashburton to deal with the payment and any paperwork. Let's see how we go, then even if this folds, there may be something else. Right! Now, let me show you round, not that there's much to show except for these bloody mirrors!"

"And what did he show you?" inquired Janet. Trudi, feeling she'd been rather rough on her friend, and also having a favor to ask, had phoned her that same evening.

"Nothing much. There's a tiny washroom. A storeroom full of all kinds of mirrors. A filing cabinet, almost empty. And that damned typewriter. I noticed an instruction book in the desk drawer, thank God. I'll need to spend my first couple of days learning how it works!"

"You'll cope, I'm sure," said Janet.

For the first time, a certain strain in her friend's voice registered with Trudi.

"Jan, are you O.K.? I mean, you're not still annoyed about lunchtime?"

"Of course not. No, you're the one entitled to be annoyed. I know I'm too pushy sometimes. No, the thing is, when I got home this afternoon, I found the house had been broken into."

"Oh Janet! How awful."

"Well, I'm trying not to make too big a thing of it. I mean, the place was a bit untidy, but he wasn't one of the dirty ones, thank God. Doesn't seem to have taken anything either, the police reckon he was looking for money. But even so, it shakes you up a bit."

"I bet it does. And me rabbiting on about my job. I'm sorry."

"No. That's really good news, that cheers me up a lot. I look forward to hearing about your new exciting commercial life next Wednesday."

"Yes. Oh, by the way, I wondered, well, would you mind going for a drive next week? Down into Derbyshire. I thought we could have a bar lunch, my treat."

"Why, yes, of course," said Janet, slightly puzzled. "That would be nice."

"Lovely. See you next Wednesday, then."

The following Wednesday was a bright but chilly December day. Janet picked her up at midday and by one o'clock they were tucking into a substantial bar lunch in the small village of Grindleford.

"I hope you're not planning an afternoon's hiking," said Janet, refilling their glasses from the bottle of hock Trudi had insisted on buying.

"No," she assured her.

"Good. Now tell me about the House of Usher!"

There wasn't much to tell.

"I spent my first day, last Thursday that was, working out that damned typewriter. On Monday, Usher showed up. There were a few letters to translate and type. And that was it. Fortunately I'd taken a good book along."

"And Usher? Did he pounce?"

"No! He bought me a drink at lunchtime though."

"Aha!" said Janet gleefully. "You want to watch him!"

"I don't think he's interested in me like that," said Trudi slowly.

"What other way is there?" mocked Janet.

Trudi smiled but didn't answer. This time she didn't need her friend to suggest that she was being neurotic.

After lunch, Trudi surprised Jan by taking charge of navigation, using an Ordnance Survey map. Janet followed, with puzzlement which might eventually become protest, the uncertain route laid out for her along a skein of narrow roads, many unclassified. The sun was still bright, but low now in the winter sky, sending long shadows from leafless trees.

Suddenly Trudi said, "Stop here!"

Janet brought the car to a halt, and Trudi was out of it before she could speak. They were on a straight and undulating stretch of narrow road running between thick hedgerows of hawthorn and blackthorn, alongside which marched a spindly line of telephone poles. About a hundred yards ahead one of the poles looked newer than the rest and there was a long gap in the hedge, repaired with stakes and wire. Beyond the hedge to the left was a plowed field rising diagonally with the swell of the ground, like the birth of a wave caught with an artist's brush.

Trudi walked along the road a little way till she came to an old wooden gate, badly in need of repair, set between two pillars of roughhewn stone which looked as if they could have been raised there by Druids. She pushed back the gate far enough to let her through and set off across the field, following the rising diagonal.

From time to time, she stopped and looked back. The first time she couldn't see Janet's car at all. The second time she could see the line of its roof and Janet's face regarding her with what she guessed was bewilderment. And on her third stop, high up the field, she could see the car and also the long line of the road where it continued its arrow-straight run on the far side of the ridge to another distant crest.

A truck coming down there would be able to reach a tremendous speed, she told herself. Downhill, an empty road ahead, foot on the accelerator, and then the exhilaration of the sudden upward swoop apparently into nothingness over the brow of the ridge on which she stood.

And immediately, panic! No longer an empty road, but not very far ahead a stationary car, leaving only a narrow passage. The foot instinctively hitting the brake pedal, the wheels locking, the tires starting to skid across the gleaming muddy surface, and suddenly the steering wheel as useless as a broken rudder in a storm-tossed sea.

She looked up to the sky. It was a mistake. The world began to reel, she felt herself in danger of being shaken off into the cold blue emptiness—her atoms, each one printed with her terror and loss, scattered forever through the universe. She closed her eyes and dug her nails deep into her palms till the earth stood still. Then she turned and walked back down to the car. Janet's face was questioning, but when Trudi got in and said, "Let's carry on. Over the hill there should be a track to the left," she obeyed silently.

The track was there, a farm road signposted *Six Mile Farm*.

The track's surface was rutted and potholed and Janet had to concentrate to pick out the least-damaging line. Trudi was mentally doing the same and finding it even more difficult. The woman she was going to see would be grieving with a nearer and probably deeper grief than her own. Trudi was suddenly astounded at her arrogance in even thinking of intruding on her at this time. The car was entering a farmyard. She wanted to tell Janet to turn straight round and head back for the road, but it was already too late. The tall stone building had an abundance of small narrow windows as though the builder lacked the art to make them double and had compensated by making them frequent. As they drove through the entrance, Trudi glimpsed a face pressed against one of these, and before the car had come to rest on the cobbled forecourt, the farmhouse door had opened and a woman emerged.

Saying to Janet, "I won't be long," she got out.

The woman remained in the doorway, for which Trudi was grateful. She wanted to explain her business out of Janet's hearing.

"Mrs. Brightshaw?" she said.

The woman nodded. She was tall and muscular, with a weatherbeaten face, a sharp chin and nose, steely gray hair and deep-set, watchful eyes. She looked about sixty or perhaps a well-preserved seventy.

Trudi said, "I'm sorry to trouble you at this time, Mrs. Brightshaw. I was sorry to hear of your husband's death."

"You knew Harold?" she said in a flat Derbyshire accent.

"No," Trudi said. "Not personally. My name's Adamson. Trudi Adamson. I don't know if you recall the accident on the road back there in the summer. Mr. Brightshaw was a witness. It was my husband who was killed."

The woman considered this, then, "You'd better come in," she said, stepping aside, adding as Trudi went by, "What about *her*?"

Presumably she was referring to Janet.

Trudi said, "No, no. She'll be all right."

Mrs. Brightshaw closed the front door and ushered Trudi into a long high living room.

Sitting down in an old wing chair before a huge fireplace in which flickered a tiny fire, Trudi said, "Look, Mrs. Brightshaw, if you don't feel like talking about your husband, please say so and I'll go."

The woman answered, "I reckon if you can talk about yours, I can talk about my Harold. And if I don't feel like it, I'll shut up. What do you want to know?"

Trudi began to explain and found herself rambling.

Impatiently, Mrs. Brightshaw said, "Let's get it straight. These lawyers are trying to say your man might've had a bad turn and stopped his car sudden like, so it was blocking the road?"

"That's right."

"And if the court believes that, it'll affect your compensation?"

Trudi hadn't mentioned money, and now she reacted against the imputation of a merely mercenary motive.

"I just want the truth, Mrs. Brightshaw," she said firmly.

"Truth! Aye. That," said the woman. "Did he leave you all right, your man?"

Belatedly, Trudi realized this was the key to whatever the

woman could tell her. Shared grief couldn't bring them together; shared poverty might.

"No," she said firmly. "He left very little. I've taken a job again after twenty-five years."

"Oh yes?" said the woman with a slight sneer. "That'd be hard for you!"

"Yes," said Trudi seriously. "Not working, but finding work, that's what's hard. At my age, in these days."

The farmer's widow nodded as if she'd at last heard a potent argument. Then she blew her nose, picked up a poker, stirred the tiny fire.

Finally she said, "Well, you needn't worry. He was parked proper all right. As tight up against the hedge as you could ask."

Trudi found herself as much puzzled as pleased by her emphasis.

"You're certain?" she asked. "Your husband told you that?"

"Yes," she said. "He did."

"And would you make a statement to that effect?" asked Trudi. "In writing, I mean."

Mrs. Brightshaw looked suddenly uneasy.

"Would I have to go to court?"

"I don't know," Trudi said. "To be quite frank, Mrs. Brightshaw, I'm not really sure about the law as it applies here. But it would be a great help to me personally, that's quite certain."

The woman continued to look so doubtful that Trudi's surprise began to turn to suspicion.

"You are *quite* certain that's what your husband told you?" she asked.

"Why do you ask?"

"Well, I wouldn't like to think you were just trying to cheer me up," said Trudi hesitantly. "And . . ."

"And . . . ?"

"And, come to think of it," said Trudi in a rush, "it does sound rather an odd thing for Mr. Brightshaw to have been so emphatic about, particularly as he doesn't seem to have felt it was worth mentioning in his statement."

The old woman nodded and said, "That's the kind of thing them fancy lawyers would say, isn't it?"

"I suppose so. If it came to questioning."

"I don't doubt it would," she said fiercely. "And I'd have taken an oath?"

"In court, yes," said Trudi, bewildered and by now a trifle uneasy.

"Then you'd better hear what I would have to tell them, Mrs. Adamson," she said with an air of decision. "Then you can make up your mind. What my husband told me wasn't what he told the police. Don't misunderstand me, he didn't lie, he just kept it simple. He told them he'd no idea how long your man's car had been stopped on the road when he noticed it. And the crash happened shortly after."

Trudi's uneasiness was now a constricting pain beneath her breasts.

"Truth was," Mrs. Brightshaw continued, "he'd noticed the car arrive twenty, thirty minutes earlier. Then another car came and stopped behind it. He heard doors slamming. Then he saw someone move from the second car to the first. It was a woman. Harold was working with his tractor, you understand, not just standing gawking. But a bit later on, he saw the second car move off. And it wasn't long after that that the accident happened."

Trudi made two false starts before she could speak.

"Why didn't he say anything about this in his statement?" she managed in the end.

"He was a kind man, my Harold," said the older woman softly. "He reckoned that if there was nothing to it, the other driver would come forward soon enough. But if it was what it looked like, there was no point in adding to your troubles by letting all and sundry know your husband was parked out in the countryside with his fancy woman."

She raised her eyes and regarded the younger woman steadily.

"But there's one thing for sure," she said. "A man doing that doesn't leave his car lying halfway across the road."

Trudi took a deep breath. She was almost too bewildered to be distressed. She heard herself saying wretchedly, "It was definitely a woman, was it?"

"It was," said Mrs. Brightshaw. "He told me he could see her head clearly above the hedge. She must have been a tall lass. Blond hair he said, I remember that. Bright blond."

A tall lass. Bright blond. Trudi felt the information register. Then she asked, "And her car? Did he say anything about that?"

"Yes, he did, as a matter of fact. He said it was a little red thing with a kind of flag on its aerial. He mentioned how small it was, particularly, because that seemed likely the reason this blond lass went to the other, which was bigger. More room for that sort of meeting. He wasn't making a joke, just giving me his reason for keeping mum. When the police came for his statement, he asked if there was a wife and when they told him yes, that made up his mind. He thought you'd be hurt enough. Like I say, he was a kind man."

"Yes, yes, he sounds like a kind man," Trudi echoed, rising. She felt surprisingly calm.

"How will you manage now that you're by yourself?" she heard herself asking, calm and concerned as the vicar's wife on a parochial visit.

Mrs. Brightshaw let the question hang, smelling more patronizing by the second, till she had shown Trudi to the door.

"I've been managing since Harold took his stroke," she said finally. "Managing's easy. It's wanting to manage that's the hard bit. But you'll have found that out yourself, I daresay."

The door closed behind Trudi and the bolt rattled home.

Slowly she returned to the car, moving in time to the childish jingle which had risen unsummoned into her head.

Three blind mice . . . See how they run . . . They all ran after the farmer's wife . . . She cut off their tails with a carving knife . . .

"O.K.?" said Janet, compressing a whole catechism into the question.

"Fine," said Trudi. "I'm fine."

"You don't look fine. You look terrible," said Janet. "Come on, what do you really feel like?"

"I feel like a widow," said Trudi savagely. "I feel like a fucking widow!"

CHAPTER
4

Trudi told Janet nothing of her discovery about Astrid Fischer till they got drunk together on Boxing Day.

She'd made a token protest when Janet invited her to spend Christmas in Oldham.

"It's your first Christmas together," she said. "And it's a family time."

"Family! What family? Mine's halfway across the world, and Frank's good for half an hour of Santa Claus with his grand-kids, then it's King Herod time. He'll be glad of an ally."

This had turned out to be true. And on Boxing Day, Carter had taken further advantage of her presence by going off to play golf with a clear conscience.

"Fair do's," said Janet. "He put golf at the top of his interests on the bureau form. I don't mind. Golf's good for a marriage. Man with his eye on the ball doesn't have much time to look at anything else."

She grinned broadly as she spoke. Their lunch of cold turkey washed down with a bottle of hock was being rounded off with liqueur chocolates and brandy.

Relaxed but not yet somnolent, Trudi said, "I think you did well there, Jan. Mebbe mail-order's the best way!"

"You didn't think so at first," said Janet slyly.

"Didn't I? I don't know what I thought. I wasn't quite right in my mind for a while, you know. I mean, it's hard. You don't know what you're like till you're not like it anymore."

She giggled and held out her glass for a refresher.

Janet said, "Dormouse philosophy is it now? Not to worry.

51

Another shot of this and I'll be able to pour you back in the teapot!"

"No, I'm serious," said Trudi. "And it's not just the drink. I woke up this morning feeling it might not be so bad to be me after all. I can't remember the last time I felt like that, Jan."

Janet looked at her disbelievingly.

"But you've had the life of Reilly!" she protested. "High-flying husband, glamorous cities, no kids to weigh you down. Don't imagine I didn't lie in bed many a night and think, that bitch is living my life!"

"I certainly wasn't living my own," said Trudi.

"What's this? Self-pity? I thought we were past that stage."

"Oh no. I may get maudlin later but right now I'm stuck at honesty. Let me tell you about my life, Jan, if you've a moment to spare. I married Trent and went off to Zürich. Only I didn't really go to Zürich. I just stayed inside the private little atmosphere that existed for me round Trent and *it* went to Zürich. We had an apartment, lovely views, a skyful of Alps. I hated those mountains. All that space threatening to suck me away, to steal my private atmosphere. But I'd have climbed them with Trent. When he was with me, anything was possible. When he was away, which in his job was often, I never stirred from the flat. I'd stock up the larder in advance and just not budge. He never knew till one time he was delayed an extra week with engine trouble and came home to find me starving."

"What did he do?"

"Got angry. Told me not to be stupid. Made me go out by myself."

"Great therapy," said Janet angrily. "Didn't you talk to anyone else? Friends? A doctor?"

"A doctor? Not that time. As for friends, how should I make friends? I didn't want to make friends. We hardly ever entertained, thank God. When we did, it was disastrous. He brought Herr Schiller to dinner once. Trent was still working for the charter company then. I suppose he wanted to make a good impression with a view of getting more work through Schiller-Reise. Everything went wrong! We had burnt salad and raw trout, I seem to recall. Trent said it didn't matter. In fact he seemed to find it rather amusing. I thought I'd ruined his future."

"But you hadn't."

"No," said Trudi sadly. "I should have known even then that ruining his future wasn't an option Trent left open to anyone, especially me. Schiller came back several times, but just for drinks! Eventually Trent announced he was taking a job full time with Schiller-Reise and we were moving to Brussels. I was delighted. Trent was giving up flying and becoming an executive. I thought he'd be home every night. It didn't work out like that. If anything, he traveled abroad even more. So the old pattern reestablished itself. And Trent found out and got angry and ordered me to go out. And I did and it seemed to be all right. At least there weren't all those mountain peaks threatening me. Till one day I was sitting in the Gran' Place feeling rather proud and woman-of-the-worldish when a storm blew up. The sky went dark and swirly, there was a tremendous wind, the air seemed lurid. Everyone ran for cover, everyone except me. I couldn't move. I knew it was me they were after . . ."

"*They?*"

"Them. Whatever's outside wanting to get inside and destroy us," said Trudi calmly. "I just sat there paralyzed with terror. No one paid much heed till the rain came. But after a while the sight of a woman sitting under a deluge attracted first attention, then concern. When Trent came back from that trip, he found me in hospital."

"What did he do? Command you to take up your bed and walk?"

"He got me the best medical treatment money could buy," said Trudi smiling. "I loved it. Suddenly I was the center of Trent's attention. When I was declared cured we moved to Paris. I felt so happy! But Trent's job took him away as often as ever, so when one day I felt the old terror returning, I almost welcomed it! Wouldn't it put me back at the center of Trent's life? Well, for a time I thought it had. But this time after the treatment was over, Trent started wondering whether it might not be better if we bought a house back in England where I wouldn't feel so isolated. It might mean our separations would be longer, but at least I'd be among 'my own folk.' I don't know if he meant it as a threat or a genuine kindness. All I know is that it was the last thing I wanted. So I took it as a threat and became a changed woman!"

"How the hell do you change something like that?" asked Janet.

"Don't forget, I had medication, I had relaxation exercises, I had self-help psycho-programs too. I put up a pretty good show of normality."

"But if you were cured, you *were* normal!"

"Oh no. Normal people look at relationships critically. All I wanted was to make sure I stayed with Trent. He was my atmosphere. Take him away and there was that awful vacuum waiting to suck me up. So I took great care of myself. When I went out, I was always ready to head for home at the first hint of fear. I refused to even try to make friends. All I wanted was to please Trent when he was home and not to displease him when he was away."

"But you never hinted at any of this when you wrote," said Janet. "Your letters were . . ."

"Dull? Just what you expected from me, I bet. I was leading a dull life, remember."

"But all those years! What did you do? How did you pass the time?"

Trudi laughed and drank some more.

"Come on, Jan. Add up the individual bits of your own life—anyone's life—and you'll find the majority of it is dull, routine, mechanical stuff. But there *were* things I did, partly to keep Trent happy that I wasn't just drifting around like a zombie and partly to stop me doing just that. Like you said, we lived in some pretty glamorous places. I did go out to the theater, cinema, galleries, museums. I even took courses, pretty basic 0-level–type things at first, but eventually I aimed higher. History, literature, whatever was available wherever we were, by correspondence mainly, though I did occasionally have discussions over the phone. Eventually I got up to degree level, there, that surprises you!"

"My God, you've got letters after your name!"

"Oh no. I never actually took the final exams. I set out once, but halfway there I changed my mind. I don't think it was agoraphobia, just terror of finding out how thick I really was."

"Come off it. Thick you're not."

"Oh yes I am," said Trudy grimly. "I managed to lead this odd half-life for more than twenty years and kid myself I was happy. And for what?"

"For . . . well, for happiness!" urged Janet. "Everyone compromises. Don't exaggerate your own compromise. You'd have gone on with it, wouldn't you? You'd have lived happily ever after if that dreadful accident hadn't happened, wouldn't you? All right, now you think you're awake. But the thing is, was that other state totally bad?"

"I think so. But the thing really is, how much longer was I going to be allowed to stay what you call happy, anyway?"

"What do you mean?"

Trudi hesitated, then thought: *Come on, don't be coy, you've gone too far to head back for home this time!*

She said baldly, "Trent was having an affair. I think he was planning to leave me."

"Good God, girl! What are you saying? I mean, why are you saying it?" said Janet in an agitated tone.

"Lots of reasons," said Trudi. "Lots and lots of reasons."

It was rather pleasant, she discovered, to have Janet's undivided attention, and she paused, savoring the feeling, as her friend regarded her with an expression of surprise bordering on shock.

"I should've guessed," she resumed. "But I never looked beyond the nose on my face, did I? Quitting his job without telling me and bringing me back to England! It's obvious he had something better to go to and he wasn't taking me with him. He was kind enough to think I'd be better off being dumped here than back in Vienna. Or perhaps he planned eventually to go back to Vienna and didn't want me still to be there. Yes, I bet that's it. Not kindness. I mean, it was hardly kindness to leave me with a measly four thousand pounds. The rest of the money's probably been transferred somewhere. I wonder if that bitch has managed to get her hands on it!"

"What bitch?" asked Janet, her voice still faint from surprise.

Now Trudi told her about Astrid Fischer. Her friend sank back into her chair.

"So that was what that trip was all about!" she said. "What a nerve, turning up at the funeral like that!"

"I suppose Trent dying was as big a shock for her as it was for me," said Trudi. "Not as big a shock as I'm going to give her, though."

Janet said, "You're going to see her?"

"Why not?" said Trudi. "I've got to go back to Vienna. I want to get a certificate of health or something from Trent's doctor and I've got to sort out the furniture in store there. I'll sell most of it, I think. I need the money. And I think I may just call in on Fräulein Fischer and see what she has to say for herself. At the very least, the bitch can be a witness that Trent was parked safely off the road!"

If she expected applause from Janet, she didn't get it. She poured herself another drink and said, "What're you looking so disapproving about?"

"Not disapproving. Just wondering if it's worth the hassle, girl. Trent's dead. Either she loved him, in which case she's had her share of pain too. Or she didn't. In which case, what's the point of dragging it all out now? Forget it. You'll just upset yourself."

Trudi burst out, "What do you mean, forget it? If it was you, would *you* forget it? No! It's just that you reckon I'm not up to it! Well, I'll show you. You're not the only one who can make decisions, *girl!* I might even give that dating agency of yours a go while I'm at it!"

She tossed her drink back dramatically and began to cough.

"Take it easy," laughed Janet. "I don't think you're ready for the Lewis Agency just yet."

"Why?" coughed Trudi. "How long did you wait?"

"Not long," admitted Janet. "But it was different. Alan and I had been drifting apart for years."

"And Trent and I hadn't?" said Trudi bitterly.

"Had you?"

"I don't know! That's the dreadful thing, Jan. I really don't know anything about our relationship. I don't know what he saw in me, why he wanted to marry me, why he stayed married to me! All these things I ought to know better than anyone. I don't! I bet you know more about me than I do myself, Jan! What does that make me? Where've I been? What sort of life have I led?"

For a second it looked as if Janet might be ready to take her question seriously. But then she smiled wryly and swung her legs off the arm of the sofa and on to the floor.

Standing up, she looked down at Trudi and said, "Not one where you got used to drinking, that's clear. A little lie-down's the best thing for you. Go on now! I'll see to the clearing up."

Trudi protested but Janet bossed her out of the room. In a last assertion of independence she paused in the doorway and said, "But I will go to that agency, you'll see."

"All right, we'll see," grinned Janet. "Now you sleep on it."

So Trudi slept on it. In her sleep, for the first time in weeks, the dream came: the flight from Trent, the slow footsteps to the door, the handle turning; and the locked door slowly opening to admit her death.

She awoke, sweating and trembling. Why had the dream come back now? For the first time she also asked herself, *Why should I dream of Trent at all in this way? Why would he hurt me in death when he never hurt me in life!*

And then she remembered and thought, *Oh yes, you did, you bastard. Yes, you did!*

PART THREE

Thou saw the fields laid bare an' waste,
An' weary Winter comin' fast,
An' cozie here, beneath the blast,
        Thou thought to dwell,
Till crash! the cruel coulter past
        Out thro' thy cell.

BURNS: "To a Mouse"

CHAPTER
1

The Sheffield branch of the Lewis Agency was situated at the top of a time-blackened building in a tall Victorian terrace not far from the squat Victorian cathedral.

There was no lift and Trudi labored up the stairs passing other offices en route; a debt-collecting agency on the first floor, an insurance brokers' on the second, a typing and secretarial bureau on the third. Two girls were standing outside this door, chattering like house sparrows. They fell silent at her approach and didn't resume their giggling conversation till she went by, her face burning with the certainty that they had guessed her destination. Only pride prevented her from retreating there and then. It was pride, or rather a kind of stubborn pique, that had brought her here in the first place. There'd been no more mention of the dating agency till Trudi had been packing to leave. Then Janet had casually tossed her a slim brochure and said, "You were asking about this, remember?"

It had been the Lewis Agency's handout. It was a smallish northern business, limited mainly to large towns in Lancashire and Yorkshire. The Sheffield address had been underlined in red.

The blurb claimed that the agency was based on sound scientific principles but it still relied on human judgment rather than computer printouts for matching its clients. While not specifically a marriage bureau, it aimed at a clientele who were looking for serious relationships, rather than just casual dates.

Trudi and Janet weren't meeting till the first week of the new year. Determined that her friend should not have the satisfaction of getting the expected negative response to her casual inquiry if the brochure had been any use, Trudi had rung up the agency on New Year's Eve. A woman called Fielding had answered in a most businesslike way and Trudi's vague general inquiries had been swiftly translated into a firm appointment the following Wednesday morning before her lunch date with Janet. She'd sat up alone that night, toasted the new year in, and gone to bed hopeful that she'd wake up in the morning a new woman.

Now here she was, the same old nervous neurotic, laboring up the last flight of stairs and wondering what the hell she was getting into.

A few minutes later she felt rather better, mainly because Mrs. Fielding was such a pleasant surprise. A comfortably plump woman of perhaps sixty with rosy cheeks and white, uncontrollably curly hair, she sat behind a desk even more untidy than her hair and cheerfully proffered a cup of tea just brewed with the help of an electric kettle and an old brown teapot. If this was demonstration that new scientific methods had not been introduced at the expense of the personal touch, it worked.

After some preliminary chat which may or may not have been searching, Mrs. Fielding said, "Shall we get down to it, Mrs. Adamson?" and extracted a blank form from the autumnal heap of paper before her.

It all proved very painless. When she hesitated about her age, Mrs. Fielding said cheerfully, "Knock a couple of years off. Everyone does it, so if you don't, you'll just end up being taken for two years older than you are."

After her own details came the details of what she was looking for. These seemed to form a fairly bland recipe when Mrs. Fielding checked through them with her.

Age 45 to 55. Height, not less than five feet nine inches. Build, preferably well-made but not fat. Nonsmoker. Social drinker. Professional man. Generally middlebrow. "Should like plays and music, but not too abstract or intellectual; town dweller, country lover; knowledgeable about food and wine, but not pretentious . . ."

As Mrs. Fielding droned on, Trudi found herself thinking with amusement how fussy a penniless widow in her mid-forties imagined she could be! She was able to feel amused because none of this seemed real, it had all assumed the dimensions of a game.

Even when she handed over the registration fee and signed a form agreeing to the payment of a further sum for each introduction that went beyond a first meeting, she could not feel it was real.

It was only when she had descended the now-empty stairs and regained the open air that the sound of traffic and the sight of people brought back reality. She felt a sudden inrush of panic at what she had done. What if somewhere out there was a man who fitted the pattern of her imagined requirements exactly? What if there were dozens of them?

She didn't have to meet anyone, she told herself firmly. That was quite clear. She didn't have to meet anyone.

That stemmed the panic for a moment, but it came back tenfold as she walked away, running over in her mind what had been said and written during the interview, and suddenly it dawned on her with terrifying clarity that what she had drawn in the limits of that stereotyped form was a blueprint for Trent.

Janet's unconcealed amazement almost made it all worth-while. Typically, however, once she got over the surprise, she launched an armada of good advice.

"First time, always meet somewhere public. Don't let him pick you up or anything like that. I did that with one and he was over the doorstep, flashing his teeth and God knows what else, before I could say hello!"

"Oh Jan! Not really?" said Trudi, amused and horrified at the same time.

"No, not *really*," Janet reassured her. "But *really* enough to be worth taking care over. So, somewhere public. Inside, not out. You don't want to risk hanging around in the rain, catching cold. Somewhere that you can sit around without attracting notice. Hotel bar rather than a pub, perhaps, though either's a bit chancy."

"How?"

"Well, I was approached by this chap in a hotel bar when I was waiting once; he fitted the general description, so I gave a big smile and chatted away merrily and thought that maybe I'd struck lucky till he suddenly produced the key to his room, asked me how much and whether I took American Express!"

"Janet!"

"Sorry. Joking again, but it was almost like that. Hey, what are we worrying about? Here. Here's the ideal place! Lots of people, but wide open, very mixed population. And it's familiar ground."

Here was the open-plan bar-foyer of the Crucible, Sheffield's civic theater, where the two friends often came for coffee or a lunchtime drink and snack.

"Now, one thing you've got to recognize, Trudi, is that men lie. Even more than us. We may trim our ages a bit, but men lie about *everything*. So you've got to use your eyes and your ears. He may say he's a brain surgeon on eighty thousand per annum basic, but check his shirts for frayed cuffs. Have a close look at his shoes. Big money buys real leather. Check his mouth. If his dental jobs have been done by some N.H. jockey on piecework, it shows. Ask him to spell *pericranium*. Tell him you're doing a crossword or something."

"But what if he's a radical brain surgeon who likes gardening, has no interest in clothes and can't spell?" said Trudi.

"Drop him," said Janet with a shudder. "You're like me, dear. Too old for radicals. Next thing. No body contact. Shaking hands is the limit. Nudges, squeezes, accidental brushes, they deserve one warning. Hand up your skirt or erection against your bum, that's it. Walk away."

"With his hand up my skirt?" said Trudi. "That could be awkward."

She still surprised herself to discover how lively and even witty she could be in the company of Janet. The renewal of their girlhood friendship had not after all meant simply a renewal of the dormouse-cat relationship. Perhaps those years of catatonic domesticity had been a necessary fallowness rather than a needless waste.

Janet said, suddenly serious, "Trudi, joking apart, are you sure this is for you?"

"What do you mean?"

"The agency. Meeting men like this. It's a step in the dark in a way. Are you sure you're ready for it? I mean, it's really no time at all . . ."

"You mean it's only five months since Trent died, and am I really such a callow, unfeeling cow as to put myself back on the market so quickly?"

"No! I didn't mean that, you know I didn't," Janet protested.

"Yes, I know," said Trudi. "But I wonder it about myself, Jan, so there's no reason why you shouldn't wonder it too. The way it seems to me, looking back, is that it was almost inevitable, like in a good play, I mean. If it had happened while I was still in Vienna, comfortable, secure, almost torpid, God knows what the effect would have been. But I'd been suddenly uprooted and dumped here at a moment's notice, in a strange town, in a strange house, without even my own furniture to keep me company. It was like being woken up out of hibernation to find it's still winter! And then, Trent's death. It was as if I had been nudged towards it somehow. God help me, it almost nudged me over the edge. If you hadn't come along . . ."

"You'd still have spewed up and been all right," said Janet sensibly.

"Perhaps. But it wasn't grief that got me to that point; it was selfish terror, I think. Just as violent in its effect, but not so long-lasting."

She fell into an introspective silence and Janet said, "Well, that wasn't what I meant anyway. I just meant that maybe you're not, well, *tough* enough to be doing this. I mean, it's all right for the bold, brash types like me . . ."

"But I thought that the whole idea of marriage agencies was to help the shy, the timid, the socially static?" said Trudi ironically. "What you really mean is, if things go disastrously wrong, you don't want to feel responsible."

"All right. That's what I really mean."

"You won't be," said Trudi. "Janet, don't take me wrong, but a good reason for me to do this is that I want to be responsible for myself. Or rather, I can feel something in me that's crying out desperately to find someone else who'll take the responsibility off me, and I've got to be careful not to let that happen, not like it happened before. I can't afford another twenty years, not at my age!"

"But I don't understand. Why go looking for another man at all if you're so worried about someone taking over and making your decisions for you?" queried Janet.

Trudi smiled and took her friend's hand.

"Darling," she said. "At the moment I haven't got another man, and sufficient be the evil, etcetera. At the moment I'm afraid I'm talking about you!"

She squeezed Janet's hand to remove any offense and went on, "And to start with, in this bold new bid for independence, I'm breaking our date on Saturday."

"Oh, hoity-toity! The Lewis Agency have fixed you up already, have they?"

"Nothing so dull," said Trudi, smiling. "And I did tell you. I'm spending a couple of days in Vienna, that's all."

CHAPTER 2

January in England was unseasonably mild, but Vienna was full of snow which a bitter east wind whipped into mini-blizzards at every corner.

At Thomas Cook's they had told her that the cheapest way

of getting to Vienna was to go on a weekend package. When she saw that the designated hotel was the Park Hotel Schönbrunn in Hietzinger Hauptstrasse, only five minutes' walk from her old apartment, she did not know whether to be glad or distressed.

She arrived at the hotel late on Friday afternoon. After unpacking, she bathed the journey off her still-skinny body, then got dressed and went out. She knew where she was going even though she did not admit it, and a few minutes later she was standing solitary in the snow, staring up at the line of windows in the high old building behind which she had (so it now seemed) slept away the last three years.

Soon the chill of the pavement began to strike up into her feet and she turned away, her mind numb with more than cold.

In a little while, she reached a small *Gasthaus* which she and Trent had occasionally visited for a simple meal. Confident of anonymity in her new guise, she entered and ordered a *schnapps*. To her horror, the owner, after regarding her curiously for a moment, said "Frau Adamson, *nicht wahr?* We haven't seen you for a little time. Is your husband joining you tonight?"

Hastily she downed her drink, muttered something about being in a hurry and rushed off into the frosty night.

Back at the hotel she went straight to the bar and had another *schnapps*. It seemed to her that she was involved in a test of strength with this city. It was determined to turn her into a ghost, driven palely by its cold winds down all the avenues of her old life, unable to communicate except by piteous weepings.

But she was not a ghost; she was a living woman, here with a purpose; two purposes perhaps, or perhaps even three. It was in pursuit of these that she would establish her identity, not by drinking here at the bar or wandering aimlessly round the streets.

She took Astrid Fischer's last letter out of her handbag and studied the address. Then she went out of the hotel again and walked the hundred or so yards to the underground station.

* * *

When Astrid opened the door of her flat, Trudi knew exactly the scene she was ready to play. The trouble was, instead of the cue of a guilty start which had been Astrid's role in her mental rehearsal, the younger woman's face expressed only a second's surprise before breaking into a wide welcoming smile.

"Trudi! This is marvelous! You should have warned me, but never mind, this is really marvelous. Come in, please!"

It was a pleasant apartment, open plan and opulently appointed. The sleeping area was raised a few feet above the rest. On the bed was a half-packed suitcase. Trudi pictured Trent under the checked coverlet. The picture didn't hurt as much as it should have, so she tried to fan her anger by wondering how much of Trent's money had gone into the expensive furnishings and decor. That was rather more effective.

"Let me get you a drink? When did you arrive? How long are you staying?"

Trudi shook her head, as much in bewilderment at how to begin as refusal of the drink. Astrid looked so young, so attractive, so sophisticated. It was no contest. What was she supposed to do?—scream like a fishwife in a ridiculous self-parodying jealous rage?

Then she glimpsed herself in the glass of a framed Japanese print on the wall behind Astrid. What she saw gave her strength. She was no longer a dumpy little Viennese *Hausfrau*, but a slender, smartly dressed woman who might look her age but no older. And what she had to be angry about was not just the deceit of infidelity but the pretense of friendship.

She said coldly, "It's no good, Astrid. I know."

"Know what?" The tone was politely puzzled, the smile still warm.

"I know about you and Trent."

The smile faded. Its slow disappearance sent a feeling of triumph and also of malice surging up through Trudi.

She said contemptuously, "You cow."

Astrid sat down, looking shattered.

"Please, tell me . . ." she said in a low voice.

"You were with him that day. You met him there, on the

road. Got in the car with him. There was a witness. You bitch."

Astrid's wide blue eyes were fixed hard on Trudi's face as though in search of some message of enlightenment.

"Please," she said. "Please. I do not understand . . ."

"How do you want it?" mocked Trudi. "In English or in German? You were his mistress, his fancy woman, his tart, *seine Nutte!* You'd been with him a few minutes before he died. You came to the funeral, talked with me later, listened to me; acting, pretending, deceiving . . . bitch!"

Astrid had sunk her face into her hands and her long blond hair fell forward in a curtain, producing an effect of concealment and removal so complete that Trudi's words, unfueled in any case by more than lukewarm emotion, stuttered to a halt.

When the girl raised her head, her cheeks were wet with tears, but her expression was one of decision, almost of calculation.

"Forgive me," she said. "I loved him. He did not love me, not so much anyway. When he left Vienna, I was brokenhearted. I followed to plead with him. He was so angry when I contacted him, he did not want to see me, would only agree to meet for a few moments somewhere quiet and remote. Nothing happened that day, believe me, Trudi. But he was there because of me. It was me who led him to his death!"

Curiously, though not unmoved by the woman's emotion, Trudi found herself a little piqued at her arrogation of total responsibility for Trent's death.

She said sharply, "Don't be stupid. He died because . . . he died!"

It seemed pointless to prolong the interview.

She turned to the door.

"Trudi, are you going?"

"Of course I'm going," she said in surprise.

Astrid brushed away her tears and said, "You have come all the way to Vienna just to say this to me?"

Trudi laughed and said, "Don't flatter yourself! This was just a little extra treat and I wish I hadn't bothered."

"Trudi! Please. Do not go. Stay a little while. Let us talk."

Trudi looked at the Austrian woman shrewdly and said, "How odd. You seem almost relieved at what's happened."

"Relieved? Yes, yes, it is true. I am glad you have come. I am glad this thing is no longer between us."

The assumption that to know all automatically meant to forgive all irritated Trudi greatly.

"What do you mean it's no longer between us?" she demanded. "It will always be between us."

"But Trent is dead," said Astrid with the air of one who offers an irrefutable argument.

"That's what I mean by always," said Trudi, once more making for the door.

"Trudi! This is foolish. You must not go like this. It was nothing, please understand. It was not important!"

"It was important enough to bring you halfway across Europe after him," retorted Trudi.

"Oh yes; important for *me*. Of course it was important for me, but that need not bother you, need it? I loved Trent, I pursued him. I admit it. But why should what I felt bother you so much? It is what you believe *Trent* felt that makes you angry, and what he can never deny now he is dead. But he denied it to me. Yes, Trudi his last words to me, to *anyone*, were a denial that he loved me or had ever loved me."

Trudi said, "Are you trying to tell me he wasn't planning to go away with you?"

Astrid said, "You knew he was planning to go away?"

"I've worked it out," said Trudy grimly.

She could almost see the younger woman's mind working.

"Not with me," she said finally.

"Don't give me that!" exclaimed Trudi. "What's the matter, Fräulein Fischer? Do you know where the money is and think you can get your hands on it?"

This assault twisted Astrid's face into an expression that might have been shock, incomprehension, guilt, or even fear.

"What money?" she asked.

"Trent left me four thousand pounds, nothing more. Don't you recall how eager you were to help me go through his papers? God, I see it all now!"

"No, Trudi, you are wrong, believe me. You of all people should know how secretive Trent was. Even if what you say about his plans to leave is true, do you think he would have let me know about his financial arrangements?"

It was a telling argument. Trudi still had no real idea of the truth at the heart of all this business, but one thing she was certain of was that Trent would never let anyone else know the whole of it.

Sensing that her visitor's rage was on the ebb, Astrid said, "Trudi, please, whatever else you believe, believe I am glad to see you. You look so much better than last time. Dare I say it? So much younger. And so alive! Please, won't you sit down and have a drink. Look, have you eaten? I can make us a little meal. Please, just for an hour. You can be angry with me for the rest of your life if you like, but let us have an hour together to sit and talk."

She took Trudi's hands and drew her back into the room. Trudi did not, could not, resist. It was like a seduction, she thought. Perhaps, having had Trent, Astrid now thought she'd try his widow. How this horrifying idea should have popped into her head she did not know, but while the thought of any sexual contact with the younger woman had no appeal whatsoever, the prospect of a drink did.

She heard herself saying with a ridiculous bourgeois politeness, "No, but you're busy. I can see you're packing."

"Oh, *that*. I'm going away tomorrow. A week's skiing. But I don't have to set off till lunchtime. Please stay."

"All right," said Trudi, sitting down. "Just for a minute. I'll have a *schnapps*."

She awoke the next morning to discover that she'd missed breakfast. It had turned into a late night. They drank, then Astrid had scrambled some eggs to sober them up, then they drank some more. And they had talked. Trudi had got Astrid's life story, which seemed so littered with unhappy affairs that the liaison with Trent was reduced to one of a long series in which Astrid was the guaranteed loser. In return Astrid had received a blow-by-blow account of Trudi's decline and resurrection since they had parted after the funeral. Astrid had been fascinated by every detail. Trudi had been flattered by such an interested and admiring audience, and, though she could not remember all she had said, had a distinct impression that she had said all.

Astrid had suggested they meet again for coffee the following morning before she set out on her skiing trip. Trudi had been drunkenly adamant; she was far too busy. Piqued by Astrid's unconcealed skepticism, she had run through her proposed timetable, padding it out a little for the sake of emphasis. Now, by sleeping in, she found she was indeed going to be rushed, even assuming her proposed arrangements could be made. She should have made them in advance she knew, but once she'd decided to come to Vienna, it had seemed imperative to maintain the impetus and come at once.

She dialed Werner's number, unoptimistic that even the Austrian work ethic would have him on call at weekends. But she had forgotten that those who serve the rich are expected to earn their fees by instant availability. No, said the weary receptionist who answered the phone, Dr. Werner was not in his consulting rooms that morning, but if it was urgent, he could be contacted at his clinic near Kahlenbergerdorf. It was urgent, said Trudi. There was a long pause. Finally the girl came back on and said that the Herr Doktor would be pleased to see Frau Adamson if she could visit him at the clinic at three o'clock that afternoon.

Happily, the antique shop dovetailed nicely with this. Herr Müller, the appraiser, had just had an appointment canceled and was able to meet Trudi at the repository in an hour's time.

The repository was a gray windowless building close to the Danube canal. A sad-faced man in a dusty white coverall checked through an equally dusty ledger, then muttered something which Trudi did not catch.

"I beg your pardon?" she said.

"He is here already," said the man surlily.

"Who is?"

"Herr Adamson."

For a second Trudi felt her mind cloud like a glass of Pernod into which a drop of water had been trailed.

"No," she said. "You mean Herr Müller."

But the sad-faced man had already turned away and was leading her without a backward glance through a graveyard of shrouded furniture.

Their steps fell dully on the concrete floor. The walls gave back no echo. The only light fell in narrow columns from a series of small bulbs in long black cylindrical shades.

Eventually her guide halted alongside a bay in which some of the dust sheets had been removed. Trudi recognized an Italian writing bureau which she had bought for Trent nearly twenty years ago. There was no sign of Müller or anyone else. The warehouseman grunted something, then slowly began to remove the rest of the covers, his expression as unchangingly melancholic as if he were unveiling memorials of some savage war. Slowly Trudi saw the past emerge, familiar shapes rising as strange and sea-changed as salvage from an ancient wreck. Here she and Trent had sat together, from this table they had eaten, in this bed made love.

Finally the job was done. The man nodded and left, his footsteps fading rapidly. Where on earth was Müller? wondered Trudi in irritation, an emotion almost welcome as it momentarily held at bay the distress she could feel gathering at this encounter with the past.

Determinedly she began to check off the furniture against her own list, adding marks to show what she wished to sell and what she thought she would keep. There was little enough of the latter. She needed the money, and the expense of safe transport to England would be large. But something she ought to have. Surely even the dormouse did not leave its hibernatory nest without a sad backward glance?

She settled for a wine table and a collection of porcelain figurines. The bureau would have been nice, but it was too large, and besides several *amateurs* of furniture had assured her it was a really excellent piece, a bargain at the price she'd paid, which at the time had seemed exorbitant. She ran her fingers over the inlay, then saw with annoyance that there were some tiny scratches around the lock. Those had not been there before. Angrily she glanced around, intending to summon the custodian to make a complaint, but he was long gone. Delving into her handbag, she produced Trent's key fob and sorted out the bureau key. To her relief it turned easily, so at least the lock was not damaged. She pulled the lid of the bureau, which formed the writing desk, and began to unlock the small internal drawers revealed. They were empty as she'd expected, but when she slid open the conventional "secret" inner drawer behind these, she saw it contained a few sheets of paper. She took them out.

Behind her there was a noise, a soft footfall.

Her mind said *Herr Müller*, but the word scarcely articulated from her constricted throat was *Trent*.

A hand plucked at the papers in her hand. She swung around, but saw no one. The air was full of a billowing grayness which descended upon her and enveloped her and crushed tightly around her with the strength of strong arms, forcing her to the floor. She tried to cry out but the grayness stifled her; she tried to struggle but the grayness constricted her. Or perhaps it was just her own terrors that paralyzed her tongue and her limbs. Awareness of this possibility brought back strength. She wrestled wildly along the floor, crashing into pieces of furniture, till at last she was out of the constricting grayness and able to draw in deep breaths of the stuffy air and then let them out again in high, rhythmic shrieks as she saw crouching over her a broad, bright-eyed man with a turbulent black beard.

"Please, please, Mrs. Adamson," he said helplessly. "It is me, Herr Müller. We are to meet here. Please. Please."

Still shrieking, she became aware that beside him stood the sad-faced custodian. Slowly the shrieks became sobs, the sobs became deep body-racking breaths, as the two men untangled her from the huge dust sheet that had been tossed over her head, and helped her into one of her own chairs.

"What has happened? What has happened?" asked Müller, who seemed beneath his fearsome appearance to be a mild-mannered and uncertain kind of man.

"Didn't you see? Didn't you see anything?" demanded Trudi.

"No. The storeman was bringing me to where you were, and then we saw you rolling around on the floor entangled in this sheet."

"And no one else? You saw no one else?"

The bearded head shook. The sad face did not respond. It seemed to be listening. Was that a distant door closing?

"Herr Adamson," said the warehouseman. And nodded his head as if this assertion explained everything.

CHAPTER
3

The warehouseman was not very helpful. *Dark, thickset*, was the nearest he came to a description. But from his cubbyhole he produced what he clearly felt was his clinching argument, one of Trent's business cards.

Herr Müller suggested calling the police, but was clearly relieved when Trudi shook her head and said it must have been just someone's silly joke. She left him to do the valuation by himself, arranging to contact the shop later. Just now all she wanted was to be out of that gloomy mausoleum into the bright winter air.

She took a taxi to the Drei Hacken in Singerstrasse. It was very crowded but that was what she wanted. Seated at a table with two young men and three girls who didn't even give her a second glance, she felt safe. She ordered goulash and *ein viertel*. After the *viertel* she felt safer and now for the first time she turned her attention to the scrap of paper which was all that remained after the other sheets had been torn from her grip.

If she'd been expecting a clue, she was disappointed. It was evidently part of a sheet on which at some time Trent had been scribbling details of some new or intended acquisitions for his collection of Orwelliana. In his distinctive hand he'd scribbled "*1984* ISBN 55 683421067 BE."

So what had the attack been all about? Could it really have been a "silly joke"? But even silly jokes had *some* point.

She ate her lunch, had another drink, gave up puzzling. It didn't help. Life was too short for puzzles. Half a liter of white wine reduced things to basics. It seemed a waste of time traveling out to Kahlenbergerdorf to see Werner. Better to go back to the hotel, have a sleep, eat a quiet dinner, sleep again, rise, pack and go home.

But where was home? That house in Sheffield? Even that was not to be hers for long.

It occurred to her that high among the basics the wine had reduced things to was money. What she wanted from Werner was a clean certificate of health for Trent, to support her compensation case.

She ordered a black coffee and then went to check the times of trains to Kahlenbergerdorf.

Kahlenbergerdorf was an attractive old village in the Wienerwald to the north of the city. Trudi had been there before and had dined in the restaurant on the Kahlenberg itself, which, at nearly five hundred meters, was the highest of the hills in the Vienna woods and afforded magnificent views over the town. But she had never heard of the Kahlenberg Klinik.

Alighting from the train, she asked directions of the village stationmaster. To her dismay he told her the clinic was in fact a good five miles beyond the village, and she was just computing the likely cost of a taxi when a tall young man dressed not unlike an SS officer without the insignia walked up to her, clicked his heels and said, "Frau Adamson?"

"Yes?"

"I am Dieter, Dr. Werner's driver. Will you come this way, please?"

He led her out of the station and opened the door of a gleaming white Mercedes with a flourish which, like his heel-clicking, contained an element of unpindownable mockery. But the suspicion of mockery was preferable to the expense of a taxicab.

They headed in the direction of the Kahlenberg for a while but then turned off the main road onto a minor road, then off that onto a forest track which ran between close-crowding, narrow-trunked trees. Another turn, and they came to a halt before a high security gate. Some unseen eye must have assessed their admissibility, for after a couple of seconds the gate swung open and they drove in.

The driveway curved upwards towards what had probably been a nineteenth-century hunting lodge which now rested patriarchally amidst a circle of lower modern buildings, all concrete and glass, and joined to the older edifice by covered ways.

The car stopped in front of the lodge and the chauffeur helped her out.

"Reception is through the main door, Madame," he said with his mocking formality.

"Thank you, Dieter," said Trudi.

"Thank *you*, Madame."

She went up the shallow flight of steps and pushed open the door of the lodge. It's possible to smell wealth, and life with Trent had given Trudi a good nose for it. This place had the opulent feel of a very good, very expensive, old-fashioned hotel. Clearly a lot of money had been spent on refurbishment, but not at the expense of character.

There was nothing so vulgar as a reception desk. A smiling young woman in an elegant dark suit came forward to greet her.

"Is it Frau Adamson? Hello. How good to see you. I'm Elvira Altenberg. Have you had a good journey? Would you like to tidy up in the ladies' room? No. In that case, let's go straight up. The doctor is expecting you."

She led Trudi up an ornately carved flight of stairs into a wide high room where velvet-draped windows displayed a spectacular view south towards the city. There *was* a desk here, but big enough and old enough and polished enough and empty enough to be far from vulgar. Behind it sat Werner.

He stood up as Trudi entered. He fitted the setting perfectly, exuding rich confidence and charm as if he were being paid by the ounce.

"Mrs. Adamson, how nice to see you again. Sit down, please. Will you have a drink? A coffee? No? Thank you, Elvira."

The smiling girl withdrew. Werner nodded encouragingly at Trudi.

"I never thanked you properly for coming to Trent's

funeral," she said. "As you probably noticed, without you there would have been few mourners."

"I had to come," he said. "Such a shock, such a loss."

"Yes. Were you surprised when he decided to leave Vienna, by the way?"

"Why, yes, I was," said Werner. "One never likes to lose a friend."

"You don't recall when he told you he was moving, do you?"

"I'm sorry," laughed Werner. "My memory isn't so good. Is it important?"

"No. I'm sorry. I was just rambling on," apologized Trudi.

"Of course. Forgive me. I did not mean to cut you off. I am delighted to sit all day and talk of poor Trent."

Trudi shook her head, as much to clear it as in denial.

"What I would really like to ask you, Doctor, is about the state of Trent's health."

"That's easy. It was excellent. He was in tip-top condition for a man of his age. But pardon me, why do you ask?"

Trudi explained. Werner listened carefully.

"Interesting. But such things can mean nothing. An autopsy on any of us might show as much. I am very happy, Frau Adamson, to give you a certificate confirming that Trent was in the best of health, in no danger of not surviving his full natural span. That may be important in deciding the amount of compensation. Forgive me for asking, but it's important to you, this compensation?"

"Oh yes. I need the money," said Trudi. "Also I like justice, Dr. Werner. Now, forgive *me* for asking, but I didn't realize you and Trent were so close."

"We became friends over the years. The attraction of opposites, perhaps." He smiled, letting her fill in the oppositions: the smooth, sophisticated, artistic man-about-town; the sturdy, physical, opportunist man of action.

"Also, he let me in on one or two business deals. He had a sharp eye for commercial growth, your husband!" laughed Werner.

"Did he? I wish he'd planted his seeds more accessibly," said Trudi bitterly. "Did he ever talk to you about his plans for the future, Doctor?"

"No. I was surprised when he was going back to England, but Trent was not a man to let you know more than he wanted."

The telephone, one of two objects allowed to rest on the dark oak desk (the other was an orchid in a crystal vase), rang.

"Excuse me," said Werner.

He picked up the receiver, listened, said, "I understand," and replaced it.

"Mrs. Adamson," he said. "It's none of my business, but I am puzzled by the implications of what you say. Am I right in inferring that you yourself had no idea what Trent was planning, and that you have found he left you unprovided for?"

"You're right in every respect, Doctor. I *had* no idea; he *did* leave me unprovided; and it *is* none of your business."

"Of course. I'm sorry. Except, I must say, I am sure Trent would not intend this. The accident must have happened at the worst of times for him. He was too careful and too sharp a man not to have put money aside. Perhaps an account, or an investment, you did not know about and which has not yet come to light?"

"Nothing," said Trudi. "We checked most carefully through his old bank records. If there'd been anything, I'm sure we'd have found it."

"We?"

"Myself and a friend. And, of course, Mr. Ashburton, my solicitor."

"Good, good. It is wise to seek help."

He was fondling the petals of the orchid. It was the gentlest of movements but Trudi guessed that in a man of his *sang-froid* it amounted to a nervous fiddling.

"Mrs. Adamson," he said. "Forgive me if once more I seem to trespass where it is not my business, but I speak now as a doctor. You surprise me. You are different from what I expected. Yes, I know we only ever met a couple of times, but Trent did tell me something of your medical history. Don't be surprised. It was purely out of his concern for you, of course."

"Of course. So you expected a pliant neurotic, Doctor?"

"No. But clearly there has been a change. Perhaps more than you yourself realize. It's a traumatic experience, grief. It can modify personality. And it can impair judgment. The post-bereavement period is a time for taking great care. What I'm saying is, I was Trent's friend and his doctor. If you ever want my help or advice in either capacity, do not hesitate to ask."

"Thank you very much," said Trudi, faintly bewildered. "I'll certainly keep that in mind."

"Yes," said Werner.

He pressed a button on his phone. A moment later Elvira appeared.

"If you leave your address with Elvira, I will see that you get a comprehensive certificate of health for Trent," he said. "Elvira will arrange for the car to drive you back to the city. No, I insist. Good luck, Mrs. Adamson. I hope we will be in touch in the very near future."

He offered his hand. She took it. He held her hand for a moment with a pressure that felt significant.

She followed the girl from the room but after descending only half a dozen of the stairs she said, "My handbag. I must have left it."

Turning, she ran back to Werner's office, knocked once and entered.

The doctor was standing with her bag in his hand. It was open.

"Oh, it is yours," he said. "I thought it must be. I was just checking."

He closed it with a snap and handed it over.

"Thank you," said Trudi. "Goodbye again."

Downstairs the girl made a note of her address and then led her outside where the white Mercedes gleamed in the winter sunshine. The chauffeur, Dieter, already had the rear door open for her.

"Goodbye, Frau Adamson," said Elvira. "And please accept my condolences on your sad loss. He was a fine man."

"You knew him?" said Trudi.

"I met him when he came to the clinic," said the girl. "Goodbye now. *Aufwiedersehen!*"

The car purred away towards the security gate, which opened as it approached.

Trudi sat in thoughtful silence for most of the journey but as they approached the center of the city she leaned forward and said, "Have you been working long for the doctor, Dieter?"

"A little while, Madame."

"I see. I was wondering, what kind of conditions does he treat at the clinic?"

The chauffeur laughed.

"For the wealthy, any condition, Madame."

He glanced in the mirror to see her reaction. Trudi smiled encouragingly.

"But mainly I believe the clinic is for addiction, Madame."

"Addiction."

"Tobacco, alcohol, drugs. They once treated a man who was addicted to Wagner, or so the nurses say."

He laughed again, but this time Trudi could not respond with a smile.

CHAPTER
4

The phone was ringing as Trudi unlocked the door of Hope House. She snatched it up and said, "Hello."

"So you are back," said Janet. "I was getting worried."

"I've just got in this very second. I've not even shut the door. Hang on."

She banged the front door shut, went through into the lounge, lit the gas fire and returned to the phone.

"Hello," she said.

"How are you? All right?"

Trudi examined the question, examined her surroundings, examined herself.

"Good Lord," she said, surprised. "How am I? I'm glad to be home! Who'd have ever imagined I'd get to thinking of Sheffield as home!"

"Great," said Janet dismissively. "And how was Vienna?"

"Interesting."

"Don't go all dormousey on me! Tell, tell!"

"No," said Trudi firmly. "I'm tired and I'm grubby and I need to brood a bit. It'll keep till Wednesday."

"Oh, hoity-toity! Couldn't we meet earlier, tomorrow say?"

"I work on Mondays now, remember?"

"Oh, all right," said Janet, disappointed. "Nothing from the Agency yet?"

"No. And there's no mail."

"I might have known they'd find you hard to place," said Janet in bitchy revenge for her friend's refusal to communicate. "What did you ask for? Robert Redford?"

It was good to be back in touch with Janet's sharp friendship, thought Trudi as she put the phone down. But it would do her no harm not to receive an instant breakdown of her friend's affairs as they happened. Also, Trudi hadn't been lying when she said she needed to brood a bit.

But as she lay in bed, she found that it was Janet's reminder of the Lewis Agency that stuck in her thoughts. That had been a mistake, she now acknowledged, an act of bravado. After her weekend in Vienna, she didn't need to go out in pursuit of complications in her life. She put it top of her list of things to sort out, and as if in response to one firm decision, her body relaxed and she fell asleep.

At Class-Glass the following morning, she found several letters from various countries. She typed out translations of each, drafted formal replies for those which needed no more, and halfway through the morning was finished. She'd brought a book, but it lay unopened on the desk as she twirled in her revolving chair and watched her face flash by in the mirror-studded wall. It would be amusing, she thought idly, to dance naked in such a room.

Then she started in fear as she glimpsed another figure reflected behind her own.

Stanley Usher was standing in the open doorway, smiling down at her. She felt herself blushing.

"Good morning," she said.

"Morning," he replied, coming into the room. "And how are you? Better than me, I bet. I spent the weekend sailing, would you believe? In this weather. I must be mad. That chap got it right who said it was like standing under a cold shower, tearing up money! What about you? Do anything interesting?"

The question was so casual as to be provocative.

"Not much," said Trudi. "I was in Vienna. It was cold there too."

"Vienna? You mean, Vienna, *Austria?*"

"That's right."

"Good Lord. Holiday?"

"Business," said Trudi. "I've put the mail in the tray there, all translated. And I've done the letters you left. Mr. Usher, is there really going to be enough work here to occupy me for two days a week?"

"Trying to talk yourself out of a job, Mrs. Adamson? Let's wait and see, shall we?"

He stayed about an hour. As he left, Trudi said, "Would it be all right if I went early for lunch?"

Usher's saturnine face twisted into a grin.

"If you can find the time, by all means!"

At twelve o'clock she was climbing the stairs to the Lewis Agency. A night's sleep had not diluted her resolution to sign off there. She could have done it by phone or by letter, but something in her required that she should from now on meet problems face to face.

This new determination enabled her to pass people on the stairs with none of her previous embarrassment, and even the presence at the Agency door of two workmen who paused in their work of repairing the lock to grin cheerily at her didn't provoke a blush.

Mrs. Fielding greeted her with preemptive delight.

"Mrs. Adamson, how extraordinary, I was just writing to you. Sit down, please do. I'm so sorry not to have been in touch earlier, but really, there didn't seem to be anyone suitable on our books. Then not an hour ago a gentleman came in who seemed to fit your requirements to a 'T.' You'd almost think he'd been cut out to your pattern, if you'll excuse the phrase! What's more, *you* fit *his* requirement profile almost as closely. It's quite amazing! Of course, there's no guarantee that you'll take to each other at all, but on paper it's a perfect match, perfect!"

She sounded so delighted that Trudi did not have the heart to reveal the true purpose of her visit. Instead she meekly accepted the duplicated sheet of details Mrs. Fielding handed her, and studied it.

James Brewster Dacre was fifty-one years old, five feet ten and a half inches tall, weighing in at twelve stones six. Divorced. Income bracket "C" (£15,000 plus per annum), Company director. Nonsmoker, nonchurchgoer, fond of the theater, reading, the countryside . . . Mrs. Fielding was right, thought Trudi. On paper, he certainly fitted the bill.

"You liked him?" she asked.

"Yes, I did," admitted the woman. "He came across very well. A little reserved, not shy exactly, but certainly not pushy. I may be entirely wrong, but I felt he was the character type I would guess you were looking for. You have to get used to seeing behind the forms very quickly in this business. And when I'm wrong, I get told pretty quickly, and also pretty sharply sometimes, so I take pains to be right! What do you think?"

"Well, on paper, he certainly looks to be the right type," admitted Trudi.

"Would you like to meet him?"

This was the moment to tell Mrs. Fielding that she'd changed her mind. Instead she found herself glancing at the office door, as if half fearful this paragon was going to be put on view this very minute.

Mrs. Fielding laughed and said, "I don't mean *now*, Mrs. Adamson. Think about it. The first move's up to you, as I explained at our first interview. He'd like to hear from you. I showed him your details—no address or phone number, of course—and after a few questions, he said yes."

"That was big of him."

"No. Just cautious. Like yourself," reproved Mrs. Fielding. "Anyway, there's his telephone number. Whatever you decide, could you let me know in forty-eight hours, so I know whether to keep you both in circulation or put you on hold."

By now it was far easier to take the number and promise to get in touch than to announce her decision to withdraw.

Mrs. Fielding accompanied her to the outer door.

"Why are you changing the lock?" wondered Trudi.

"We had a break-in over the weekend," said Mrs. Fielding. "Most distressing. No need to worry, our filing cabinets are secure. But they took some stamps, the petty-cash box and my little transistor."

"How awful," said Trudi.

The workman stood aside to let her pass.

One of them smiled and said, "All right then, luv?"

Trudi found herself smiling back at him.

"Grand," she heard herself saying like a native. "And how are you, *luv?*"

That night she found herself seriously considering what to do about James Brewster Dacre. The real question seemed to be, which was the greater act of independence from Janet—to make contact or to withdraw?

Better still, she told herself savagely, would be to do what she herself wanted. But choice, like self-knowledge, was never so simple.

She diverted her mind to a simpler or at least more concrete problem. Money. She was still some way from being destitute but it came as a surprise to her how rapidly even a relatively frugal existence ate away at cash. When the house lease ran out, she could foresee real problems. There was the money from the furniture sale to come, but on past performance, that wouldn't go far. The only consoling thought was that she hadn't yet disposed of Trent's watches and the other bits and pieces which Janet had stored in the shoebox. Any sentimental value they possessed had been considerably diminished by the discovery of Trent's affair with Astrid. Not even the Orwell first editions could feel complacent about their future now, she told herself bitterly.

But first things first. She was mad to have things so attractive to any casual burglar lying around the house. She ought at least to have them inventoried and valued. She went in search of the shoebox.

There were two watches, one a Rolex and the other a gold Cartier. Cufflinks, also gold. Another set, diamond studded. An ornamental ingot, 24 carat, on a fine chain. He had liked his gold, had Trent, she thought. All this must be worth a few bob, she told herself hopefully.

Her eye fell on the wallet they'd found in the cheap jacket. She opened it. Janet had removed the money it contained, she recalled, but there were still the credit cards, which she ought to have destroyed.

She took them out and got a pair of nail scissors and prepared to cut them in half.

Then she paused in simple puzzlement.

The plastic oblongs were not in fact credit cards but a check card and a cash card from the same national bank.

But it wasn't this unremarkable discovery that stayed her hand. It was the name of the card holder, clearly printed on each of the cards.

Not Trent Adamson, but Eric Blair.

Eric Blair.

She sat for many minutes studying the cards like a Tarot reader who sees a future she does not care to foretell.

Eric Blair. The name somehow was familiar. A business friend of Trent's perhaps? She was almost certain she had heard him mention it. But that still didn't explain why he had the cards. In this imitation leather wallet. In that awful Terylene suit.

Hypotheses were forming and collapsing in her mind like the crazy snow shapes whipped up by a blizzard. She felt a strong urge to ring Janet, but fought against it. What she needed was a distraction from these whirling thoughts, not an extra ringmaster to keep them galloping round.

The phone was in her hand. There was, she realized, in all the world only one other number she had any reason to dial.

She did it so unconsciously that she started in shock when a voice said in her ear, "Dacre here. Hello!"

The line wasn't good. Through the crackles, the voice sounded level and featureless.

"Mr. Dacre? Mr. James Brewster Dacre?"

"Yes."

"I'm Mrs. Adamson. Trudi Adamson."

"Ah yes, Mrs. Adamson."

A pause. Time now for a long, subtly probing conversation, then a decision. But Trudi found she had no art for subtle probing on the telephone.

She said bluntly, "Shall we meet?"

"Yes, I think so. Where? When?"

"Twelve-thirty tomorrow. The Crucible Bar," said Trudi, recalling Janet's advice.

"I'll be there," said the voice. "Goodbye now, Mrs. Adamson."

The receiver was replaced. Trudi banged hers down as if in an effort to beat him to this punch. She reckoned that in terms of businesslike brusqueness she was at least level on points.

It occurred to her that they hadn't arranged any recognition signals. So what? she told herself. I probably won't turn up anyway!

She went to bed.

CHAPTER 5

It was going to be Trent.

Sleep had come hard the previous night. Distraction from one worry had simply given her another. Now at last the two had combined and the solution was simple. Trent, who had become Eric Blair, could just as easily have become James Brewster Dacre. Wasn't the profile of requirements she had given Mrs. Fielding a simple blueprint of Trent? Then there'd been the break-in. Trent had been there, read her file, smiled that bleak, knowing, humorless smile. It all fitted. In her sleep she could flee him, escape into wakingness. Now he had found a way to follow her. Good old Trent! He always came back!

She drank her vodka. It was the second in ten minutes. She'd arrived early to give him the test of identifying her, but looking around, it didn't seem a problem. There was no one but young people here today, lively, extroverted, casually dressed, all familiar with each other. Her age, her dress, her aloneness, must have made her stand out like a creature from another world!

It was a good image if Trent did appear. Takes a one to know a one. The outstretched hand, the cold touch, and then she'd be away to whatever shadowy world Trent now traveled in.

She finished her vodka and stood up. She had tasted freedom and no one, not even a ghost, was going to lull her back into that long coma from which she had woken with such pain.

"Mrs. Adamson?" said a voice.

She looked round. A well-made man with heavy, rather watchful features and a slightly unruly sweep of grizzled brown hair was addressing her.

"I hope I'm not late," he said. "I'm James Dacre."

He held out his hand. She took it. His clasp was warm, dry and firm. Build apart, he looked nothing like Trent.

She laughed in nervous relief, saw what an odd response this must appear, pulled herself together and said, "Yes. Trudi Adamson. How do you do?"

He said, "Let me get you a drink."

She said, "Thanks, but, would you mind, I think I'd rather walk. If that's all right?"

"Of course," he said, standing back to let her past.

She glanced at the bar as she left. No one was paying them the slightest attention, and the average age of the customers suddenly seemed to have risen by ten years. Perhaps it was foolish to have exchanged its comfort and warmth for these cold streets, but as they walked in silence for a while, the instinctive wisdom of her decision made itself felt. There is a companionableness about walking side by side that makes conversation unnecessary until it comes naturally, and then it is the easier between strangers because it is not face to face.

"Have you lived in Sheffield long?" he asked.

"Not long. We'd more or less just arrived when my husband died."

"I'm sorry."

"It was a car accident."

"Yes. Mrs. Fielding told me. It must have been dreadful."

"What about you?"

It was a question interpretable in many ways, but she did nothing to make it specific.

"Not long," he said. "I'm from the North Riding originally, but I've worked abroad most of my life. I got divorced last year. It fizzled out. No recriminations, well, not many. And I thought I'd come back to settle."

"But not in the north?"

"No," he said. "I went up there, but the roots are all broken except for a few ancients who want to talk about the even more ancient and long dead. But I thought I'd stay in Yorkshire, give it a try."

"Any children?" asked Trudi.

"No. You?"

"No."

"Chance or choice?" he asked, adding, "Chance, in our case," as though to make easier the first positive step towards an exchange beyond the merely informational.

"Choice," she said, not meaning to lie but recognizing the lie as she spoke it. The choice had been Trent's, not hers. She had merely reflected it, as usual.

"Well, it's a free country," he said. "But it can leave you lonely."

"That's why you went to Mrs. Fielding? Because you were lonely?"

"I suppose so. Is there another reason?"

She was amazed to hear herself reply casually, "Sex, I suppose."

He smiled briefly and said, "I suppose that's a possibility. But a man after that would be better off joining one of these swinging-single clubs. There are more widows than widowers, it seems, so there's plenty of choice."

"Sounds like a male pipe-dream," she said.

He laughed and said, "You have a nice turn of phrase. Yes, I suppose they're O.K. if you like playing musical beds."

"Which you don't? What's your game, then?"

"Sorry?"

Trudi suddenly realized she was being quite uncharacteristically aggressive.

She said, "Sorry. What I mean is, if that's not what you're looking for, what is it?"

"Just to get to know someone," he said slowly. "There's more to life than quick pleasures, I reckon, though I don't mind quick pleasures. But they weren't what I was after when I went along to the Agency. No, I was looking for something a bit more solid. I'm hoping for something that will see me through."

"See him through *what*, for God's sake?" demanded Janet.

"Life, I suppose."

"Christ, it's like buying your last pair of shoes! And what happened after that?"

"Nothing much."

"Nothing much?" exclaimed Janet. "So much has happened to you since last time we met that I need another ten months to ask all my questions! And all you can say is *nothing much!*"

To tell the truth, Trudi was quite enjoying the storyteller's sense of power when the narrative grips the listener like a drug yearning. Her trip to Vienna, her confrontation of Astrid, the assault in the repository, the Eric Blair mystery, the meeting with James Dacre, all these had radically interfered with Janet's enjoyment of her cod and chips.

"All we did was walk and talk."

"No lunch? Mean bastard!"

"He offered. I said I wasn't hungry."

"Silly! It's a good test, see where they take you, how they behave. What's he do?"

"It says *company director* on his details."

"It probably says *St. Michael* on his Y-fronts, but that doesn't mean he keeps a halo down there. Haven't you noticed, the docks of our courts are jam-packed with company directors? What did you find out about his company?"

"Nothing," admitted Trudi. "But his fingernails weren't broken or dirty and his cuffs weren't frayed and his toe-caps weren't cracked, so that's all in his favor, isn't it?"

"Satire now, is it? I'm not sure I didn't prefer you when all I could get out of you was a mouselike squeak! So, when are you seeing him again?"

"Tomorrow," said Trudi. "In my lunch break. I'm seeing him in a pub this time and we're going to have a bite to eat."

"Well, I'll expect an updated report immediately," said Janet. "Now let's get back to the other things. This Blair character. Are the cards still valid?"

"Yes. For another month, I think."

"Then there's a chance the account still exists."

"So what?"

"So the bank must have an address! I wonder how we can get it."

"Can't we just ask?" said Trudi.

Janet laughed.

"Not nowadays. Very distrusting places, banks. Never worry though, I'll put my mind to it."

"But why should we want an address?" asked Trudi.

"Come on! Either there's a real Eric Blair, in which case you've got his bank cards. Or there isn't a real Blair. In which case Trent made him up. In *which* case, if there's any money in that account, it could belong to you."

A thought struck her.

"Of course, the way these cash cards work, all you need to do is stick it in the dispenser, key your personal code and then it'll tell us how much is in the account, won't it?"

"Except for one thing," said Trudi. "We don't know the personal code."

"It's only four figures," said Janet dismissively.

"That's a lot of possible combinations. Key the wrong one twice and the machine keeps the card. I know. It's happened to me. I've a rotten memory," said Trudi.

"All right, killjoy. I'll work on it. Now, this other business in Vienna. God, what an exciting life you live! It's like something out of *Dynasty*. You've no idea who'd want to attack you?"

"None. And it wasn't much of an attack," protested Trudi.

"Brave now, are we? Let's have a look at that bit of paper you found."

Obediently Trudi dug into the depths of her bag.

Janet studied it and said, "What's *ISBN* stand for?"

"International Standard Book Number. They're in every book, as you'd know if you ever read one. And *1984* is a book by George Orwell, you see."

"Don't go clever on me," said Janet darkly. "All right, so this means nothing. It's what was on the paper the mugger took away from you that bothers me. I'll work on it. You put it right out of your mind for the time being. All you need to work on is keeping your knees together till you find out a hell of a lot more about your precious company director!"

Trudi laughed at Janet's words but that night they kept on coming back to her. The next day, as she poked at the lemon in her gin and tonic, she heard herself saying, "What exactly is it that you direct?"

"Direct?"

"Trade or profession—company director," she quoted. "That's what you said."

"Oh that!" He sipped at his beer. They were sitting in a pub not far from the Class-Glass office.

"It's a business consultancy. Well, it will be when I get it going."

"Oh. Is that what you did abroad?"

"More or less," he said. "I suppose I was a kind of troubleshooter. Sorted out problems."

"What kind of problems?"

"Very dull ones, mainly. Does it matter?"

"I was just interested in what you did," she said, piqued.

"Sorry. I didn't mean to be rude. What I meant was, does it matter what a man does? I mean, are there some jobs that would turn you off? Like a policeman, say? Or a soldier?"

She considered.

"I don't think I'd jib at either of those," she said. "But I'd be a bit chary of an undertaker, I think. Or a mass murderer."

"I see. Well, a man makes a living the best way he can," said Dacre. "Circumstances limit choice. Look at you."

She'd told him about Class-Glass and Stanley Usher. It had sounded boring to her, but Dacre had that gift of close listening which draws out rather more than the speaker intends.

"Oh, I don't mind. It's boring, but it's better than nothing."

She glanced at her watch and said, "Damn. It's time for me to go back and be bored already."

Her regret was genuine. She was feeling nicely relaxed in Dacre's company. He had dry quiet wit and so far had proved very unpushy.

"If you're not busy, would another five minutes matter?" he asked

"Oh no," she said seriously. "Not at all. And I doubt if Mr. Usher will be looking in today. But being there is what I get paid for. That's what matters. No, no need for you to move. You haven't finished your beer. Thanks for the sandwich. I've enjoyed it."

"Me too," he said, smiling.

There was a pause. Is this it? Trudi wondered. A smiling farewell, a decision not to proceed? Would she mind?

She wasn't sure, but she was sure she'd mind not knowing.

He said, "Will you be in town tomorrow?"

"I might be."

"How about lunch? Proper sit-down lunch, I mean."

"All right. But Dutch."

"Cuisine, you mean?"

They laughed together. It was a good feeling.

"Let's meet in the Crucible bar again, shall we? And go on from there. Twelve o'clock?"

"That'll be fine," said Trudi.

When she got back to the office, the phone was ringing. It was Janet.

"Where've you been? Having your wicked way with Mr. Faker?"

"Dacre. I do get a lunch break."

"That's what they call it now, is it? I'll want a full report on that later. But listen, I think I may have made a bit of progress. Not me really, but Frank."

"Frank?" said Trudi, taken aback. "I'm sorry. What's Frank got to do with anything?"

"He's my husband, remember?" said Janet. "Oh look, I can guess what you're thinking, and no, I don't go running back and repeating everything you tell me down to the last detail. But I do talk to him, Trudi. And it's just as well I do. All I told him was that you'd come across this check card in the name of Eric Blair and we were wondering how to get his address from the bank in case he was a business contact of Trent's. All he said was, go and have a word with the manager. Very helpful! I know what that would get us. No information and the cards confiscated. But then Frank suddenly had a real inspiration. One a decade's about his limit, I should think, so we were really lucky. *Eric Blair*, he says. *That's familiar. I came across it in the* Telegraph *crossword the other week*. That's one thing he's got in common with Trent. He's a devil for his crosswords. Anyway, *I'll tell you what it is*, he says. *Eric Blair's George Orwell's real name!* There! See how it fits? Trent wants a fake name, what better than his hero's real one! Just the way his mind would work. I'm surprised you didn't spot it yourself."

"It did sound familiar," admitted Trudi, trying to conceal a sudden rush of resentment at her friend's discovery, or at least the manner of retelling it. "But why on earth *should* he want a false name?"

"Why not? It was you who reckoned he was going to leave you. Perhaps he was going to go the whole hog. Now, don't go broody on me, will you? Listen. Frank's not the only one due an inspiration. You know those cash cards? Well, the first time you use them, if you don't like the number they've given you, you can select another that you'll find easier to remember. Now suppose that's what Trent did? See what I mean? No harm in giving it a try, is there? Have you got the card with you?"

"Yes, it's still in my purse. But what number are you suggesting I should use?"

"Why, 1984, of course, girl. 1984!"

There was a branch of Blair's bank only a few minutes' walk away. She hesitated, recalling her rather smug little speech to James Dacre about being paid to be here. But she found she was too impatient to wait till after work.

Scribbling a note saying *Back in five minutes*, she left the office.

At the cash dispenser, she had to wait. When her turn came, she was almost ready to abandon the affair, it seemed so futile. But she thought of Janet and inserted her card. The display panel invited her to key her four-figure code.

She pressed *1 . . . 9 . . . 8 . . . 4* and waited.

Silence. A blank.

Then the message flashed up.

WRONG NUMBER KEYED

PLEASE KEY CORRECT NUMBER

She felt almost relieved. She realized that deep down in her subconscious there must be a strong desire for time to close its water over Trent and leave her to strike out for whatever possible future there might be.

It seemed an almost symbolic act to press the CANCEL button, but for some reason her finger remained poised.

Trent was a careful man. An aide-memoire was useful, but he wouldn't make it too obvious. Suppose he'd reversed the number?

And if he hadn't, well, the machine might retain the card, and that would be one way of ridding herself of that problem!

She keyed *4 8 9 1*.

Silence. A blank screen.

And then almost shockingly the display lit up with a chart inviting her to key the service she wanted.

Her mind numb, she pressed BALANCE.

And waited.

Twenty seconds passed. She counted them.

Then once more the display flickered into life.

It took her another twenty seconds to register the green letters and figures.

And even longer to get the commas and decimal points into the right place.

Finally she believed what she saw and leaned against the bank wall for support.

At close of business on the previous day, Eric Blair's account had stood at £250,992.86p.

PART FOUR

I doubt na, whyles, but thou may thieve;
What then? poor beastie, thou maun live! . . .

BURNS: "To a Mouse"

CHAPTER
1

The following lunchtime, the Crucible bar felt like a very pleasant and familiar haven.

She had returned to her office the previous afternoon wondering whether to tell Janet. But the phone had rung as soon as she got in and there'd been no way not to.

Janet had been amazed, excited, and endlessly speculative. Finally Trudi had cut her short with lies about work. She had rung her again that evening and renewed the game till Trudi had protested, "Jan, I know you mean well, but, look, it's all a bit much for me. I want to forget about it if I can. For the time being anyway. I mean, there's nothing I can do, is there?"

"Nothing? You've got the card, you know the code, you can start taking the money out, that's what you can do for starters! Is there a withdrawal limit, I wonder? Only one way to find out. Hit that dispenser till it cries *enough! no more!*"

"Jan, I can't do that," said Trudi. "I don't know whose money it is. I don't know where it's come from. I suppose I ought to go to the police."

"*What?* Don't be daft, girl. They'd all be off to the Costa del Crooko on the proceeds! No, if that's the way you're thinking, stick to your first plan. Try to forget it! For the time being anyway!"

Trudi had gone to bed and tried to forget it. It proved

impossible, and when she slept, she dreamed of Trent, only this time when he turned towards her and reached out, his hands were full of banknotes. As usual she woke in terror. The house was still. She lay in the dark and thought of her father, that kind, quiet, loving man who had never altogether lost his German accent. Had he lived to make old bones, she guessed she would never have left him, but grown old as his daughter, companion, friend, and finally nurse. She had placed an absolute trust in him. When he died she had transferred that trust wholly, blindly, to Trent.

It was not a fair burden to load him with, she told herself in the darkness of her bedroom. If in the end he had found it unbearable, that was not a betrayal, not in any real sense.

She was still pursuing her vain quest for comfort at dawn.

Janet had returned to the attack the following morning, wanting to come to Sheffield to talk things through, as she put it.

Trudi had said bluntly no, it was impossible, she had a lunch date with James Dacre and there was no way she was going to break it.

"All right," said Janet rather waspishly. "But don't tell him about the money, else you'll never know whether it's you he's after or not, will you?"

In fact there were times during lunch when she had felt very tempted to confide in her companion.

They had gone to an Italian restaurant, simple and moderately priced. She guessed that if she hadn't reemphasized in the Crucible bar that they were going dutch, they'd have eaten somewhere rather more upmarket. Perhaps crystal glasses, discreet waiters and acres of white napery would have been better. The noisy, friendly informality of this place, plus the smallness of the tables and a bottle of Orvieto, quickly broke down a lot of barriers.

She found herself talking about Trent and their life abroad quite freely. With very little urging, she told him about the accident.

He said, "And this was when? Five months ago?"

She put her glass down rather hard and said abruptly, "Yes. Not long, is it?"

"I'm sorry, I didn't mean . . . Please believe me . . ."

"Probably you didn't, but you must be thinking, she was pretty fast off the mark after twenty-five years of marriage!"

"Why should I think that? I know how these things work. The closer you are to someone, the less other people matter, the bigger the gap when you lose them. After a full life, it's hard to live with emptiness."

It was a graciously romantic diagnosis. Trudi resisted the urge to deny it, to tell him savagely that her life had been full of nothing but pretense and torpor, and that the emptiness she wanted to fill stretched back for probably two decades. This wasn't the time or the place for such heart-barings, nor was she yet altogether certain he was the person.

But the temptation to lay the odd facts about Eric Blair before a neutral eye was strong. It was only the feeling that somehow this would be disloyal to Janet that held her back.

After lunch Dacre said, "In a hurry?"

"Not really."

"Then what about a walk? Indoor or out. I can arrange both."

"Clever old you. That would be nice."

He led her to his car, which was parked nearby. Trudi studied it carefully, preempting Jan's questions. It was a gray Ford Sierra, about a year old, with GB plates and 20,000 miles on the clock.

He drove swiftly and carefully the short distance to a large park which housed, according to the signs, the city's Art Gallery and Museum.

They walked in the park first. Dacre talked about his upbringing in a small farming community in the Cleveland Hills. Finally he paused, invitingly.

"Not much to tell," said Trudi. "My father was an Austrian refugee. He got out not long after the *Anschluss* in 1938."

"Was he political?"

"Not in any active sense. Just anti-Nazi. He was Jewish, you see. Not Orthodox. I never knew him to go to any kind of religious ceremony. And my mother wasn't Jewish. At least I don't think so."

"I'm sorry?"

"I mean, I didn't know her. She died shortly after I was

born. Complications of some kind, I don't know. My father didn't talk much about it. He couldn't. It really broke him up. He was very reserved, very suspicious in many ways. He came to the promised land, you see, fled his own country, and he was interned here when the war began, and mother died, and when he was released, he had a hell of a job getting hold of me to bring me up. He taught me to tread very softly, to suspect people's motives, never to answer the door after dark, to keep myself to myself . . ."

"He didn't teach you all that well!" laughed James Dacre.

"Oh, I'm sorry! I'm going on a bit, aren't I? It must be the wine . . ."

"Don't be sorry! It's interesting. So your family came from Austria? You must have had an interesting time chasing up relatives when you lived in Vienna?"

"No," said Trudi. "I had no contacts there. My father made no effort himself after the war. Perhaps he reckoned that everyone was dead, I don't know. As for my mother's family, all I ever gathered about them was that they disapproved of my father. That was enough to condemn them in my eyes. If he had felt it best to close the book as far as the past went, I could see no reason to reopen it."

"Simple curiosity, perhaps?" murmured Dacre. "Look, it's getting a bit chilly. Why don't we go inside? If the art doesn't appeal, perhaps we can get a cup of tea."

Trudi heard herself saying, "Why not come home with me? I'm not much of a cook, but I can brew a cup of tea."

He didn't hesitate but said, "Thanks. I'd like that. If you're sure . . ."

"Of course I'm sure. It's only a cup of tea!"

Before they'd got out of the car park, she realized she was far from sure, not about the tea but the wisdom of inviting him back. They performed the journey into the suburbs almost in silence. As they approached the house, Dacre said, "I think you've got visitors."

Trudi didn't know whether to be annoyed or relieved as she recognized Janet's green Escort in the driveway. Dacre parked by the curb and Janet got out of her car and came to the gateway to meet them.

"Hello, Trudi," she said. "I was in Sheffield, so I thought I'd just look in on my way home, see how you are."

Her sharp eyes were quartering James Dacre as she spoke. She probably knows more about him in a single glance than I've found out in three meetings, thought Trudi resignedly.

She performed the introductions. Janet and Dacre shook hands. Now there was a short hiatus.

Well, she's not going to diplomatically retire, thought Trudi. This time her feelings came down heavily for annoyance rather than relief.

"Let's go in, shall we?" she said rather stiffly. "And I'll make us all some tea."

"No, look, I was only going to have time for a quick cup anyway. I really ought to be off," said James Dacre.

"Don't let me chase you," said Janet, solidly planted in the driveway.

Trudi gave her a hard look, and at least she had the grace to withdraw a couple of yards towards the house.

"There's no need to go," said Trudi.

"Of course there isn't," smiled Dacre. "I mean, there's no need *here*. But I'm telling the truth. I would have had to make my excuses soon in any case."

"Well, thanks a lot," said Trudi.

"No need to thank me. We went dutch, remember? But it's my treat next time, I insist."

"Next time?"

"If that's O.K.? I'll be in touch."

As if the literal meaning of his words had suddenly struck him, he leaned forward, brushed her lips with his, climbed into his car and was gone.

"Come on, Beauty. The prince's kiss is supposed to wake you, not put you to sleep!"

Trudi turned and said wearily, "Oh Janet, you know I like to see you but . . ."

"But you wish I'd run under a juggernaut on the motorway? I'm sorry. Mind you, it's just as well I was here, if you ask me. At it on the pavement like a pair of pooches already, what would you have been like in the hallway? No, seriously, I am sorry to butt in, but I had to see you. I've got it, see? Eric Blair's address! What do you think of that?"

"Come inside and I'll tell you what I think," said Trudi. Inside Janet explained.

"Frank was taking me out to lunch today, but when I got to his office, he'd had to go out on a valuation. While I was waiting, I got this idea. I rang the two main Sheffield branches of our mystery man's bank, said I had an inquiry and gave the account number from the check card. First one said it wasn't theirs, so I laughed and said *Silly me!* But the second said, yes, what was the query? I knew they wouldn't just dish out information ad lib, so I said that Mr. Blair had been into the office of the estate agent where I was assistant manager and put down a deposit on a property he was interested in. Unhappily, within hours of his being here, complications had arisen. We needed to contact him urgently, but the stupid junior who had dealt with him in my absence hadn't got his address. His check was the only clue. Could the bank help? They asked for my number and said they'd get back to me. I guessed they were checking it really did belong to an estate agent's office. They were back on in five minutes, someone rather more important sounding, saying that they too were eager to get in touch with Mr. Blair. Nothing wrong? I said, all upset like I would be if I found I was holding a dud check. Oh no, on the contrary, they said. Mr. Blair was a customer in very good standing, only a trifle elusive. Should I contact him before they did, perhaps I could urge him to get in touch. And his last known address on their records was . . ."

Here Janet waved a piece of paper triumphantly.

". . . Well Cottage, near Eyam, Derbyshire."

She sat back, clearly ready to be overwhelmed in congratulations.

"Eyam? What's that?" said Trudi.

"It's a village, idiot. Quite famous, really. Don't you know anything? It's the plague village."

"Sounds charming."

"Stupid! It was three hundred years ago. The great plague was ravaging London. Someone brought it to Eyam, probably in fleas in a bale of cloth. When the villagers realized it had broken out, they went into voluntary quarantine, no one in or out till the epidemic was over. They died in droves; whole families were wiped out. All so it wouldn't spread all over the country."

"That was noble," said Trudi sincerely.

"Yes, wasn't it? But from our point of view the interesting thing is it's only a couple of miles from Grindleford and hardly any distance at all from where Trent had his accident. I rang the local post office and they gave me directions. Look, I've got it marked on the map here. It's outside the village, above it to the north, nice and isolated, it seems."

She spread out a newly purchased Ordnance Survey sheet and stabbed her finger down on it.

"That's great, Jan," said Trudi without much conviction. "You've been very clever. But you could have told me all this over the phone."

"Still moping over your lost date, are you?" said Janet. "You'd better get your priorities right! Yes, I could have told you over the phone, but I couldn't take you there, could I?"

"Take me there? You mean now?" said Trudi aghast.

"When else? Let the thought be father to the deed, that's my motto. So get upstairs and bring those keys of Trent's. Yes, *keys*, girl. To unlock doors with, remember? And better put your green Wellies on! We're going for a walk in the country!"

CHAPTER
2

The drive to Eyam took less than half an hour, but it was almost dark when they arrived. The sky above was relatively clear but the sun had set early into a mountain range of cloud looming menacingly on the western horizon.

It was probably a charming little place, thought Trudi. But the chill twilight, the emptiness of the streets, the sense of exclusion she always got from lighted windows, plus what

Janet had told her of the village's tragic history, combined to make the clustering houses and winding ways forbidding and sinister.

They drew up in front of a church. The land rose behind it, dark and mysterious, so that the church, whose windows glimmered dimly, stood like a staging post to that gloomy hinterland.

"We needn't have come into the village," explained Janet. "But I thought it best to get our bearings proper. Don't want to be banging on the wrong door, do we?"

"You could have stopped somewhere more cheerful," said Trudi.

"The church, you mean? It's very interesting, that. You should take a look sometime. List of all those that died in the plague. And the gravestones too, fascinating. Once drove over here with Alan and the kids when they were little. Had a picnic, I recall."

"You had family picnics in graveyards?" said Trudi. "What did you do for birthday treats? Visit abattoirs?"

"Easy," said Janet, looking at her curiously. "Don't be so uptight."

"I'm sorry. I just don't feel I want to do this, not at night anyway," replied Trudi, more vehemently than she intended.

"No? I'm sorry, I didn't realize it was bothering you so much," said Janet, immediately repentant. "You know me, I get carried away and I tend to carry everyone along with me! Look, let's forget it for tonight anyway. I'm sure I spotted a *les Routiers* sign back there. What about a drink, a spot of grub, then back home, and leave our exploring till the sun's high in the sky?"

Trudi considered, then sighed and shook her head.

"No," she said. "All I'll do is get a couple of drinks in me, then get brave and say *let's go anyway!* So we'll end up wandering around when it's pitch dark and we're full of Dutch courage. I'd rather go now, stone sober, while there's still a glimmer of light, and we'll be finished while the pubs are still open!"

"That makes sense," said Janet. "All right. I think I've got it now. Here we go!"

She doesn't trust me with the map! thought Trudi rebelliously. On the other hand if, with a bit of luck, they got completely lost and had to abort the mission, it wouldn't be her fault.

Her luck was out. With a rally driver's panache and sense of direction, Janet sent the car rocketing out of the village up a steep hill. A twist of the wheel took them off the metaled surface onto what felt like a flight of worn concrete steps. They bounced along for several minutes, turned again onto even rougher terrain, then the car came to a halt with a seatbelt-testing suddenness. Janet killed the lights.

"Here we are," she said triumphantly.

Trudi looked out. They seemed to be parked close against a hedge under a tree which cut off what light remained in the sky. Of human habitation there was not a sign. Suddenly the glow of those windows in Eyam no longer seemed excluding but most welcoming.

"*Where* are we?" she asked.

"Here. Well Cottage."

"But *where?*" said Trudi, helplessly.

"A hundred yards further on," said Janet confidently. "I thought it best not to drive right up to the door. You never know. I did tell you to bring your Wellies."

"Never know what?" demanded Trudi nervously.

But Janet was already out of the car. She flashed a torch into Trudi's face.

"Come on," she said.

By the time they'd walked the hundred yards, Trudi's eyes were beginning to adjust to the gloom. Her first glimpse of the cottage made her wish the adjustment had not taken place. It was a squat, single-story building, crouched beneath a shading yew and flanked by thickets of briar. The rough stone walls were made even more blankly unwelcoming by the heavily shuttered windows. Painted dark brown, these shutters proved on examination not to be wood but metal, and quite impenetrable.

"At least it means there's no one at home," said Janet. "By God, he didn't mean anyone to get in here, did he? Look at this door. You'd need a road drill to break through that! Good job I made you bring the keys."

Trudi's last hope was that the keys wouldn't fit, but it

proved vain. It took two of them to unlock the door, but all too soon it was swinging back on well-oiled hinges.

"We're in, Meredith!" Janet proclaimed triumphantly. "Now let's see what Mr. Blair's been up to in his little hidey-hole."

The torch beam showed that the front door entered straight into a living room, sparsely furnished with a table, a wooden chair and one armchair.

"Not exactly a love-nest, is it?"

Trudi's foot disturbed something. Looking down, she saw a couple of envelopes which had dropped through the narrow letter box. She picked them up. They were both addressed to E. Blair.

"Open them," commanded Janet.

One contained an electricity bill, long overdue for payment. The other was a letter from the bank in which the manager expressed his unease at such a large sum of money lying fallow in a current account and urged Mr. Blair to get in touch.

"Electricity is there?" said Janet. "Let's see."

She waved the torch around till she found a light switch, pressed it and a bare bulb on a short frayed flex cast its unflattering light on the room.

There was another door in the wall to the left. It led into a narrow stone-flagged corridor, also lit by a bare bulb. Two more doors faced each other. One opened onto a small bedroom containing a metal bedstead with a thin mattress, the other onto a kitchen with an old pot sink, a cooker, a small kitchen table, a kitchen chair and, incongruous in such company, a large upright freezer on which a red light glowed like a watching eye.

Janet led the way back to the living room.

"What now?" said Trudi, oppressed by the place.

"Let's search," said Janet.

They searched. It didn't take long, there was so little to search. The bedroom offered even less. They ended up once more in the kitchen. All that required looking into here were the drawers in the table and a cupboard under the sink.

Janet took the drawers. A wooden spoon, a plastic spatula, one knife, one fork.

"He wasn't planning on entertaining much," she said.

Trudi didn't reply. In the sink she'd found a pot mug and a teaspoon. Now she opened the cupboard. It had no shelves and contained four dully gleaming cylinders. She started as she looked inside.

"Gas for the cooker," said Janet, kneeling beside her. "What did you think they were? Bombs?"

But Trudi wasn't looking at the cylinders. On them rested a small saucepan, a tin of ground coffee and an old metal percolator. She reached inside and drew this out.

"What is it?" asked Janet.

"It is—was—his," said Trudi dully. "This was Trent's. He had it when we married. He always said it made better coffee than anything else we got. I didn't even notice it was missing."

The Welsh woman put her arms around her shoulders and squeezed hard.

"Bastards," she said inclusively. "Come on. I don't think there's anything else for us here. I'll buy you a drink and we'll toss a few theories around."

They stood up.

Trudi found herself strangely reluctant to leave without any real clue to what Trent had been up to here.

She said, "What about the freezer?"

"What about it?"

"If the electricity bill's not paid, anything in there will go rotten when the current's switched off."

"What are you suggesting? That we pile my boot up with frozen fish fingers and take them home?"

Trudi didn't answer but went across to the freezer, pressed down the handle, and pulled. The door didn't budge.

"He really was security conscious," said Janet. "Even protected his fish fingers. Come on, girl, let's go."

Obstinately, Trudi ignored her. She examined the bunch of keys she was carrying.

There was a small flat one. She inserted it into the freezer lock and turned it.

"There," she said triumphantly. "I've done it."

And pressed the handle and opened the door.

Who shrieked first was hard to say.

But Trudi certainly shrieked longest as the man standing

inside the cabinet slowly reached out towards her and touched her with his icy hand.

Then, still shrieking, she flung herself aside as she realized he was not reaching but falling, stiff and solid, to crash full-length against the stone-flagged floor.

CHAPTER 3

"We've got to tell the police," said Janet.

"I suppose so," said Trudi.

They were on their second large Scotches and this was the third time they'd had this conversation, each time with less conviction, since they had fled from Well Cottage and driven madly down the hill back into Eyam. They'd stopped at the first pub they'd encountered. Neither of them could have given its name. It had been a pub, that was all, offering warmth, light, company, and Scotch.

"Another?" suggested Trudi.

"I'm driving," said Janet. "Make it a small one."

Trudi got the drinks.

"We've got to tell the police," she said on her return.

"I suppose so," said Janet.

"Only . . ."

"Yes?"

"I don't know."

"You know," said Janet, regarding her friend closely. "You're a bit of a marvel. Here's bold, brassy old me still shaking. While you . . ."

"I'm still shaking inside," said Trudi in a low voice. "But it wasn't so awful when . . . Well, to tell the truth, I thought it was Trent. When I saw him standing there, I thought it was Trent, come to get me. Once I realized it wasn't, it was still terrible, but not as terrible as *that*. Am I making sense?"

"What's sense?" wondered Janet. "You were saying, or at least I think you were trying to say, why we shouldn't tell the police."

"I don't know. Perhaps we should. I mean, of course we must!"

"As good citizens? You're right. Except that I'm a lousy citizen. But we've got to tell them. Only perhaps not straightaway."

"Why not?"

"Well, principally because I'm very happy just sitting here, and there's still a long time till last orders," said Janet. "More to the point, once the police are in, we're out. Instead of asking our questions, we start answering theirs. Big solid men with faces like flagstones and tongues all blue from licking little stubs of pencil. They'll give us less rope than a flying picket!"

"So what are you suggesting? That we sit here till it's closing time and we're legless, *then* ring the police?" said Trudi.

"Don't be silly. No, all I'm saying is, we ought to be sure that we know at least as much as they do before we contact them."

Trudi digested this with the help of a large mouthful of whiskey.

"You've lost me," she said. "We already know more than they do. And they won't know anything unless we've told them it."

"Wrong," proclaimed Janet. "They'll know everything they can find out about that *thing* in the freezer. And you can bet your Social Security check they won't be telling us any of that!"

"I haven't got a Social Security check."

"No, but you'll be needing one pretty soon if you can't get your hands on some of that cash in E. Blair's account. You can kiss goodbye to that once the police come in, of course."

"I haven't *got* it, so I can hardly kiss it goodbye,"

protested Trudi. "Janet, are you saying now we *shouldn't* tell the police?"

"No. I'm saying that first of all we owe it to ourselves to find out all we can about that man."

"But how?"

"Go through his pockets," said Janet boldly. "Look for identification. See if we can spot how he was killed."

The only real response to the implied suggestion that they should return to Well Cottage and search the frozen corpse was hysterical derision. Trudi made the mistake of controlling it and attempting a rational objection.

"But he's frozen *solid*, Jan. You can't look in pockets when they're blocks of ice!"

"He should be defrosting nicely by closing time," she said. "Not *oven-ready* by a long chalk, but we should be able to get in his pockets at least!"

The two women regarded each other, each aghast in her own way at the callousness of the comment and at its implications. But whiskey, warmth and friendship are strong solvents and gradually their fears and inhibitions melted into slightly hysterical amusement at the absurdity of men, life, and the whole of God's creation.

They were still laughing when they left the pub some time later. Janet's difficulty in fitting the key into the ignition and her crashing of gears as they set out up the hill struck them both as screamingly funny. But by the time they were bumping along the track to Well Cottage, the funniness had faded and only the screaming remained in their minds.

This time they drove right up to the cottage gate.

"I thought we left the lights on," said Trudi, looking at the darkened building.

"I don't remember anything except running like hell," replied Janet.

Slowly they went up the path. The door was shut.

"You closed the door behind you, didn't you?" said Janet.

"Was I last out? I thought you were."

"Dead heat, if I remember, girl," said Janet.

Trudi unlocked the door.

"After you," she said.

"Don't go polite on me."

"All right. I'll go first through this one but you go first into the kitchen."

Their attempts at lightness sounded forced and unconvincing.

At the kitchen door they hesitated, both looking down. Then they looked up at each other, realizing they'd both been searching for a telltale pool of water seeping beneath the door. Now with one accord they pushed it open.

They were keyed up for the repetition of horror.

What they saw was both less and more shocking than what they were expecting. For a long moment they stood completely still. Then Janet flicked the light switch on, but the illumination from the corridor had not deceived their eyes.

The body was gone.

The red light still glowed on the freezer.

"It's not possible," said Janet.

For answer Trudi reached forward, pulled at the cabinet handle and jumped back.

Slowly the freezer door swung open, spilling its internal light onto the kitchen floor. But nothing else. It was quite empty.

"Perhaps," said Janet in a low voice, "it was an ice sculpture and has melted away to nothing."

For answer, Trudi stooped and touched the bone-dry floor.

"I think," said Janet, "in that case, we ought to go."

They didn't speak as they switched off the lights, locked the door behind them, got into the car and slowly drove back towards Sheffield.

CHAPTER
4

Janet stayed the night at Hope House.

"I'm not driving off into the dark and leaving you alone after *that*," she said firmly.

"Frank will hate me," protested Trudi.

"No, he won't. I'll tell him the car's playing up. He won't want me belting over the Snake on a winter's night in a dicey car," said Janet confidently.

She was right. Trudi listened to the phone call enviously.

"I feel guilty. He was very worried," said Janet.

"I wish I had someone to feel guilty about."

"You concentrate on the worry. That's what you've got plenty of."

Curiously, as they talked about the events of the evening, they discovered their positions had merged. Janet, eloquent for delay earlier, was now uneasily wondering if they should not instantly contact the police. Her change of heart seemed to have little to do with social conscience, everything with Trudi's well-being. And perhaps her own.

"A frozen body, that's one thing. Could've been there for months. Years! Don't ask me why! But a vanished body's different. That's here and now, girl. Whoever took it was too close to us for comfort. You may need protection."

Trudi shook her head.

"Protection from what? And what are the police going to do? Put a bobby at my gate?"

"You've changed your tune, girl," said Janet. "You were all for the police before."

"Was I? I suppose I was just plain terrified. I still am. But listen, Jan, all this is to do with Trent, isn't it? How or why, I don't know. But without knowing, I don't just feel I can hand it over to the police. I owe Trent that much, don't I?"

"Trent's dead, Trudi!" said Janet savagely. "You owe him nothing! What should be concerning you, my girl, is your own living future. Everything connected with that husband of yours has brought nothing but aggravation since he died. You want rid of it. Offload it onto someone else. That's what we pay the police for!"

Trudi said in a voice close to tears, "I'm sorry, Jan, I should never have got you mixed up in this in the first place . . ."

"Don't flatter yourself," snapped Janet rather ill-temperedly. "I got myself mixed up without any help from you!"

"All right. But what I'm saying is, it's my problem, *whatever* it is. I don't want to end up being a silly hysterical widow, bothering the police with her neuroses."

"Neuroses! Assault? Murder? False identity? Hundreds of thousands of pounds in a bank account? Come on, Trudi!"

The mockery in Janet's voice took Trudi back to their schooldays when she had been foolhardy enough to voice a suggestion or opinion running counter to the Welsh girl's ideas. *Then* she had usually subsided into a tearful silence. *Now* by contrast she found that the scorn dried up her desire to weep.

"Assault," she said crisply. "Someone threw a dust sheet over me in Vienna. Murder: What murder? There's no body, nor any sign there ever was one. Impersonation: A man called Blair bought a holiday home in Derbyshire and it's all locked up. What's wrong with that? People don't usually take country holidays in the middle of winter."

"And the money in his account?"

"So he's a rich man. Or perhaps I read the figures wrong."

"Well, that's one thing we can easily check out. Tomorrow we'll go into town and take a look together."

Janet seemed content to shelve her arguments for involving the police at this point. Indeed she seemed almost relieved. Perhaps she didn't relish telling Frank what had happened, thought Trudi as she got into bed.

She dreamt of Trent that night, but not a nightmare. In fact it was less a dream than a simple memory of a picnic they'd had in the Vienna woods during their last spring there. Recently Trent had been very distracted, and she'd been delighted when he suggested this outing.

After they'd eaten he'd said, "It doesn't bother you anymore, this?" gesturing up through the steepling pines to the vault of the sky.

"No. Especially not with you here," she replied.

"And without me?"

"I wouldn't have come. I can't drive."

He looked at her with what she now recognized as his normal expression when looking at her, a mixture of puzzlement, concern and exasperation.

He said, "Twenty years. Where's it gone? More than twenty years, and . . ."

"And what, Trent?"

"And . . ." Still he hesitated, then he shook his head slightly and concluded, "And we've never made love in the open air!"

He came to her then. She was surprised. After some initial terrors, she'd always been a willing partner in sex, though her own satisfactions had been emotional rather than physical, enjoying the act because it brought Trent so close to her. His demands, never great, had diminished over the years and it was the unexpectedness of this approach, especially here and now, that surprised her. Trent was a careful and, on the surface at least, conventional man, and the woods were a popular picnicking spot. Indeed they could hear the sound of a transistor not too far away as he unbuttoned her blouse. But she did not protest; if Trent judged it safe, then safe it must be.

But as she lay on the car rug and looked up at the cloud-flecked sky and felt his hot hardness pushing into her, she felt a second and greater surprise. She had missed this not simply because of the closeness with Trent but because . . . because . . . . The beginnings of a mindless physical pleasure pushed thought out of her mind. She felt herself relaxing, giving her entire being over to it . . . Then suddenly Trent had finished, had withdrawn, was rolling away from her and pulling on his pants.

She'd lain there, looking up at the sky but not seeing it. It was as if the shock of frustrated pleasure had half opened a door, and she felt almost strong enough to push right through it and to ask Trent, who stood on the other side, "Yes? What about all these years of married life? What do we have to say to each other about them?" Only rarely before in their marriage had this door opened, and never so wide as now.

But before she could speak, Trent had said, "Someone's coming. Hurry up, Trudi!" and she'd realized she was still lying naked, legs splayed, and the sound of the transistor was getting louder.

By the time they got home, that door had closed. All that remained was the afterglow of a fine day spent in Trent's company, and a sense of security which confirmed the wise structure of her life.

But now in the dream, it was the beginnings of delight she most remembered, and here dream and reality parted, for now Trent looked down at her body as he rose and smiled and said, "Next time, Trudi, I promise."

She awoke and recollected that there had never been a next time. For Trent perhaps, but not for her. But the memory of that smile and promise were oddly comforting, almost as comforting as the domestic noises and smells rising from the kitchen below.

Her unexpected sense of well-being lasted through breakfast till Janet said, "Right, let's dump the dishes and get right off to town."

"Town?"

"You haven't forgotten? We're just going to check on Mr. E. Blair's account. And after that, well, we've got to think seriously about the police."

That her friend was right, Trudi couldn't deny. She wasn't even sure why she herself should feel so reluctant. She'd always been a member of the law-abiding, police-respecting class; hadn't she?

The interrogative phrase tagged itself on unexpectedly. She frowned and considered what had been intended as a simple assertion of incontrovertible truth.

She'd been brought up in a country and an era when children were still taught to trust the police, but, looking back, she realized she'd always been afraid of them. Nor was it simply natural timidity. It was her father's example. What persecution by the Nazi authorities he had undergone before he fled to England she could only guess at. What suspicion and what indignities were heaped upon him in England during the war she had been too young to notice. But now she recollected that he shunned uniformed authority as much as possible, and she wondered how much of this feeling had been communicated to his worshiping daughter. Similarly with Trent. He preferred to sort out his own problems. Once, while living in Amsterdam, their flat had been burgled. He hadn't called the police. *The cure can be worse than the disease*, he had said, and simply spent a lot of money reinforcing the flat's security.

Trent. Her father. The two strong men, strong influences, in her life. Both police-distrusters. Perhaps it was no wonder she felt reluctant to follow Janet's advice.

She found herself wondering what James Dacre's advice would be and then pushed the thought away. He might be a candidate for strong man number three, but he was still a long way from elected.

It was Saturday and the center of Sheffield was crowded. They had to stand in a queue at the cash dispenser outside the bank. Janet took up a position to block the screen off from the woman behind them.

"O.K., girl," she said. "Let's take a look."

Trudi inserted the card, pressed *4—8—9—1* and then the BALANCE button.

A longish pause. Then the green letters glowed on the screen.

The message was simple.

ACCOUNT CLOSED. CARD RETAINED.

Disbelieving, Trudi punched other buttons at random.

Finally the screen cleared. And then the message inviting the next customer to insert his card came up.

"Are you finished, luv?" inquired the woman behind them.

"Oh yes," said Trudi. "Sorry."

They walked slowly away.

"It was there," insisted Trudi. "I saw it."

"I believe you," said Janet. "The account was certainly open yesterday when I rang the bank, remember? Maybe we shouldn't have been surprised. People who can make a body disappear will have no trouble with money. *I* can make money disappear! Oh, Trudi, why didn't you help yourself while you had the chance?"

"What do we do now?" asked Trudi, ignoring the reproach.

"Suddenly you want advice again, is it?" said Janet without much satisfaction. "Well, we can still go to the police. Tell them we found a body and a quarter of a million pounds, but now we've lost them both. Maybe we can persuade them to take us seriously, and maybe forensic experts will find some traces in that freezer, and certainly financial experts should find some traces in that bank. But . . ."

"But?" echoed Trudi.

"I don't know. Trudi, don't take this wrong, girl, but there's nothing you haven't told me, is there? Nothing you know and I don't?"

"All I can promise you is, anything you don't know, I don't know either," said Trudi.

"And you still don't want us to go to the police?"

"No," said Trudi, much more definitely than she felt.

"All right. I'll go along with that. On one condition."

"What's that?"

"You do nothing, absolutely nothing, without telling me first. O.K.?"

"Does that include my sex life?" asked Trudi. "What if I get carried away on a tide of irresistible passion?"

"In that case, I want his address," laughed Janet. "Seriously, a bargain?"

"Bargain," said Trudi.

Janet spat on her hand and held it out in a gesture resurrected from their schooldays. Trudi slapped it with hers.

"Right," said Janet. "Now, where do you reckon a woman of good standing can get a drink in Sheffield at this hour on a Saturday morning?"

PART
FIVE

I'm truly sorry Man's dominion
Has broken Nature's social union,
An' justifies that ill opinion,
 Which makes thee startle . . .

BURNS: "To a Mouse"

CHAPTER
1

The weekend dragged by slowly but also, to Trudi's relief, uneventfully. She was half expecting James Dacre to ring and when Sunday night came without any contact, she was surprised to detect in herself a strong sense of resentment.

On Monday morning, she was pleased to find a fairly considerable body of mail to deal with at Class-Glass. Even so, by eleven in the morning it was all sorted out and she was faced with the prospect of several more hours of catching up on her reading.

There was a tap at the office door.

"Come in," she called.

"Hello," said James Dacre. "I was in the area and I thought I'd call and see what your place of work was like. Are you busy?"

"Only on getting to the end of this chapter," she said, holding up her book.

"And then?"

"Then I sit and reflect."

He glanced at the mirrors and smiled.

"I'm sorry we didn't get our cup of tea on Friday," he said. "Was everything all right?"

"Why do you ask?" she said sharply.

"Your friend seemed rather anxious to see you, that was

120

all," he said. "I just hoped there wasn't any kind of emergency."

"No. Janet is just rather single-minded," replied Trudi. "When she wants to see you, she wants to see you."

"There are worse qualities. Are you doing anything tonight?"

Trudi still hesitated. She realized she was frightened where her growing intimacy with Dacre might lead. Would she have the strength not to confide her troubles to him? Did she have the right to risk involving him?

Whistling quietly to himself, Dacre took a turn round the room as though to give her time to think. He stopped in front of a heart-shaped mirror pierced with a painted arrow and studied his reflection as though it were a gallery painting.

"Of course, if you're busy," he said. "Perhaps Mr. Usher's giving you work to do at home. What kind of chap is he, by the way?"

As if in answer, the door opened and Stanley Usher appeared.

"Good Lord," he said. "Don't say we've got ourselves a real live customer?"

"Afraid not," said Dacre. "Just a friend of Mrs. Adamson."

Trudi introduced the two men, feeling absurdly guilty at being discovered alone with Dacre.

He excused himself after a couple of sentences of meaningless chat with Usher. At the door he said interrogatively, "Tonight, then?"

"Yes. Fine," said Trudi.

"I'll pick you up at seven."

With a cheerful wave, he left.

"Nice chap," said Usher. "I should have asked. He's not in the finance business, is he? I thought he looked familiar and the most I see of other fellows is when I'm trying to raise a loan from them."

"No," said Trudi. "I don't think so. I haven't known him long."

Why she made this disclaimer she didn't really know, nor why she didn't impart the little bit of information she had acquired about Dacre's job. In fact, through the long dull afternoon, sitting with no work and nothing for company but her book and her multiple reflections, she found herself at a loss to explain most of her reactions in the past few months. There had been extraordinary events and revelations, that was true, but when she examined her own behavior, it was just as extraordinary. Concealing a killing, getting drunk with her husband's mistress, meeting a man through a dating agency—these alone in prospect would have had her rushing for medical help a year ago! But it was at a less dramatic level that she perceived perhaps the most worrying changes. She no longer knew how she was going to react to the ordinary circumstances of everyday life. She no longer felt in full control of her own thought processes. For instance, how was it possible that she, Trudi Adamson, whose attitude towards sex had always been more dutiful than enthusiastic, could find herself slipping off into reveries about what James Dacre would look like naked, and how it was going to feel as he entered her! And the real shock came when she realized that these hypotheses were not just idle, but anticipatory. It was going to happen, possibly—no; *probably* tonight.

By the time he came to call for her, a strong reaction had set in and she received him rather coolly. He didn't seem to notice, but accepted with a friendly smile a glass of sherry and an invitation to take a seat while she completed her preparations.

Looking at herself in her dressing-table mirror she found she was straining her ears for the sound of his footsteps on the stairs.

You're going mad! she told her reflection. *It's the menopause or something!*

She jumped up and grabbed her handbag. The sooner she got out of the house the better. Then she started violently as, below, the front door bell rang.

As she went down the stairs, James Dacre came out of the lounge.

"It's all right. I'll get it, James," she said.

When she opened the door, she saw two men standing there, one behind the other. The nearer one, who wore a belted raincoat and had a sharp though not unfriendly face beneath a thatch of salty gray hair, said, "Mrs. Adamson?"

"Yes."

"Detective Inspector Workman, madam."

He produced a card which he held out for her inspection. It had a photograph and quite a lot of print. She registered the photograph but little else. Her eyes were drawn to the second man, at present little more than a silhouette, familiar in Viennese winters, of square fur hat and heavy overcoat with a thick fur collar.

As if interpreting her gaze as a question, Workman said, "And this is a colleague, Herr Walter Jünger of the Austrian Justice Department."

The fur-hatted man moved forward so that the light fell on his face and Trudi felt light and substance begin to slip away from her. She leaned against the door jamb and grasped at the solid wood for both support and reassurance.

For a second she had been certain that she was looking at the man whose frozen body had fallen out of the freezer at Well Cottage.

"Are you all right, ma'am?" said Workman anxiously.

"Yes, of course," she lied, her eyes still fixed on Jünger's face, her mind telling her that the similarity was superficial. In any case, this man's round, rather squashed-up face was marked by a long scar from the left corner of his mouth to the underside of his jaw which definitely had not been on the corpse.

Jünger, who looked to be about sixty, gave a little bow and said in German, "I am delighted to meet you."

"English, please," said Workman gently. "May we come in?"

"We were just going out," said Trudi.

"We'll try to be as quick as possible," said Workman.

Trudi led them into the lounge. James Dacre stood aside at the door and said, "Shall I wait out here?"

Before Trudi could reply, Workman said, "And you, sir, are?"

Trudi interrupted to say coldly, "This is Mr. Dacre, a friend of mine. No, James, I think I should prefer you to stay in here, if you don't mind."

She glared at Workman, challenging an objection.

He turned away indifferently and murmured something to Jünger.

"What's this all about, please?" inquired Trudi.

"I'm sorry, ma'am," said Workman. "It's just that we're helping the Austrian authorities with some inquiries they're making. A couple of questions first, just to make sure there aren't any crossed lines. Do you know a women called Astrid Fischer of . . ."

He consulted a piece of paper and with some difficulty read out Astrid's address.

"Yes, I do," said Trudi.

"Have you seen her recently?"

"Yes. I saw her, when was it? A week last Friday."

"And not since?"

"No. I left Austria on the Sunday, and Astrid was going away on a skiing holiday on the Saturday. Look, what's this all about?"

"Why did you go to see her, may I ask?"

Trudi felt both anger and fear welling up inside her. She glanced towards Dacre, who read this as an appeal for help.

"I really think that if it's Mrs. Adamson's help you want, you ought to make the nature of the inquiry clear before she answers any further questions," he said gently.

"Why? Has Mrs. Adamson got any reason not to be absolutely frank with us?" said Workman, irritated.

James Dacre laughed. He had a rich, deep laugh, slightly unexpected from his rather dour and guarded expression.

"We've all watched too much television to be bothered by that old insinuating stuff, Inspector," he said. "Mrs. Adamson has every reason not to reveal details of her private business to a couple of strangers who may be investigating nothing more serious than a drunk-driving charge."

"You don't find drunk-driving serious?"

"Not as serious as invasion of privacy," said Dacre, with sudden force.

"James, it's all right. I don't mind answering their questions. But I would like to know what it's all about. Is Astrid all right? Nothing's happened to her, has it?"

Workman glanced at Jünger, who shrugged and said in accented but very correct English, "Astrid Fischer did not join her friends for the skiing holiday. At first they did not worry. They thought she must simply have been delayed. But by Monday they were worried and started making inquiries. They rang hospitals, inquired about road accidents, checked with her office. There was no trace of her. Finally they contacted the police. This was last Thursday. Even in Austria, Frau Adamson, citizens do not cooperate readily with the police."

He smiled faintly, the unscarred end of his mouth curving more than the other.

"So finally on Friday, the police, concerned that there may have been an accident to Fräulein Fischer in her apartment, broke in."

He paused.

"And?" said Trudi impatiently. "Did they find her?"

"Oh yes. They found her, Mrs. Adamson," said Jünger.

He leaned towards her and despite herself she saw once again the rigid figure toppling slowly forward out of the freezer. Perhaps he glimpsed this fear in her eyes and interpreted it as a sign of guilt, for his voice suddenly grew hoarse with an accusatory vehemence.

"They found her on the floor near the telephone. Not that it would have helped her much if she'd got to it, Mrs. Adamson. A massive overdose of heroin had been injected into her veins, and once that happens there's no turning back, is there?"

"You mean she's dead?" said Trudi foolishly.

"What do you think? Yes, she's dead! Of course's she's dead! Dead as your husband, Mrs. Adamson!"

She took a step towards a chair, but it was too far away. The light was ebbing once more. Neither Jünger nor Workman attempted to move and James Dacre was too slow to catch her as she fell.

CHAPTER 2

When Trudi woke up, she was lying on her bed still fully clothed. Her shoes had been removed and her blouse unbuttoned at the throat. There was a cold wet hand towel neatly folded and draped around her brow.

She could hear voices somewhere in the house. She sat up and felt pain stab at her forehead, but not unbearably. The towel fell onto her lap and she saw there was a smudge of blood on it.

Immediately the memory of Astrid came into her mind, and she screwed up her eyes in a pain much stronger than the physical one.

The door opened and Dacre came in.

"Are you all right?" he demanded. "Lie back."

"How long have I been like this?"

"Ten minutes. You fainted. Also you banged your head on the coffee table as you went down. I don't think it's much, but you should see the coffee table."

He smiled. Reassured, she lay back, then sat up again immediately.

"Those men . . ."

"I've given 'em their marching orders," said Dacre grimly. "I suggested that their heavy-handed methods had done enough damage for one day and told them that the only person you'd be talking to tonight was the doctor."

"Doctor?"

"Yes. I thought we'd better get a quack out to look you

over. I'm sure it's just a cut and a bump, nothing more, but best to be sure."

"And Workman and Jünger?"

"They've gone. Reluctantly. But they'll be back tomorrow, I suspect."

The door bell rang.

"That'll be the doctor. Lie still."

The doctor was a fat, breathless man smelling of pipe tobacco. He examined her with a thoroughness which might have surprised or even annoyed her if she'd been in the frame of mind to take much notice.

Finished, he packed his bag, nodded farewell, and left.

A few moments later, James Dacre returned.

"All decent?" he said.

"Yes. He looked at the oddest places for someone examining a bump on the head."

"Did he? Well, he's one of the old school. Slow but thorough."

"Is he your doctor then?"

"That's right. I didn't know who yours was or even if you've got one. I hope you don't mind."

"Of course not," said Trudi. "What did he say?"

"Nothing to worry about. You'll have a bit of a swelling, and a bit of a headache, but a couple of aspirin and a good night's sleep will see you right. I'm afraid our trip to the pictures will have to wait till another night."

He glanced at his watch. She was suddenly terrified that he was going to leave her.

"James, you'll need to eat something. Let me cook you a meal."

"No way," he said. "A kitchen is no place for a dizzy woman. I use the term medically, of course. No, I'll scramble us some eggs later if you feel up to it. All right?"

"That'd be fine," she said. "Fine."

Dacre realized she'd started to cry almost before she herself did.

"Here, what's the matter?" he said, sitting on the bed and putting his arm rather clumsily around her shoulders. "My cooking's not that bad."

"Scrambled eggs," she sobbed. "That's what Astrid made

for me the last time I saw her. I went to quarrel with her and we ended up getting drunk and eating scrambled eggs and then she . . . then she . . ."

She leaned her head against his chest and sobbed uncontrollably.

He held her tight and did not speak till the outburst died away.

"I'm sorry, I'm sorry," she gasped.

"That's all right, I understand," he said gently. "She must have been a good friend, this Astrid."

"A friend?" She laughed only slightly hysterically. "Oh no. Not at all. Like I say, I went around to quarrel with her. You see, I'd found out she'd been having an affair with my husband!"

After that the whole story came out, about Trent's death, Astrid's visit, Trudi's discovery at Six Mile Farm, her trip to Vienna, the confrontation in the apartment.

That was where it should have stopped, but with the floodgates open, reticence seemed impossible, and she found herself telling James Dacre about the attack in the repository, Werner's clinic, Eric Blair's account and the body at Well Cottage.

Finally she reached an end and fell silent.

He was regarding her with a look of mingled bewilderment and perplexity.

"Well, that's done it," she said in a wide miss at cheeriness.

"Done what?"

"You'll be going to Mrs. Fielding and asking for your money back."

He smiled, then his expression became grave.

"Trudi," he said. "Do you know what any of this means?"

She shook her head.

"I don't know what to do," she said in a small voice.

"Are you asking for my advice?"

She said, "I've no right to involve you. I'm sorry."

He said, "How much of this will you tell Workman and the Austrian when they come back tomorrow?"

"I don't know. Most of it's nothing to do with Astrid killing herself, is it?"

Her voice rose on the *is it?* He regarded her steadily without speaking.

After a while, she nodded and said dully, "Yes, I can see that too. She wasn't about to kill herself after I left. I know that. And they wouldn't have sent a man all the way over here if it was simply a matter of suicide, would they?"

"It doesn't seem likely, Trudi," he said.

"I'd better tell them everything."

He considered this, then to her surprise shook his head. "No. I mean, at least sleep on it before you decide."

He rose with a look of decision.

Alarmed, she said, "You're not going?"

"Only to the kitchen," he said.

"And afterwards?"

What she sounded like, she did not know.

He said, "Don't worry. I won't leave you by yourself. Not tonight."

She ate a little of the scrambled eggs, drank some tea. She screwed up her face when he told her no alcohol but did not make an issue of it. Her head was throbbing gently but she felt well at ease in his company.

Finally he gave her a couple of aspirin and a glass of water.

"Get those down," he ordered. "And then get into bed. I'll just be next door, so if you want anything, just shout. Good night."

"Good night, James," she said.

She didn't anticipate a restful night, but in any event she slept soundly. When she woke up, there was a slight residual headache but nothing more. She rose and went to the bathroom. When she came out, Dacre was standing in the open doorway of the bedroom next to hers. He was dressed only in his underpants, with a blanket draped over his shoulders.

"I thought I heard a noise," he said. "How are you?"

"Fine. Did I wake you? I'm sorry," said Trudi.

"No. It's time to be up." He glanced at his watch. "Nearly eight o'clock. I gave myself a generous nightcap of your Scotch last night. I'm afraid it did the trick."

"How was the bed?"

"Fine. Only thing was, I couldn't find any sheets and the blankets were a bit tickly."

She said, "James, when I asked you to stay last night, well, I wouldn't have minded if you'd really stayed. With me, I mean."

He studied her carefully and suddenly she was aware that all she had on was a flimsy cotton nightdress. But instead of shrinking modestly, she forced herself to stand still and look at his deep chest with its crucifix of dark hair running down across a slightly thickening belly to join with the line of crinklier hair just peeping over the band of his Y-fronts. She recalled Janet's joke about St. Michael and smiled.

He said, "I wouldn't have minded either, but not in those circumstances."

"Circumstances?"

"You were unwell, upset."

"Chivalry, was it?"

"If you like."

She smiled.

"I think I do like. Thank you," she said. "But that was last night. This morning I'm not upset and I feel fine."

Is this really me talking? she asked herself in amazement. *And if it is, why am I talking like this?*

She said, "I'm sorry. Look, I was forgetting what I told you last night. I shouldn't have involved you like that. And I'm glad we didn't get involved even more. Thanks for being such a help. Perhaps we can get in touch again when I've got all this nonsense sorted out, if you wanted to hear the end of the story, that is."

He smiled and shook his head.

"No," he said.

"No?"

"No, I don't want to hear the end of the story. I want to be in it. For a while anyway."

He stepped forward, the blanket fell from his shoulders and he kissed her passionately. When he stepped back, the Y-fronts were looking inadequate.

"Your room, I think," he said. "Unless you want to be tickled to death."

* * *

There were no physical fireworks and the earth didn't move, but when they finally drew apart, the residual headache had completely vanished and she felt a glow of relaxed well-being she hadn't known for months. Perhaps for years.

"O.K.?"

He wasn't asking for compliments, she realized, merely commenting on her self-absorption.

"Yes," she said. "I imagined this, you know."

"Imagined?"

"When you said you'd pick me up last night. I started to imagine this."

"And did it live up to your fantasies?"

"I don't know," she said gravely. "I stopped myself imagining. It didn't seem decent. But it feels good. Yes, at the moment I feel so good I've no room to feel guilty."

"What have you got to feel guilty about?" he wondered.

"Oh, nothing," she said. "Nothing special, I mean. But I know myself. Or at least I'm getting to know myself. And eventually I'll start thinking about Trent and then I'll feel guilty."

She giggled, a sound almost as unexpected to herself as to Dacre.

"What's funny?" he said.

"I don't know. This is my first time at this, you see, and it just struck me that probably rule number one is, don't start talking about your husband two minutes after your lover has just, well, finished."

He considered.

"No. That's rule number two."

"And what's number one?"

"Make quite sure that your lover has in fact finished before you start talking at all!"

It was corny, but when he embraced her again she realized it was true. This time their coupling pushed her far beyond well-being towards something fiercer, a journey she had begun to make that time with Trent on their last picnic in the Vienna woods. Perhaps if she'd made that journey sooner, broken the pattern of domination and submission in bed at least, perhaps then they might have . . . Downstairs the doorbell rang.

"Damn!" she cried. "Why do policemen have to start so early?" She sprang out of bed. It was absurd but she felt sure that Workman would pick the lock or smash the door down if she didn't open it, and come running up to the bedroom in search of her. Dragging on her dressing gown she ran down the stairs. The bell was still ringing. Workman must be leaning on the button.

Bloody man! she thought, but not very angrily. She was feeling too good to be angry, too good to worry that she probably looked a mess.

No, not a mess. She probably looked like a woman who'd just gotten out of bed with a passionate man, and she found she didn't much care about that either.

She made herself slow down in the hallway. The bell stopped ringing as she started to unlock the door. Through the frosted panel, she could see the outline of only one figure. Perhaps the Austrian had gone home.

She composed her face into an unwelcoming blank and began to open the door. The second the catch was free, the door was thrust back towards her with great force and a figure rushed in, forcing her sideways against the wall.

"Where is she? Come on! Where is she!"

It was Frank Carter, his amiable face distorted with anger.

"Frank! What's the matter! What's happened?" she cried.

He didn't answer but regarded her with an expression of disgust. She realized her dressing gown had fallen open, and now she drew it tightly around her as Carter turned and, crying, "Janet! Janet! Are you there?" went running up the stairs.

Doors opened and banged shut. Then suddenly there was silence.

Distantly she heard James Dacre's voice say quietly but menacingly, "Can I help you, friend?"

A moment later, Carter came down the stairs, his anger clearly unabated.

"What's the matter, Frank? Has something happened to Jan?" demanded Trudi fearfully.

"Bitch," he said. "You came back into her life, that's what happened. Bitch!"

"What are you talking about?" said Trudi. "What's going on."

"Yes. Why don't you tell the lady what's going on?"

James Dacre had slipped into his trousers and shirt and was halfway down the stairs, moving with great quietness for a bulky man.

"Who the hell are you anyway?" sneered Carter.

"Frank, this is James Dacre, a friend of mine. James, this is Frank Carter, my friend Janet's husband. Frank, where's Janet?"

"How the hell do I know?" he demanded. "She walked out last night. I was sure she'd be here."

"What happened, Frank? Why did she walk out?"

The anger was beginning to slip from him, not because he wanted it to go, but because he did not have the kind of emotional machinery which could sustain a high head of rage for long. Twice he had spurred himself to the fury point, once the previous night and again this morning. But the lasting imprint on his inner being was bewilderment and shock.

"We quarreled," he said. "She left."

"Why? What did you quarrel about? Why did you think she was here?"

"Because of this," he snapped.

He reached into his jacket pocket and pulled out an envelope. From it he took a photograph and handed it to Trudi, reverse side upward.

On it was scribbled: *What do you think your old lady gets up to when she visits her slag chum in Sheffield?*

Trudi turned the photograph over and looked at it.

Immediately she was back to the previous night with the air thickening and eddying round her reeling head like mist round a ruined tower. This time she forced herself back to light through the darkness, though leaning back against the wall for its needed support.

The photograph came back into focus.

It showed Janet, naked, leaning forward across a bed, her face twisted with pleasure but still instantly recognizable.

Behind her, and apparently entering her from behind, was a naked man.

His face appearing over her shoulder was even more contorted with delight, but it was just as easily recognizable.

It was Trent Adamson.

CHAPTER
3

It took surprisingly little time to convince Carter that Trudi knew nothing of Janet's whereabouts. Just as violent rage was too foreign to his make-up to be sustainable long, so the need for the comfort of sympathetic conversation was too strong to be long denied.

They sat and drank coffee round the kitchen table and Carter talked.

"It came second post so I didn't get it till I got home last night. Janet was out. She goes to a townswomen's group on Mondays. So she says."

He looked at his listeners with the dark-ringed bitterness of a man into whose life doubt has come.

"I just sat looking at the photo from time to time. I couldn't believe it, you see. I'd just sit and have a drink and after a while it didn't seem possible, then I'd take it out and have another look, and then it started all over again!

"She came home after nine. I'd drunk quite a lot. I'm not a big drinker."

He glanced at Trudi as if for confirmation. She nodded and said, "No you're not."

"I started soon as she got in. I asked her where she'd been, who she'd been with. I was yelling. Pretty soon she was yelling back. You know Janet."

He fell silent for a moment as if studying that assertion.

"I said . . . all kinds of things. I told her I should've known that only dirty tarts would let themselves get picked up through a dating agency."

He passed his hand over his face. Trudi felt Dacre glance towards her at this revelation, but she did not meet his eyes. She was watching Carter, who was now fingering the photograph, face down on the table, as if to draw the strength of self-justification from it.

"She said I must be having a nervous breakdown and she was going to ring the doctor.

"Then I showed her the photo.

"It was a real shock to her, I could see that. She went white. She didn't say anything. I yelled at her. She still didn't speak. I hit her."

He looked at the palm of his right hand as if it didn't belong to him.

"That's when she left. I heard the car drive away. I just sat and drank some more. It got to midnight. She hadn't come back. I knew she wasn't going to come back. I wanted to know where she was. I was . . ."

His face screwed up in the effort of recalling his feelings.

"I was worried," he said. "I was angry. I felt sick. I wanted to know that she was O.K., I wanted to yell at her some more, I wanted to . . . I wanted to hear her say it was all a mistake. Not her. A fake. I don't know . . .

"Anyway, all I could think of was, she might be here. With you. Because of what it said on the back of the photo."

His fingers touched the message.

Trudi said, "Did Jan see what was written there?"

"What? I don't know. Maybe. Perhaps not, though. I don't think she turned it over. What's it matter? I looked up your number. It was in the address book by the telephone. And I tried to ring. All I got was the engaged signal. I tried for an hour. Nothing!"

Trudi glanced at Dacre, who said, "It was me. I left the phone off the hook. Didn't want to risk you being disturbed."

Then in his stern voice, he added to Carter. "Mrs. Adamson was ill last night. The doctor said she had to rest."

Carter regarded him indifferently.

"Is that so? I tried again at six this morning. Still engaged. So I thought I'd come and see for myself. I just wanted to talk."

"Yes, you looked and sounded like a man who just wanted to talk," said Dacre ironically. "Well, now you've searched the house and talked to Mrs. Adamson, I hope you're happy that she knows nothing about your wife's whereabouts, or indeed any of this business."

He tapped the photo with his index finger. Carter looked up from it to Trudi, who said, "Honestly, Frank, there's been nothing like that when Jan visited me. Nothing."

"She's stayed the night often enough. Last Friday she rang up and said she was staying with you. Did she?"

"Oh yes. That's right."

"And what did you do that night, eh?" he asked harshly.

We went to Eyam and found a body, thought Trudi.

"Nothing," she said. "We just sat and talked. Really, Frank."

Dacre intervened again.

"The man in the picture, do you know who he is?"

"Oh yes. Well, at least I've seen him."

Trudi, despite being seated, felt the wave of faintness sweeping over her again.

"Who? Who?"

"It's her brother," said Carter, amazingly. "No, it's probably not, that's just what she said, the bitch. But that was my first thought. Her own brother! You see how easy I was to fool!"

"I'm sorry, I don't understand," said Trudi.

"Shortly after we started going out together, I ran into the two of them in Manchester," said Carter. "They were having a drink together. I remember she was surprised to see me. Well, she sort of hesitated, I recall, and then introduced this man as her brother Jack. There was no reason to lie, not then anyway. We hadn't got ourselves fixed up properly then. We were both free agents. But I see now she was looking ahead, planning for the future. A great planner, Janet!"

He laughed and said, "When we were making our wedding arrangements I remember I said, 'Hey what about your brother Jack? Shouldn't we ask him?' and she looked at me as if I was daft for a moment and then said, 'Oh no, he's working abroad just now, he couldn't possibly make it.' God, what a fool I've been! Here, do *you* know him? Come on, Trudi, you can at least tell me that? Have you ever seen him around when you've been with Janet?"

He stared half accusingly, half appealingly, at Trudi. She felt James Dacre's gaze on her too.

"No," she said with an effort she hoped was concealed. "I don't know him. I've never seen him in my life."

And suddenly she recalled how very much Trent disliked having his picture taken and how assiduous he was at removing photos of himself from display.

Perhaps if I asked nicely, Frank would let me have a print taken from this one, she found herself thinking madly.

Finally Carter left, mainly because James Dacre practically shepherded him through the door.

"If she gets in touch, you'll let me know?" he pleaded as he went.

"If I hear from Janet, I'll certainly tell her she ought to let you know," said Trudi.

Finally he went. James Dacre, who had gone to his car with him, came back into the kitchen.

Trudi said, "I'm sorry. You must be convinced you've strayed into a madhouse now. If you decide that this is the last straw, I'll understand."

He regarded her steadily and said, "You knew him, didn't you?"

"Who?"

"The man in the photograph. You knew him. I could tell."

"Could you?" she said with as much indifference as she could muster. "I must get dressed before the next act begins."

"Who was he, Trudi?" said Dacre sternly. "Who was that man?"

She said wearily, "James, you've had two orgasms inside me and I've had a very pleasant feeling, but that doesn't mean you own me."

He looked ready to accept her challenge for a moment then he relaxed and said, abashed, "I'm sorry. I was just . . . I'm sorry. I'd no right to ask that question."

"Well, as long as we're agreed about that, I'll make you even sorrier by answering it," said Trudi as she went by him through the door. "It was my husband, James. My dear departed husband, Trent."

CHAPTER
4

James Dacre stayed only long enough to make and drink a cup of coffee. He was kind and sympathetic, like a teacher with a child who had fallen in the playground, but there was a distance between them. He made no further direct reference to the events of the morning or of the previous night, but glanced at the kitchen clock, said he had an urgent business appointment and he'd be in touch later. And left.

It seemed to Trudi that the revelation about Trent had really been the last straw for him. It gave her another reason for regretting having made it.

The full enormity of the implications of the photograph had not sunk in till she was alone. At first she tried to control her response by fitting the pieces together like a private detective. She now recalled Janet's disproportionate shock at Trudi's Boxing Day revelation that Trent had been having an affair, and her relaxation (now seen as relief) when she discovered that it was Astrid that Trudi was talking about.

She recalled also that it was Trent who had urged her to make contact with Janet once more. It was when she tried to puzzle out his precise motive for this that she found she was drifting out of the saving limits of cerebral induction and into the trackless wastes of trauma.

Trent and Janet! How long? The photograph had been taken in the last few years: those passion-contorted faces had been middle aged: but when were the seeds of the relationship sown? She felt something in herself close to death as her mind ran back over the years to those very first days. When she first met Trent, he'd been Janet's boyfriend, hadn't he? Or at least, the object of her aspirations. How far had things gone between them? Janet had concealed her disappointment, though not her amazement, when Trent turned his attention to her dormouse friend. And then she'd been assiduous in promoting the "romance." Never had she given the slightest hint that she'd slept with Trent, but she'd flown regularly with him till he gave up his job in England, and Trudi had heard lurid office stories about the good times flight and cabin crews had on overnight stops abroad.

After their marriage and the move to the Continent, Trudi had rarely returned to the U.K., but Trent was frequently away from home. Indeed, as he moved from flying to executive status, his trips seemed to become more rather than less frequent. Did they take him to England? Occasionally perhaps. Or perhaps often. Her own interest in their duration and destination had never been great. It wasn't that his domination of her life didn't remain complete. On the contrary, it was so complete it didn't even require his physical presence, merely the certainty that, however far he went, good old Trent would always come back.

So; Trent and Janet; her husband and her best friend (oh, how banal!) lovers perhaps for the past twenty-five years! Had they talked about her, mocked her appearance, her sexual performance? Or worse, had they perhaps talked kindly of her, affectionately, even pityingly, as of a much-loved family pet?

Rage, revulsion, disbelief; flight, suicide, revenge; her mind went reeling between emotions and courses of action till she felt herself spinning back through the months to that day she got the news of Trent's death.

Like a perfectly timed cue, the doorbell rang. She went to

answer it, certain that she would find a policeman standing on the step.

She was right. But not a young constable this time, nervously twisting his cap in his hand.

"Come in, Inspector Workman," she said.

His arrival was like a switch, lighting up the present once more. Whether his departure would return her to the shadows she couldn't foresee. But for the moment she was calm, alert, self-contained.

"Herr Jünger isn't with you?" she said.

"He'll be along shortly," said Workman. "But I thought I'd get here first and have a little chat. Are you all right this morning, Mrs. Adamson? You gave us a fright last night."

"I thought it was the other way round."

"Yes. I'm sorry. Herr Jünger's English is good, but he hasn't quite got the fine control working, has he?"

He smiled tentatively, inviting her to join him in the old English pastime of being amused by daft foreigners. She found herself smiling back.

"Will you have a cup of coffee?" she asked.

"That'd be lovely."

As they drank their coffee seated in the lounge, Workman came to the point, or the alleged point, of his visit.

"The thing is, we like to cooperate with our colleagues abroad, you can understand that. Crime's international these days. But our first duty's still to our own people. It's not always easy to make this clear in circumstances like yesterday, with Herr Jünger being there, and all. So I thought I'd get here early and put you fully in the picture."

He sat back, smiling, and sipped his coffee.

"Yes?" said Trudi.

"Pardon?"

"You said you were going to put me fully in the picture."

"Yes, that's what I've been trying to do, Mrs. Adamson."

"No," said Trudi firmly. "You've told me that if, or maybe when, Herr Jünger starts being nasty to me, I'm not to worry because you will be nice. But what's it all about, Inspector? What does Herr Jünger really want from me?"

He looked at her shrewdly.

"I think," he said at last, "that what he'd really like is for you to go back to Vienna with him to help in their inquiries."

Trudi considered this, and Workman's reasons for saying it.

I'm never going to trust anybody again! said part of her mind, that part most closely in contact with the reeling universe from which the doorbell had summoned her.

"When I read that in the papers," she said slowly, "helping with inquiries, I mean; when I read that I usually assume it means someone's been arrested."

"Come now, Mrs. Adamson." He laughed. "What could anyone want to arrest you for?"

"Over here, nothing," she said.

"And in Austria."

"Nothing again."

"So what's the problem?"

"No problem," she said. "Except that while I'm here, Herr Jünger can't even threaten me with arrest, can he?"

"But why should he want to? I mean, as you say, you've done nothing . . ."

"Don't treat me as naïve! I'm tired of being treated like an idiot child!"

She realized she'd raised her voice to a level not much below shrieking. She took a deep breath and reacquired control. At least now she knew how close to snapping she was.

She said quietly, "I've done nothing, but here in my own house in my own country, Jünger can only question me with my consent and your cooperaton. Even if I confessed to mass murder in Vienna, he couldn't arrest me, could he? He'd have to get you to hold me while he applied for extradition. But in Vienna, it wouldn't matter if I was arrested or not. I'm sure you've all got your local methods of keeping people 'helping with inquiries' as long as you like. I don't know what Herr Jünger wants, but I don't fancy wasting a week in custody finding out!"

Workman produced a packet of cigarettes, offered them, said, "Do you mind if I do?"

"If you must," she said.

"Must?" he said musingly, examining the cigarette he had already removed from the packet.

He replaced it and put the packet on the table.

"There," he said. "Just to show who's in control. Look, Mrs. Adamson, don't you think you're being just a little paranoiac? I'm not saying you should go running off to Austria this very minute. But listen to Herr Jünger at least. Trust him. O.K., so it's obviously not just about this Fischer woman dying of an overdose of heroin. You're not stupid, and I'm sorry if anything I've said suggested I was treating you as such. All I'm saying is, if you can have a nice all-expense-paid trip to what must practically feel like your home town and help the Austrian police sort out what sounds like a very nasty business, where's the problem? I mean, why be so suspicious? If the Austrians really wanted to get you in a dungeon under a spotlight as you seem to suspect, wouldn't they have boxed clever and just waited till next time you visited Vienna and then pounced?"

"What makes you think there'd be a next time, Inspector?" asked Trudi.

"I don't know. Your husband's affairs. Selling your furniture. Or simply attending Astrid Fischer's funeral. It seems to me there could be plenty of reasons for a next time."

Trudi finished her cooling coffee.

As far as she could recall she had not mentioned the previous evening the reason for her last visit to Vienna. She did not believe Workman was psychic.

The doorbell rang.

"Excuse me," she said.

It was Jünger, nicely on cue. Perhaps the house was bugged!

When she returned to the lounge, the inspector was smoking. He caught her glance and, peering at the cigarette in his fingers, he said with apparently genuine amazement, "Christ! How did that get there?"

Jünger produced a big Austrian cigar and said, "You permit?"

Trudi said, "Why not?" and Workman, about to stub his cigarette out, paused, took a long last draw, then extinguished it.

As Jünger made himself comfortable, Trudi watched for

some signal to be passed between the two men, but was unable to detect anything. On the contrary they seemed to be ignoring each other.

His cigar lit, Jünger leaned forward. To her surprise he began to speak in German.

"I believe your German is very good," he said. "Our friend here doesn't speak a word. First, I want to say I am sorry for having caused you such a shock last night. It was ill-mannered to say the least. Second, very quickly, before we are interrupted, I want to say I was a good friend to your husband. Say nothing of this here. But please agree to come back to Vienna with me."

"Excuse me," said Workman. "I'm sorry, Herr Jünger, but our agreement was, English only."

"Forgive me, Inspector," said the Austrian. "It was a slip of the tongue."

"Some slip," said Workman. "What did you say?"

"Only that I was sorry Frau Adamson became ill last night and hoped she was recovered. Frau Adamson, let me now explain things more clearly. Astrid Fischer died of an overdose of heroin. She had been an addict, we know that, but she had taken a voluntary course of treatment some years earlier. The puncture scars on her body were all old except the one that killed her. Why should she have chosen that moment to restart the habit? No, we do not believe this injection was self-administered. We believe you must have been the last person, other than the killer, of course, to see her and speak to her. We would like from you several things. One, a detailed account of your conversation that night. Two, an examination of Fischer's apartment to see if there are any changes there from when you last saw it. Three, a study of photographs of possible suspects to see if you recall seeing any of them in the vicinity of the apartment that night. There are other ways you can help also, but these are the most important. Some of these things you could do here in England; all of them can be done more efficiently in Vienna. We would be grateful if you could return there for perhaps two days only to assist us. Your expenses will, of course, be taken care of and any loss of income recompensed."

"Income?"

"Yes. You have a job, the inspector tells me."

Another snippet of information from the well-informed inspector!

Trudi said in rapid German, "And what about my husband, what's this got to do with him?"

"Please, Frau Adamson, leave it till later!" urged Jünger.

And, turning apologetically to Workman, he said, "The lady wants assurances that we will not keep her beyond two days. I have promised. Perhaps you will witness my promise, Inspector."

"Gladly," said Workman solemnly with a small gesture of his right hand which might have been a parody of a judicial oath-taking.

Do they really expect me to fall for *that?* wondered Trudi.

But she had made up her mind, with or without reassurances. Jünger's reference to Trent had had its probably intended effect.

Also, she had a feeling amounting to certainty that very soon Janet would try to contact her in Sheffield. That was an encounter she wanted to delay as long as possible.

"All right, Herr Jünger," she said in German. "I agree. I will return with you to Vienna."

And saw from the flicker of triumph in Workman's eyes that, as she'd suspected, it had all been a game and he understood German perfectly well.

But it didn't change her mind.

PART SIX

Thou need na start awa sae hasty,
    Wi' bickering brattle!
I wad be laith to rin an' chase thee,
    Wi' murd'ring pattle! . . .

BURNS: "To a Mouse"

CHAPTER
1

Jünger worked fast. It was arranged that she would be picked up that same afternoon and driven to Manchester airport where they would catch a flight to Paris with a connection to Vienna.

Left alone, Trudi picked up the telephone and rang the emergency number Stanley Usher had given her. She let the phone ring for five minutes but there was no reply.

As soon as she replaced the receiver, it rang. She hesitated to pick it up, fearing to hear Janet's voice. It kept on ringing and in the end she snatched it from its rest, clamped her hand over the mouthpiece and listened.

"Trudi, is that you? Hello? Hello?"

"James!" she cried in relief. "Hello. Yes. Sorry. It's me."

"Hello," he said. "I was just ringing to see how you were. I was sorry to have to rush off and leave you alone."

"I'm getting used to that," said Trudi. "Being alone, I mean. I'm fine, thank you."

"Good. Look, what about a spot of lunch? Could you manage that? Just a drink and a sandwich."

It was very tempting. Dacre's seemed the one friendly voice in all the world. But there was no time. She had to pack and be ready at two o'clock. In any case, she had a fear that if she saw James, she might break down and cry on his shoulder and put him off forever.

She didn't want that.

"I'm sorry, James, I can't," she said.

"Oh," he said neutrally. "Pity."

He thinks I'm giving *him* the brush-off! she told herself. She rushed to explain.

"And so I'm off to Vienna again," she concluded.

"Trudi, you're sure this is wise?" he said in a worried voice.

"Why shouldn't it be?"

"I don't know. But there's something going on, that's clear. And you're in danger of being sucked into it. I know you say that Jünger's given you reassurances, but dealing with the authorities abroad is like boxing in America—you need a knockout to get a draw!"

His odd analogy made her laugh.

"I'll be all right," she said almost gaily. "I'm probably more at home in Vienna than I am in Sheffield!"

"That's not what it says on your passport," he answered grimly. "Trudi . . ."

"Yes?"

"I enjoyed . . . this morning. The important bit, I mean."

"So did I, James. So did I."

There was a pause. She willed him to suggest he might come out to the house to have his sandwich and drink with her there.

But with an abruptness which she was beginning to suspect was habitual rather than indicative, he said. "Well, I hope you have a good trip, Trudi. Take care," and rang off.

Immediately she was furious with herself for waiting for Dacre to make the suggestion. What phantom of old-fashioned decorum had kept her quiet?

None, she answered herself immediately. Not genteel etiquette (which would have been doubly absurd when you considered how they had met in the first place) but a simple, earthy fear of seeming pushy.

The trouble is, I've forgotten how to behave naturally, she told herself. Like a pupil in a new language, I'm so frightened of getting it wrong that I prefer to say nothing at all.

She set about her packing. Two days, she had told Jünger. Two days, he had agreed.

But she found herself dropping in little extras "just in case."

Jünger was prompt, in fact a little early, which she was glad of. As he carried her cases out to the car, she said to him, "Can we go through the center of town? I have to leave a message at my workplace. It won't take a moment."

"Of course," he said. "I'll tell the driver."

The car was a black Granada with no official markings, nor was it clear whether the driver had any official standing, except for one thing. He was a young, blond-haired man with a moustache. Trudi couldn't be sure, but she half recognized him as the man she had suspected of watching her months earlier.

She was amazed how little this suspicion worried her. But what's toothache to a woman with a cracked skull? she asked herself wryly.

She directed the car to the Class-Glass office. When it stopped, she got out, ran across the pavement and climbed the stairs. She'd written a note explaining her absence to Usher and her intention was to leave it on the typewriter. But when she pushed open the office door, that went right out of her mind.

"Oh Jesus!" she said.

Someone had been into the office and wrecked it. Instead of her reflected face in the mirrors, all she saw now were empty frames or at most a jagged ruff of glass. As she advanced into the room her feet crunched on shards and splinters of mirror.

It hadn't been a wrecking job incidental to burglary. The desk with its typewriter and telephone stood untouched. As her eyes noted this, the phone rang and the sound made her startle as if she were the intruder surprised.

She picked up the receiver.

"Hello?" she said.

"Mrs. Adamson?"

The voice was familiar, reassuringly so, though she didn't place it immediately.

"Yes."

"Oh good. Ashburton here. I've been trying to get you at home. I thought I might as well try your office though I didn't think this was one of your days."

"Oh no, it's not."

Quickly she explained what she was doing there and then went on to describe the state of the office.

"The thing is, Mr. Ashburton, I've got a plane to catch and I'm behind schedule already. Could I possibly ask you to get in touch with the police and, of course, Mr. Usher?"

"Good Lord! That's terrible. What's the world coming to? Yes, I'd be glad to help in any way, but I'm not sure if you should really leave the scene of the crime, so to speak."

Despite the situation, Trudi smiled at the little solicitor's care for the law.

"It'll be all right, really. Ask for Inspector Workman to be told. Workman. He'll put it right. Look, what was it you wanted to contact me about?"

"Just a point in connection with your claim. But nothing urgent if you're in a hurry, my dear."

"Mrs. Adamson! Please. We are going to be late!"

It was Jünger from the foot of the stairs.

"Yes. I must fly. Go, I mean. And fly. Goodbye."

She replaced the receiver, but she didn't head for the door straightaway.

As she spoke to Ashburton, something had been tugging at her eyesight. She assumed at first it was some kind of accidental *trompe l'oeil* by which one of the shattered mirrors seemed to show space behind it rather than its backing or the wall.

But the more she looked . . .

She went close. No optical illusion, this. Where the glass had fallen out, there was a hole through which she could see a small room, only a few feet square, with a wooden chair and a doorway.

The mirror was the heart-shaped one in which James Dacre had admired himself. She removed a piece of the glass still held in the frame and turned it over. Its reverse was unsilvered and when she held it up to the window and examined it from this side, she saw that light came through.

Outside there were footsteps on the stairs.

Oh God, she thought. *Let Workman sort it out!*

She met Jünger as he reached the landing.

"I'm sorry," she said. "The phone rang. I got held up."

Jünger did not reprove her, but gave her the silent disapproval treatment. This suited Trudi very well. She sank deep into her own thoughts as the car climbed out of Sheffield and wound between the snow-freckled moors of the southern Pennines. This was the Snake Pass. Last time she had traveled over here, she had been with Janet. Her friend, her guide, her mentor. Her betrayer.

Once she saw a green Escort coming towards them and shrank back in her seat, certain it must be Janet's. It wasn't, of course, but it reminded her how much this journey was really a flight.

At Manchester, Jünger took charge of everything. This was how it had been with Trent, the sharp edges of modern travel smoothed down to a few longueurs. Then she had taken it for granted. Now she found herself half resenting the Austrian's smooth organization, which was somehow more macho than any noisy, bullying bellowing could have been. She walked after him to the check-in desk. The girl had just tapped up a couple of seats on her screen.

Trudi looked and said, "Make one of those a nonsmoker, will you, Mrs. Adamson."

The girl glanced queryingly at Jünger who sighed and said, "All right. Two in the nonsmoking . . ."

"No!" said Trudi. "Just one. I don't see why you should suffer for me, Herr Jünger."

"But we should talk . . ."

"There will be plenty of time to talk in Vienna," she said, savoring the small triumph.

The plane was on time. She took her seat by the window and stared out at the unedifying prospect of a modern airport, wondering if she was doing the right thing. She felt someone take the seat beside her but did not look up.

"Now, this is very handy," said a familiar voice. "I thought you'd be handcuffed to our Austrian friend if not actually chained up in the hold."

It was James Dacre. The flip remark did not chime with his naturally serious mien, but it matched the feel of determined embarrassment that emanated from him.

"James! What are you doing here?"

"Business in Vienna," he said, holding up a briefcase unconvincingly. "I thought I might as well have some company on the flight."

She shook her head in disbelief. Even the briefcase looked new and empty.

"And this business has come up since midday?" she said.

He grinned sheepishly.

"All right," he said. "I've no talent for play-acting, clearly. After I put down the phone, I thought about what you'd said—going back to Vienna with Jünger, I mean—and I got to thinking. I've led a rather dull life, Trudi. There've been crises and excitements, of course, but they've been the conventional kind that happen to everybody. When I met you through the Agency, you seemed just the right type for me."

"A quiet dull little dormouse, you mean," said Trudi.

"Is that what I mean? Perhaps. But not without other attractions. Anyway, suddenly in the last twenty-four hours, there's all this."

He made the kind of gesture the first man to see the aliens in a science-fiction movie might make when he got back home.

"My first instinct last night was to run for cover," he said.

"But you decided venery was the better part of discretion," she said tartly.

"No. I resisted the discretion without thought of sex," he said seriously. "That came later. And then that fellow Carter turned up. You know what I thought? Just for a second, I thought that it was some complicated setup, like in the old pictures. You know, where the private eye busts into the hotel bedroom with a flash camera!"

"My God!" said Trudi.

"I'm sorry. Well, I soon realized it wasn't, but I needed to get away to think. It didn't take me long to realize that I needed to have a serious talk with you. I rang up and asked you to meet me at lunch, and you sprang this thing about going back to Vienna. I thought hard and long, Trudi. And I decided that either I got involved or I got out. I can't sit on the sidelines, that's never been my way. I picked up my phone. I had a choice. Ring the Lewis Agency and put myself back in the system, or ring a travel agent and put myself on this plane."

The stewardess leaned over and asked Dacre to put on his seat belt as they would soon be taking off. The interruption gave Trudi a chance to examine her ambiguous feelings.

Part of her was delighted to have James Dacre's company.

And part of her wanted to ask him in bitter mockery what he expected from her for his noble decision—applause?

The plane was taxiing forward. She stared out of the window as though fascinated by the passing scene. Soon the preparatory roar of the jets released her from that pretense. The plane began its takeoff run. So absorbed was she in the problem of her relationship with Dacre that she missed that moment of pure terror when it seemed impossible for this huge weight of metal and flesh to unstick itself from the ground.

But that other and consequent moment of exultation when the plane soared, and the earth dwindled, and with it all its problems and irritations, did come.

Releasing her seat belt, she turned to Dacre and said with a smile, "At least I'll be able to accept that luncheon invitation now. And I won't count anything we're likely to get on this plane!"

CHAPTER
2

Jünger took James Dacre's presence in his stride, nodding at him as though at a familiar if casual acquaintance, when he came back to check that Trudi was comfortably settled. There was something perhaps a touch satirical in the way he held open the door of the car

that met them at Vienna and motioned Dacre to get in beside
Trudi, but it wasn't till they drew up outside the Hotel Regina
in Rooseveltplatz that he actually addressed the Englishman.

As the driver removed the luggage from the boot, Jünger
opened the car door on Dacre's side. As Dacre climbed out,
Jünger said, "Frau Adamson's room is 451. Perhaps you
would see her luggage gets there. I do hope you can get a
room on the same floor, Herr Dacre."

Then he slid into the vacated seat, and the driver, who had
abandoned the cases on the curb, sent the Mercedes speeding
away.

Trudi began to protest, but Jünger merely said, "Forgive
me. First things first and there is little time if I am to keep my
promise and send you home after only two days. Herr Dacre
would, I think, prove to be a distraction."

The car took them the short journey to Astrid's flat. Almost
before she was aware where she was, Trudi found herself
climbing the stairs to the olive-green door.

Jünger had a key.

"Enter, please," he commanded. "Look around. Take
note. Let me know what you see that may be different from
your last visit."

He opened the door. For a second Trudi saw Astrid's
narrow, lively face, heard her high surprised voice.

A blink of the eyes, a shake of the head, dissolved that
ghost. But a reality more devastating than any phantom
awaited her as she entered the apartment.

On the long table between two armchairs in front of the gas
fire were the remnants of a meal. Plates with traces of egg on
them and forks left lying askew. An open pickle jar. A basket
with half a mildewed bread roll. A bowl of rotting fruit. An
ashtray with an apple core and several plum stones in it.
Three wine bottles, two empty, one almost. Two tall hock
glasses.

These were the relics of their meal together that night;
Astrid's last meal; Astrid's last night.

Her closeness to Astrid's death had not registered till this
moment. She remembered offering tipsily to help with the
dishes. Astrid had laughingly rejected the offer, saying she
liked to wash up after guests had gone, it got her sober before
going to bed.

She dragged her eyes with difficulty from the table and turned them to the bed on the mezzanine level. The half-packed suitcase lay there, the legs of a gay red ski suit trailing grotesquely over the side just as they had been on the night of her visit.

She began to walk round the apartment. It felt like sleep-walking. Jünger stood by the door and watched her.

When he spoke, it was merely a prompting, "So?"

"It's all the same," she said dully. "Only that. I don't remember that."

She pointed at a piece of black plastic sheeting about four feet square, against the skirting board under the wall-mounted telephone.

"No. That wasn't there," agreed Jünger. He drew it back.

On the wood-block floor beneath was drawn a chalk outline, irregular, vaguely rhomboid, like an depiction of Great Britain on an ancient map.

"She tried to reach the telephone, I think."

Trudi gasped and put her hand to her mouth. There was little humanoid about the chalk shape. Worse was the tiny space Astrid Fischer must have crumpled into. Suddenly the wavering white line took on significance. She saw a body drawn back into itself in an effort to shut out the abyss. Back arched, knees tucked tight under the chin, head forced down hard, body as fetal in death as it had been in birth.

She said, "May I sit down?"

"Oh, yes. It is all right now. All the forensic examination is finished."

She sat in the same chair she had used that night. Her hand, trailed lifelessly over the arm, touched glass. She looked down. It was the brandy balloon she had left there and that smudge on the rim was the mark of her own pale lipstick.

"Excuse me," she said.

She went into the bathroom and let herself be violently sick.

When she came back Jünger said, "I'm sorry. The flight and that airline food . . ."

"No," she said. "Neither, as you know, Herr Jünger. It's all this. Just as I last saw it. Except that Astrid was alive and well, laughing, full of life."

"Yes," said Jünger. "Now, tell me, Frau Adamson. Why did you visit her that evening?"

"She was a family friend. She used to work for my husband when he was with Schiller-Reise, the travel company."

The Austrian put his hand to his face and massaged his fleshy cheeks.

"So, a social visit only?"

"Yes," said Trudi.

She had not known what she was going to say about the purpose of her visit till this very moment. Back in Sheffield she had felt she would probably tell the truth. Here the truth seemed irrelevant, almost unseemly.

Also, despite her long sojourn in this country, she felt suddenly afraid of what powers a man like Jünger might have if he decided it was necessary to pressurize a witness.

The Austrian made no effort to pursue this line of questioning. Indeed he yawned widely as if the fatigue of his journeyings had married with a growing boredom with this case and his mind had turned to home and bed.

"Forgive me," he said. "You must be tired, too, I think. Nothing has changed here, you are sure?"

"Not as far as I can see. I'm sorry."

"No need. It is helpful in that it suggests how little time must have passed between your departure and . . . well, whatever happened. But time enough for all that tomorrow. A car will come for you at eight-thirty in the morning. I'm sorry it is so early, but the sooner we start the sooner we finish. Now my driver will take you back to your hotel and the anxious Herr Dacre. Good night, Frau Adamson."

"Good night," said Trudi, bewildered but not displeased by this sudden dismissal.

He opened the door and ushered her out.

"You're not coming?" she said.

"No. The driver will pick me up on the way back. Good night."

Trudi paused in the doorway. A question had formed in her mind but she was not altogether certain she wanted to ask it.

But if concealing things from others was part of her new game plan, concealing things from herself wasn't.

"Herr Jünger," she said. "How did you know it was me who visited Astrid Fischer that night?"

He looked at her with a faint expression of surprise as though the question were unnecessary.

Stooping, he picked up the brandy balloon her hand had brushed and held it towards her. Now she saw there was a change. A faint white dust clung to the outside of the bowl.

"Fingerprints, of course. Frau Adamson," he said. "You left your fingerprints."

He laughed as if amused at her simplicity and she found herself smiling back and nodding as if in accord with this judgment.

But as she descended the stairs, her legs once more felt weak as she tried to imagine a reason for the Austrian authorities having a record of her fingerprints.

Back at the hotel, James Dacre was waiting in the lobby. She told him she wasn't hungry but was very tired and would go straight to her room. But after a shower and a change of clothing, hunger revived. As her mind by now was running round like a mouse on a treadmill, she knew that any attempt at sleep was likely to be fruitless.

She rang Dacre's room and told him of her change of heart, and they met in the restaurant. Over supper, they talked about everything but the reason for her presence in Vienna. From time to time as she relaxed she strayed in that direction, but always he steered her away as if sensing that the time was not ripe. After their meal, they walked from the hotel towards the Votiv Kirche but the chill of the night soon drove them back indoors.

When they reached her room, she did not hesitate but opened the door, stepped in, and drew him after her. It was a need not to be alone that was strong inside her, but the sex was good and released that last notch of tension. Now she was able to talk without the risk of recreating the state of fear and panic which followed her visit to the apartment.

They talked deep into the night, or rather she talked, he listened. Then they made love again and she fell asleep, as happy as she had been for more years than she could recall.

* * *

The next morning she would have been late for the car if Dacre had not woken her. He was dressed and shaved, and a breakfast tray stood on the table by her bed.

"You'd better get a move on," he said. "Otherwise friend Jünger will probably arrive with a gang of storm troopers to drag you from your bed."

She smiled and stretched luxuriously, realized the bed-clothes were pushed down to her thighs, and pulled them up over her in modest confusion. Dacre seemed to enjoy the rôle change hugely.

"I'll see you in twenty minutes," he said, grinning broadly as he withdrew.

She took half an hour. Keeping the official car waiting presented her with no problems this morning.

Dacre appeared immediately when she tapped on his door.

"James," she said, "what are you going to do today?"

"First of all, I'm coming to Jünger's dungeon with you, to check whether he's letting you out on parole at lunchtime or not. It won't do any harm for him to be reminded that you have a friend in the vicinity, anxious for your well-being.

"Then I suppose I'll see the sights. What are the sights, by the way. My knowledge of Vienna is restricted to *The Third Man*."

"Well, you can still go up on the big wheel at the Prater, if you want," said Trudi. "And I presume the sewers haven't changed much. Otherwise it depends on your taste. Muse-ums, churches, the Opera, the Riding School, or you can just sit in a café, drinking lovely coffee and gorging delicious cream cakes. But beware of your figure."

"It hasn't affected yours so I notice," said Dacre inno-cently.

"You should have seen me this time last year," laughed Trudi. But the phrase *this time last year* brought the shadow of the past with it, and her lighthearted mood began to fade as she got into the waiting Mercedes.

She half expected to be taken to police headquarters. Instead they turned off fashionable Kärntner Strasse down what looked like a service lane for shop deliveries, passed through a solid wooden gate and came to a halt in a narrow yard.

Jünger was waiting in a mean little doorway. He expressed no surprise at seeing Dacre but preempted his questions by saying, "I anticipate Frau Adamson will be with us till midafternoon. Let us say four o'clock to be safe."

"No lunch break?" said Dacre.

"Of course. We will provide lunch here. It saves time, permits us to finish earlier."

"And tomorrow?" insisted Dacre. "Will you be wanting to see her tomorrow?"

Jünger shrugged, the gesture oddly Gallic on his solid Austrian frame.

"Who knows?" he said.

With this Dacre had to be satisfied.

He kissed Trudi gently on the cheek and turned away. Obedient to the pressure of Jünger's hand, she stepped over the threshold.

Behind her, the door shut with as solid a thud as ever echoed through a castle keep.

CHAPTER
3

They walked at a pace more quick than comfortable along the grid of gray corridors punctuated by unnumbered doors. Jünger was a half step ahead and whenever she tried to catch up to make conversation possible, he matched her acceleration.

Finally she halted. He kept on going for a dozen paces before stopping also and turning to regard her somberly.

"Is something wrong, Frau Adamson?" he asked.

"I'm not moving another step till I know where we're going," she said, more shrilly than she intended.

"We're here," he replied, pushing open the door he was standing next to.

Feeling foolish, Trudi advanced and went into the room.

Behind her Jünger said, "Fräulein Weigel will take care of you."

The door closed. She turned, half bewildered, half angry. There didn't appear to be a handle.

"Take a seat please, Frau Adamson," said a woman's voice.

There was only one seat to take, a hard kitchen chair placed opposite a plain deal table. Above the table hung a bulb in a heavy frilled shade which directed nearly all the light downwards, though enough filtered to the room's corners to show that it was devoid of window, decoration, or other furniture.

Behind the table sat a woman, or rather a girl. She looked little more than eighteen and her severe black blouse might have been part of a school uniform. Her face, fine-boned and delicately beautiful, had the rather self-consciously stern expression of a head prefect. Her hands rested palms down on the table on either side of a slim file.

Trudi sat down. The girl flipped open the file.

"Shoesmith, Gertrud Adele. Known as Trudi. Daughter of Wilhelm and Gertrud Schumacher. Born London, England, June 15th 1939. Married Adamson, Trent—"

"Hold on," protested Trudi. "What is this?"

"I am just checking your particulars, Frau Adamson," said the girl, not looking up. "It is necessary procedure."

"Well, all right. I'm Trudi Adamson. I know that, now you know it. Where's Herr Jünger?"

"Close. Please, let us continue. I must complete the checks."

The girl flicked over a page of the file.

"For God's sake," said Trudi, standing up. "I haven't come here to hear my life story."

Now the girl looked up. An expression which might have been annoyance or bewilderment passed over her face.

"Wait here," she said.

She rose and went to the corner of the room. A door, which Trudi hadn't spotted, opened. She passed through, and the door closed behind her.

Trudi didn't hesitate, because hesitation would almost certainly have meant inaction. She went round the table and began to examine the file.

It was all there, her life history. Birth, school, exams, work, marriage, where she'd lived, where she'd traveled, friends, acquaintances, interests, tastes, everything up to and including her time in Sheffield. Janet was there, and James Dacre too, with a note on his background and on the circumstances of their meeting.

Her face burned at the thought that this child, this Fräulein Weigel, not to mention God knows how many others, should have access to this information.

And another part of her mind marveled at the smallness of the space her life folded into and the dullness of the existence and personality here contained.

She turned the sheet.

Photographs, more than a dozen of them.

Again they followed her through to the present, though they only started after her marriage. Most she recognized as snapshots from her own album. Only the last three were new to her. One showed her with Trent. A dumpy figure walking away from an airplane. It must have been taken on their arrival in England the previous year. Trent was a step behind her, and even this telescopic shot seemed to have alerted that old sensitivity to the camera, for his head was bowed and his left hand was scratching his nose.

The other two showed her in her new widowed persona. In the first the slight, still unfamiliar figure was standing head-on to the camera waiting to cross a road. Shops behind her she recognized as belonging to Sheffield. She was taken aback at the look of unhappiness on her face.

The final picture caught her in quite a different mood. She was glowing with joy, her head tipped back, her mouth opened wide in laughter. The print had been cut and probably enlarged so that background details were vague, but she knew where and when it had been taken. Her last lunchtime drink with James Dacre.

She flipped over the page. There was just one more sheet. It consisted of a photocopy of two sets of fingerprints, left hand and right hand.

Beneath them was her name.

Carefully she closed the file and replaced it as she'd found it. But the futility of that act was already clear to her. The file had been left here for her to examine. Perhaps they were somehow watching her examining it while they examined her for her reaction. What should it be? Anger? Fear? Bewilderment?

The door opened. Fräulein Weigel said, "In here, if you please."

Obediently she went through into a brightly lit room which had a medical smell about it, an impression reinforced by the presence of a small middle-aged woman wearing a white overall. There was a further door opposite the one she had entered. By this stood another woman, broad-shouldered, slab-faced, like an Eastern European shot-putter. Or a concentration-camp guard.

There was no furniture at all in this room.

"Please turn and face the wall. Lean against it with your hands as far apart as they will go, your legs spread wide," said Fräulein Weigel.

"No!" cried Trudi. "What is this? Please, where's Jünger? I demand to see Jünger!"

"Shortly," said the girl. "Please, Frau Adamson. It is merely procedure. It is necessary to search you. Everyone who comes here must be searched."

"Not me," said Trudi fearfully.

"It is easier with your cooperation," said the girl, glancing towards the burly woman by the door.

Now was the time to resist, to scream, to flee.

Only the conviction that this was all part of a deliberately debilitating plan kept Trudi from hysterics.

She turned to the wall and leaned against it as she had seen suspects do in American thrillers. What happened next confirmed the memory. Her feet were kicked further apart till she was completely off balance. Hands ran through her clothes, over her body, checking every bump, every unevenness. Next some kind of electronic detector was moved in a slow zigzag up and down her frame. Finally, just as she thought it was over, she suddenly felt her wrists seized in a grip like a clamp and to her unutterable horror her pants were pulled down over her buttocks and a hand slipped between her thighs and entered her.

She screamed in pain, in outrage, in sheer amazement. It was all over in a couple of seconds, but she carried on screaming. Then she realized the grip on her wrists had been removed. Drunkenly she staggered away from the wall, pulled her pants up, and turned around.

The burly woman was standing a couple of feet away, regarding her indifferently. The white-overalled woman was moving away, peeling off a surgical glove. Fräulein Weigel, serious as ever, said, "This way, please," and walked briskly to the further door and opened it. Trudi followed with unsteady steps. As she passed the woman in white, she paused and swung an open-handed blow at her face with all her might.

Her forearm was caught before the slap could connect. The burly woman held it, one-handed, with ease. The woman in white didn't even look at her.

Sobbing, Trudi pulled away and went after the girl through the door into the corridor. That part of her mind which she had begun to value as *herself*, independent, rational, captain of her fate, mistress of her soul, was screaming at her that beyond these walls, within a few meters, lay Vienna—a free city in a democratic state, a city she knew well, had lived in for many years, which contained people she knew, which contained a British consulate and James Dacre.

But this screamed reassurance came from a vast distance, from some perilous ledge to which *herself* had retreated and to which *herself* was clinging with most precarious hold.

They were climbing stairs now, endless mean little flights which turned back on themselves every twelve treads. Once she looked down into the narrow well. It was dark and receding apparently into infinity, except that somewhere in the gloom she thought she glimpsed a pallid face peering up at her. After that she looked no more but concentrated on following Fräulein Weigel. There was a moment on each flight when the girl had turned up the next and was no longer in view ahead. Trudi felt a crescending panic that at each turn, her guide would have disappeared or, worse, been substituted by she didn't let herself think what, except that images of Trent kept on stealing into her mind.

At last it happened. The girl had gone. Trudi gasped aloud in fear, and louder still as a voice behind her said, "This way."

She turned. They had reached a long landing and she had simply been looking the wrong way. Behind her stood Fräulein Weigel, and she was holding open another door through which, miraculously, fell a shaft of mote-filled sunlight.

Slowly Trudi approached the threshold and halted, feeling as Dante must have felt when he beheld the stars again.

It was a fine, airy, elegantly proportioned room with delicate ceiling moldings picked out in gold and burgundy, a marble fireplace in which glowed a wood-log fire and three high windows which gave a view across a tumble of rooftops to the familiar outline of Steffl, the great South Tower of Saint Stephen's Cathedral. The morning sun was still low in the sky. Trudi stood in its thin rays and felt them like a benison.

"It is a nice view, isn't it?"

Startled, she turned to see the owner of the voice. Only now did she realized that she had entered the room and walked straight across it to stand in the window.

Jünger was standing by the fireplace, evidently having just risen from one of a pair of *bergères* in the high rococo style which stood in front of it.

"Oh, I'm sorry," began Trudi, instinctively starting to apologize for her rudeness in ignoring him, then memory of what she'd been through came rushing in.

"I want out of here, Herr Jünger," she shouted. "I don't know or care who you are, I'm bringing charges, even if I've got to go to the European Court to make this stick!"

His face filled with bewildered concern.

"Please, Frau Adamson, what is the matter?"

She told him, using words she once would not have used, even to Trent.

He said, "Excuse me," and left the room.

She sat in one of the chairs and warmed herself at the fire. She hadn't realized she was so cold, even to the point of shivering.

The door opened. It wasn't Jünger but a boy in a white

shirt and black trousers with a red stripe. He was carrying a tray with coffee pot, cups, cream, sugar and a plate artistically laden with *Torten*.

He moved a small table between the two chairs, placed the tray on it, bowed and smiled in response to Trudi's thank-you and left.

After a while Trudi poured herself a coffee. It was excellent and her tattered nerves repaired enough for her to note that the *bergères* were apparently genuine mid-eighteenth century, and to resist the temptation of the *Torten*. She was drinking her second cup when Jünger returned, his face creased with concern.

"You're having coffee. Excellent. A cake to go with it? Or some brandy perhaps? No? Frau Adamson, I am devastated. It has been a ghastly error. The instruction was to process you; it is a necessary procedure for all visitors, however high, nothing more than simple identity check and an electronic scan, then you are given a security label. Look, I have yours here."

He handed over a plastic-covered lapel badge which contained her photograph and a deal of small print. She let it lie on the table.

"Unfortunately," he continued, "owing to some administrative idiocy, Fräulein Weigel had you classified as an interrogatee. I am so sorry."

"And that's it?" cried Trudi. "Listen, Herr Jünger, visitor or interrogatee, I'd still be outraged! I don't believe it can be legal to do that to *anyone*."

Jünger shrugged and said, "There are people out there who would stop at nothing to get bugs or even bombs into this building. Our procedures are necessary, believe me. But I will see that those responsible for this mishap are disciplined."

"Starting with Weigel, I hope. I got the impression she got rather too much enjoyment from her work."

"Fräulein Weigel? Perhaps. Not without reason. But I have spoken severely to her already and will do so again. Now I hope we can put this unhappy start behind us."

Trudi shook her head.

"Not yet," she said firmly. "Weigel had a file. There were

details of my life in it. Photographs I didn't know had been taken. And fingerprints. That's how you knew I'd been at Astrid's, you said. Fingerprints. What I want to know is, what does it all mean? Why should this office of yours have a file on me, like a criminal?"

"No," said Jünger. "Not like a criminal. Like a citizen who has come near crime and needs protection."

"Protection? Who from? And on whose authority?" demanded Trudi.

"Authority? My authority, I suppose. But better to ask, at whose request."

"All right then," said Trudi. "If you must play games. At whose request?"

"At your husband's, Frau Adamson. At Trent's. You see, he was working for me, I mean for the department, when he died. It was at his request that we opened a surveillance file on you."

Trudi sat very still. The heat seemed to have gone out of the fire.

She said, "That brandy you offered me, I think I'd like it now."

CHAPTER
4

"In 1945 at the end of the war, Vienna was in ruins; physically, administratively, morally. The Allies were trying to restore some kind of order, but they were constantly diverted by squabbling after their own interests in competition with each other. The only truly efficient organization in the city was that which feeds on war rather than suffers under it—crime. There was a huge and complex black-market system. Food, petrol, medical supplies . . ."

"I saw *The Third Man*," said Trudi, recalling James's remark.

Jünger laughed humorlessly.

"Yes. A nice entertainment. But this was far from entertaining. Men died. Others made fortunes. As civic order was restored, so these men had to seek solid cover for their activities. Opportunism is the criminal virtue of chaos; organization, of order. The black-market bosses developed their own specialties. If you decided to concentrate on protection, you got yourself a union; on gambling, a night club; on prostitution, an employment agency. And if you decided to stay closer to the old black market and expand into a large-scale international smuggling operation, you looked for something which would offer you fluidity of movement, familiarity with frontier officialdom, up-to-date information on cross-border movement, legitimate reason for flight and ship charters, established contact points in major cities . . ."

He paused invitingly.

"Schiller-Reise," said Trudi dully.

"That's right. You get yourself a travel agency. A good, efficient, respected and prospering travel agency. After that, all things are possible. It is our belief, our *certainty*, that Schiller-Reise has for many many years been the legitimate cover for a highly sophisticated smuggling operation."

"What makes you so certain?" asked Trudi, anticipating the answer.

"Your husband, Frau Adamson. He was our inside man, our star witness. No, not in any professional sense. He was just a good citizen who, when his suspicions were roused, very properly went to the authorities. We listened, checked where we could, found what he said fitted with much of our own information. And then . . ."

"Then what?"

"We asked him to help us. What he had given us was enough to snip off a few important shoots, that was true. But we wanted the whole tree, roots and all. So we asked him to keep watching and reporting. He agreed."

Trudi finished her brandy. Jünger refilled the glass without needing to be asked.

"Herr Jünger," she said. "Has all this got anything to do with my husband's death?"

Before he answered, he poured himself a glass and sipped it appreciatively.

"Shall I be honest? I do not know, but naturally I had suspicions. The English police, however, could find nothing that was not consistent with accident. The fire worried me, however. It is not as easy as it appears in American films for a car to set on fire. Every day there are numerous accidents often resulting in the total write-off of automobiles, yet how often do they go up in flames? The car was reexamined by incendiary experts."

"Who said?"

"That they could see how a device might have been used, but if it were, then it was made out of such inflammable materials as are used in normal car construction and was therefore itself consumed undetectably by the flames."

Jünger spoke gloomily. *He wants Trent to have been murdered!* thought Trudi.

She said, "Why did my husband leave Schiller-Reise and return to England? He must have told you, surely?"

"In a manner of speaking," said Jünger. "He told us he had been posted to the U.K. to take over Schiller-Reise's operations there. He said nothing about having resigned from the company. I read the reports of the statements you made to the police after his death. It seems you knew nothing of this either?"

"Nothing at all, not until the funeral when Astrid Fischer told me that I needn't expect any pension," she said with bitter recollection. "Why should Trent have lied to us both?"

"Perhaps he didn't," said Jünger.

"You mean, perhaps he didn't resign from Schiller?" said Trudi incredulously. "But how could they get away with saying he did. My lawyer made inquiries about pensions, insurance . . ."

"And was doubtless shown a letter of resignation. I have seen it too. It looks genuine."

"Looks? But why shouldn't it be? Why would the firm do

something like that? To save on a widow's pension? I can't believe it!"

Her mind was racing. She drank more brandy. It was like increasing the octane rating of fuel for a high-powered machine.

"And what about the records of his new appointment? They'd have to be destroyed also. But what if there wasn't really any new appointment, they just wanted him away from Vienna, somewhere where he could be got rid of and they could then produce the records which showed he'd resigned and had nothing more to do with them!"

"Who are *they*, Frau Adamson?"

"I don't know. Whoever it is at Schiller-Reise who is running this smuggling racket. They found out that Trent was working for you. Perhaps they thought that by getting him out of the country, they'd get him away from your investigations. Perhaps . . ."

She paused as another thought entered.

"Astrid. Astrid would know that she was lying to me. Astrid had been sent to lie to me. Astrid had been sent to make contact with Trent.

"Astrid was with him shortly before the accident!"

"What's that you say, Frau Adamson?" said Jünger, sitting up straight.

Trudi explained about Mrs. Brightshaw.

"But you said nothing of this!" he said accusingly.

"Who should I say it to, unless the compensation case came to court? But I said it to Astrid! That's why I went to see her, Herr Jünger. Not an old friend paying a surprise visit, but a jealous wife come to seek satisfaction!"

Jünger massaged his jowls and said, "Yet you stayed to eat a meal, drink a lot of wine."

"Yes, I did," said Trudi defiantly. "Women can be civilized, in fact it's probably easier for us than for men. Besides, it's one thing quarreling over a live man but it seems a waste of time quarreling over a corpse."

She stopped, shocked at her own vehemence. She found herself glaring at Jünger as if defying him to look amused. It was unnecessary. His face was deadly serious.

"So. Astrid Fischer. Here, at last, is what it is all about,

your visit here, I mean. You say you left her full of wine,
happy, content?"

"Oh yes. We'd had a lot of laughs."

"So certainly not in a state in which her old need might
suddenly grow active again. And besides, why should she
have heroin available? Unless of course she was more deeply
implicated . . . a courier perhaps . . . but her skiing
holiday would not take her out of the country. Though it
would be a good opportunity to meet a contact from abroad,
of course."

He was speaking half to himself.

Trudi said, "I'm being very stupid. This smuggling racket
is concerned with drugs?"

"It's concerned with large profits, Frau Adamson," he
said, looking at her curiously. "There was a time when butter
could bring you as much profit as heroin in central Europe,
but those days have gone. Sometimes they seem almost like
the good old days now! Strange, isn't it? But to answer your
question, yes, of course it is a drug operation. That's where
the huge profits lie. Though with them come peculiar
dangers, and not just from the law."

"What do you mean?" asked Trudi.

"The natural growth of big business is towards monopolies," said Jünger. "Monopolies control production and
prices. They are good for businessmen, bad for consumers.
Therefore civilized countries inhibit them by law. But for
those who work outside the law there is no control, except
fear and strength. But to get back to our business. There is a
chance that perhaps Fischer overdosed by accident. I do not
believe so. She was shut up, I believe. And why? Because
she talked to you perhaps."

"More reason to shut me up, surely," said Trudi reasonably. She hoped Jünger would deny it.

"Yes, I see that," he said, frowning. "There is much I
don't understand. But to our business, Frau Adamson. There
is work to do."

They spent the next hour going over Trudi's account of the
evening and her conversation with Astrid. The interrogation
broadened to include Trudi's life with Trent and her contact

with other employees of Schiller-Reise. She realized how very little she knew about them. She recognized a few names and she could recall a couple of faces, but putting names and faces together was quite beyond her. She sensed Jünger's growing exasperation. He'd set a tape recorder running and at one point he stabbed his finger on the pause button and said, "Frau Adamson, please! You are a lively and intelligent woman, that I can see. Are you telling me that you had no interest in your husband's job, or his colleagues? That you managed to live in Vienna for three years and never became involved socially with any of them or their families?"

"We lived very quietly wherever we lived," she said defensively. "Trent preferred it that way."

He looked at her almost disbelievingly, then restarted the machine.

"What about Herr Schiller himself? Did you see much of him?"

She frowned and said, "Once or twice a year the firm would hold a sort of convention. We all gathered here in Vienna. I saw him then, of course."

She'd never liked these gatherings. There'd been something of the nature of a military parade about them, with honors worn and strict precedence adhered to. The fact that Trent had always been in the top stratum hadn't made matters easier for her. Nor had the many kind attentions lavished on her by Schiller done much more than embarrass her.

"And on other occasions?"

"Yes. If ever he was visiting the branch where Trent was working, he always came to stay with us."

"So you were friendly?"

"I suppose so. But not . . . friends. To tell the truth, I didn't care for him much. And he was always so kind and interested. He was always asking if we were starting a family yet. I used to get embarrassed. But he was Trent's boss, so I had to put up with it."

"Very dutiful," said Jünger drily. "And you moved here to Vienna to live shortly before Schiller had his first stroke?"

"That's right. I think everyone thought he would die, but he seemed to make a marvelous recovery. Trent saw him a lot, of course. I only saw him a few times before. He looked remarkably well, I thought."

She recalled him easily, a tall lively man with a shock of white hair and bright blue eyes which never seemed to leave you. It wasn't till you got close and saw the terrapin creases of his age-tanned skin that you realized just how old he was.

"Herr Jünger, are you saying that Herr Schiller was behind all this?"

"Would that surprise you?" said Jünger.

She thought and realized it wouldn't. He studied her closely as if dubious about her reaction. She said, "He is so highly respected. The State President has honored him."

"Everyone makes mistakes, Frau Adamson," said Jünger. "There are those who say that if the Allied War Crimes Commission had done *its* job properly, Herr Schiller would have spent the first two decades of peace in jail instead of making a fortune. But he no longer concerns us, I'm glad to say. He is, I gather, completely decrepit, eking out his days in some nursing home where the rich go to die."

Again he was watching her. What was he looking for? Pity? Callous indifference?

He sighed and said, "Now let us look at some photographs."

From a desk drawer, he took a leather-bound album and opened it before her. They might have been a pair of distant relatives, newly met, poring over old family snaps together.

Some of the photos *were* very like family snaps, casual, unposed, with the subject (marked with a red cross) often clearly unaware he was being taken. Others had the grim formality of police-file portraits.

Trudi went steadily through the thick album, shaking her head at most pages. A couple she nodded at, both former colleagues of Trent's, though she had no names for them. Jünger made spidery notes on a pad. Trudi turned the page.

And gasped.

Alert, Jünger said, "What is it? You recognize him?"

The marked man, drinking a glass of wine at a café table, she'd never seen before.

But behind him, slightly out of focus, was another table with two men sitting at it.

One of them, head as always half turned away but instantly recognizable to herself, was Trent.

But it wasn't this that had caused Trudi to react.

The man he was sitting with was the man who resembled Jünger—the man she had last seen falling out of the freezer at Well Cottage near Eyam.

"No. Not him. But *him*."

Her finger stabbed down on Trent.

"Yes. I am sorry, Frau Adamson. I had overlooked that photograph. Forgive me."

Herr Jünger did not give the impression of a man who overlooked things.

Trudi said, "The man with Trent, is that you, Herr Jünger? There is a certain resemblance . . ."

Jünger looked and shook his head and said shortly, "No." Then, as if relenting, he added, "Yes, there is said to be a resemblance, though not by members of the family. That is my brother, Gerhardt. He is . . . was . . . a policeman. A practical policeman, I mean. I was the one for the files, the paper, the organization; Gerdt was always more interested in events, people, flesh and blood."

"You say he *was* a policeman?"

"He disappeared some months ago, Frau Adamson. At the same time as your husband's death. He was our liaison with your husband, you see. He had established a cover as a salesman, moving around a great deal. We expected him to surface after your husband's death, to give his analysis of the situation. He didn't. After so long a time, we can only fear the worst."

His tone was studiously neutral.

"I'm sorry," said Trudi helplessly.

"Yes. Thank you. Shall we carry on?"

The rest of the book was unproductive—though probably in her present confused state of mind, Trudi could have looked at a picture of herself without recognition.

As she reached the last page, a phone rang. Jünger went to the desk and answered it. He listened for a while, then said, "Yes. I'll see to it."

Returning to the fireplace, he said, "Frau Adamson, a change of plan. You have been most helpful but we will not require you this afternoon after all. You may have lunch here, as I promised, but, alas, I will not be able to join you. Or, if you prefer, you may of course leave."

Trudi glanced at her watch. It was twelve-fifteen.

She said, "In that case, thank you, but I'll make my own arrangements. And tomorrow?"

"The car will come for you at the same time. Once more, my apologies. In Fräulein Weigel's defense, I should say that her own sister is a registered drug addict, so she has cause to feel strongly about those suspected of links with the trade. This does not, of course, excuse the administrative incompetence shown in your case."

There was a tap at the door. Jünger opened it to reveal Weigel.

He said, "Frau Adamson is leaving now. Please show her out."

They shook hands and Trudi went into the corridor.

"This way please," said the girl briskly.

How severe would her reprimand be? wondered Trudi. Jünger's words had struck a small spark of sympathy in his bright and comfortable room, but here in the dim corridor which brought back sharp memories of her earlier humiliation, it was soon quenched. The best she could resolve was to accept any proffered apology with cool courtesy.

The girl stopped by a door and pressed a button almost invisible in the wall. The door, which looked just like all the others, slid aside to reveal a lift. At least they were going to be spared all those stairs. Trudi entered. Weigel followed. The lift began to descend.

There was no indicator and the cubicle was ill-lit and rather stuffy. The descent seemed to take forever. Weigel stood staring straight ahead. Far from looking apologetic for her earlier error, she gave off waves of cold hostility. Trudi's initial anger had cooled during her talk with Jünger, but now its embers began to glow once more.

"Look," she said reasonably. "You made a mistake before. Everybody does. It doesn't hurt to admit it."

Suddenly the girl swung round to face her.

"A mistake, Frau Adamson?" she said, her voice vibrant with dislike and contempt. "I don't believe so; the only mistake I see is letting you go out of here!"

The lift halted with a suddenness that threw the two women against each other. Trudi felt the other's taut young body pressing her back against the wall.

Then Weigel drew back and turned away. The door opened onto a well-lit vestibule with a marble floor. Weigel stepped out, halted, turned and said in her previous neutral voice, "This way, please," and walked away. The heels of her flat shoes clacked on the marble floor in stark contrast with the utter silence of her movement along the gray corridors.

Too shaken to be angry yet, Trudi followed. A uniformed commissionaire opened a tall double door and she found herself looking out, not into the mean little courtyard through which she'd entered the building, but into a quiet elegant street of tall houses with the noise of Kärntner Strasse off to her right.

She did not pause but stepped out onto the pavement with eager haste.

"Goodbye, Frau Adamson," said Weigel behind her. "Till tomorrow."

And the door closed.

CHAPTER
5

Back at the hotel she looked for James Dacre, but he was nowhere to be found and his key was on the rack. Not expecting her "release" till midafternoon, he must have gone off sight-seeing.

Trudi was disproportionately disappointed. Her mind was full of the morning's revelations, not to mention Weigel's extraordinary behavior, and she had been looking forward eagerly to pouring them out. She looked into the hotel dining room. Its air of quiet efficiency and the discreet spacing of the tables, which would normally have attracted her, seemed alienating and merely contrived to accentuate her aloneness.

The headwaiter approached, smiling. She shook her head and withdrew. She wanted either the complete loneliness of her room or the bustle of a crowded *Beisel*. Rather to her surprise, she opted for the latter. After leaving Dacre a note, she set out once more.

It was barely one o'clock but the day was already darkening as cloud built up from the north, smudging out the morning's wintry blue. Soon there would be more snow to refresh the dingy relics of the last big fall.

Shivering, she stood on the pavement waiting for a break in the traffic. She paid no special attention to the long white Mercedes that slid past until it stopped, a few meters beyond her. The rear door opened and a voice called, "Mrs. Adamson!"

As she turned towards the car, Dr. Werner stepped out. She now recognized the limousine as the one which had brought her down from the clinic at Kahlenbergerdorf the previous month.

"It *is* you," said Werner, coming towards her. "I thought I recognized you. How are you, my dear lady?"

"I'm fine," she said. "And you?"

He smiled faintly, as if to suggest the question was superfluous to a man whose clothes cost more than many men earn in a month.

"Well enough," he said. "But I'm eager to hear what has developed in the sad business we talked of last time you were here. How long are you staying? Were you perhaps planning to call on me again? I hope so, if only socially. Be assured, I would be most hurt if I discovered you were visiting our city without paying me a call!"

He had charm enough to get away with such insincerities, and just in case he didn't, his dark intelligent eyes invited her to be amused at his Viennese floweriness.

Before she could reply, the northern clouds drifted a couple of feathery flakes onto her chilled lips.

"But we can't talk here," he said. "Come into the car. Where are you going? Can I give you a lift?"

Taking her elbow, he hurried her along to the Mercedes. Dieter, lean and muscular in his SS uniform, said, "Good day, Frau Adamson." He spoke courteously, but she still sensed mockery in his tone.

Trudi paused, half into the car, and said, "I was just going for lunch. Somewhere simple like Drei Hacken, I thought, but I can easily walk."

Werner's eyebrows, which were almost as elegantly groomed as his luxuriant hair, arched themselves in reaction to her choice either of eating place or of locomotion.

He said, "If you are uncertain, then you must be eating alone. Please, won't you keep me company? I was just on my way to the clinic. We have really first-class cuisine there. You'll join me? I insist!"

"I've got an appointment later," she said feebly, getting into the car.

"No problem. Dieter will drive you back whenever you wish."

He rapped on the partition which cut them off from the driver. The limousine pulled quietly away, its long wipers already moving to clear a sight-path through the snow-curded air.

Trudi leaned back in the soft warm comfort of her seat and closed her eyes.

"You are tired, Frau Adamson?" asked Werner solicitously.

"No," she said. "Just enjoying the treat. I'm a public-transport person now, Dr. Werner."

He smiled again and shook his head slightly as if in disbelief.

He was right. She was lying. What she'd really been trying to work out was a route from Werner's city surgery to Kahlenbergerdorf which would take him sensibly past her hotel.

It was impossible. But she didn't know what necessary diversion he might have had to make, did she?

Nor was she certain, she who had spent so much of her life in an incurious torpor, at what point careful suspicion became chronic neurosis.

She left the matter in abeyance. One thing did seem certain, however. Whether the meeting was accidental or planned, Werner's enthusiasm for her company derived neither from natural courtesy nor from lust for her lily-white flesh.

* * *

By the time they reached Kahlenbergerdorf, the snow was so heavy that it could as easily have been obscuring skyscrapers as cottages. Once they were beyond the village and onto the forest road, there seemed to be no way of distinguishing the path ahead. Dieter, however, seemed untroubled by either visibility or road conditions, and Trudi, far from being afraid, let herself be lulled by the sense of cozy cocooning given by the warmth within and the swirling whiteness without. Werner was content to share her mood and, apart from a few sociable trivialities, said nothing during the journey.

Finally the car stopped.

"We are here," said Werner.

"Are you sure?" said Trudi doubtfully, peering out of the window.

Werner laughed, the chauffeur blew the horn, a door opened, leaning a rectangle of yellow light against the whiteness, and two orderlies emerged, one sweeping the snow aside with a broad broom, the other carrying a huge umbrella.

"Is this for you, or do they imagine I'm a rich patient?" inquired Trudi.

Werner frowned. Perhaps it was bad taste to joke about rich patients in front of the staff. Trudi giggled to herself, wished she had Janet here to share the giggle, then remembered.

Inside, the elegant Elvira Altenberg greeted her with pleasure, though without surprise.

"Frau Adamson, how nice to see you again. Herr Doktor, here is your list of calls. I think the top two need immediate attention, the others may wait till after lunch."

"Thanks," said Werner. "Will you excuse me for five minutes? Elvira will look after you."

He ran lightly up the staircase.

The young woman said, "Will you come this way, Frau Adamson?"

She led her through a large oak door.

The room they entered was a medium-sized lounge, very comfortably furnished, with a small bar in a corner. Two men and a woman were seated in armchairs drinking glasses of wine. They looked up and smiled at Elvira.

"What would you like to drink?" asked the younger woman.

"An orange juice," said Trudi firmly.

Nodding as if in approval, Elvira went to the bar. The trio of wine drinkers rose and exited through a door whose momentary opening let in the sight of a small dining room and the sound of half a dozen diners. Trudi sat down in an armchair in the box bay. In better weather it probably afforded a spectacular view but all that was visible today was a swirl of snow.

"It looks bad out there," said Elvira, sitting beside her. She too was drinking orange juice.

"Yes," said Trudi. "I was just thinking that perhaps I shouldn't stay too long. I don't want to get stuck."

Elvira laughed and said, "No one wants to get stuck, least of all Dr. Werner. We have a snowplow and a tractor and most of our vehicles are four-wheel-drive. Once down to the village, you'll find that the authorities are very good at keeping the public road open into the city. Ah, here is the doctor already. Dr. Werner, shall I get you a drink?"

"A Perrier water only, thank you. There, that didn't take long, did it, Frau Adamson? What do you think of our staff facilities?"

He sat down in the chair vacated by his secretary.

Trudi said, "They seem excellent."

"That's the aim," said Werner. "We set out to attract the top echelon of patients to the clinic, I make no bones about it. They are used to nothing but the best, so it is the best that we must employ. And they in their turn require excellence in their working and relaxing conditions. Thank you, Elvira."

The young woman placed a glass before him, smiled at Trudi, and left.

"Trent would have been flattered to be numbered in the top echelon," said Trudi.

"Herr Adamson? Well, certainly so I would have regarded him, of course."

"Would have? But he *was* your patient."

"Happily only for minor ailments in my city practice," said Werner.

"You mean he was never a patient here at the clinic?"

"Good Lord, no!" said Werner in surprise. "What makes you say that?"

"I don't know; something Fräulein Altenberg said about meeting him here," said Trudi, affecting vagueness.

"Elvira? Ah! You must have misunderstood! Of course, she would meet him when he came visiting."

"Visiting?"

"Why, yes. He came regularly to visit Herr Schiller, his old employer."

"Herr Schiller is here?" exclaimed Trudi. She recalled what Jünger had said. *Schiller is old and decrepit and eking out his days in a nursing home where the rich go to die.*

"You didn't know?" He was looking at her curiously. "No, obviously not or you could not have imagined your husband came here for treatment. Herr Schiller has been with us for nearly a year now. He requires intensive nursing, more than can be provided in his home, so I persuaded him to transfer here. To be honest, I thought it would be a short-term stay, but he rallied marvelously in this environment. If he were to leave, however . . ."

"I understood this was an addiction clinic, Doctor Werner," said Trudi.

"That is our main area of work, but in some cases we do offer general nursing care and specialist treatment where we have the expertise. I have been Herr Schiller's physician for many years, so when it became clear that he had to be admitted to hospital, it was hard for me not to bring him here."

He leaned back in his chair and studied Trudi carefully, as if assessing her response to his explanation. It reminded her of the way Jünger had looked at her.

"Would it be possible for me to see Herr Schiller?" she asked.

He frowned and said, "That depends on his state of health today. Was there any special reason . . . ?"

"No. Only, I have met him a few times, and as he's ill, and I am here, it would seem a kindness . . ."

He nodded appreciatively.

"It's a generous thought. And perhaps a visit from an

attractive woman would do him good. But I doubt if it will be possible. But we'll see. Shall we go in to lunch?"

In the dining room there was one central communal table for a dozen people and in the box bay another two tables set for two and four respectively. Presumably when staff members wanted a more private conversation over a meal, they used one of these. Werner led Trudi to the center table, however, sat her down there and introduced her casually to her immediate neighbors. For a while the conversation was general; but soon the group dynamic took over and the talk veered back to shop. Werner smiled apologetically at Trudi, shook his head and said "No comment" when his opinion was canvassed during a slightly heated debate, and used the argument as a cover to ask Trudi, "What is the situation now with your compensation case? Have there been any significant developments since last we talked?"

Trudi considered all that had happened in recent weeks, shook her head and said, "Not really. You know the law."

"Ah yes. The law. It's the same everywhere. That's the main difference between our professions. For lawyers, the longer the better. For doctors, the quicker the better."

Trudi felt that this proposition might bear close scrutiny but perhaps not here and now. She concentrated on the excellent food for a while. There was no wine on the table, only mineral water, and Werner, noticing this, said, "I'm sorry. We're subjecting you to our restrictions. On duty, one drink before a meal and no alcohol with. But there is no need for you to be so deprived. You are not facing an afternoon ministering to the sick!"

He made to summon the woman who had served them, but Trudi said, "No, the water's fine, really. And don't forget, I too hope to be visiting the sick. Herr Schiller, remember?"

"Only if he is well enough, which I doubt," said Werner.

A blond young man sitting opposite, who had been introduced as Dr. Klarsfeld, intervened to say, "Herr Schiller? No need to worry there, Franz. I was with him just before lunch. He's the best today he's been in weeks."

"Thank you, Paul," said Werner, a touch chillily. "But, of course, in his condition, rapid swings of health are to be expected. By now he could have drifted off again."

The dining room door opened and Elvira came in. She went up to Werner and spoke into his ear.

"Excuse me," he said. "Some urgent business. Please, Frau Adamson, finish your lunch. I should be back to join you for coffee."

He went out with his secretary. Others at the table drifted off back into the lounge to smoke and drink coffee. Klarsfeld remained politely at the table though he had finished eating a few minutes earlier.

"Please," said Trudi, "don't let me keep you from your coffee."

"No trouble," smiled the young doctor. "I'll tell you a secret: the coffee's not very good actually. At least I don't think so, though the others say I have a perverted taste!"

"In that case," said Trudi, "I shan't have any either. I wonder, perhaps you could show me to Herr Schiller's room?"

"Of course. But you haven't had any dessert."

"I'm cutting down on sweetness," said Trudi, rising. "Do we have to go outside?"

"Oh no. The old lodge, which is where we are now, is linked by corridors to all the clinical complex. We can't have medical staff coming on duty with frostbite and pneumonia, can we?"

"I suppose it wouldn't be a good advertisement," said Trudi.

As they descended the stairs together she asked Klarsfeld how long he had been at the clinic. It turned out to be a couple of years, his first "big break," as he put it. He was unstinting in his admiration of Werner.

"A fine doctor and a fine man too. He does his best for everyone, staff and patients alike. Some men in his position would keep all the plums to himself, you know, trips to conferences, that sort of thing, but not Franz. I've been to Milan, Cairo, and Paris in the short time I've been here."

"Did you go with Dr. Werner to the London conference last year?"

There was no conscious ulterior motive in asking this question, but the moment she'd asked it, Trudi recognized her obliquity.

"London? Last year? let me see, I don't recall . . ."

"Last August," prompted Trudi.

"Last August? No, I think you're mistaken. Franz was away on holiday in August, I recall. But no conference."

"I must have got it wrong," said Trudi negligently. "Tell me about your work here. What do you specialize in?"

Klarsfeld chattered happily about his job and his hopes as they walked along the corridor linking the lodge with the first unit of the clinical complex. Here everything changed from old-world to hi-tech, but the unstinted luxury of appointment remained constant. Nothing but the best would do, from light fittings and doorknobs up to, presumably, medical equipment.

"Here we are," said Klarsfeld, ushering her through a door into what looked like a small office. It contained a desk with a telephone, an easy chair, and a wall-mounted TV monitor above a bank of visual display panels along which points of green light bounced or undulated. On the monitor an old man could be seen, lying in bed with a nurse sitting at the bedside reading a book. Her voice came over the monitor. Trudi recognized the story instantly. Her father had used to read it to her when she was a child. It was *Heidi*.

She looked at Klarsfeld in puzzlement.

He said, "No, it doesn't mean he's gone infantile, but in his condition, long-term memory does tend to be much sharper than short-term and there's an attendant urge to relive old times, old pleasures, perhaps a kind of leave-taking. How long is it since you've seen him?"

"Over a year," said Trudi. "I didn't know him well, though my husband used to work for him. He's dead now. He died last year."

"I'm sorry," said Klarsfeld. "Does Herr Schiller know this?"

Trudi shrugged.

"Possibly he'll have forgotten anyway. And it's very likely, from what you say, that he won't remember you at all. So don't be disappointed. Shall we go in?"

He pushed open a door opposite the one through which they'd entered. The nurse looked up, smiled, and kept on reading till the end of the paragraph.

Then she said, "You have visitors, Herr Schiller."

The old man turned his head towards them. Reduced on the monitor, he had looked like a rather thinner version of his old self. In the flesh, or rather in the absence of it, the changes were much more shocking. He had the emaciated skeletal look familiar to the postwar generation from concentration-camp photographs. Only the eyes peering at her from cavernous sockets gave the lie to that image. There was nothing here of that blank despair. These eyes still glinted alertly as he studied the newcomers.

"Good afternoon, Herr Schiller," said Klarsfeld. "Do you know who this is?"

The eyes moved slowly over Trudi's face.

"Perhaps you've forgotten," said Klarsfeld, laughing. "Not to worry. It's not always easy to remember, is it? This is—"

Interrupting him with a vehemence which was shocking from such an unlikely source, Schiller cried, "No! Of course I haven't forgotten, you fool. How should I forget? This is Trudi, isn't it? Trudi! My dear, dear Trudi!"

The remembering was surprise enough without the totally unexpected enthusiasm.

"That's right," said Trudi, moving forward. "It's Trudi."

And now another change came over the old man's face. The smile which had stretched his narrow lips vanished and his features contorted with an emotion not far removed from terror. He slid down in the bed, shaking his head and crying, "No, no, no! It's not Trudi! Trudi's dead, she's dead. The Jew killed her! Go away! Go away!"

His left hand shot out sideways, clawed at, then knocked over a silver photo frame which stood on a bedside table. It fell heavily to the ground but did not break on the resilient cushion floor.

Klarsfeld took Trudi's arm as she stood in helpless horror.

"Would you mind leaving for a moment? It would be best, I think."

She turned and went out of the room. She realized she was trembling.

In the monitor, she saw Klarsfeld and the nurse leaning over the old man. A sense of voyeurism came over her and she turned away and sat in the easy chair. Slowly she regained possession of herself but her nerves were still sufficiently raw for her to start as the outer door suddenly opened.

It was Werner. His gaze touched her for a moment then swung up to the monitor.

"What has happened?" he demanded.

"Nothing. Herr Schiller got a bit upset . . ."

But the door from the patient's room had opened now and Klarsfeld came out.

"What's going on, Doctor Klarsfeld?" asked Werner harshly.

"A rather excited reaction, that's all. I've given him a sedative. No damage done. It was so curious, Franz . . ."

"It was avoidable, Doctor, and that's all that concerns me. I warned that there might be a problem but you clearly rate your own judgment more highly than mine."

Klarsfeld looked taken aback by the violence of this attack. Embarrassed, Trudi stood up and said, "It was really my fault, Dr. Werner. I'm sorry. Look, it's really time that I ought to be getting back to town. I've got an appointment . . ."

"I'm sorry," said Werner. "That's what I came to tell you. The snow's so deep that our own plow has got stuck. I'm afraid you will have to stay with us till the blizzard dies and the authorities can clear the road from the village."

But Trudi didn't respond. She was staring into the monitor.

The nurse had retrieved the silver photo frame and replaced it on the table, but this time angled so that the picture it contained was visible. Visible but not comprehensible.

Trudi pushed open the door again and peered inside, needing direct eye contact. Immediately Klarsfeld took her arm, clearly eager to regain credit with Werner, and drew her back.

"Please, he must rest, Frau Adamson."

"Yes," said Trudi. "Of course."

But her eyes had seen enough to confirm what the monitor had incredibly suggested.

Schiller kept the photograph of a teen-age girl by his bed. The young face smiling out of the ornate frame had been changed by the years, but no change is so great that the mind loses the image of what once it was.

And Trudi knew beyond all doubt that the young girl whose recorded smile comforted the old man's twilight pain was herself.

CHAPTER 6

Trudi awoke. It was dark dark night. She could see nothing, but she could hear. There were footsteps somewhere, not in the room, but outside, approaching the door, too soft almost for her straining ears, but plucking like a plectrum at her straining nerves.

They stopped. The door. Where was the door? She didn't know, except that it must be where the footsteps had halted. She'd locked it but drew no comfort from a mere key.

Was that the handle being turned, or just the squeak of her mouselike terror, the crackle of her short-circuiting brain?

It stopped. Silence. Then the steps retreated, fading like a dying man's pulse, till all was still.

She lay for many minutes, how many she did not know. Slowly she reached for the light switch, could not find it, stretched further. Her fingers touched curtains.

In one convulsive movement she rolled out of bed, seized the curtains and flung them open. No light, nothing, it was as dark as ever, darker than any night could be.

Then, hands and mind arriving at the solution together, her fingers fumbled with the window catch, pulled the hinged frames inward, fumbled again, and then her outstretched palms pushed with all her strength. The shutters burst open and the light of a full moon, reflected off a sea of virgin snow, dazzled her more than the midday sun.

The snow was almost up to the windows. They had been right to close all the shutters against its wind-driven weight. But now all was still and the great arc of the frost-scoured sky glinted like polished quartz.

She breathed deep, feeling the chill on her skin beneath her borrowed nightgown like a lover's caress. She was aware now of the cord of the light within easy reaching distance of the bed, but she made no move to put it on. Just to stand here and breathe the cold air and see the bright champaign was all she desired.

Then there was movement. Away to the left where the forest was thinnest. A man on skis. He flashed across a huge clearing, crouched low, expert, effortless. Then he was among the trees, flickering behind them like an old film for a little while. And now he was gone.

Impossible to make him out at this distance except that his build was broad and solid. Like Jünger's. Or James Dacre's.

Or Trent's.

Her sudden shivering was not due to cold alone, but she closed the window, though not the shutter, and scrambled back into bed.

Her watch told her it was not much after midnight. She had gone to bed early, escaping the frustrations of finding herself an unwilling guest at the clinic. She'd rung the hotel in the afternoon; Dacre hadn't returned, so she left a message explaining her situation. At that point she'd still had hopes of getting away the same evening. But when the snow kept on coming and help from the village didn't, she resigned herself to staying the night.

She'd expected James to ring up but he hadn't, not before six o'clock anyway, and at that time it was discovered that the snow had brought some lines down and the telephones were out of order.

Werner had been as apologetic and attentive as his own frustrations would permit, though whether he was missing an important medical appointment or a night at the opera wasn't revealed. Klarsfeld she hadn't seen again and when she asked after him at dinner she was told he was on duty. The other staff members had treated her with friendly courtesy but inevitably they had drifted off into shop talk after a little while.

So to bed, early, with a paperback novel borrowed from a bookcase in the staff sitting room. It still lay open by her pillow at page one, for she had found that no imagined world could win her from the mind-aching bewilderments and terrors of her own. Finally sleep, light as mourning crepe, had settled on her soul to be snatched easily aside by the first real or fancied noise.

She realized now that it was not going to be so easily regained. Her whole being, mind and body alike, felt electric with a craving for action. She considered the possibilities with a coolness that amazed the dormouse which still cowered in its tiny nest at her heart's deep core. Only one offered any real hope of an advancement of knowledge, and that so small as to be microscopic.

But small hopes are nourishment to a mind starved of understanding.

She rose again and quickly got dressed.

It proved remarkably easy to get to Schiller's room. Trudi had not been in a hospital since she'd had her appendix out at the age of fifteen, but none of the still dimly remembered National Health Service clatters and clangs and nightly alarms disturbed the midnight peace of the Kahlenberg Klinic.

Her main fear was that there would be a nurse in the outer room, but this proved groundless. In fact, the TV monitor wasn't even switched on, and for a second Trudi feared this might mean that Schiller had been moved. But instantly she was reassured by the green points of light tracing out the message that the old man still breathed and functioned in the next room.

Quietly she entered. A dim night light fell kindly on the ancient face. She went to the bedside and picked up the silver photo frame.

Her face looked back at her in double, reflected in the glass as she was now and peering through it as she had been then. No reason for anyone else to recognize it. Not even her recent incidental dieting could peel off all those years. But it was her, certainly . . .

Except that, had she ever had her hair like that? She

couldn't recall it. She studied the photo more closely. It was a close-up, blown up, she surmised, from a full-length negative, for there was a faint fuzziness which gave the print a rather attractive romantic glow. Background detail was therefore nonexistent.

Exasperated, she turned the frame over and twisted the wing screw which held the mounting in place. Now the print slid out to made close examination easier.

There was some writing on the back and a faded photographer's stamp.

It read *Brüder Schmidt, Wipplingerstrasse, Wien.*

And the writing in a cramped Gothic script said *Fräulein Gertrud Schiller. 17.*

Slowly, necessarily, Trudi sank into the chair which the nurse had occupied.

She turned the print over again to look at the face once more, the face which was hers and yet not hers. *Gertrud Schiller.* Her face. Her name. *His* name. This old man who lay dying close by.

Trudi.

So shallow was the breath which bore the word that she was ready to think it was merely the syllabling of her feverish mind.

"Trudi."

Only a slight increase of volume, but this time it was undoubtedly the old man who spoke.

"I'm here," she said.

A hand moved on the counterpane. She reached out and took it. It was like a tiny bunch of dry twigs.

She said, "Who are you?"

Silence, then the reedy voice echoed, "Who are you?"

"Trudi! I'm Trudi Adamson, Herr Schiller."

The hand moved, or rather trembled a fraction. But it was a withdrawal. She released it gladly. The contact had not been pleasant.

"Ah yes. The Jew's daughter," said Schiller, his voice stronger. "And yet, Trudi also. Strange."

"You mean, my mother?" said Trudi taking verbally with slow reluctance the steps her mind had already overleapt.

"Yes."

"You are my grandfather?"

A long pause here.

"Yes."

Trudi could not look at him. Her eyes were focused on the photograph before her. The young girl smiled up at her, happy, secure, uncaring. Seventeen. Sometime in the thirties. Europe lurching towards war. Hitler peering greedily over the Austrian frontier towards Vienna where some faces smiled welcomingly back at him and others regarded him with the blankness of terror. Her father had spoken to her of these times, though never openly and fully. Always it had been in hints and hesitations which perhaps he imagined were sparing his young daughter the horror of full knowledge, but which in fact had only served to stimulate her fearful imagination.

"You were a Nazi, Herr Schiller," she said.

"Oh no," he denied with an unconcern more convincing than vehemence. "Never that. Nazi is political. I was never political."

"A Jew-hater, then."

"That's so," he agreed with an equal insouciance. "Some of my best rivals were Jews. Before 1938, I had to deal with them on equal terms. I didn't like it, but I did it. Business is business, as they say. After 1938, things changed. I cracked the whip then."

There was a nostalgic satisfaction in his voice which chilled the blood.

"Good days," he sighed. "Good days. Perhaps the best. I was legitimate, you understand. A businessman only. It was the war that changed things. Not me. It was crime that changed. When those in charge are willing to pay through the nose for what the law forbids, then crime becomes legitimate! Surely you must understand that, my little Jewess? Hasn't that been the guiding principle of your race ever since they bribed their way out of Egypt?"

Trudi wanted to leave. Her whole being cried to her to be gone while there was still room to doubt the relationship that was being implied between her and this mummified evil.

But one thing she did know for certain was that there was no longer any warm nest for her to hibernate safely in, and knowing that, she had to know everything.

"My mother . . ." she said.

But the old man wasn't yet ready for that strand in his life's coil. He wanted to dwell a little longer on what he saw as his triumphs.

"After the war, the Americans came. After the pure-blooded Aryans, these mongrels! Latins, Negroes, Anglo-Saxons, Orientals. Jews even. I dealt with them all, and you know what, *liebchen?* They were all the same! The British too. Even the holy, preaching British. My enemies had said, when the Allies come, *then* we'll have you, *then* we'll see you tried and punished. Fools! All the Allies wanted was to rescue 'poor little Austria' from the horrid Hun. A couple of token trials perhaps, but for the rest, an untainted past, a bright future in which all things were possible—wealth, power, respect, even the presidency itself!"

He laughed like the wind in dead leaves.

"So I made sure *I* wasn't a token. I had money. I needed a man. I found him. I'm good at finding men, you should know that, my little Jewess! It was just a precaution, you understand. I'd probably have survived anyway. These new conquerors needed men like me to keep them well fed and comfortable, to pleasure them and make them rich! Normally a job for the Jews, my dear. Only, just then, there weren't many Jews to do it!"

The door burst open and a nurse came in.

"What are you doing here?" she demanded. "Herr Schiller must rest!"

Trudi, whose senses seemed to be drug-sharp tonight, felt fear through the indignation. She guessed that this nurse should have been on station in the anteroom but had gone off on her own business.

"Get out!" she snarled. "I have permission."

The nurse hesitated, then left. But she would probably check up.

Trudi said urgently, "Tell me about my mother!"

"Your mother?" said the old man vaguely.

"My mother. Your daughter. Trudi!"

She thrust the photograph before his dulling eyes. Slowly the gleam of understanding, or something close to it, returned.

"Trudi! The Jew had her. His oily skin, his greasy lips, his skinned *thing* . . . Oh, they have charms and drugs, they have ceremonies . . . When I found out I thought . . . but too late . . . already he had infected her with child!"

He struggled into an upright position.

"But what's a child? A Jewish child? A life like a candle flame. Snuff! and it's out! And I knew experts . . . I told her I forgave her. I told her to send him to meet me. And I told my friends too, friends who would receive him like a gift of meat to tigers! But she didn't trust me! That too he had done. He had entered her mind and taught her not to trust me! He came early and when he saw I had brought my friends, he fled, and she fled with him. Switzerland first, but I could reach them in Switzerland, they were cunning enough to know that. So on they went to England. And there she littered, and there she died, but none of this did I know till later when the new peace gave us leisure to take up old wars. Then I sent out searchers, then I took up the trail . . ."

The door swung open again.

Klarsfeld's voice cried, "Frau Adamson, what's going on? Please, you shouldn't be here. You must leave immediately."

Ignoring him, Trudi cried, "And then? What did you do then?"

But the interruption had done more than interrupt the flow of the old man's speech. It had broken some vital thread, for once more all animation left his skinny frame and he slid back down beneath the bedclothes like a line of seaweed washed off a harbor wall.

Trudi rose to her feet, not in obedience to the doctor's repeated command, but because she recognized there was nothing more to be learned here for the time being. Perhaps forever.

Pushing past the nurse, who regarded her with the complacency of one whose own dereliction of duty has been subsumed by another's greater guilt, she set off back to her room. Halfway down the walk to the old lodge, she encountered Werner. He halted and looked set to address her reprimandingly but without breaking her stride she said, "I've been talking to Schiller," and left him staring after her with an expression of alarm on his face.

Back in her room, she locked the door and sat at the window, staring out at the pleated snow.

It was strange. A week ago, she would not have claimed to be happy. But looking back now at that time before she knew about Astrid Fischer's death, and Trent's betrayal of her with Jan, and her own descent from Herr Schiller, it seemed a golden age.

After a while there was a knock at the door.

Werner's voice called, "Frau Adamson, may I come in please?"

"No," she said flatly.

There was a moment's silence, then footsteps moved slowly away.

Trudi was still sitting by the window at first light when the distant roar of an engine, then a long plume of regurgitated snow, told her the road from the village was being reopened.

When she left her room it was still early, but she had screwed up her will to the point where she was going to leave the clinic even if it meant walking back to Vienna.

It proved unnecessary. What she'd started to think of as a prison, or at best a trap, became simply a place of work as she made her way downstairs. In the staff room, there was hot coffee, and white-coated acquaintances from the previous night's meal greeted her with friendly remarks about the weather.

Elivra came forward and said, "Would you like some breakfast before you leave, Frau Adamson?"

A smell of fresh-baked rolls from the dining room nearly tempted her, but she said, "No."

"In that case, the car is waiting. Dr. Werner sends his apologies, but he is working. He hopes he may see you again before you leave Vienna."

"Thank him for his hospitality," said Trudi thinly. "Tell him I certainly hope I shall have the chance to pay another visit. I should like in particular to resume my conversation with Herr Schiller."

Her Parthian shot misfired pathetically. The young woman's face lengthened with the solemnity of condolence.

"I'm sorry," she said, "but of course, you cannot know. I regret to say that Herr Schiller passed away last night. Quietly. In his sleep. A sad loss; a blessed relief. *Aufwiedersehen*, Frau Adamson. *Aufwiedersehen*."

CHAPTER
7

Back at the Hotel Regina, Trudi was luxuriating in a hot bath when the telephone rang. Her first thought was that it would be James Dacre checking to see if she had returned. But when she answered it, the voice was the receptionist's telling her that Herr Jünger's car had come to collect her.

"Tell him to wait," she said. "And would you have some coffee and rolls sent up to my room?"

The receptionist started to say she would transfer the call to room service but Trudi replaced the phone. Ten minutes later as she was dressing there was a tap at the door. She opened it and saw the tray of coffee and rolls before she saw that it was Dacre carrying it.

"Welcome back," he said. "I intercepted a waiter."

"I thought you'd got a new job," said Trudi. "Come in."

She poured herself some coffee and buttered a roll. Dacre reclined on the bed, watching her. His silence, she guessed, was aimed at making her give an account of all her adventures since last they met. In fact, she'd been looking forward to an audience as a mirror in which to reexamine her experiences, but now the opportunity was here, she felt strangely reluctant. There are intimacies far beyond sex, and she was even less used to admitting strangers to her mind than she was to her body.

A longing for Jan came over her, and though, as on every other occasion she'd found herself missing her friend, it was immediately drowned by bitter anger, the echo of the longing still reverberated deep down.

"Well?" said Dacre.

It felt like a triumph that her silence had provoked him to break his. Immediately she was ashamed. This was no way to treat a man who was her lover and who had been as assiduous in her protection as he had.

The telephone rang.

It was Jünger.

"My driver has just contacted me to say he is still waiting to collect you," he said. "The thing is, I have to leave town at noon. Something's come up unexpectedly and I shall be away for a few days. I don't think there is a great deal left for us to do together, but if there is a hold-up on your side, perhaps it would be best if I let one of my assistants deal with you. In fact, he could come to your hotel and save you the bother of coming here if you are not feeling well. . . ."

"I'm feeling fine, Herr Jünger," interrupted Trudi. "I shall be with you in five minutes. Good morning."

She replaced the receiver firmly. Had she been manipulated? she was already thinking. Yesterday, the thought of not having to go to that sinister building again would have seemed delightful, and she wouldn't have been much bothered at the prospect of missing Jünger himself.

Now, however, she was determined to see the man, come what may.

James Dacre said, "Trudi, what's going on?"

"I'm sorry?"

"All I know about what's been happening to you since you went into that blockhouse yesterday morning is a couple of messages, one saying you'd got out early and would see me later, the other saying you were snowed in out in the woods somewhere and would see me when you could!"

"That's about the strength of it, James," she said finishing her coffee and putting her coat on. "Look, I've got to dash now. Jünger's leaving at noon, so that should be me finished. We can have lunch and the afternoon together and then head for home as soon as we like. I'll see you here at, say, one o'clock. Be here, James, and then I shan't have to leave a message, shall I?"

It all sounded more cumbersome than she intended. She was still learning the art of the light touch. She went over to him and kissed him and that didn't quite work either. But she had no time to sort out these deficiencies at the moment, and she'd already stopped thinking about them by the time she got into the car.

Prepared to do battle with Fräulein Weigel, she was almost disappointed to be dropped not in the gloomy courtyard but at the entrance she'd left by in the elegant street off Kärntner Strasse. The uniformed commissionaire ushered her through the tall doors, put her in the lift, pressed a button, and when the lift halted and the door slid back, Jünger himself was standing there.

In his comfortable office, he offered her coffee.

Trudi refused and said, "Herr Jünger, I spent last night snowbound in the Kahlenberg Klinik, or perhaps you know that already?"

He made a gesture which could have meant anything and she did not press the point.

"While I was there, I had the chance to talk with Herr Schiller," she said. "Herr Manfred Schiller, head of Schiller-Reise, remember?"

"Of course. I told you he was in a nursing home, I seem to recollect."

"But you didn't mention the Kahlenberg Klinik."

"There was no reason."

"Not even when you cross-examined me about my last visit to Vienna and I told you that I'd been there to talk with Dr. Werner?"

"I noted the coincidence, did not think it worth mentioning," murmured Jünger.

"No? And perhaps you didn't think it was worth mentioning either that Schiller was my grandfather!" she shouted.

To his credit—or perhaps not—he didn't affect surprise but merely sighed deeply and said, "Well, either you knew it or you didn't."

She took this in and said in bewilderment, "But if I had known, then of course . . ."

". . . of course, you would have mentioned it," he completed the sentence, smiling. "Perhaps. But can I be sure you always mention everything you know to me, Frau Adamson? Is there nothing you have held back? About

Schiller-Reise for instance? Or about what has happened since your husband's death?"

Avoiding this unattractive diversion, Trudi said, "But I didn't know about my ancestry, Herr Jünger. And now I only know part of it and I can't find out more, not from Schiller. He's dead, you see."

"So I understand," said Jünger, unsurprised once more.

"You know already?" She digested this. "Is this anything to do with your change of plan?"

"In a way." He sighed again. "You see, Frau Adamson, Schiller-Reise, or at least that level of it with which I'm concerned, is like a kingdom. When the king is dying, the battle for the succession begins. Sometimes it seems to have been settled beyond all doubt. But there is always room for debate and sometimes the obvious heir might not be approved by the colonial governor if the country is a tributary state. No, it's not until the king is dead and his successor crowned that you can be really sure."

"Schiller's dead now," said Trudi. "Who's the likely heir?"

"Oddly enough, in strict legal terms, I suppose you are!" said Jünger. "He has no other family."

"He had *no* family!" she exploded. Then, calming down, she said, "Tell me what you know about him."

"What do you know already?"

"Only what he told me last night," she said, and outlined what had been said.

Jünger nodded and said gently, "Then you know just about everything. He was a rabid anti-Semite. The *Anschluss* was for him a heaven-sent opportunity to pay off old scores and make a lot of money while he was at it. When he discovered his daughter was seeing your father, he must have been enraged. He probably ordered her to break off the liaison and then learned that she was pregnant and proposed marrying her lover. The best that can be said for Schiller was that he was probably genuinely afraid of what this might mean for his daughter's safety. But, even without the Nazis, I don't doubt he would have used every device, legal and illegal, to stop his daughter marrying a Jew. Now, he had the simple solution of turning Schumacher over to the Gestapo. But the plan went wrong, your father got away and your mother went with him. Schiller probably chased them as far as Switzerland, but they put themselves temporarily out of reach by moving to England, and now the war was close to breaking out. After the war, he had other things to occupy him for a while. He came close to being put on trial, but some documents mysteriously disappeared and he was downgraded from Category-Three, militarists, activists and profiteers, to the fifth and lowest category of Nazi, nonoffenders. I suspect the first bit of hard information he got out of England was that his daughter was dead. That would be a matter of record. When he became aware of your existence I don't know, but you must have presented him with what in his own terms was a moral problem. His own flesh and blood, yet . . ."

"I know," said Trudi dully. "The Jew's daughter. The cause of his own daughter's death."

"Just so. Well, there you have it. I'm sorry you had to find all this out in this way, always assuming . . ."

"Yes?"

". . . that you *have* just found it out."

Trudi said, "What other assumption is there?"

"Ask yourself, Frau Adamson."

She asked herself, nodded and said, "Of course. It seems too much of a coincidence, doesn't it? Schiller's granddaughter not knowing she is Schiller's granddaughter, but so clearly connected via her husband with the firm."

He nodded. His unblinking gaze never left her.

Trudi's mind was racing now, devouring in huge strides what might have taken an age of painful plodding not long before.

She said, "*Trent*."

"Yes?"

"I know I'm telling the truth even if you don't. If I discount coincidence, which I must, that leaves just one link. Trent. In the sixties it was, when he gave up flying. We left Zürich and went to Brussels where he started to work for Schiller-Reise proper."

"Proper?"

"I mean, he'd worked for them before, or rather the Swiss charter company had. I can remember meeting Herr Schiller

early on in Zürich. I remember how he looked at me . . .
Could it be he realized then who I was? I was still young. I
still looked like my mother's photo. Could that be why he
gave Trent the job?"

"To keep tabs on you? Perhaps," said Jünger.

He looked as if he might be about to say something else,
then shook his head as a climber might do who has
experienced an unaccustomed giddiness on a steep traverse.

Trudi thought she could guess the reason why.

"I think you know a lot more than you tell me, Herr
Jünger," she accused.

"Why do you say that?" he inquired mildly.

"Because whenever we talk, I feel that it's like . . .
well, like a fencing match. We exchange blows, not
information."

He nodded as if he liked the idea—or its expression.

"If it is a fencing match, Frau Adamson," he said, "that
implies both sides have a weapon."

She laughed and said uneasily, "I'm just a defenseless
woman, anyone can see that."

"Perhaps. Or perhaps you too know a lot more than you
tell."

For the first time it came fully home to Trudi that Jünger
really considered her a possible danger, or a threat, or an
opponent of some kind. A life of self-effacement had left her
with so little self to efface that to be taken so seriously was
like stepping out of a shower onto a floodlit stage.

She opened her mouth to protest, closed it again as she
recalled all the things she did know, but had not passed on to
Jünger.

Especially about his brother, deep frozen in that plague-
village cottage.

He smiled at her humorlessly, as though interpreting her
silence as the admission of guilt it was. But her recognition of
how seriously he took her had forced another revelation into
her mind. She voiced it instinctively as it formulated itself.

"Nothing that happens here happens accidentally, does it,
Herr Jünger?" she burst out. "That business when I came
yesterday, those awful women, that *assault!* That was no
administrative error, was it? That was done according to your
express order!"

He stood up and buttoned up the few buttons of his old-fashioned Austrian jacket. So constrained, he should have looked rather absurd, like a man in a corset, but he managed instead to look more like a weary knight strapping on his breastplate for yet another foray.

He held out his hand and said, "I must go now, Frau Adamson. *Leb'wohl*."

"Not *wiedersehen?*" said Trudi.

"I don't care to tempt fate. Not too often."

They shook hands.

The meeting had only taken half an hour. Obscurely Trudi felt that the initiative she had thought to grasp by insisting on seeing Jünger himself had been wrested from her.

"What about Astrid?" she asked. "Why was she murdered?"

"That is a good question to ask yourself, Frau Adamson," he replied.

The door opened and Fräulein Weigel appeared. Jünger turned away. This was her dismissal and, though Trudi resented it, she did not know yet how to resist it.

As she followed the young woman to the lift, she felt her inward agitation growing, an as yet unchanneled urge to action. Something must happen, was going to happen, and she wanted to be for once an initiator, not a passive object. Perhaps this was how Samson felt on his way to the Philistine games.

And look what happened to him! she thought ruefully, and chuckled aloud. Chuckling was not a common activity of hers and possibly the sound came out odd, or perhaps it wasn't a sound the poker-faced Fräulein Weigel was used to hearing in this building, but she shot Trudi a sternly reproving look as she summoned the lift.

As they descended, Trudi said conversationally, "So, it turns out you were only following orders after all, Fräulein?"

Weigel stared ahead indifferently, which irritated Trudi into adding, "Like Eichmann and the rest."

This got through.

Weigel glanced at her contemptuously and as the lift stopped, said, "You may be right, *gnädige Frau*. It is after all perhaps still a version of the Jewish problem."

As the doors opened, Trudi hit her. She did not plan it. And it happened so quickly that she was already feeling the amazement that followed the blow before she truly experienced the anger that launched it. Nor was it a slap but a full-blooded punch, the first she could recollect ever having thrown. It caught the woman on the side of the mouth. And Trudi's last image before she marched across the marble floor and out of the double door, which the commissionaire had difficulty in getting open in time, was of Weigel's lips parted in pain and shock, with a smear of blood across the porcelain perfection of her left upper incisors.

PART SEVEN

But, Mousie, thou art no thy lane,
In proving foresight may be vain: . . .

BURNS: "To a Mouse"

CHAPTER
1

She told James Dacre everything. Any cautious reticence she may have intended was swept away in a flash flood of horrified amazement as she reran that moment in the lift. Of all the self-revelations she had experienced since Trent's death, this one affected her the most.

Like Doubting Thomas, James inspected her hands as if needing the ocular proof of her story. There was a brown smudge on her right knuckles. She dabbed at it with a moistened handkerchief and discovered a cut in the skin and was relieved to think it was her own blood, not Weigel's.

"So," said James Dacre, regarding her quizzically. "Always something new about you, Trudi. This is not at all what Mrs. Fielding led me to expect."

"You'd better ask for a rebate," she retorted.

Then she burst into tears. When Dacre reached forward to comfort her, she pushed him away, as angry at her own emotionalism as she had been shocked by her violence. He accepted the rebuff with the tranquillity which characterized his actions, and which proved probably more calming than an embrace.

"James," she said, wiping her eyes with the bloodstained handkerchief, "would you mind, before anything else, let's find out the earliest flight home."

"Home," he said as if the word intrigued him. "All right."

He went to the telephone. Trudi noticed for the first time that he spoke German fluently, though with an unmistakably English accent.

"Nothing direct to Manchester," he said. "But there's a flight to Heathrow tonight at five with seats available. Shall I book?"

She nodded. He made the booking, then, turning to her with a smile, said, "Now what about some lunch?"

By an unspoken agreement, they dropped all reference to the problems and puzzles of Schiller-Reise and spent their few remaining hours in Vienna like tourists. James Dacre proved to have a genuine gift for enjoyment and when his curiosity outstripped Trudi's expertise—as it did frequently— it was an occasion of mirth and a springboard for a game in which Trudi mixed her own fantasy with historic and architectural fact and Dacre tried to catch her out.

They arrived late for check-in, a sin underlined by the desk girl's pointed look at her watch before feeding them into her computer. Giggling, they went through into the departure lounge and waited for their flight to be called.

"You know something, James," said Trudi. "Of all the time I've spent in Vienna, the happiest part has been these last couple of hours."

"That includes the night before last?" queried Dacre mockingly.

"Beds don't count. Beds can be *anywhere*," retorted Trudi.

He was observing her quizzically, but she sensed an underlying genuine puzzlement.

"What's the matter?" she said.

"Nothing. Like I said earlier, you've changed a lot. Or . . ."

"Or?" she prompted.

"Or perhaps you haven't. Listen, that's our plane, isn't it?"

* * *

On the journey home the euphoria slowly evaporated. Dacre seemed to be tired, and dozed—or pretended to doze. Trudi studied his face, calm and assured even in repose, and felt a barrier between them. Her father had once tried to explain about this barrier. He had been a little drunk at the time. "It shuts us off from each other, each man from each other," he had said. "Sometimes it is as broad and unbridgeable as the Atlantic and you can sit and look at another man's face—eyes, nose, teeth and smiling mouth—the same as yours, the same as all men's—and yet between you is a gap to sink a regiment, or a race in. Sometimes it is almost not there. Like between me and your mother, Trudi. Like between you and me. But it still exists, in every case it still exists. That you learn. That you cannot forget."

The plane landed at Heathrow. The airport building had blossomed glass and concrete during the past twenty-five years, yet enough remained to bring back memories. Interestingly they brought no pain, though the images of Trent and Jan flickered prominently among them. It was curious—*them* she recognized almost unchanged; the big barrier seemed to be between herself and the little office mouse who avoided where possible crossing the middle of a room but always stuck to the wall.

"You look tired," said James Dacre.

"Do I?"

"Yes," he said firmly.

Outside the terminal, he hailed a taxi.

"Saint Pancras," he said.

"James," she inquired during the long ride, "who's paying for this?"

He laughed and said, "We'll find a way of putting it on Herr Jünger's tab, shall we?"

They spoke little on the train. Now she really was tired. At Sheffield, as they waited for another taxi, she said, "James, your car must still be at Manchester. I'm sorry. This has all been a terrible inconvenience for you."

He said, "Is that how I'm to regard it? A terrible inconvenience?"

"I didn't mean . . ."

"No. I know you didn't." He smiled and went on. "But it

is a nuisance not having the car. I noticed on the departure board that there's a train to Manchester in ten minutes. I could be across there and back with the car in a couple of hours. Would you mind doing the last stage home by yourself?"

"I'm not entirely helpless," she retorted.

"I didn't think you were. But that's not why I worry about you."

"Why then?"

A taxi drew up. He opened the door but she didn't move.

He said, "Trudi, what's between us, well, it's gone further than I . . . thought possible. I'd like to think it could last, become permanent. Think about it."

She said with an effort at lightness, "Is this a proposal? If so, of what?"

He didn't answer but kissed her fiercely. She broke loose, got into the taxi and wound down the window. He looked at her more grimly than a man who had just made such a declaration should.

"I'll be in touch," he said and banged the cab roof.

She looked back as the taxi nosed its way into the main road, but already he had vanished.

"What am I going to say?" she asked herself. And found she had no answer.

The streets glistened with a fine cold rain and the traffic moved along in a hissing haze. There were few pedestrians and by the time they turned into the gloomy corridor of Linden Lane, there were no other vehicles in sight except for a few parked cars. The cracks of light through curtained windows were as exclusive here as she had felt them that night in the plague village of Eyam.

Hope House was in total darkness. Would she have felt more reassured to see it ablaze with light? Dark or light, it didn't feel like home. Though with James by her side . . . she felt herself slipping towards a decision.

The taxi driver dropped her case on the pavement without leaving his cab.

"Night, luv," he said.

She thought of asking him to accompany her to the front

door but even as she balanced new fortitude against old fears, the cab moved away.

Slowly she began to walk up the drive. The moment she passed through the gate, she'd had a sense of being watched. But who wouldn't? It would take a stronger nerve than hers not to be affected by walking up a dark driveway to an empty house on such a wet and windy night! So, confounding her particular fears in a general susceptibility, she pressed on towards the front door. One thing being frightened of the darkness of the garden did was to turn the house from a cold unwelcoming hulk to a haven of light and warmth.

Something moved. Away to her left. It was surely nothing. The wind in the shrubbery. Rain spattering on the waxy pallor of evergreen leaves. Nothing.

It was almost completely dark. Ahead the hulk of the house, no detail visible except the outline of the dreadful garden gnomes which guarded the front porch and whose pale gray stone seemed to possess its own ghostly fluorescence.

Definitely a movement now! Mind multiplying natural explanations—wind, rain, a cat, a dog—and feet racing also as she ran the last few yards, knowing she was pursued, and thrust her key like a talisman at the outer porch door.

Incredibly she found the lock first time, twisted the key, turned the handle, and stumbled into the porch. Dragging the key out, she twisted the ring to find the key to the inner door. In her panic, the bunch slipped from her hand and fell to the floor. Stooping, she began to search for it, her breath coming in those short, uncontrollable gasps produced by the mind's certainty that there is not enough oxygen in the world to fuel the blood raging through a tumultuous heart.

The key . . . the key . . . she had to find the key . . . but what need of a key when the door was open?

Slowly she looked up. The open door; a pair of feet— brown shoes, slip-ons, slightly scuffed; dark gray slacks, a black sweater; and so on and up until she found herself looking into the face of Stanley Usher.

"Welcome home, Mrs. Adamson," he said.

He reached his left hand down towards her as if offering

assistance. But in his right was a snub-nosed automatic, and so it was little surprise when the outstretched fingers seized her hair and began to forcibly drag her into the entrance hall.

"Play time's over, Trudi," he said.

Behind him was another figure. Vague as yet, but more menacing somehow than her physical assailant. She had to stop herself being dragged into the house. Resistance brought unbearable pain, yet perhaps the pain of having her hair ripped from her scalp would turn out to be preferable to what lay inside. She was sobbing and moaning, her very terror acting like a gag. At least she must scream!

She drew in a long ragged breath and screamed with all her might.

The effect was devastating. The porch seemed to dissolve around her in a huge explosion of glass. She'd heard of such effects but thought they only happened to vast divas in old comedy films. The grip on her hair was released and she could look up. Usher was falling backwards, his arms raised to ward off the ferocious attack of one of the garden gnomes. Simultaneously Trudi felt her hand seized from behind and a voice screamed, "Run, Trudi! Run!"

She turned and ran. Hand in hand with her rescuer, she ran down the drive and into the street, turning left with the certainty of a good dancer responding to the gentlest pressure of an expert lead.

A car stood at the curbside. It was the car she recognized before acknowledging the identity of her partner. The door was unlocked. She fell into the passenger seat and almost before she could pull the door shut behind her, the engine was growling cruelly and they were accelerating like a pair of teen-age joyriders down the quiet suburban street.

Breathing was all her concern for a while. She'd not realized till now that breathing could kill you, tear you apart with overdemand, lungs inadequate as a topsail in a hurricane. Slowly she tacked with it, directed it, controlled it. Soon her breath was fast and deep but regular. Soon it would reach a level where speech would be possible, where questions could be asked and answers demanded.

But here she was preempted. Here the questions which

were burning on her tongue came flaming forth from her rescuer.

"For Christ's sake, girl, what's going on?" cried Janet. "Trudi, what the fuck have you been up to?"

CHAPTER
2

They sat at a corner table in the lounge bar of a big city-center hotel. Janet had scattered their coats across the other seats, but twice already they had been approached by what she called "toad-faces," middle-aged salesmen with lust-young eyes glittering through their wrinkles, asking if the chairs were taken.

"Yes, boyo. By my husband, the wrestler. He needs at least two of them," retorted Janet.

What Trudi had really wanted to do was go and find James Dacre and collapse into the safety of his strong arms and tell him yes, yes, yes, she would marry him instantly, here, now! Even though she knew he'd still be en route for Manchester, she had gone to a phone booth while Janet was getting the drinks and dialed his number. Perhaps he'd missed the train, perhaps . . . her heart leapt as she heard his voice! But it was only an answering machine. She told it where she was, begged him to come and fetch her as soon as he got the message.

This vicarious contact was some comfort, and as light, warmth, drink and even the single-minded interest of the toad-faces further soothed her panicking spirits, she found herself not totally distressed that James couldn't be with her straightaway. Not that she didn't want him, close and permanent, but there were serious matters to be sorted out privately between herself and Janet.

"Well, girl, you'll want to get Trent out of the way first, I expect," said the Welsh woman with a matter-of-factness that didn't quite come off.

"No," said Trudi, rather to her own surprise. "When we start on that, we may quarrel, and I'd rather get the nonquarreling bit sorted first. Jan, what happened back there at Hope House?"

Janet looked at her with interest. Her dark intelligent eyes had rarely left Trudi's face since they sat down. It was as if she was bent on showing she wasn't going to flinch from the expected onslaught.

"Where've you been, on a personality assertion course, or something? All right, let's do it that way. I've no idea what happened back there, and that's the truth. All I know is I wanted to get in touch with you. I'd talked to Frank, see, and he'd said he'd been round to your place, looking for me. I realized you'd not said anything about who Trent was . . . Trudi, I know how it must seem to you, seeing that picture . . ."

"Later, Jan, later!" said Trudi vehemently. "The house!"

"All right. I rang. I've been ringing off and on for a couple of days. No reply till late this afternoon, the phone was picked up. I spoke but no one answered. Then it was replaced. I went straight round there. I thought . . ."

"You thought I might be doing my pill-spewing act again," suggested Trudi. "I think I'm past that now, Jan."

Again that interested appraising look.

"I'm glad to hear it, girl. Anyway, I went round. No reply to my knocking. I wandered round the house. Nothing to be seen through the windows. Everything locked and barred. No sign of anyone at home. Yet I felt . . . watched."

"I know the feeling," said Trudi. "Didn't you think it might just be me?"

"I wondered about that. It was a possibility, of course. But I doubted if you'd have been able just to watch."

"Why not? A little mouse cowering beneath a sheaf of wheat—isn't that what you'd expect from me?"

"Once perhaps. Not lately. Not now," said Janet. "Anyway, I told myself I was being stupid, probably I'd dialed the wrong number and got an answering machine that had gone wrong. The house was empty. I should go away and ring again tomorrow. I got in my car and drove round the corner.

"There I stopped. I sat in the car for ages, wondering what the hell I was doing. Finally I thought, I'll be getting arrested for curb-crawling if I'm not careful! So I got out and walked back. I went into the gate of the house next door, the empty one that's up for sale. I sneaked up the garden and found myself a spot where I could watch the side of Hope House. God knows how long I stood there, but it seemed an age and it was cold and wet, and I was beginning to think I should be certified, when I saw a movement. Just a shadow behind the bedroom window at the side. I stood and stared for another age, but nothing more. Then I heard the phone ring. At least I think I did, but my ears were straining so hard that I could probably have heard angels singing with a little more effort. But if it did ring, it stopped so quickly that it must have been answered. I waited. Then your taxi came. I heard it. I heard your footsteps up the drive. But I couldn't be sure it was you, and I had to be sure before I yelled or anything. Then suddenly you started running and I knew it was you! You were in the porch like a startled rabbit! Through the glass I could see the inner door opening and someone standing there, and he grabbed your hair and I knew I'd been right and I should have yelled earlier, or gone down to the gate to intercept you, or rung the police, or anything!

"Instead, I had to do the best I could. I picked up that bloody gnome and I hurled it through the porch window! Even as I did it, I thought, This could kill Trudi!"

"You missed me," said Trudi. "But I've still got glass in my hair."

"Sorry. But with a bit of luck that bastard who attacked you will still have concrete in his teeth! Then I grabbed you and ran. And here we are, Trudi, safe and sound. Here we are."

They sipped their drinks in silence. Another pair of hopeful toad-faces approached their table, but Janet fended them off with a ferocious glower. Trudi touched her head. Her scalp was still tender from Usher's assault. Who the hell was he? What did he want from her?

Why wasn't she at the police station, demanding the C.I.D. find the answers to these questions?

One reason was here, sitting alongside her. Unfinished business that she did not know how to begin.

She said, "You say you've spoken to Frank?"

"Yes. I gave him a day to cool off, then I rang. Whatever happened, we had to talk."

"And?"

"We talked. I told him I was sorry but what I did before we got married was no business of his. I told him that in any case, for what it was worth, it could never happen again as the man was dead."

"It doesn't matter if the man's dead? Yes, I've heard you use that argument before."

"When?" demanded Janet.

"When I told you about Astrid and Trent. It soothed your own conscience, did it?"

"Not much," admitted Janet. "I'd met you again, and got to like you again, and in a way I was more worried about you finding out with Trent dead than I'd ever been while he was alive."

"Jan, tell me the lot, will you? Now. Leave nothing out. Let me be sure that when you stop, there'll be no more to take me by surprise."

"All right," said the Welsh woman, suddenly brisk and businesslike. "Here goes. Down and dirty. Me and Trent first went to bed together when I was twenty. I was still doing my training course and I was on his plane and we got chatting and . . . well, that was it. We overnighted in Bonn I think it was, and he popped my cork. Oh yes, I mean it like I say. I was still a virgin, despite all those wild stories at school. Us girls from the valleys know all about long-term negotiation and all that! Well, after that, I thought I had it made, see. Young stewardess marries mature pilot, just like in the magazine stories. Only Trent didn't seem inclined to take things further than the odd supersonic bang when our trips coincided. But I was young and naïve and kept my hopes up till the night I was daft enough to introduce you into the equation. After that there was nothing to do but bow out gracefully and look around for consolation.

"And there was Alan. He had a lot of go in him, did Alan. And when he realized I wanted a husband as well as a lively date, well he was happy to go along with that too. I did want a husband, see. Not for me the gay life, really. Hubby, nice house, two point four nice kids, holidays on the Costa whatever, that suited me down to the ground. That wasn't Alan's idea, though. Fair do's, he gave me the framework all right, especially when we moved north. House, kids, comfortable life, package holidays at good-class hotels, it was all there. Except that soon as I got pregnant first time, he was away wining and dining and dancing band banging! God knows how many, but the first one I found out about—that was really ironic!—was an Aer Lingus stewardess, a broth of a girl with nipples like shamrocks—I quote Alan's own words. He saw no reason not to admit all when I accused him, in fact I think he got his rocks off telling me about them. Nevertheless we soldiered on—it's marvelous how that framework I was telling you about can hold together a cracked marriage—and to tell the truth there were good times too. And there was always Trent.

"He never lost contact with Alan, that was clear. I'd sometimes wondered if they had some little arrangement going at Heathrow—one or two things I noticed—everyone was at it, of course, and no one really minded, long as you didn't get too greedy—but a pilot and a customs officer, they could really have a ball! Anyway, like I say, I bumped into Trent by accident in Manchester one day, and we had a drink, and one thing led to another, and we ended up in a hotel bedroom. Afterwards he mentioned he saw Alan from time to time but thought it best if neither of us mentioned we'd met. And after that, from time to time, I'd get a call and . . . well, I worked it out that he probably rang me when he was meeting with Alan, so he'd know it was safe to talk. It wasn't all that often, Trudi, believe me. Sometimes six, nine months would go by. Once it was a whole year . . ."

"But you kept up a steady average?" observed Trudi. "Let me see, twenty-five years at say one and a half times a year. Why, you almost did as well out of him as me!"

"Yes, he said . . ." She tailed off and then tried to resume on a different line, but Trudi was too quick.

"You talked about me, did you? That was nice, as we were all such good old friends. What did he say?"

"He said that you weren't much interested, Trudi, that was all!" burst out Janet. "He said that he doubted if you'd really be much bothered if you found out!"

"And you believed him?" said Trudi.

"Oh no. I'm a woman, remember? That's the kind of thing men say about their wives, isn't it?"

"I wouldn't know," said Trudi. "All those years, Jan."

She tried to speak flatly, but the simple words must have come out as a bitter reproach.

"Oh please, don't . . . it didn't mean anything . . . it just happened . . . it could've been anyone . . ."

"Could it, Jan?"

Janet paused, her mobile features went curiously still, she regarded Trudi quietly for a long moment, then she said, "No, you're right. Honesty's the game tonight. Every time I screwed Trent I paid you back for marrying him! How's that for honest? It's not all of it, by a long chalk, and put bluntly, it's as false as anything else, but it's part of the truth, I can see that. I've never really faced it before. I mean, *you*, Trudi, my little pet mouse, and he'd picked you over me! It was a shock I tell you. Oh, I put on the makeup and I smiled and said 'How marvelous!' but old Pagliacci Evans was all broke up under the Max Factor. It was a slap in the face, see? It didn't make any kind of sense! Oh I'm sorry, Trudi, that was all those years ago, I was young and daft and self-centered and I couldn't understand . . ."

"Couldn't understand all my well-hidden attractions, you mean?" said Trudi savagely. "And that photo of you and Trent, you didn't look so young then, all droopy boobs and spare tyres, weren't you? Had you started understanding by then or not? Tell me that!"

"What big claws you've got suddenly, Trudi," said the

Welsh woman softly. "No, I never started understanding. Never. Not that I didn't . . ."

She broke off, made a business of lighting a cigarette, looked irritatedly into her empty glass.

"Fancy a refill, love?"

She looked up at the smirkingly hopeful toad-face who was leaning over the table and said, "Right, thanks. G. and T., treble. My friend will have the same. Ice and lemon, don't forget."

Uncertain, the man retreated.

Trudi said, "You were about to say, not that you didn't ask Trent why he went for me. So. What did he answer?"

"Trudi, this is daft. This is nothing to do with you and me, here and now. You've got trouble, and there's no time to scratch around and dig up old graves!"

"What did he say?" insisted Trudi.

And when Janet still hesitated, she added impatiently, "Oh come on. I'm not just picking at sores. Things have happened you don't know about. I need to hear this, Jan, believe me!"

"All right. Keep your hair on," said Janet. "There's not much to hear, anyway. I asked him why once. Well, a lot of times actually. Why he chose you. But he only ever answered once. I mean, he usually said something like *Why not?* or grunted, or told me to stop yacking. But this time, I think he was a bit pissed maybe, and he laughed, not very nicely I should say, and he turned to me and he said—these were his exact words as far as I can remember—'Listen, you Welsh witch, marriage with Trudi's been worth more to me than ten lifetimes screwing you could ever have got near, now are you happy?' And he laughed again."

"What did you think he meant?" said Trudi.

"I don't know," admitted Janet. "I think he was putting me down, that was part of it. But there was something else. I mean, he *meant* it, and all I could think was that he was saying that he really loved you, except that . . ."

"Yes?"

"The way he laughed, it didn't sound like that's what he was saying," said Janet. "I'm sorry, Trudi, but you did ask."

"I know it," said Trudi.

She was looking sideways at a thought like that fabled monster of the woods which you only see at first from the corner of your eye, flickering distantly between the tree trunks; but as you walk on, you realize that your paths are not parallel but convergent. She had seen it first in Jünger's office that same morning, and here it was again, coming closer and closer.

Trent hadn't married her and *then* found out she was Schiller's granddaughter.

No. Trent—ambitious, opportunist, amoral Trent—had found out who she was and then married her.

But this was not the total truth about the monster. There were other greater horrors of deed and feature which the flickering trees so far only allowed her to suspect, but which their final, inevitable meeting would fully reveal. Her mind was driving her inexorably towards that meeting. She tried to turn aside from it. Not here! Not now! There was too much to think of, too much to decide. Her mind would burst . . .

"Look, push off, boyo. You want crumpet, you ring room service, why don't you!"

Janet's voice, angry at yet another toad-face assault, brought her out of the gloomy forest of her thoughts. Gratefully she looked up, ready to reward the lecher with a consoling smile. But there was no lechery on the face that regarded her, only concern.

"Mrs. Adamson, I thought it was you. I just wanted to say hello, but . . . are you all right, Mrs. Adamson? You don't look well."

"Oh yes," she said, tears suddenly stinging her eyes. "Really, I'm fine, Mr. Ashburton, fine. Won't you sit down?"

CHAPTER
3

"**I** was dining with friends, well, clients really. It was curious something we were talking about made me think of you, and then as I casually glanced in her on my way out, there you were. At least, I thought it was you. Well, of course it is, isn't it?"

Mr. Ashburton laughed. Clearly there'd been seeds of jollity buried in his usual dusty dryness and whatever he'd drunk that night had set them sprouting. Trudi found herself wondering if perhaps after all there might not have been something toad-faced in his "casual glance." But no, she couldn't really see the little solicitor essaying a pickup. She sensed something in him which would shy away from the sheer unpredictability of the venture. Jolly he might be, Jack the Lad he definitely wasn't.

"What made you think about me, Mr. Ashburton?" she asked.

"Well, it was just that I got talking to my dinner companions about Mr. Usher . . ."

"Usher! What about him?"

He looked taken aback by the fierceness of the interruption.

"Your employer," he said, as though wanting to make sure they were talking about the same man. "You recall we spoke on the phone just before you left for Vienna—how was your trip, by the way?"

"Fine, fine," said Trudi. God, she'd almost forgotten about the wrecking of Class-Glass and that sinister little cubbyhole with the one-way window. So much had happened in the last couple of days that hours seemed stretched into weeks.

"I rang the police as you requested. They got in touch with me later and seemed naturally keen to speak with Mr. Usher. I gave them the address and telephone number I had, but they got in touch with me again today to say that they still hadn't been able to contact him. They were most persistent in their search for information, I must say. All I could say was that I first encountered him some four or five years ago when I acted for him in the purchase of some premises, a small warehouse in fact. That was when he told me his business was snapping up failing businesses and he often needed to store items he couldn't dispose of immediately. Since then I've acted for him in one or two minor matters, but nothing of any size."

"What about the purchase of Class-Glass?"

"No, indeed," said Ashburton vigorously. "And there's an odd thing. I learned from the police that, far from buying it as a failing business, he'd set it up himself. Now isn't that odd? It was this I was discussing with my friends this evening. In a most general way, you understand. Even in situations like this there is still a duty to client confidentiality."

He regarded them solemnly through his owlish glasses. Janet said, "I bet there is."

Jollity broke through again and he grinned unexpectedly.

"I was surprised. They all seemed to know *of* Usher, but not much *about* him. I could feel a certain reserve in their comments, though whether this was out of suspicion of a not-quite-rightness or a feeling that he was not the kind of man it was safe to gossip about, I do not know. I must confess I myself had never had any such reservations. He was a client, straightforward in his dealings, prompt in his payments. I would not have recommended you to his employ else, Mrs. Adamson, believe me."

He spoke so earnestly that Trudi found herself patting his hand and saying, "I do, Mr. Ashburton, I do."

Something else occurred to her.

"Tell me," she said. "It wasn't by any chance Mr. Usher that recommended you to my husband, was it?"

He looked thoughtful, then nodded, beaming. "I believe it

was, Mrs. Adamson. I believe it was! Mention of your late husband puts me in mind of why I was trying to contact you in the first place. A small matter in connection with your compensation case . . ."

"To hell with the whole business!" exploded Trudi, amazing herself as much as the others.

Taking a grip on herself, she said in a voice quiet with restraint, "What I mean is, I don't think I care to pursue the case, Mr. Ashburton. I've got other things on my mind. Besides, the way things look to me now, I should be paying that truck driver a reward, not suing him for compensation!"

The statement came out flatly, without emphasis, and Ashburton regarded her in wide-eyed bewilderment. But Janet clearly detected the bitterness and the strain from which it arose. She shot an accusatory glance at the little solicitor, who rose hastily and said, "Perhaps you would care to call at my office some time tomorrow, Mrs. Adamson, so that we can discuss this in surroundings more conducive to . . . er . . ."

"She'll be there," promised Janet when it became clear Trudi was not about to answer.

Ashburton retreated, his face marmoset-like with concern. Janet said, "Trudi, I don't know what's happening, but this time we've got to go to the police."

"No!" said Trudi. "I've been to the police. I didn't care for it."

It was a silly response to a sensible suggestion, but sense and silliness seemed to have been so mixed up in her life that she could only play it by ear, and *no* to the police sounded pretty right.

"You haven't got some daft notion that Trent's still alive and you're protecting him, have you?"

"No."

"You're sure? That *no* lacked the punch of your new emphatic style."

Trudi smiled wearily.

"Snarling wears you out," she said. "That's why lions spend most of their time sleeping, I suppose."

"Is it? So now you're a dor-lion instead of a dormouse?"

"Maybe. But I'll emphasize my belief in Trent's death if

you like. I believe it so much that I'm going to get married again, and you know I'd never dare risk bigamy."

"Trudi! You mean that chap I met, whatsisname . . ."

"Yes, whatsisname," said Trudi.

She stood up. She felt a strong need to be away from here, to be moving towards James. What if he came back and didn't run his answering machine but went straight to bed? She resolved to be sitting on his doorstep when he got back from Manchester.

Janet was rising too. Gently Trudi pushed her back into her seat.

"No," she said. "I'm on my own now, till I get to James, that is. That's where I'm going now, so no need to worry. And don't look so glum. It's not goodbye. I'll be in touch."

"You mean you've forgiven me?" said Janet, half satirical, half sincere.

"Not on your life, but I'll need to see you again to make you squirm some more, won't I?"

Trudi regarded her friend seriously as she spoke. Then slowly she let her tight lips relax and stretch into the broadest of grins.

"Cow!" said Janet, her face rubbery with relief. "Look, ring me, promise? At home. Frank and I are getting back together again, I think, even though he's a bit tiresome with his besmirched-honor act. Whatever, I think the old sod can be relied on to pass a message. Trudi, you'll take care?"

"You can bet on it," said Trudi.

She headed for the door, sailing like a bride beneath an arch of toad-face leers.

In the hotel foyer, the receptionist repeated the word *taxi* as though savoring a neologism.

"I could ring," she said. "But if you walk towards the City Hall, you'll likely pick up one a lot quicker."

Would the same advice have been offered if I'd been wearing my silver lamé evening gown and a tiara, wondered Trudi.

Very probably! she answered herself. This was, after all, South Yorkshire.

To her surprise, the thought was almost affectionate.

The rain had stopped, though the air was still misty and

damp. Headlights swam through it like bathyscaphes exploring the ocean bed. She waved at a couple of taxi shapes but they drifted by, occupied or preoccupied. A third was at least more positive and accelerated away at her wave, but a pair of headlights behind swung in to the curb alongside her. It wasn't a traditional taxi, but she was used to a mixture of London cabs and ordinary limousines with hackney licenses, and had her hand on the door handle before suspicion rang a bell.

Then it was too late. The door was open and her wrist was seized.

Stanley Usher, a strip of plaster across his brow and an unpleasant smile across his face said, "Come on in, Mrs. Adamson. I've got someone who's very keen to talk to you."

He jerked her inside as she began to scream. She felt the blow to the stomach which turned the scream into a choking gasp for breath.

But the blow to the head which turned the hazy street lights to darkness she never felt at all.

PART EIGHT

A daimen icker in a thrave
'S a sma' request:
I'll get a blessin wi' the lave,
And never miss 't! . . .

BURNS: "To a Mouse"

CHAPTER
1

Trudi awoke.

Now she felt the blow which had rendered her unconscious. Her head ached and her straining eyes created sparks and shards of light in their effort to make sense of her surroundings. Finally she began to make distinctions between the internal and the external.

She was lying on a hard mattress in a darkened room. Her wrists and ankles were bound, but this was an unnecessary refinement. In her mind she had been here many times before and knew there was no escape. One strip of light there was which could not be blinked away. It lay on the floor, seeping in beneath the door, and beyond that door on bare stone flags she could hear the sound of footsteps getting near.

She lay as still as the mouse which huddles in its cornfield nest and hears the approach of the coulter, and knows what it means, but does not know how to fly.

Nothing remained in her life, no spur of action, no prick of hope. Nothing of past, present or future touched her senses, only that crack of light beneath the door and the footsteps which were approaching it.

She had been waiting for them all her life. They belonged to the secret police who strike with the dawn; to the cruel rapist who lurks in the shadows; to the man she had loved, come here to kill her.

Now they were close. Now the line of light beneath the door was broken by a growing shadow.

Now the footsteps halted.

Slowly the door handle began to turn. Slowly the door swung open. In the threshold loomed a figure, bulky, still, menacing.

Now it was in the room and advancing.

Her mouth gaped wide as her desperate lungs drew in one last, long, ragged breath . . .

And now she let it out in a great gale of laughter. She roared, she writhed, she almost rolled off the bed in her mirth. Even the sharp slap he gave across her cheek didn't quell her almost entirely hysterical mirth.

"I'm sorry. I'm sorry," she gasped. "It's just that . . . with the light behind you . . . you looked bigger somehow . . . I'm sorry, I don't mean . . . but I thought . . . it's just relief really . . . I thought that . . . and it's only you, little you! So it's all right."

"Well, that remains to be seen," said Mr. Ashburton, sitting on the edge of the bed. "But I think I understand, my dear. You thought perhaps it was Trent, come back to haunt you? Or not really dead at all? Well, it was almost like that, you know. He was such an ingenious man, your husband. Perhaps it was only fitting that in the end he should be the victim of his own ingenuity."

Trudi tried to struggle upright, but it proved impossible. Frowning, Mr. Ashburton leaned forward to study her bonds, then undid the cords which bound her wrists.

"You must forgive Usher. A man of excesses, I'm afraid. I'll have a word with him. There, is that better?"

It was and it wasn't. Now she could push herself up the mattress to rest her back against the wall, which was an improvement. But at the same time the last dregs of her merriment drained away as Ashburton's easy assumption of authority over Usher persuaded her that the little solicitor was no fit object for mirth, even hysterical mirth.

"Where am I?" she said.

"Don't you know? You've been here before, I think."

She peered past him through the open door. At first the whitewashed stone corridor, which was all she could see, meant nothing to her, then realization came. It was Well Cottage at Eyam.

"That's right," said Ashburton. "I see you remember. An economical choice, I thought. And with all mod cons."

Trudi recalled the frozen body of Jünger's brother and shuddered. She felt her hysteria returning. Something dreadful was about to happen. She'd been knocked unconscious, kidnapped, tied to a bed. She wasn't worth a ransom to anyone, so it was herself they wanted, what they imagined she knew.

She screamed, "I know nothing. Nothing! I don't want to know anything. Please, it's all been a mistake, you've got it wrong. It's not worth it . . . whatever you're going to do . . . it's just wasting time . . ."

She threw in the last phrase as her mind tried to control her fear; it was the nearest she could get to a rational argument.

"Wasting time," mused Ashburton. "We've plenty of that, I assure you. I'm still not sure about you, my dear, but in case you think that sounds hopeful, let me tell you what I *am* sure of. Either you know what I want to know and are acting your head off to conceal the knowledge. Or you really imagine you don't know, but in fact you probably do, unawares. Either way, I'm going to get it out of you, you'd better believe me."

"Yes, yes, yes," babbled Trudi. "I believe you. And you've got to believe me, I know nothing. Anything I do know, you're welcome to. What is it you want, Mr. Ashburton? Please, just tell me. Why are you doing this? What do you want? Who are you?"

Ashburton looked at her thoughtfully and smiled.

"All right," he said mildly. "Let's play this way for a little while. Let's assume you may be unaware of precisely what it is you know. I'll make sure you know everything, and after that you can't plead ignorance, can you?"

Suddenly Trudi had no desire to know everything. Knowledge wasn't power, it was terror. How happy her days of drowsy ignorance now seemed. She recalled once asking Trent about his work and he had smiled and said, "Do you really want to know?" And she, drinking what tasted like affection from his smile, had shaken her head and replied, laughing, "Probably not." At moments like that she had felt really close to him, protected by him. How she longed for that protection now. Ashburton was pressing his hands together and preparing to speak. Now fear of what was going to happen when he stopped made her pray he might go on speaking forever.

He said, "I'm a simple provincial solicitor, Mrs. Adamson. I am also the U.K. representative of the Schiller organization. Not Schiller-Reise, which for historical reasons never established its own agency in this country, but the other, less public side of the business. I see you know what I mean. I will not exaggerate my own importance. For many years the U.K. was surprisingly impervious to our marketing campaigns. We did steady business, but compared with the Americas, Asia and even the European mainland, we really were a third-rate power."

"You mean, Britain didn't have a drug problem," said Trudi.

"That's one way of putting it, yes. Even the Swinging Sixties, with London as their fulcrum, saw only a relatively small rise in demand compared with the States. The English are hypocrites even in their excesses, you know; on the surface all long hair, free love and pink shirts, but with marriage, mortgages and nine-to-five still very much the framework of existence. It took the Seventies to see a real change, and the Eighties to confirm it. Our operation must have doubled in the last two years alone. Suddenly from being a minor post, mine became a key job. I was not surprised when it was suggested I might think about retiring. I am, after all, in my sixties and to be quite frank, the business was becoming a little too strenuous for me. And nor, I admit, was I very surprised when I learnt who was to be my successor."

"Trent," said Trudi, becoming involved despite her fear.

"That's right. I'd known him for some years, of course. He made fairly frequent liaison visits. And one of our major input points was directly under his personal control."

"Manchester Airport," said Trudi.

"You see, you do know such a lot! Yes, he had a contact there who worked directly for him rather than for Schiller. He was very insistent on this. I believe it caused a lot of resentment, but many things your husband did caused resentment. But he, of course, was in a privileged position. I do not doubt you know the reasons for that, Mrs. Adamson?"

He raised his eyebrows in forensic invitation.

"Because I am Manfred Schiller's granddaughter," said Trudi.

"You know that too? But you didn't know it when you married, did you? Your husband, however, did. Oh yes, he knew."

His tone was admiring. Up to this point, despite everything, Trudi had been finding herself unable to see far beyond her image of the benign, faintly comic little solicitor. Now for the first time she began to feel fear.

"Who are you?" she demanded. "What's your connection with all this? I mean, how did someone like you get involved?"

Before Ashburton could answer, there were footsteps in the corridor outside. He went to the door and Trudi heard the mutter of voices without being able to distinguish the words. Then he returned.

He said, "I'm sorry. He gets impatient. But I've told him to take a stroll. Enjoy the night air. It's a fine night now. The cloud's cleared. No moon, but stars enough to spangle an ocean. Do I surprise you? Law's a drab business and we who practice it of necessity take on its coloring, but underneath, my soul is a rainbow, Mrs. Adamson. Why take up the legal profession, then? My parents' choice. They scrimped and saved to get me articled. The war seemed to change all that for me. I could see no future in the law. If you had the money, could buy yourself a partnership, live off the fat of other people's troubles, then it could be a pleasant enough existence. But for someone like me, the penniless son of a Sheffield steel worker with no connections, it promised to be a gray, grinding existence. Then in 1945 I found myself in Vienna, attached, in a very minor capacity, to the War Crimes Commission. Ah, I see you're ahead of me, Mrs. Adamson. And you still want me to believe you a fool!"

"You met my . . . you met Schiller," said Trudi.

"Indeed. Or rather, he met me. Sought me out, you might

say. He was not a war criminal of the first water, you understand. He held no Party rank. No villages had been razed at his command, he did not have lampshades made out of Jewish skin, nothing of that. But where his own profit and Party policy had coincided, he had been energetic and ruthless in pursuit of both. He was definitely in the frame, as our policemen are so fond of saying now. His turn would come. There were certain papers, certain affidavits, certain records . . . it was suggested to me that I should remove them for a consideration. I refused. I pointed out that their complete disappearance would do nothing but rouse suspicion, possibly of myself, and draw closer attention to Herr Schiller. But, I went on, for a rather larger consideration, I would perform the more subtle task of filleting the evidence against him, removing enough to have him downgraded from the profiteer category to *follower* or *nonoffender*. You look shocked, Mrs. Adamson. Don't be. It was nothing. There were much bigger villains than your grandfather, men who had been active and committed members of the Gestapo, classified as mere *followers* and now actually working for the Allied intelligence services. What good to pursue one businessman whose racial attitudes and business ethics, to be honest, differed very little from many of my present clients!

"I acted. I worked. I was paid, with a bonus. I performed one or two more small services for Herr Schiller before I was demobbed. And, because he is a man of foresight and vision, he asked me how he might get in touch with me in England should the need ever arise. I didn't expect ever to hear from him again, of course. I'd no idea of the extent of his interests. I came home, got my qualifications and used my newly acquired wealth to buy myself a partnership in the firm that now bears my sole name. And one day a man walked into my office with greetings from Herr Schiller and a request that I should perform him a small service. This was the first of many such requests. I won't go into details but gradually I became Herr Schiller's man in the U.K. It was suggested at one point I might move to London. I resisted. I said, here I was known, respected. In London I would be nothing, or worse, an oddity. Besides, if you wanted to be at the center of the United Kingdom in practical terms, then where better than Sheffield?"

Trudi recalled the police sergeant who had spoken to her after Trent's death. He'd said Sheffield would be a good center and she'd wondered for what?

Now she knew.

Ashburton resumed.

"It was some years later that I received a request a little out of the ordinary run of things. I was asked to check on the background and provenance of a man living in the South. I was told that he was a teacher of German and that his name, as you must have guessed, was Shoesmith. It was suggested to me that he might have changed his name from Schumacher to Shoesmith when he applied for British citizenship. With this clue things were easy. During the war, aliens domiciled here were as well documented as major criminals. It was just a matter of knowing where to look. I was able to get chapter and verse on him from the time he left Austria, even to the maiden name of his wife. When I saw this was Schiller, I sat up and took notice. As requested, I sent my report direct to Herr Schiller in Vienna. I knew nothing of his family circumstances then, but I made it my business to find out by subtle indirect means. I had the feeling that he would not take kindly to anyone prying into his business. I also kept a distant eye on Mr. Shoesmith née Schumacher, teacher of German.

"Not long after, two things happened. Were they connected, I wondered? But I couldn't quite see how or why. And then some time after that, a new man came into my office and showed me his credentials from Herr Schiller. And in that moment, though I didn't blink an eye, I saw all things clear. Do you know what I'm talking about, Mrs. Adamson?"

"No," said Trudi. "No. No. No."

"I think you do. I think you've known for a little while now. Not long, but long enough. The two things were, first, your father was killed; second, you got married. And the man who came to my office, the new rising star of the Schiller organization, was your husband, Trent Adamson. It was he who first spotted you, I guessed. Learning something of your background from your friend, the name Schumacher rang a bell. He was already smuggling for Schiller in a small way and he'd learned something of the man's history. Well, he would, wouldn't he? Trent was always a great man for knowing things. Information helped a man jump the right way when the chances came and your husband was a great one for chances. He told Schiller. Schiller got me to check it out. And then . . ."

"Then what?" demanded Trudi.

"Then your father dies. Which is what Schiller wants. You get married to a man whose location and career are in Schiller's control, which is also what he wants. And Trent's career prospers, which is what *he* wants. So much satisfaction can hardly be ascribed to coincidence, I feel. Don't look so distressed, my dear. As I say, I'm sure you've worked all this out for yourself. Indeed, what I find hard to believe is that a woman of your obvious intelligence didn't work it all out a great deal earlier. Surely you must have sensed something odd, something not quite right in your life all those years?"

"Which years?" said Trudi dully. "You don't notice time when you're sleeping."

Ashburton took off his spectacles and polished them, blinking at her with what looked like genuine sympathy.

The door, which he'd half closed, was suddenly flung open. Usher stood on the threshold.

"For Christ's sake, man! What the hell's going on? Give me two minutes with the cow. I'll guarantee she'll talk!"

"Patience, I beg you. Patience," said Ashburton.

"Patience! If we'd hit her hard from the start like I said, we'd be long gone by now. All this shilly-shallying, all this clever-clever stuff—they're all out there now, you know, out there looking, you'd better believe it!"

"In a general sense, yes. But there's really no chance that anyone is out there in a simple geographical sense. So go away! This matter will be resolved in a very few minutes!"

He put on his spectacles as he spoke. It was like the assumption of a badge of authority. Reluctantly, Usher withdrew.

"Who's out there? What does he mean?" asked Trudi.

"All kinds of people," said Ashburton vaguely. "You'd be

surprised what interest there is in you. You see, what's happening in the organization at the moment is rather like the dissolution of the Roman Empire. No one's quite sure where the power will end up, everyone's struggling to make sure they don't get the dirty end of the stick, and the Vandals, in the form of various law-enforcement agencies, are at the gates.

"A couple of years ago with Herr Schiller growing old, your husband looked set fair for the succession. Your grandfather had never been able to bring himself openly to acknowledge you. You were after all the Jew's daughter, and the cause of your mother's death. But you were all he had of family. Had you had a child of your own, a son in particular, I think that would have brought him into the open. But it never happened, and the best he could do was elect Trent to the role.

"Trent's rise had created resentment and curiosity, but it was a long time before any of his rivals discovered the reason for his success."

He smiled as he spoke and Trudi said, "It was you. You sold the information."

"So sharp! Perhaps I did. Not that it seemed very helpful to Trent's enemies. The best they could think of was the old-fashioned idea of getting some compromising photographs and either using them to shock old Schiller or perhaps drive you into a divorce and thus cut the connection. Your friend, the Welsh lady, obliged—unwittingly, I hasten to add. You have enough to forgive her for, I wouldn't want to suggest anything worse. I don't know what effect the photos might have had on Schiller, but he never saw them. He had his first stroke. It took him out of the game for over a year. By the time he got back everything was in a turmoil. Trent was in the thick of it, of course. You must have been aware of something?"

Trudi thought of the even tenor of her life in Vienna, the slow drift from dawn to dusk, the drowsy cocoon of rich food, fine wine, good living; theater, cinemas, television, dress shops, furniture shops, cafés . . .

She could not believe she was remembering herself. She shook her head helplessly and said, "No."

"No? Well, possibly Trent went out of his way to keep you unaware," said Ashburton comfortingly. "He had enough on his plate. You see, we know now that in the middle of all this he was also approached by the police. Of course, you know that from Herr Jünger!"

"Jünger told me that Trent came to him and said he suspected that something crooked was going on at Schiller-Reise."

Ashburton laughed.

"Is that what he said? Does that mean he believes in your innocence, I wonder? Or is it a bluff to persuade *you* he believes in it? A bluff, I think. I see from your expression that your experience with Herr Jünger has not been altogether happy. Well, you must forgive him. He will have worked out by now that something very nasty has happened to his brother and must suspect you know what it is. Which, of course, is true, isn't it?"

"No! I only know he's dead!"

"Yes? Well. Let's play the game a little longer then. Nearly two years ago, your friend's husband, Alan Cummings, died suddenly of a heart attack on his way to work in the Customs and Excise office at Manchester Airport. He picked a bad day to die. A shipment was on its way from Holland that day which needed a friendly eye to ensure its safe passage. Alas, the friendly eye was now glazed, permanently. The shipment was discovered. It was a triumph for our clever customs officers. But one of them, cleverer than the others, wondered why it had in fact been so easy to find. Surely the traffickers would have shown more ingenuity in concealing it—unless, of course, they had been confident that the finders would also be the keepers. That's when they started to look closely at Cummings. The trail quickly led to Trent and Schiller-Reise, tying in with other leads and suspicions in Austria. Trent was alerted, probably through your friend, the widow Cummings, who told him of their strange postmortem interest in her dead husband's affairs. Jünger, I suspect, is telling the truth in part at least. Trent, wanting time, probably did actually approach him, not as the innocent who has stumbled on a crime, but as the guilty willing to do a deal. Jünger agreed. He wanted the whole setup. And Trent had his time.

"He also had Jünger junior as his liaison and his minder. Over months, he fed the police enough tidbits of information to keep them happy. But by an amusing paradox, his own need for time forced him to protect his great rival in the organization, the only other man capable of inheriting complete control from Schiller. You see, once Jünger got him, then the whole operation would be folded up, including Trent."

"But you said he'd done a deal."

"Oh yes. I've no doubt he'd have got away with five years instead of the twenty he thoroughly deserved. But you don't imagine Trent would settle for that! No. He wanted freedom, security, wealth. So he kept quiet for the time being about his main rival for the throne, which was easier than you think, as—unlike the others—this man had no overt link with Schiller-Reise. Again I see you're ahead of me, my dear!"

"Dr. Werner," said Trudi.

"Of course. Even I have only found this out in recent months. He's so highly respected in every field, social, cultural as well as professional. And that clinic of his! Some of the most advanced treatment in the world in the field of drug addiction is carried on there. It's incredible, isn't it? He gets paid at both ends."

"Why did he come to Trent's funeral?"

"A good question. Panic. A mistake. Though of course he'd no idea then that the police were involved. Trent wanted to be in England. He needed a legitimate reason and he got Schiller, in one of his last acts of authority, to appoint him my successor. Werner's suspicions were roused, of course. He started looking into the areas of business that Trent was responsible for. And what he found was—nothing! Almost literally. Trent had been clearing out the organization's coffers for months and covering up his tracks with exquisite care. Then, almost simultaneous with this discovery, Werner was told that Trent had died. He flew to England at once."

"Why? Trent was dead? Did he expect to be able to examine the body?"

"Oh no. It wasn't Trent he wanted to see. It was you. He wanted to get to you before anyone else did. He wanted to find out for himself what you knew. Like me, he found it hard to believe that you could be totally ignorant. And things were in such a turmoil, he could not bring himself to trust anyone else."

"But he didn't stay after the funeral."

"Because Astrid Fischer turned up. He'd never met her, you see. But now he recognized her as a former patient at his clinic and he knew who'd been picking up the bills for her treatment. I don't mean specifically, but in general terms. She had friends in high places, the kind of friends to whom an organization like Schiller's was either a threat to be removed or an attraction to be absorbed. The realization that they must have put Astrid in to keep an eye on Trent made Werner realize that the absorption program had gone much further than Schiller himself had ever revealed."

"You mean Astrid was spying on Trent?" said Trudi, wondering why she felt so indignant at the idea.

"Initially. But Trent, I think, was sharp enough to suspect, and attractive enough to get confirmation through an affair. What he discovered must have convinced him that the time had come to get out, even without the realization that the authorities were on his heels.

"Anyway, the sight of Astrid stopped Werner short and made him realize just how foolhardly he'd been to come out so openly and turn up at the funeral. He retreated as fast as possible to await events."

But Trudi wasn't interested in Werner.

"What are you saying about Astrid, then? That she had something to do with Trent's death?"

"Oh no. On the contrary. She was I think besotted by him, or at least sufficiently infatuated to have let herself be used. But when he died, she suddenly became aware of her situation. She'd been seen with Trent, if only by an old farmer. She wasn't to know that chivalry would keep his mouth shut! Her masters had ways of finding out things. So she controlled her grief and set about putting herself in the clear and ringing back in to report on what happened and ask for instructions. She was told to attend the funeral and pass on to you the information that Trent no longer worked for Schiller-Reise.

"Well, she must have thought she'd got away with it. But

these are hard people to satisfy. They questioned her, I should think. Then gave her a bit of rope. You see, there were very large sums of money involved, money they hoped she might lead them to. Or yourself, Mrs. Adamson. Or yourself."

"Who are *they?*"

"Just people," he said vaguely. "And Werner too, of course. And myself, I shouldn't let modesty forbid me to mention that, I feel! So when you suddenly appeared for your long heart-to-heart with Astrid, eyebrows were bound to be raised. It must have been decided that one of you needed rather more pressure applied. Fortunately for you, the choice fell on Astrid."

Trudi shuddered and said, "Why did they have to kill her?"

Ashburton shrugged.

"They probably pumped her full of something to get her talking. So they pumped her fuller of heroin to shut her up. Don't feel too sorry for her, Mrs. Adamson. Indirectly, you see, she was responsible for your husband's death. There are still those who don't really believe he *is* dead, but I'm sure of it. You see, what had happened was this. Trent, concerned about his future, had created for himself a new persona as Eric Blair. He bought this cottage. And all the time he was helping himself to every penny of Schiller money he could lay his hands on. Now all he had to do was put himself out of reach of the authorities on the one hand and his colleagues on the other."

"So he planned to die."

"He *planned* it?"

"Oh yes. Almost exactly as it happened. But with one essential difference. It wasn't going to be his own body that was charred beyond recognition in the car. He required, of course, another body with the same general specification of build and age. And by a happy coincidence, he'd been provided with one in the shape of Gerhardt Jünger, his attendant policeman. Such an elegant solution! His shadow became his substance. Exit Gerhardt, popped into the freezer out there to keep him fresh until required. Now all he had to do was prepare his own demise, burnt to death in a car accident. Cars, of course, don't burn all that easy, but it wouldn't be difficult for a man of Trent's skills to make some modifications to the fuel system so that on impact it could go up like a torch. When the chosen moment came, he would defrost Gerhardt, load him into the car, drive ever so gently up onto one of the lonely cross-Pennine roads, which he'd already reconnoitered, get his foldaway motor scooter out of the boot, put Jünger into the driving seat, blow a tire and run the whole thing over the edge.

"Then, ah then, who knows? Back here and lie low, perhaps? Or perhaps he had other hideaways, other arrangements? Who knows? Only Trent, and he can never tell us. For he had made an error. He thought his sexual power over Astrid extended to her mind, and that she would go along with all he said unquestioningly. But he underestimated her. Perhaps his life with you had persuaded him that all women were docile, blinkered and easily deceived."

The edge of cruelty gleamed momentarily in his voice, but Trudi was too wrapped up in the narrative to be affected by it.

"Go on," she said.

"Astrid sensed something was wrong and knew she had to find out what, either to join in or report on it to her masters. Trent probably assured her he would be in touch soon after his return to England. But once he was out of her sight, she realized just how very little she trusted him! So without a word to anyone, she followed him to Yorkshire. There was no point in making you suspicious by turning up at the house, so that last morning she probably just sat at the end of Linden Lane and waited. When Trent appeared, she followed him. Perhaps she kept well back in the town or perhaps the traffic was heavy enough to separate them. But once they got into open countryside she closed up. He was heading here, probably, but she had no way of knowing how long he would drive. So she flashed her lights and got close. When he looked in his mirror and saw who it was, his stomach must have turned over.

"But he was a man of endless resource. He stopped on that lonely road and waited till she joined him. What a story he doubtless told! Culminating, I imagine, in an invitation to Astrid to join him in his flight to distant parts when the time came. Perhaps he just wanted her out of his hair for a couple of days till he could implement his plan. Or perhaps he was already modifying it in his mind and thinking of having Astrid's body in the burnt-out car too as extra authentication!"

"You make him sound monstrous! Completely cold-blooded!" burst out Trudi.

"Do I? I really don't mean to," said Ashburton apologetically. "He was an opportunist. He took the nearest way to his own advantage, always. A monster would have killed *you* and left *your* body in the car as authenticating evidence, I think. But he avoided putting you in harm's way, didn't he?"

"He *what?* He betrayed me, used me, stole half my life from me, intended me to think he had been burnt to death, left me penniless . . ."

Indignation was strangulating her voice. Ashburton was shaking his head.

"Oh no. He left you well provided for, my dear."

"What?"

"Oh yes. There were certain securities he had, plus of course the lump-sum payment and the substantial pension due from Schiller-Reise. Only our masters clearly decided in the circumstances the best thing to do to get you to show your hand, if you had a hand to show, was to squeeze you financially. *That* would have sent you scurrying off to the money if anything would."

Trudi's features rounded in amazement, contorted in anger and finally, just as explosion seemed inevitable, relaxed into tearful amusement.

"Laughter again?" said Ashburton. "It's good to see you so merry."

"It's not merriment," said Trudi in a low voice. "More disgust. I just realized that, after hearing this monstrous tale, the thing that was making me more indignant than anything else was that you hadn't let me have my pension! Isn't that pathetic? Perhaps I'm really as money-grubbing as you after all, Mr. Ashburton!"

"Hang onto that thought," said the solicitor, eyeing her dubiously. "But I do hope you mean that you wanted your pension in *addition* to all the money Trent appropriated. Mr. Usher certainly intends to proceed on that basis, and he's a hard man to divert once his mind's made up. But we are delaying our story's ironic climax.

"Finally Astrid drove away, convinced by Trent's silver-tongued reassurances. Trent sat a little longer, doubtless adjusting his plans to this new factor. And over the hill came the fertilizer truck. Now, I believe Trent had probably already started making the modifications which would turn his car into a fire bomb when the time came. Remember, he had to guarantee a conflagration sufficient to render Gerhardt Jünger unrecognizable. Naturally he would leave the final adjustments to the very last minute, and the car was safe enough for normal driving. But when the truck hit him, what thoughts must have gone through his mind! What prayers that his preparatory adjustments would prove totally ineffective!

"But of course he was not an ineffective man. Suddenly the mock funeral pyre he had so carefully been preparing for himself became the real thing! And what a confusion it threw us all into. Because of course all the parties concerned suspected that this must be a trick, that Trent must really still be alive, and that you were possibly privy to the plot.

"So the long watch began. There was a kind of unspoken truce between the organization and the police, both watching, both knowing the other was watching, both applying little bits of pressure to try to force you to show your hand. But what was your hand? Your behavior so extraordinary, so erratic? A suicide attempt—could it be real? A marriage agency—could it be part of a plan? Sometimes you seemed like a bewildered child, at others a calculatingly mature adult. Sometimes, as when you got onto the Blair account, we were sure you knew. Sometimes, as when you went to see Fischer, we were sure you didn't. We tested you with the offer of a little job. You accepted with gratitude! Bluff or reality? At least it gave us a chance to sit you down somewhere where we could watch you at our ease and listen to your conversations on the telephone or with visitors. It was suggested that perhaps Trent's mistress, not his wife, was the key. We searched her house. We even sent her husband a copy of the photo I mentioned, hoping to provoke a reaction. It did but not a useful one. Nor did your reaction when you saw it suggest that Trent was still alive and answerable. All we knew was that somewhere, probably in a bank, under a false name, was the Schiller money, accessible only to whoever had the necessary identification and the access number. Neither the organization nor the police knew how to get at that money. You were the only hope, and so the truce continued while everyone concentrated on watching you!"

"But why's it still going on?" demanded Trudi. "What interest am I to anyone now that you know the bank and know the number and know the name and have got the money?"

Her voice was zooming to a hysterical shriek, but it wasn't this that made Ashburton sit up, alert as a hare scenting danger in a summer meadow.

"What do you mean?" he said quietly. "Who's got which money?"

"You have! The money from the Blair account. The two hundred and fifty thousand pounds. It was in the bank, then it wasn't. It was you who got it, wasn't it?"

"Oh, yes," said Ashburton. "It was us."

He regarded her steadily for a while, then he began to laugh. It wasn't a pleasant sound.

"I wish I could make up my mind about you," he said. "Idiot or consummate actress? Which is it, Mrs. Adamson? Do you really not know? Two hundred and fifty thousand pounds, you say! Do you think this is all about two hundred and fifty thousand pounds! That was your husband's working fund, that was for day-to-day expenses and for the odd emergency, that was his small change!"

"Small change?" echoed Trudi. It was finally coming home to her that in whatever direction she looked of human cruelty and human greed, there were no limits that her puny mind could reach.

"What do you mean, small change?" she went on, her voice echoing shrilly in her skull like a mouse-squeak in a tomb.

At last Ashburton seemed to lose patience.

"For God's sake, Mrs. Adamson, will you drag it out for ever? Do you imagine that your ingenious husband, who married you to further his criminal career and almost certainly killed your father for the same reason, was going to retire with peanuts! His personal pension fund that he contrived to syphon out of the Schiller organization and that we suspect you know the location of amounted to just over twelve million pounds! *Twelve million pounds!*"

CHAPTER
2

She'd been wrong before when she thought she'd hit bottom.

Now here they were at last, the real depths. There was no lower deep waiting to receive her now. She was sunk beyond all hope of recovery, but also beyond all fear of any further fall. It shamed her that money should at last have been the key that opened the full truth to her, but she saw now that it had been money, Trent's money, Schiller's money, that had woven for her that warm, luxurious, drowsy nest where she had drowsed all those years, thinking herself safe from the dawn knock or the evening frost.

How kind they'd been, how unconsciously kind, those greedy calculating men who had withheld from her the money which should legitimately have been hers after Trent's death. With it, she would surely have simply contrived to build herself another cozy refuge from the outside world. Without it, she had been forced into life, into feeling, into decision. Not kind, but cruel! How cruel they had been!

But how right in their calculations! Had there been money available, any money from whatever source, to buy back her old oblivion, she would surely have gone scurrying towards it and taken them with her.

Was the disease cured even now? Twelve million pounds! It had taken the size of the sum to persuade her finally of

Trent's involvement in her father's death. What had seemed impossible, unthinkable, had suddenly become an unavoidable truth when she at last realized the rewards Trent had been playing for. What that told her about Trent was horrifying. What perhaps it told her about herself was horrendous. All that money, doubly stolen, the filthy profits of misery, pain and degradation, how would she have acted if indeed she had known where Trent had put it, if she had in fact discovered the secret of access to it? Janet had urged her to dip her hand into the Eric Blair account while she'd had the chance and perhaps on that second visit to the cash-point she might have done so. Would she then have been able to resist taking a tiny, unmissable slice off twelve millions? A little spoonful of interest? Surely whatever the stench that arose from the main deposit, the interest was clean?

It was nice to have a moral problem to wrestle with. It took her mind off her other much more concrete problems as she lay here in the dark, waiting.

It was a long wait. Ashburton had left her, presumably to confer with Usher. Perhaps he was taking his time in order to build up her fear. Or perhaps Usher needed the time to heat up the instruments of persuasion.

It suddenly occurred to her that before he left, Ashburton had made no attempt to retie her wrists, yet all this time she had been lying here, she had never thought to try the bonds about her ankles!

A huge self-contempt welled up in her, drowning for a moment the despair and horror which the little solicitor must have recognized as incapacitating beyond any physical restraint. So she must have appeared to Trent, passive beyond his requirements, not moving except at his gesture or command.

Yet this was not her nature. Surely if the past months had taught her anything, they had taught her that?

Her fingers scrabbled at the cord which bound her ankles, but it was too late. The door opened and Ashburton was in the room.

"Bothering you, are they?" he said sympathetically. "Here, let's have them off."

His little fingers worked more dextrously at the knots than

her own had managed and in a couple of seconds her feet were free.

"That better? Good. Come through into the kitchen for a moment, please, Mrs. Adamson."

She stood up and almost collapsed against the bed. Her left leg had gone quite dead without her being aware.

"Touch of cramp? Here, lean on me," said Ashburton solicitously. *Solicitously!* Well, he should be solicitous, shouldn't he? she thought madly as she limped through the doorway on his arm like a dowager making what might be her last entrance.

They went down the narrow passage and into the kitchen. She stopped on the threshold. Usher was sitting at the bare wooden table drinking from a mug. He scowled at her from under lowering brows and she felt a pang of fear, sharp as heartburn. At the same time she smelt coffee, and her fear had to give way to a strong lust for a taste of the pungent liquid.

"I expect you'd like a cup of coffee?" said Ashburton. "Mr. Usher, please."

"There's only one mug," growled Usher. Ashburton turned the blank of his spectacles on him and, after a moment, he rose ungraciously, went across to the old marble sink, flung the dregs of his coffee into it and refilled it from the percolator Trudi had recognized on her first visit. Once again she wondered whether it was sentiment or taste that had made Trent bring it. At least she knew now it could hardly have been economy!

That thought made her grimace a smile.

Ashburton said, "Feeling better now?"

He sat her down on the creaky wooden chair. Usher returned with the coffee, which he banged down before her like a disgruntled waitress. She seized it in both hands and, even though the liquid was thick, black and very hot, she drank deeply.

Ashburton sat opposite her. Usher returned to the sink and leaned up against it, regarding her with a cold speculation far worse than hate. The solicitor glanced towards him and said in a low voice, vibrant with concern, "Please, Mrs. Adamson. Tell us what you know. It will be best for everyone."

"I don't know anything," she said. "Most of all I don't know how much they need to pay a man like you to behave like this!"

He smiled. "I see your problem. No, I wouldn't get so *physically* involved for a mere honorarium, certainly not. But you haven't quite understood how things stand. You see, Mrs. Adamson, things are falling apart. True, to start with, I was working close with Dr. Werner and, by chain of authority, with the shadowy men in whose eyes the Schiller organization is but a small subsidiary of a huge business empire. They have grown impatient, or distrustful, I fear, and are taking a hand themselves. The shattering of the mirrors at Class-Glass was one of their ploys, I would guess. That was what persuaded Mr. Usher and I to start working for ourselves. You see, they know about us, but we know very little about them, which makes us expendable. So, like Trent before us, we've decided to get out with our own pension fund!"

Trudi felt very cold. She drank more coffee and tried not to think of the pain which must inevitably begin.

Ashburton said, "The positive side of this is that I am in a position to make firm offers without reference to any other party. Believe me, Mrs. Adamson, I'd be most grateful for any help you can give us. I mean, ask yourself seriously, what would you do with all that money? Wouldn't half a million satisfy all your foreseeable needs? We could easily spare you half a million. Properly invested, it would give you an income of around fifty thousand per annum. A good-looking widow with that kind of money could really enjoy herself, Mrs. Adamson."

"I can't help you," she said.

"A million. We could go to a million. You'd have your pick of life's good things with a million. All the pleasures of the high life, if that's what you wanted. Or perhaps a little hideaway somewhere, a place to be at peace in, safe from the trials and tribulations of this harsh world, perhaps that would be more to your taste."

"I don't know, Mr. Ashburton," she said. "I've grown quite fond of the trials and tribulations of this harsh world in the last few months."

"Have you now? Well, be that as it may. You're an intelligent woman, despite all your efforts to appear retarded, and you must be aware that there's a negative side to my offer."

Trudi glanced towards Usher and nodded.

"Quite right, my dear," said Ashburton. "Mr. Usher has some rather brutal ideas about persuasion. I'm a much more patient and reasonable man, however, and after a free and frank discussion, you'll be glad to hear that my point of view prevailed."

"I'll tell you in a minute if I'm glad," said Trudi.

"Quite simply, I think we can achieve the desired end of your cooperation just by locking you up till you change your mind."

"You mean, starve it out of me? Whatever *it* is, I mean."

"Something like that, my dear."

Trudi's mind was racing. If Ashburton really meant he was just going to lock her up and wait for hunger or thirst to break her will, that at least would give her time. To do what, she couldn't yet imagine. But there must be people out looking for her by now. Jan and James, to name but two. And they both knew about Well Cottage, Jan because she'd been here, James because she'd told him. There was no reason, of course, why they should look here to start with, but as time went by and they got more worried . . .

Just how much time *had* gone by? she wondered.

She glanced at her watch. It had stopped at ten-thirty, presumably at the time she'd been attacked. Ashburton caught her glance and said, "I see you've decided to spin matters out, Mrs. Adamson. Very well."

He leaned towards her and knocked on the table, three short raps, one long, the Morse V-for-Victory, the opening bar of Beethoven's Fifth.

"When you feel like talking, knock like that. It's best to have an agreed signal so we shouldn't have our hopes raised by any indiscriminate banging. Try it."

"I don't think I'll be needing it," said Trudi. "I know nothing, Mr. Ashburton. *Nothing*."

"We'll see."

Desperately she drained her mug. She was going to need every drop of sustenance she could get.

She stood up and began to walk towards the door.

"Mrs. Adamson," said the solicitor gently.

She halted and looked back at him.

"Yes?"

"Not that way."

"What?"

"You've misunderstood me, I think. It's not the bedroom we are going to lock you in."

He smiled as he spoke and glanced to his right. She turned her head to follow the gaze.

Usher had moved from the sink to stand beside the tall upright freezer which had housed Gerhardt Jünger's dreadful corpse. His hand was on the handle. As she watched he pulled and the door swung slowly open.

For a second her mind anticipated another corpse, but the freezer was completely empty, and in that same second, its gleaming white emptiness was suddenly the source of far greater horror than any contents no matter how grisly they could have been.

"No!" she screamed. But Ashburton had her left arm, and Usher was by her side grasping her right, and she felt herself lifted bodily off the ground and thrust into the freezer before she could scream a second denial.

"Remember. Dah-dah-dah-DUH!" said Ashburton.

And the door slammed shut, and gleaming white became pitch black.

She was screaming now, not words, but long high ululations of terror. She flung herself against the door and beat at it with her fists but there was not the slightest movement. Desperately she tried to pull herself together, to calm her trembling body and crash her freewheeling mind back into the gears of logical thought.

But her efforts were vain, or at best, counterproductive. For the subzero temperature was ready to shake her with cold if she managed to control her fear, and all that her reason could tell her was that she was likely to suffocate before she actually froze to death.

But it was the dark that was worst of all. Never before had

her eyes known a darkness so complete that no amount of blinking and straining could etch a visible shape in it. Her hands traced out shelf supports, corners, the interior light holder, but to her sight she was in total eclipse.

She slumped down till she was wedged in her narrow coffin. Her mind was trying to move away from the certainty of death to any hypothesis which involved life, but all she could come up with was that here at least corruption would be held at bay for a little while longer than usual. What was the recommended use-by period for fresh-frozen humans?

I'm making jokes! she realized. I'm freezing, suffocating, panicking, and I'm making jokes. That's something to be proud of, perhaps.

She essayed a laugh, drew in a long draft of freezing air, tried to gauge its oxygen content, decided it didn't much matter as it was taking the lining off her lungs anyway, and let it out in what wasn't a bad effort at a chuckle, all things considered.

I think, she told herself, I think I might bear all things if only I could see the sky again. Just once more. All I have to do is knock. Dad-dah-dah-DUH! Then I'll be out in the kitchen. And if I can get across to the sink and pull back that old scrap of curtain, I must surely get a glimpse (oh what I would give for a glimpse!) of that starry infinity, that airy openness. Suddenly all trace of her *old* terror had vanished. How easily could death be borne if it merely meant being sucked into that turbulent calm, that crowded emptiness!

But to die in this constricting box, this sterile coffin . . .

There was nothing to gain by staying in here.

She freed one arm, raised it to knock.

But there was something to lose by going out, wasn't there?

She tried to remember what it was, couldn't; raised her arm again to knock, couldn't. Was it act of will or simply physical incapacity? She didn't know. Somewhere inside she was beginning to feel warm. It was, of course, illusion; the mind's response to the extremity of cold which in the end kills kindly, anesthetizing the nerve endings it sinks its teeth into. Perhaps it wasn't going to be so bad after all. Perhaps before the blackness outside seeped completely into her being, this freezing airless tomb would be transformed into just such a snug and warm little nest as she'd spent the best part of her life in. Perhaps . . .

Light erupted before and behind her. She spilled out onto the kitchen flags. Ashburton stooped over her, spectacles shining like flying saucers.

She opened her mouth, couldn't speak, tried again, failed again.

"Yes?" he cried. "Yes?"

She managed a mutter.

"Louder!" he insisted. "I can't hear."

She drew in a breath. It didn't sear her lungs. Flexibility was returned to the muscles of her mouth.

She spoke.

"I didn't knock," she said. "I didn't knock."

He hit her then, a swinging punch to the side of her head. She rolled with it, but could not roll away from the sickening pain of it. She curled into a fetal ball but that brought no protection from the foot which drove viciously into the base of her spine, setting her rolling again. But there was no chance of evasion, and, having moved from threats to violence, the little solicitor seemed to have lost all control. He followed her round the room stamping and kicking, his teeth bared as he gasped with the effort and sweat smearing the gleaming blanks of his glasses. She tried to get to her feet but her right knee had gone and her leg folded under her. In any case, the effort was futile for she found she had collapsed against the legs of Usher, who had just come through the kitchen door.

He looked down at her without any discernible emotion and said to Ashburton, "I was right. There's a car down the lane."

"Hell. Who?"

"I couldn't see anyone. Might be nothing. Farmer up early to milk his sheep or something. But we ought to be ready."

What readiness consisted of was easy to see. He pulled a large automatic out of an arm holster. Trudi looked up at Ashburton and saw him produce a smaller version of the same. She felt approval. Little men shouldn't carry big guns.

"What about her?" said Usher.

"She'll keep. You're not going anywhere are you, my dear?"

A final kick in the ribs and they were gone. She heard a key turn in the door; it seemed an unnecessary precaution; she had no intention of ever moving again.

Minutes ticked by. At least she assumed they did. She had no machinery, internal or external, for measuring their ticking.

She sat up. It was unpremeditated. It didn't feel like a physical act at all. It wouldn't have surprised her to find she was having one of those out-of-the-body experiences and would soon find herself floating around the ceiling, looking down at her own poor battered frame.

A stab of pain from her spine to her head persuaded her she was still inside that poor battered frame. This time she had a decision to stand up. It wasn't quite as effective as the previous unpremeditated move, but she finished up on her feet, leaning on the kitchen table.

What now? She thought of shouting, tried it, decided not to bother. At best that pathetic squeak was going to bring either Ashburton or Usher in to shut her up permanently.

But whoever was out there had to be warned. Did they know the cottage was occupied or were they merely coming up here on spec? Or perhaps they had no interest whatsoever in the cottage; perhaps some perfectly innocent stranger was going to be sucked into this mess.

Whatever the case, any chance she had of survival must rest with whoever was out there.

She launched herself from the table and reeled across to the sink. Her left leg didn't seem to have any feeling at all, and her right had a great deal too much. She took hold of the square of flowered curtain and pulled it aside. No welcome light flowed in, not even the pale glimmer of night sky. Of course the shutters were up, those impenetrable metal shutters by which Trent had kept out any casual thief who might disturb his plans.

No wonder Ashburton had been happy to lock her in here.

At least she might find herself a weapon. She dragged open the drawer in the old wooden unit which boxed in the sink. Memory dragged open too. Nothing had changed since last she looked. A plastic spatula, a wooden spoon, a tin opener, and most ferocious of all, a cheap flimsy knife and fork which wouldn't need Yuri Geller to bend them.

She slid to the floor partly in despair, partly to look in the cupboard under the sink. Nothing had changed here either. One small saucepan and three spare cylinders of gas for the cooker. She slumped forward and let her head rest on the smooth, cool, dully shining surface of the cylinders. Why couldn't they be bombs? she thought in the crazy fantasy of despair. They looked like bombs, why couldn't a merciful God turn them into real bombs?

Suddenly she opened her eyes and jerked upright so fast she cracked her head on the roof of the cupboard. She ignored what was after all only a fractional increase in pain and reveled in a huge increase in illumination.

Bombs? Who needed a merciful God? Of course these cylinders were bombs! Her intuition had been right. Her craziness lay in denying it. Weren't they full of gas and wouldn't gas explode?

But how? But how?

She tried to drag one of the cylinders out of the cupboard but in her weakened state could hardly move it. That was no use. But yet again she realized that she wasn't thinking straight, or perhaps wasn't thinking laterally, which was more like it. The cylinders were in an ideal spot already, in a confined space beneath the heavy sink but with plenty of cracks in the cupboard for gas to seep slowly through.

She grasped at the wheel which controlled the valve on the nearest one and tried to turn it. Nothing happened. She tried again. Again nothing.

Oh Christ, she thought, *am I being the stupid little woman who doesn't even know how to change a fuse? Let me think. Which way to open, which way to shut?*

She concentrated on the thought of shutting off and turning on central heating radiators. Counterclockwise to open. And that indeed was what she had been doing here!

The triumph of being right gave her fingers new strength. She turned, the wheel moved. Again, and gas was hissing out.

The others were easier. She rose and closed the cupboard.

Then, using the remnants of her newfound strength, she dragged the table across and wedged it tight as it would go against the cupboard door.

Now what? To her surprise, she knew exactly what. She turned the jets in the oven on and closed the door. Then she switched on one gas ring, struck a match from the box which lay on the windowsill, and lit it.

Eventually something must happen. She didn't know how long it would be or how devastating. Perhaps it would be too late, or perhaps it would be too feeble. It didn't matter. She'd done her best. There was nothing more to do.

For the first time it occurred to her that if the effect were devastating, she was going to be the nearest thing to be devastated. Did it matter? Probably not. Samson must have felt like this when he got hold of the temple pillar.

Me Samson! she laughed. Then she became indignant with herself.

I should think not! He was a thick macho thug who got stitched up by a clever woman. What would Delilah have done?

The answer wasn't pleasant, but the longer she looked at it, the more she could see it was the only answer.

Also the longer she looked at it, the more chance there was it wouldn't do her any good anyway.

She staggered back to the freezer.

First thing was to turn it off. At least she wouldn't freeze to death.

Second thing was to fix it so it wouldn't lock itself on her.

She examined the handle and the catch, recalled reading that burglars did things with plastic credit cards but couldn't remember exactly what, and in any case she was right out of credit cards. Sod it! she would just have to use a simple wedge and hope for the best.

She tore off her blouse, twisted it into a shank, knotted it round the freezer door handle and stepped inside.

It was quite ingenious. By pulling on the blouse she could bring the door shut tight enough to give her some protection while at the same time the thick shank of cloth prevented the door from locking her in. She felt the pride of real achievement. Whatever else they said about her, they'd have to admit she'd been clever in this.

Now there was nothing to do but wait. At first she relaxed her hold on the blouse so that a crack of light ran round the door.

Then she started thinking about gas seeping in here with her and the possible effect when it finally ignited. This made her pull the door shut as hard as possible till the thin line of light vanished.

She was shivering violently. She assured herself it had nothing to do with terror. Even though the freezer was switched off, residual temperature was incredibly low and without even the flimsy protection of her blouse, her upper body was trembling with cold. How she longed now for that insulating flab which years of Viennese cream cakes had layered her with.

No I don't! she told herself sharply. All those layers of insulation—physical, emotional, economic—I'm better off without them! I'm like an old mural that's been coated by time and decorators and improvers till it's become an almost impossible task to strip off the addendae and reveal the original. Well, it may not be a masterpiece they've thinned me down to, but by God, it's genuine!

But such defiant thoughts can only be sustained for a short while, and Trudi soon found herself slipping into a frivolous rehearsal of her appearance before the great Judgment Throne in the sky, where, asked how she had spent her last moments on earth, she replied, "Shut in a freezer, waiting for a bang!"

Which was a long time coming.

She could not resist opening the door a fraction to take a peep.

Simultaneously she heard someone unlocking the kitchen door.

Oh no! she prayed. Not this! Not anticlimax. I've come so far, I've done so well. Don't take it all away from me now!

The door opened. Through her crack she saw Usher appear, his automatic still in his hand. In other circumstances the drama-school look of disbelief which twisted his face would have been comic. He peered twice around the room, then shouted, "Ashburton, for Christ's sake, the bitch has gone!"

A moment later the little solicitor appeared.

"Gone? That's impossible," he said.

His sharper eyes turned at once to the freezer and he laughed.

"Not gone," he said. "Just rehearsing the next stage, I think. Get back out there and keep watch. I'll take care of this."

He began to advance, but Usher was now also looking at what was there rather than simply at what wasn't.

"What's that table doing over there?" he said. "And why's that burner on?"

Ashburton halted and looked towards the cooker. Suspicion pinched his face like frost.

"Oh you cunning little bitch!" he cried as his sharp solicitor's mind leapt to a conclusion.

He turned towards the freezer once more, his eyes promising vicious retribution. Then, realizing that for once he'd got his priorities wrong, he turned back towards the cooker and hurried forward to switch off the burner.

Those two-seconds delay were fatal. His fingers reached the tap but they never turned it off. Trudi, leaning back in the freezer and pulling on her blouse with all her might in a last doomed effort to shield herself from Ashburton's rage, heard the explosion like the roar of a space shot and felt its impact on the metal box like the force waves as the rocket labors up from the gantry.

The first explosion was followed by a second larger one. Perhaps the oven had gone first, then the cylinders in the cupboard. Trudi started to shriek. She knew that shrieking could do no good but she felt like shrieking and didn't see why she shouldn't indulge herself this once.

After the explosions and after the shock waves came a silence. At least here in the freezer it was silent. She stopped screaming to listen to the silence. It was also dark, absolutely dark. And she realized that she was no longer pulling on the shank formed from her blouse, but holding it loose in her hands. She ran her fingers down it till she came to the frayed charred end.

She pressed her palms against the door and pushed. Nothing happened. She pushed again and it was like pushing at a wall of rock. She was beginning to feel like shrieking once more. Oh for weight! Oh for strength! Samson, I'm sorry for bad-mouthing you like that! she gasped internally.

And, flinging her whole body against the door, she felt it give, then slowly peel back from its magnetic strip and tumble like a gangplank straight before her.

It was early morning. A star-spattered sky was beginning to flush a pale peach at its cloudy edges. Birds, momentarily stilled by the rowdy human competition, picked up their parts again and resumed their song. All this was visible and audible through the ragged gap in the wall where the sink and cooker had been. There were flames too and a bit of smoke, but nothing to bother a traveler newly returned from the Underworld. Besides, these old stone houses didn't offer much sustenance for a greedy fire. But it seemed like a good idea to leave it to its feasting.

She walked forward, slowly, painfully, concentrating on keeping upright and not looking at the two sacklike objects her peripheral vision kept on insinuating into the corner of her eye. She got the impression that one of them had an old pot sink on top of it with a pair of little feet protruding like the Wicked Witch of the West's in *The Wizard of Oz*. The trouble with people who got what they deserved was their tendency to hang around afterwards and make you sorry about it.

She was out of the house now and standing knee deep in damp grass. She breathed deeply. It was the best breath she had ever taken in her life. It was the best sky, the best birdsong, the best damp grass. There were people running towards her, voices shouting. Their figures and voices were both obscured by the morning mist. Funny, she hadn't noticed the morning mist before.

Just before it came billowing up to smother completely her eyes and ears, she recognized the approaching figures as James and Jan. But when she opened her mouth to greet them, that let the mist right into the center of her being and they were scarcely in time to catch her as she fell.

PART NINE

Still, thou art blest, compar'd wi' me!
The present only toucheth thee:
But Och! I backward cast my e'e,
                    On prospects drear!
An' forward, tho' I canna see,
                    I guess an' fear!

BURNS: "To a Mouse"

CHAPTER
1

For the next forty-eight hours Trudi swam in and out of consciousness, like a dolphin soaring briefly through air before vanishing again into the sea.

It was partly the sedatives the doctors gave her, but choice played a large part too. She enjoyed those turquoise depths as long as they held nothing but shells and bones and silence.

Janet grabbed her on one of her forays above the surface.

"I had another couple of drinks after you left the hotel," she said. "All right, I let one of them toad-faces buy! I didn't feel like driving home just then. And suddenly I looked up and saw James coming into the bar. He told me you'd left a message on his machine saying you were here, I told him you'd gone off to his place. We soon got ourselves into a real tizzy, I tell you. We got into his car and went looking. Hope House, Class-Glass, round and round. Nothing. I rang Ashburton, thinking he might have seen you after you left. When *he* didn't answer either, I didn't know what to think. He was such a little weed, you couldn't really think any harm of him. Shows how wrong I usually am about men, doesn't it? It was then I went to the police. Not that they showed much interest, asked if you'd been drinking, asked if *I'd* been drinking! Sauce. James got a bit of a grip of them but I couldn't see them doing much before daylight. It was then I thought of Well Cottage. Seemed a long shot, but there was nothing else to shoot at. So out we came. When we saw a car parked outside, we started scouting around like a pair of Indians, I tell you. Then boom! suddenly war breaks out, the place goes up like a bomb. And then, like a bloody miracle it was, out of that hole in the wall, through the smoke and the flames, you come walking like you're strolling over the lawn at a garden party. You were smiling, girl, bloody well smiling! I could have wept."

Trudi smiled again and slipped back under. There were a couple of wrecks down there this time, old lives lying on their sides with their bare ribs open to the waters, the fish, and any curious mermaid.

James Dacre caught her next.

"Trudi," he said. "Darling. I was wild with worry. I should never have left you by yourself. It's not going to happen again, I promise you that. Trudi, I love you, I really do. Say you'll marry me, say it!"

But Trudi was away with a back-flip and speeding down cliffs of pink coral in search of sunken treasure.

When she next broke surface, Herr Jünger was sitting by the bed.

"*Guten Tag*, Frau Adamson," he said heavily. "A few points to clear up."

She didn't want to hear more and submerged instantly. Only this time the water seemed darker and not so warm as it had been, and something came floating slowly along, tumbled by invisible currents and nuzzled by hungry fish, and as it rolled by her she saw it was the body of Gerhardt Jünger.

She burst back into the air, gasping for breath.

Jünger did not seem to have noticed her absence.

"Schiller-Reise is in the control of the courts and has ceased to do business," he was saying. "Most of its executives are in police custody for interrogation, as are several of its foreign representatives in their particular countries. It will be a long job to sort out the innocent from the guilty. Meantime we will assume they are all implicated equally."

"That's a large assumption," said Trudi.

"You think so? I found no problem with it," said Jünger, genuinely puzzled.

"In England, things are done differently."

"You tell me so?"

Jünger glanced across the bed and Trudi realized for the first time that Inspector Workman was in the room also. He smiled and nodded at her.

Jünger said, "In your statement, you said that Ashburton definitely implicated Dr. Werner."

Trudi was amazed. She had no recollection of having made a statement. Clearly there had been other visits to the surface which had gone unrecorded in her mind. But not, it seemed, in Jünger's notebook.

"What has happened to Werner?" she asked.

"He went suddenly on a study visit to South America," said Jünger gloomily.

"What? No assumption of guilt?"

"We had no evidence of direct links with the Schiller organization, only suspicion," said Jünger. "And your husband had been most assiduous in his refusal to implicate him."

"I suppose he thought that once he did that, you would wind the whole thing up, including him," mocked Trudi. "Perhaps he didn't trust you. I can't say I blame him."

"What do you mean?"

"You've misled me pretty consistently, haven't you?" she accused.

"We were not sure of your role," he said unapologetically.

"And you're sure now?"

He didn't answer and Trudi laughed.

"So you *can* be honest, Herr Jünger. You really did think I knew where the money was, the twelve million! Well, I didn't, and I don't. Do you?"

Jünger said, "It is possible Werner found out. It is possible it is in South America and he intends to buy himself security there."

"Tell me, Herr Jünger, what would have happened to all that money if you *had* recovered it?"

Jünger looked at her surprise and said, "It would have been confiscated to the State, naturally."

"And the State would have done what with it?"

"Surely you know what States do with money, Mrs. Adamson?" said Workman, speaking for the first time.

"With twelve million? Well, the British State would probably buy an American missile, or build another motorway for Euro-juggernauts, or give the top twelve hundred earners ten thousand pounds worth of tax relief each."

Workman sighed and said, "You've changed, Mrs. Adamson. Or perhaps you haven't. Your husband was also a lover of George Orwell, wasn't he? But that didn't stop him from being a nasty, ruthless crook making money out of drugs and degradation, did it?"

Trudi regarded him steadily but she wasn't really seeing him. She was examining herself for hurt, or resentment, or guilt, or shame.

She found herself quite pleased with the result of the examination.

She said briskly, "You're absolutely right, Inspector. But being absolutely right doesn't make you absolutely guiltless, does it? Any responsibility I personally have for these things I will expiate personally. I do not need your help any more, I suggest, than you really need mine. Perhaps if either of you wish to talk with me again, you will give me sufficient notice so that I can have a legal adviser present."

"Like Mr. Ashburton?" said Workman maliciously.

"Mr. Ashburton was, I recall, remarkably complacent about his relations with the local police," said Trudi sweetly. "Good day."

She closed her eyes and kept them closed till she heard them leave the room.

When she opened them, she found James Dacre had taken Jünger's place.

"I've been waiting for them to go," he said. "Is everything O.K.?"

"Why?"

"They didn't look happy."

Trudi laughed and said, "Then everything's O.K."

He smiled uncertainly.

"Trudi," he said.

"Yes?"

"What about us?"

She said, "Shall I tell you something, James? When I was lying there in Well Cottage, trussed up like a chicken on the bed, waiting for someone to come and wring my neck, I was half convinced that it was Trent who was going to come into the room. The half that wasn't convinced it was Trent knew for certain it would be you."

"Me?" he said reflectively.

"Yes. I'd got it all worked out. There'd been a break-in at the Lewis Agency the weekend before you registered. Mrs. Fielding said that some small items had been stolen, but that the records were completely safe. Well, she would say that, wouldn't she? Or perhaps she thought she was telling the truth, but a real professional could probably unlock a filing cabinet and leave no trace, wouldn't you say!"

"To what end?" said James Dacre.

"To look into some silly woman's file, see what she was shopping for, and come up with the required goods, perfectly packaged, a couple of days later. An introduction so random it could not possibly be suspect."

"But why should anyone . . ."

". . . want to meet me? Good question, if not very gallant! All kinds of people have been keen to meet me recently for all kinds of reasons. Why not one more?"

"Trudi, you're not being serious about this, are you? Even if you were once upset enough to have such a crazy idea, surely we've gotten close enough for you to know how I feel . . ."

"Oh yes," said Trudi. "I think I do know how you feel, James. And I know how I feel too."

He reached forward and took her unresisting body in his arms.

"That's all that matters, surely? Whatever happens, I love you, I need you, I want you to be with me, always. Forget these crazy ideas. Trudi, I love you . . ."

He kissed her. She responded with equal passion for a while, then pushed him away.

"Not in a National Health bed," she said. "And no, don't press me, James, not in any sense. From now on, I'll be making all my decisions vertically. But one thing's certain.

I've had my fill of surprises, about other people and about myself. My New Year resolution, backdated, is that I won't make a move without knowing all the available facts. Now why don't you run along? I'm beginning to feel quite well after that little interlude. I think I might try a turn round the room, and I'd prefer not to have witnesses if I fall on my face!"

He didn't argue but went to the door. Here he paused, his expression closed, unreadable.

"I envy you, Trudi," he said unexpectedly.

"*Me?*" she said in genuine astonishment. "What on earth for?"

"Because you're finding you're strong enough to face up to things. That's a rare and enviable talent. Only . . ."

"Yes?"

"Don't run before you can walk."

He left. Trudi lay in bed, puzzled and uneasy. She had never been paid the compliment of envy before and was taken aback to feel it like a threat.

"*Will* you marry him?" asked Janet.

"Possibly," said Trudi into the phone.

"That doesn't sound very positive."

"Well, I've only been on my feet for a few days," said Trudi enigmatically. "How's domestic life with you?"

Janet had returned to Frank in an effort to repair relations between them.

"All right," said Janet doubtfully. "He keeps looking at me askance, there's no other word for it. It was quite fun being treated like the Great Whore of Babylon at first, but it begins to pall after a while."

"Well, you can't blame him. That picture! It wouldn't have been so bad in the missionary position with your eyes closed!" said Trudi, laughing.

There was a silence.

"Trudi, are you all right?" said Janet finally.

"Apart from being very hard-up and close to eviction, I'm fine. Why?"

"You just sound . . . I don't know . . ."

"Because I can laugh about that photo? What do you want

me to do, girl? Don't think I've stopped thinking what you did was really shitty. And if you ever did anything like it again, I'd claw your eyes out, believe me. You're on probation! That understood, I can laugh. O.K.?"

"O.K.," said Janet. "O.K. Listen, how hard-up are you? I've got a bit put by. If I loan you some money, then you'll have to like me, won't you?"

"I like you, I like you," said Trudi. "And I'll bear it in mind. But it's not necessary just yet. I'm selling up the last of Trent. I got diverted last time by finding those bankers' cards, but this time I'm clearing out the lot."

"Including Orwell."

"Including Orwell. And when I've spent all that, then I'll probably come running."

She'd almost changed her mind about selling the books by the time the dealer came to the house. She'd done better than she expected with the watches. Rolex, like Rolls-Royce, evidently held up well in the secondhand market. But there seemed no harm in getting a valuation at least.

Mr. Murtagh, the dealer, was short, stout, pebble-glassed and yellow-waistcoated, easy to imagine in the shady mustiness of an old bookshop. His advertisement had promised expertise in the fields of antiquarianism, topography and rare editions.

"If I could inspect the volumes," he said after accepting the offer of a cup of tea.

Trudi unlocked the cabinet.

"Help yourself," she said.

When she came back he was well into his task of inspection and note-making.

"Won't be long," he said. "Oh, here, this will be yours."

The book he'd just picked up, which was *1984*, had opened at a point where a folded sheet of paper had been inserted.

Trudi took it, opened it and felt her head swimming.

"Excuse me," she said with amazing calmness. "Do have some tea when you're ready."

She went out into the dining room and sat down at the table.

The paper was half-covered in writing. There was no heading, no date, but it began *Dear Trudi* and the hand was Trent's.

She took a deep breath and began to read.

> *Dear Trudi,*
>
> *If it works, I'll be dead in theory, alive in Brazil, and you'll never read this.*
>
> *If you do, then it hasn't worked and I'm really dead. By daylight there's no reason why it shouldn't work, but at four in the morning, it all seems mad fantasy. Not just the plan either. Midday, I feel quite chuffed with myself and reckon I've come a long way for a poor orphan boy from the East End. Midnight, I don't seem to have moved at all, and all I want to do sometimes is what I wanted to do then, which was curl up small and warm under the scratchy blankets and go to sleep and never have to come out into the cold unloving world again.*
>
> *I've envied you all these years, Trudi. Nothing ever seemed to bother you. You never got anxious or inquisitive over anything. I often wondered if you didn't know exactly what I was up to and just didn't care! So I've not got many qualms about my plan as far as you're concerned. It'll be a shock, but not much of one. I'm no great loss, there'll be plenty around to point that out. And with a bit of luck, you'll be with Jan when you get the news, so that'll help you over the first shock.*
>
> *As for the people who'll come sniffing around after I've gone, they'll have lots to tell you about me, I shouldn't wonder. Don't bust a gut trying to work out what's true. Just remember one thing, whatever they say about me, they're as bad, most of 'em! Don't trust anyone, especially if they say they're my friend. I've got no friends. And don't be taken in by so-called professional qualifications. Lawyers, doctors, cops, they're all after one thing. Money. Well, it's what I was always after too. Onward and upward, per ardua ad astra, local lad makes good!*

I sometimes wish I'd never seen an aeroplane. I sometimes wish I'd never stirred east of Ilford or west of Bethnal Green.

Now, money

There it stopped.

There, thought Trudi, he heard me coming down the stairs, and stopped writing and slipped the sheet into the book.

He knew it was safe there. He knew that if his plan worked, he'd have the Orwells with him. That's why he said he was thinking of showing them to a dealer in Manchester when he took me over to see Jan.

That was when he planned to do it. When he was supposed to be coming to collect me. Somewhere high up on the Snake Pass. Knowing I'd be safe with Jan.

She began to cry. Tears flowing unstoppably, she examined why she was crying. And discovered it was relief. Up to this point, unspoken but ineradicable, there had been the conviction that Trent's plan had involved killing her too, leaving her body in the car with Jünger's as additional verification.

But she'd been wrong. In many many ways.

"Mrs. Adamson!"

She rose, wiped her eyes, studied her face in the mirror over the fireplace, thought *What the hell!* and went through to rejoin Mr. Murtagh.

"I'm finished," he said. "It's an interesting little collection, less likely to be purchased as a whole than as individual items, so that's how I've priced it. Here's what I could offer, and I've rounded up the total as you can see, in case you wish to sell the lot."

She took the sheet of paper he offered her. On it in an ornate, not very legible hand were written the book titles with notes of publisher and condition alongside and a very clearly printed price.

She ran her eyes down the list, paused at *1984*. The letter had been in *1984*, hadn't it? And on that doodle of Trent's she'd found in the bureau in Vienna, there'd been a reference to *1984*. Was he trying to tell her something? No. That was absurd. The paper in the bureau had been there for ages from the look of it. There could be no connection.

She said, "You haven't made a note of the ISBN's. Isn't that important?"

"It would be if these volumes had them," he said dryly. "It would mean they were worth next to nothing. Standard Book Numbering didn't start till 1967, so first editions of a man who died in 1950 would certainly not have them."

"Later editions, though?"

"Oh yes. Reprints after 1967, certainly after 1970 when it became International SBN, would have them."   -

"Excuse me," said Trudi.

She went upstairs, leaving Mr. Murtagh rolling his eyes behind his pebble glasses in wonderment at the mysterious ways of womanhood.

It took her a few moments to find the piece of paper. Downstairs she showed it to Murtagh.

"The edition of *1984* referred to here, was a copy of it in my husband's collection?"

"There was only the first edition," he said looking at the writing dubiously. "ISBN 55 683421067 BE. That doesn't sound like any ISBN I've ever come across, I'm afraid. Might be a translation, of course. Some foreign edition, but it doesn't sound right."

"Translation?" said Trudi.

"Yes." Murtagh returned the paper and said, "About the collection . . ."

"Thank you. I'll let you know."

The book dealer looked rather disgruntled as he left, but Trudi didn't notice. She was back in the lounge before he'd opened his car door, looking at the two sheets of paper she now possessed in Trent's hand.

"Translation," she murmured.

"I was trying all kinds of daft things," she told Janet over the phone. "Like trying to prove Bacon wrote Shakespeare by working out a code!"

"I didn't know that!"

"Shut up! I knew Trent did crosswords and things and that led me to be too complicated. Then it struck me. *1984*. He'd used that as his cash-card personal number, but reversed. Suppose that's what he'd been doodling. His personal number. And if 1984 really means 4891, then ISBN 55 683421067 BE might mean EB 760124386 55 NBSI!"

"Gosh!" said Janet with heavy sarcasm. "You've really cracked it! I mean, it's so obvious! How did I miss it? I mean, what the hell are you on about, girl?"

"Don't you see?" said Trudi impatiently. "EB. That's Eric Blair. Then a number. Ashburton reckoned the money would be in a numbered account somewhere and that's what this sounds like."

"And NBSI?"

"That's the easiest of all when I see it that way round. When we lived in Zürich, I used to see those initials every time I wrote a check. Don't you remember when you went through Trent's papers? All those banks, and the Zurich one was *die Neue Bank Schmidt-Immermann*—NBSI!"

"But we checked all those accounts," objected Janet. "They'd all been closed as you and Trent moved onward and upward, or downward as it now appears."

"Of course they had. They were all ordinary day-to-day current accounts in Trent's real name. This was different. Trent would want somewhere to put away all the unofficial earnings he was making, wouldn't he? What better place to use than a discreet Swiss bank that he knew and trusted. Not in his own name, of course. He didn't trust them *that* much! That was probably when Eric Blair appeared. And it would amuse Trent a lot when he realized that he could reverse the bank's initials to ISBN and give himself a safe aide-memoire. So when he started robbing Schiller a couple of years ago, he had the setup there already. He didn't have to risk leaving traces by starting something new. And the use of Blair's name and the 1984 code in Sheffield just naturally followed on!"

"Well, it's a very pretty theory," said Janet, her voice full of doubt.

"Theory nothing. I've rung the Neue Bank Schmidt-Immermann. I've told them who I am, that my husband, alias Eric Blair, is dead, and that I would like to get my hands on the money. They have invited me to attend in person with proof of identity, evidence of Trent's death, and details of the alleged account."

"*Alleged?* Huh!"

"They're not going to admit it's there till they're sure I'm entitled," said Trudi.

"And will you go?"

"I'm all booked, aren't I?"

"By yourself? I mean, what about James? Have you told him?"

"Not yet," said Trudi. "Not yet."

CHAPTER
2

It was a piebald day, with a blustery wind scattering patches of sun and shade all over the countryside.

Trudi sat in the departure lounge at Manchester Airport and waited for her flight to be called.

"Trudi! Hi!"

It was Janet, slightly breathless, but with not a hair out of place in her elegant coiffure. She wore what looked like a brand-new-model suit in a rich dark green that clung to her figure like moss to a young birch tree.

"You look gorgeous," said Trudi.

"We like to please. No James, then?"

"You sound certain. He could be in the loo."

"I checked at the flight desk," grinned Janet. "You don't think I'd play gooseberry, do you?"

"Gooseberry. You mean . . ."

"I'm coming with you!" she cried, producing a ticket. "You don't think I'm letting you loose after all that money by yourself, do you?"

If she'd expected delight from Trudi, she was disappointed.

"All right," she said. "What's the matter?"

"Nothing," said Trudi. Then she added, "Look, Jan, if you've got some notion of looking after me . . ."

"No bloody fear!" retorted Janet. "I've seen what *that* leads to. You're on your own. Except . . ."

"What?"

"This time I thought I'd like to be right on the spot when a bit of money swims into your reach."

"All right," said Trudi. "You can come."

"Well, thank you kindly."

"What did Frank say?"

"Don't know," said Janet. "I left him a note."

"Saying what?"

"Saying I wasn't cut out for the rôle of golf widow and perpetual penitent, so I was taking off till the Pope's three-wood started sprouting twigs."

"Oh dear. Listen. That's our flight, I think."

They gathered their things together and made for the departure gate.

"And what did James say?" asked Janet.

"Don't know. I left him a note too," said Trudi.

"Oh. What did *you* say?"

"Not much. I told him where I was going, and why, and when I expected to be back."

Janet said no more till they were seated, belted, extinguished, and taxiing along the runway.

"You're living dangerously, you realize that, I hope. He won't wait around forever. How long will you keep him waiting?"

"Forever, if it takes that long to be sure."

"Good God, girl! I don't mind you being choosy, but you can go too far. What do you want the poor sod to do? Pass a written test?"

"Yes," said Trudi thoughtfully. "I rather think I do. For starters. Look, Jan, it's not easy judging people and I've discovered I've no talent for it. Look at Trent. I thought he was the Rock of Gibraltar and you thought he was a cocky little chancer. And what was the truth of it? He turns out to have been even more screwed up than I was. It was just our reactions to the big nasty world that were different. While I hid in my corner he put a brave face on and ran boldly out to nibble at the cheese!"

"You'll be sorry for him next!" said Janet.

"Perhaps. But not as sorry as I'd be for me if I made the same mistake again."

"James doesn't seem screwed up to me."

"No? Well, there's all kinds of screwed up. I like James. But I need to be sure I know all about him. Otherwise, after my experience, you get to wondering . . . well, I told him that I got to wondering. He knows how I feel, I think. We'll just have to see. Whoops! Here we go!"

The engines climaxed. The runway markers glided by till they formed a continuous line and the gray concrete surface was smudged by their speed. Then suddenly the ground began to dwindle and slow down and they were floating on air.

Janet peered out at the matchbox view.

"You know," she said thoughtfully. "We must be a great disappointment to Mrs. Fielding."

"I don't know," said Trudi. "Perhaps she left Mr. Fielding a note."

They laughed together as the plane broke through a layer of thin cloud into the rich-blue, high-arched, sunlit empyrean.

They were still laughing, though not at the same joke, as they landed in Zürich.

Trudi had booked in at the modest but comfortable Hotel Rosengarten on Bleicherweg, a long way from the district where she and Trent had lived. This was not going to be a nostalgic return.

Janet managed to get a room on the floor above. They gave themselves an hour to shower and change, then met in the bar for a drink. Despite Trudi's reluctance to take trips down memory lane, Janet insisted she be given a guided tour of the city center. She made it as neutral as possible, pointing out the sights as they strolled through the streets and down the quays. And she was careful to pick a restaurant she'd never been in before for their meal. Chance favored them. The food was good, the service excellent and the wine more plentiful than they intended.

As they returned arm in arm to the Rosengarten, Janet suddenly became serious.

"This money, Trudi. If you *can* get your hands on it, what are you going to do with it?"

"What would you do?"

"I don't know. All money's filthy lucre, right? But some's filthier than others. I don't much like where this lot has been, do you?"

"It's been in the bank."

"You know what I mean," said Janet with tipsy earnestness.

"Do I? I suppose by the same token, everything I've ever possessed or enjoyed has been contaminated?"

"Don't be daft! Trent had a real job, earned real money. It might have been a cover, but he had to do the bloody work, didn't he? And this life of sodding luxury you led! All right, so you were never short of a bob or two, but you were pretty easy pleased, weren't you? No motor yachts or private jets; and you didn't exactly end up laden with gold and jewels, did you? Unless you're one of those way-out ladies who's got diamond-studded labia."

"Janet!"

"No? Pity. I've always wondered about that. Anyway, as I was saying, this lot's different, isn't it? This really is the nasties. People suffered, and were degraded, and died, to spew out this lot."

Trudi didn't reply. They strolled on in silence for a while, then Janet said, "Cat got your tongue?"

"Don't know any cats, do I?" said Trudi. "Know a mouse though. Not a dormouse. Church-mouse, maybe. Or perhaps a chapel-mouse from the sound of her!"

"Chapel or church, girl, makes no difference. Right's right, and there's an end!" said Janet, very Welsh, very fierce.

"And here's our hotel. Let me buy you a nightcap. How about a champagne cocktail?"

"You can't bribe me!"

"No? And where precisely would modom like her diamond studs then?"

Janet collapsed giggling in the revolving door and the receptionist gave her a glance which said clearly that it wasn't just British soccer fans that should be barred.

They had their drink, then headed for bed.

"What time's your appointment?" asked Janet as they parted.

"Eleven-thirty."

"Oh, good. Time for a late breakfast. Nine-thirty shall we say?"

"Fine. Good night."

"Good night."

As Trudi got ready for bed, she wondered if she should be alarmed at the ease with which the lie had slipped out. Her appointment at the bank was for ten o'clock. By the time Janet came down for breakfast, she'd be on her way. It was very important for her to go to the bank alone. She knew Janet would understand this in retrospect, but in advance deceit had seemed easier than explanation.

She slept badly. Food, drink, and nervousness at the prospect of her morning appointment combined to set her mind and stomach churning. At last, about five A.M., she felt a blessed drowsiness slipping over her. He last thought was that she hoped the alarm call she'd booked for eight would be persistent enough to rouse her.

She awoke at the first ring, picked up the phone, said thanks, replaced it, yawned, rolled over in bed, and gaped her mouth wide in a silent shriek.

Seated in the room's easy chair at this side of the bed was a man. He looked very much at ease. But then, he'd had the practice, hadn't he?

Slowly she let her mouth close, letting out her breath in a gentle sigh.

"Good morning, Mrs. Adamson," said the man.

"Good morning, Dr. Werner," said Trudi.

PART
TEN

The best laid schemes o' Mice an' Men,
Gang aft a-gley, . . .

BURNS: "To a Mouse"

CHAPTER
1

"**B**efore we plan our day, you might like to make a phone call," said Werner. "Room 407, I think it is."

Trudi picked up the phone, asked for 407, listened.

The receiver was lifted. No one spoke.

She said, "Jan?"

Suddenly her friend's voice came on, breathless, scared but fighting for control.

"Trudi, what the hell's happening? there's a man . . ."

The line went dead.

"That's the situation then, dear lady," said Werner. "I'm so glad you brought your friend. I was uncertain how best to proceed till I saw her. Now we can make our arrangements in an atmosphere of mutual respect and cooperation. I'll make some coffee while you dress, shall I?"

He busied himself at the coffee machine. Trudi went into the bathroom, her mind unable to deal with anything except the thought of Janet. She washed, returned to the bedroom, got dressed with the unselfconsciousness of the totally preoccupied, and sat down on the bed.

"Coffee," said Werner handing her a cup. "And a croissant? I didn't think you'd want to go to the dining room, so I took the liberty of buying a couple of croissants on my way here."

"No, thanks," said Trudi.

"Please," insisted Werner. "We don't want to faint, do we?"

"What's he doing to Janet? Who is it with her?" demanded Trudi on a rising note.

"Be calm, Mrs. Adamson. Just a friend. No harm will come to anyone as long as we all keep our heads. All you have to remember is that I am now your financial and legal adviser. I have full accreditation here," he said, tapping an elegant maroon leather document case at his feet. "And have no fear. My name and my title remain the same, and it's all quite genuine! You did not know I was a doctor of law as well as medicine? Ah yes, in the old days I would have been addressed as Herr Doktor Doktor Werner! But such archaic usage will not be necessary at the bank when you turn to me for advice."

"What do you think's going to happen there?" demanded Trudi. "They're not going to pack a suitcase full of used notes, are they?"

"I think not. No, it's all done by microchip nowadays. There will be three stages. One: You and I will establish our credentials. Two: You will issue your instructions. Three: We will return here and wait for a phone call confirming those instructions have been carried out. And then we'll say goodbye, Mrs. Adamson."

"Instructions? What instructions?"

"Simply to transfer the money to another account in the merchant bank of Shelley and Cable in the City of London. Very natural that you should want your money at home. And Shelley's, though one of the younger merchant banks, has a good reputation for soundness of funds and sharpness of investment."

"But I don't have an account at Shelley's."

"Oh, you do, my dear. In fact, you've had one for a little while. It was opened for you on my instruction after Trent's alleged death. There was in fact a good deal of money due to you from Schiller-Reise. Though for your benefit there had to seem to be none, for the benefit of the firm's legitimate accountants the money had to be seen to be paid. This is always the quandary of the left hand knowing what the right is doing, but not vice-versa. I need hardly say, however, that the account is not just in your name, but that I myself have legal access to it. The money your husband embezzled will remain in Shelley's only long enough to register on their computer. Then it's on to . . . well, best that you don't know its final destination."

"Brazil?"

"Perhaps," smiled Werner. "Incidentally, I'm sure it's unnecessary to add that that part of the account which is yours by right of widowhood will not of course be touched."

"Ah. You only murder children, not rob widows?"

"That's how you see it? Well, it's a point of view. I can understand how you feel, of course. In my area of work, I've seen so many very very sad cases. It's a terrible problem and I'm conscious of how little progress we've made toward its solution. But I pride myself that I've made a not insignificant contribution myself . . ."

"You!"

"Why, yes," said Werner indignantly. "In my work at the clinic."

"You must be slightly mad!" mocked Trudi.

"I hope not. What I've been working to achieve is dependency without deterioration. Drugs provide a real way out of the terrors and traumas of modern life. Visit any psychiatric hospital. You will soon realize that what I say is true. I wish I had my clinical tapes here. I would let you hear for yourself how many of my patients claim that their first experience of drugs made them feel *whole* for the first time in their lives. I'm surprised that you were never tempted, Mrs. Adamson. All those fears and uncertainties and doubts and hesitations and regrets, all to be smoothed away! To be calm and confident and serene! Is this not worth a risk or two? Is this not a gift a scientist might find worth giving?"

Did I say *slightly* mad? thought Trudi. He's utterly insane!

But this time, because she was starting to believe it, she didn't say it.

She glanced at her watch.

"There's still a little time before we need go," he said. "Please. I know how the human mind works. These are dangerous, the moments of waiting. There is such a strong pull towards sudden desperate action. Remember your friend who is also waiting. And remember, Mrs. Adamson, it is only money we are concerned with. Why should you risk yourself for mere money, which I do not believe in any case you would be allowed to keep?"

"Who'd stop me?"

"The law, perhaps. Or your own conscience." He shrugged. "Failing that, it would probably be taken from you by force."

"By force? Like you're doing, you mean."

"Oh no," he said. "You've already had a taste from Ashburton of what a man will do for his money. Please believe me, there are others beside whom Ashburton was a kind, gentle, innocuous creature."

"Others? Haven't the police rounded up most of the others?"

"Most of the Schiller people perhaps. But the organization was not an independent free-standing thing. Once perhaps. In the fifties and early sixties as it grew. But in business as in the jungle, you either eat or are eaten. Ah, I see you do know something of this?"

He's very sharp, thought Trudi, who had been casting her mind back to what Ashburton had told her. *I'll have to watch that.*

"Something Ashburton said," she replied. "What was he talking about? The Mafia, that sort of thing?"

Werner smiled sadly. With his fine features and distinguished graying hair, he was a rather attractive man.

"If I knew who I was talking about, I think I might be too frightened to talk," he said. "Ignorance gives me a kind of courage."

"Courage?" echoed Trudi. "You mean that having the money will put you in danger too?"

"Having it? No. Having the effrontery to have it, yes. You see, when a business folds, the major shareholders think they're entitled to lay claim to its assets. These people think that this is *their* money. They don't actually need it. Twelve million here or there doesn't much concern them . . ."

Trudi closed her eyes at this point. She recalled her amazement when Ashburton had been so dismissive about the quarter-million in the Blair account. Now here was someone referring to twelve million in the same way. Where could it end?

". . . but what does concern them is being seen to get their due. It's a matter of principle with them."

"Principle!" choked Trudi. "Well, if it's so dangerous, why are *you* taking the risk, Dr. Werner?"

"Because I *do* need the money," he said vehemently. "I need it to reestablish my work in . . . where I'm going. Now I think it is time for us to go, Mrs. Adamson. Remember, keep your head, if in doubt ask my advice—it will seem the most natural thing in the world—and soon you will be safe, and your friend will be safe, and all this danger you're in will have passed to me."

"Doctor, you're too kind," said Trudi.

They went out of the hotel together—a middle-aged woman of means, well dressed, well groomed, cool and collected; her professional adviser, smooth, elegant, sophisticated, deferential without sycophancy, concerned without involvement.

They took a taxi. In it Werner studied the various documents that Trudi had brought with her at the bank's request. Familiar with them, he placed them in his smart leather case.

At the bank, he paid off the taxi with an accountant's tip, a precise ten percent.

"Remember . . ." He hesistated in his admonition, as if uncertain what it would best suit his purpose for Trudi to remember.

"Remember, it's only *money*," he said finally.

The bank was a rather curious building. To reach it you had to walk across a cobbled patio adorned with a quincunx of modern statuary, four tapered aluminum tubes in the corners all inclined towards a cast-iron spiral in the center, which egregious arrangement purported to represent the Spirit of Enterprise. The bank itself had a ground and first floor which belonged to the cobbles and two further floors which belonged to the tubes. In other words, two layers of plate glass rested incongruously upon a solid, granite-block, nineteenth-century base.

Inside, Trudi got that quiet, efficient, well-upholstered feel you get in the reception area of a first-class Swiss hotel.

Mention of her name brought a smiling young man in a severely cut dark suit who introduced himself as Herr Dietl, personal assistant to the manager, Herr Hussmüller.

They all shook hands and Dietl ushered them into a roomy mahogany lift, which sped them effortlessly upwards. When its doors opened, they'd traveled in time to a long bright corridor tiled in some modern mosaic, with one side lined by the huge plate-glass windows which, perhaps symbolically, looked down upon the Spirit of Enterprise.

They followed Dietl to an unmarked door. He tapped. A green light flashed in a panel above the lintel. Dietl opened the door and stepped inside.

"Herr Hussmüller," he said. "Mrs. Adamson and her adviser, Dr. Werner, to see you."

The stocky, graying man behind the huge desk rose slowly and offered his hand.

"Come in. Have a seat," he commanded.

Dietl made small adjustments to the two chairs already arranged before the desk and gestured for them to sit. He then went and stood behind and slightly to the right of Hussmüller's chair as the manager sank back down.

"Formalities first," said Hussmüller. "You have some documentation, I believe, Mrs. Adamson. And perhaps you too, Herr Doktor Werner, would favor us with some accreditation."

"Certainly, Herr Hussmüller," said Werner.

His case was on his knee. He glanced towards Trudi as he opened it, and smiled. Perhaps it was a smile of reassurance that she was doing well, Trudi thought. But it didn't feel like it. On the contrary, if a smile can convey hatred and threat, then this was it.

While she was still wrestling with the problem, Werner's hand came out of the case. In it was a small automatic.

With cool deliberation, he shot Dietl in the chest and Hussmüller through the shoulder. It was curiously undramatic, the gun belched gently rather than exploded, and Trudi's reflexes couldn't even produce a programmed scream as the weapon swung round towards her head.

"Bitch," said Werner. "Do you think I haven't checked to see what Hussmüller looks like?"

He could have killed her then, but he hesitated. Male chauvinist scruples? wondered Trudi whose mind was whirling madly as though in compensation for her paralyzed body. And just as she saw in his face that he'd been converted to the feminist egalitarian position, the door burst open.

The uniformed security guard, summoned by the alarm button at the foot of the manager's chair, took a bullet in the cheek and fell screaming. As though released by the sound, Trudi went diving for the protection of the solid-oak desk, crashing into the side of it with such force that for a second she was sure the snap shot Werner took at her diving body must have struck home.

He was coming after her, leaning over the desk to fire at point-blank range. She looked up at the contorted handsome face. The look of rage turned to pain as the courageous security man, who had struggled to his knees, launched himself at Werner's splayed legs and, more by luck than judgment, delivered a swinging uppercut to his crotch.

The doctor twisted round to club his attacker to the ground. Trudi, ignoring the pain in her shoulder, got to her feet and, grabbing at his thick, gray hair, pulled back with all her might.

And tore the top of his head off.

He turned to face her.

She looked in horror from the obscenely silken wig in her hand to the obscenely naked dome of Werner's skull. He could have shot her then, but the mad rage was perceptibly dying in his face, which without the wig looked nearer fifty than thirty. For a second they stared into each other's eyes.

Then he turned, clumsily hurdled the recumbent guard, and was gone. She heard his footsteps beating a tattoo along the tiled corridor.

Glancing at the wig, she said, "One up to Delilah."

A groan brought her back to her surroundings. The man in the manager's chair was still conscious.

"Herr Jünger, are you all right?" cried Trudi.

Jünger said something very obscene in German. Taking this as reassurance, she turned her attention to Dietl. He was slumped on the floor, gray-faced but still breathing, and the security man's moans told her that he had survived the second attack. She grabbed at the phone on the desk and screamed, "Ambulance! Quick!" at the astounded switchboard girl.

And now her mind switched from the violence she'd just witnessed to the possible violence to come.

"Janet?" she screamed at Jünger. "Is someone taking care of Janet?"

Jünger looked at her in bewilderment.

"Oh Christ! You don't even know!"

She ran out of the room now as if she hoped to pursue and apprehend Werner. There was no sign of him. Nor was the corridor full of alert policemen—just bewildered faces peering through half-opened doors.

Surely Jünger would have someone downstairs ready to stop Werner? But it wasn't Jünger's operation, was it? Not here in Switzerland. He'd probably used up all his influence to get agreement to his impersonation of Hussmüller, and now he was paying for that bit of vanity.

The Swiss police had a good reputation, though. They must be waiting below, ready to pick up the doctor if they saw him coming out alone.

Then she looked at the wig dangling like a hunting trophy in her hand and realized that she'd managed to give Werner the perfect disguise. Completely bald and aged fifteen years, he would only be spotted by the very sharpest of eyes.

She went to the great plate-glass window in the corridor and peered down, seeking some evidence of a police presence below, or the kind of excitement that would go with the arrest of an armed man. But cars drifted along the street and pedestrians moved across the cobbled patio with nothing in their speed or manner to indicate anything out of the ordinary.

And there he was, Werner, unmistakable to her alone, with his bald head gleaming against his dark-gray jacket, strolling casually away from the bank like any law-abiding citizen going about his business. Another few steps would take him onto the crowded sidewalk, and then he would be able to vanish into this populous city and ring his confederate at the Rosengarten Hotel with any instruction for Janet's fate he cared to give.

She should have rung the hotel herself and told them to block any calls to Jan's room! Instead she had acted like a lunatic, running out into the corridor on a ludicrous doomed attempt to overtake Werner.

It was still not too late. She was just turning away from the window when she saw a man step out from behind one of the tubes of Spirit of Enterprise. He moved right into Werner's path. Werner had to stop. They stood almost face to face. They seemed to be speaking, then the man began to walk away. He was wearing a nondescript trilby whose brim from Trudi's angle made it impossible to see his face. But now her attention was back with Werner. He too had started moving again, but in contrast with the others' measured steady stride, he was staggering obliquely, his hand against his breastbone. He got as far as the silver tube of the quincunctial sculpture. Here he paused, took his hand from his chest and rested it against the tube to support himself. Then he made one more effort, pushed himself upright, held the position for perhaps three seconds, and slowly sank to the ground.

On the gleaming aluminum surface Trudi could see quite clearly the print of his hand in dark red, already drying to russet.

She looked back now in search of the man in the trilby. He'd disappeared. No! There he was, sauntering gently towards the pavement crowded with people determinedly ignoring the midmorning drunk slumped against the Spirit of Enterprise.

In a moment he would step into the throng and vanish.

But now he hesitated. Now he turned round and stood, head bowed, face completely hidden, as if meditating some problematical course of action.

And suddenly, decision! He reached up, removed his hat with a flourish, and turned his face full to the window at which she stood. It must have been impossible for him to see her at that distance behind plate glass. But he would know, if she were there, that she could see him.

For the space of three seconds he stood. Then he replaced

his hat, turned, and was absorbed into the stream of pedestrians on the pavement.

There were people standing nervously over Dr. Werner now, but Trudi didn't watch them. Her eyes remained on the pavement, though she was not really seeing that either.

She had told James Dacre she had to know everything. And now she did.

They found Janet huddled in her bathroom clutching the tooth glass, which she had decided was a marginally more potent weapon than the toilet-plunger.

In her bedroom, neatly laid out on the bed, was a dead man with a bullet hole in the middle of his head. Even with this distraction Trudi was able to identify him as Dieter, the chauffeur from the Kahlenberg Klinik.

Janet couldn't throw much light on his killer. Dieter had ordered her into the bathroom and warned her to stay quiet. Some time later—she'd lost track of how long—there'd been a noise from the bedroom like a thick book being closed hard. Then a new voice at the bathroom door had commanded, "Stay in there!" in a tone she had neither cared nor dared to disobey.

There were tears on her face as she described her experience, but in the space of three large duty-free whiskies she passed from nervous collapse to righteous indignation.

"You knew, didn't you!" she yelled at Trudi. "It was a setup! You'd told Jünger about the bloody account and agreed to come across here in the hope that Werner would show up. And you never breathed a word!"

"I couldn't," retorted Trudi. "I tried to warn you off coming, but you're so damn pushy! I never thought you'd get involved . . ."

"That's been your trouble from the start, never thinking!"

"Don't give me that! It hasn't been my thoughtlessness that got you involved, it's been your guilt!"

"Guilt, is it? Well, let me disenchant you, girl. I don't feel guilty, I *never* felt guilty. Why *should* I feel guilty? I was doing you a favor. I was doing *him* a favor. For God's sake, looking back, I've spent the best part of my life doing ungrateful people favors!"

"Well, do me one now!" yelled Trudi. "Shut your big Welsh mouth and don't open it again in my presence except for drink or breath, both of which it seems to me are wasted on you!"

It was at this point that both women realized they'd stopped being angry and had started to enjoy the argument. Paradoxically the realization stopped them arguing, but stopped them enjoying it also.

"Oh Trudi, I was so scared."

"Not half as scared as I was," said Trudi. "Are you going to drink all that bottle, or do your friends get a spot?"

They drank and exchanged stories once more, Janet paying more attention this time to Trudi's perils and other people's pains.

"And Jünger and this man, Dietl, how bad are they?"

"Jünger will be bossing people around in a week or so. With Dietl it's more serious, but he should pull through. The guard too, though he has a fractured skull."

Janet shuddered.

"Some bedside manner that Werner had. How did he know you were coming to Zürich, Trudi?"

"There was a bug on my phone. The police found it when they put theirs on, but they decided to leave it there."

"And who the hell killed him, and why?"

"People," said Trudi vaguely. "People who don't like loose tongues or loose ends."

"This lot who were really behind Schiller, you mean? But they didn't get the money, did they?"

"No. They'd have liked it, of course. They'd have done a great deal to get it. I'm not really sure how much. But in the end they'll be happy to stop Werner getting away with it. Or Ashburton, or Usher. Or Trent. I suppose there's a sort of principle involved."

"God save me from principles like that! Well, what now?"

"Back to the U.K., I suppose. Sort out my pension."

"Your pension!"

"Oh, yes. It's all there at some merchant bank in the City. The twelve million may be filthy lucre and therefore untouchable by the morally pure like me and you. But I can't see any reason not to claim my pension. And if you can, I'd be grateful if you kept your big mouth shut!"

"Charming. And then?"

"And then I'd better start looking for somewhere to live. You wouldn't care to share a flat, would you?"

"In Sheffield?"

"Why not? It's a good center, so I've been told."

"Sounds a nice idea, " said Janet. "Long lease or short lease?"

"Oh, long, I would say."

"You've made up your mind about James, then?"

"I think so."

"But you said you'd wait till you had all the information."

"I think," said Trudi carefully, "that I've now got all the information I need, or am likely to get, to help me reach my decision."

Janet looked at her closely. Even all that Scotch didn't take the edge off those sharp Celtic eyes, but Trudi met her gaze with smiling candor.

"All right, girl," said Janet. "I'll let myself be satisfied with that. For now. But I hope you're not going to let Trent put you off men forever."

"I don't think so. Why should he?"

"Because, despite the sentimental memories you seem to be developing about him, because he was a Grade-A, pure-bred, unadulterated rat!"

Trudi considered this.

"Maybe," she said. "Only I think maybe he only passed for a rat because of the company he kept. He was really more of a mouse. He'd have loved to huddle up cozy, only he kept on smelling cheese."

"You think so? Well if it pleases you, all right. Trent was the dormouse. You were just the doormat! But now he's dead."

"Yes," said Trudi. "And I . . ."

She thought of Trent writing his lonely letter in the dark hours of the morning, saying how he envied her.

She thought of James Dacre, who'd envied her too and loved her enough to save her friend and let her see the truth about himself though he didn't have to.

She thought of the future. One day the phone would ring, she was sure of that, and then she'd find out if her mind was really as made up as she had assured Janet.

But sufficient until the day . . .

". . . and I'm alive," said Trudi Adamson.

"I'll drink to that."

They clinked their glasses together and drank.

MORE MYSTERIOUS PLEASURES

HAROLD ADAMS

MURDER

Carl Wilcox debuts in a story of triple murder which exposes the underbelly of corruption in the town of Corden, shattering the respectability of its most dignified citizens.   #501 $3.50

THE NAKED LIAR

When a sexy young widow is framed for the murder of her husband, Carl Wilcox comes through to help her fight off cops and big-city goons.
                                                                #420 $3.95

THE FOURTH WIDOW

Ex-con/private eye Carl Wilcox is back, investigating the death of a "popular" widow in the Depression-era town of Corden, S.D.
                                                                #502 $3.50

EARL DERR BIGGERS

THE HOUSE WITHOUT A KEY

Charlie Chan debuts in the Honolulu investigation of an expatriate Bostonian's murder.   #421 $3.95

THE CHINESE PARROT

Charlie Chan works to find the key to murders seemingly without victims—but which have left a multitude of clues.   #503 $3.95

BEHIND THAT CURTAIN

Two murders sixteen years apart, one in London, one in San Francisco, each share a major clue in a pair of velvet Chinese slippers. Chan seeks the connection.   #504 $3.95

THE BLACK CAMEL

When movie goddess Sheila Fane is murdered in her Hawaiian pavilion, Chan discovers an interrelated crime in a murky Hollywood mystery from the past.   #505 $3.95

CHARLIE CHAN CARRIES ON

An elusive transcontinental killer dogs the heels of the Lofton Round the World Cruise. When the touring party reaches Honolulu, the murderer finally meets his match.   #506 $3.95

JAMES M. CAIN
THE ENCHANTED ISLE
A beautiful runaway is involved in a deadly bank robbery in this posthumously published novel.   #415 $3.95

CLOUD NINE
Two brothers—one good, one evil—battle over a million-dollar land deal and a luscious 16-year-old in this posthumously published novel.
#507 $3.95

ROBERT CAMPBELL
IN LA-LA LAND WE TRUST
Child porn, snuff films, and drunken TV stars in fast cars—that's what makes the L.A. world go 'round. Whistler, a luckless P.I., finds that it's not good to know too much about the porn trade in the City of Angels.
#508 $3.95

GEORGE C. CHESBRO
VEIL
Clairvoyant artist Veil Kendry volunteers to be tested at the Institute for Human Studies and finds that his life is in deadly peril; is he threatened by the Institute, the Army, or the CIA?   #509 $3.95

WILLIAM L. DeANDREA
THE LUNATIC FRINGE
Police Commissioner Teddy Roosevelt and Officer Dennis Muldoon comb 1896 New York for a missing exotic dancer who holds the key to the murder of a prominent political cartoonist.   #306 $3.95

SNARK
Espionage agent Bellman must locate the missing director of British Intelligence—and elude a master terrorist who has sworn to kill him.
#510 $3.50

KILLED IN THE ACT
Brash, witty Matt Cobb, TV network troubleshooter, must contend with bizarre crimes connected with a TV spectacular—one of which is a murder committed before 40 million witnesses.   #511 $3.50

KILLED WITH A PASSION
In seeking to clear an old college friend of murder, Matt Cobb must deal with the Mad Karate Killer and the Organic Hit Man, among other eccentric criminals.   #512 $3.50

KILLED ON THE ICE
When a famous psychiatrist is stabbed in a Manhattan skating rink, Matt Cobb finds it necessary to protect a beautiful Olympic skater who appears to be the next victim.   #513 $3.50

JAMES ELLROY
SUICIDE HILL
Brilliant L.A. Police sergeant Lloyd Hopkins teams up with the FBI to solve a series of inside bank robberies—but is he working with or against them?   #514 $3.95

PAUL ENGLEMAN
CATCH A FALLEN ANGEL
Private eye Mark Renzler becomes involved in publishing mayhem and murder when two slick mens' magazines battle for control of the lucrative market.   #515 $3.50

LOREN D. ESTLEMAN
ROSES ARE DEAD
Someone's put a contract out on freelance hit man Peter Macklin. Is he as good as the killers on his trail?   #516 $3.95

ANY MAN'S DEATH
Hit man Peter Macklin is engaged to keep a famous television evangelist *alive*—quite a switch from his normal line.   #517 $3.95

DICK FRANCIS
THE SPORT OF QUEENS
The autobiography of the celebrated race jockey/crime novelist.
                                                            #410 $3.95

JOHN GARDNER
THE GARDEN OF WEAPONS
Big Herbie Kruger returns to East Berlin to uncover a double agent. He confronts his own past and life's only certainty—death.
                                                            #103 $4.50

BRIAN GARFIELD
DEATH WISH
Paul Benjamin is a modern-day New York vigilante, stalking the rapist-killers who victimized his wife and daughter. The basis for the Charles Bronson movie.   #301 $3.95

DEATH SENTENCE
A riveting sequel to *Death Wish*. The action moves to Chicago as Paul Benjamin continues his heroic (or is it psychotic?) mission to make city streets safe.   #302 $3.95

TRIPWIRE
A crime novel set in the American West of the late 1800s. Boag, a black outlaw, seeks revenge on the white cohorts who left him for dead. "One of the most compelling characters in recent fiction."—Robert Ludlum.   #303 $3.95

FEAR IN A HANDFUL OF DUST
Four psychiatrists, three men and a woman, struggle across the blazing Arizona desert—pursued by a fanatic killer they themselves have judged insane. "Unique and disturbing."—Alfred Coppel.   #304 $3.95

JOE GORES
A TIME OF PREDATORS
When Paula Halstead kills herself after witnessing a horrid crime, her husband vows to avenge her death. Winner of the Edgar Allan Poe Award. #215 $3.95

COME MORNING
Two million in diamonds are at stake, and the ex-con who knows their whereabouts may have trouble staying alive if he turns them up at the wrong moment. #518 $3.95

NAT HENTOFF
BLUES FOR CHARLIE DARWIN
Gritty, colorful Greenwich Village sets the scene for Noah Green and Sam McKibbon, two street-wise New York cops who are as at home in jazz clubs as they are at a homicide scene. #208 $3.95

THE MAN FROM INTERNAL AFFAIRS
Detective Noah Green wants to know who's stuffing corpses into East Village garbage cans . . . and who's lying about him to the Internal Affairs Division. #409 $3.95

PATRICIA HIGHSMITH
THE BLUNDERER
An unhappy husband attempts to kill his wife by applying the murderous methods of another man. When things go wrong, he pays a visit to the more successful killer—a dreadful error. #305 $3.95

DOUG HORNIG
THE DARK SIDE
Insurance detective Loren Swift is called to a rural commune to investigate a carbon-monoxide murder. Are the commune inhabitants as gentle as they seem? #519 $3.95

P.D. JAMES/T.A. CRITCHLEY
THE MAUL AND THE PEAR TREE
The noted mystery novelist teams up with a police historian to create a fascinating factual account of the 1811 Ratcliffe Highway murders. #520 $3.95

STUART KAMINSKY'S "TOBY PETERS" SERIES
NEVER CROSS A VAMPIRE
When Bela Lugosi receives a dead bat in the mail, Toby tries to catch the prankster. But Toby's time is at a premium because he's also trying to clear William Faulkner of a murder charge! #107 $3.95

HIGH MIDNIGHT
When Gary Cooper and Ernest Hemingway come to Toby for protection, he tries to save them from vicious blackmailers. #106 $3.95

HE DONE HER WRONG
Someone has stolen Mae West's autobiography, and when she asks Toby to come up and see her sometime, he doesn't know how deadly a visit it could be. #105 $3.95

BULLET FOR A STAR
Warner Brothers hires Toby Peters to clear the name of Errol Flynn, a blackmail victim with a penchant for young girls. The first novel in the acclaimed Hollywood-based private eye series. #308 $3.95

THE FALA FACTOR
Toby comes to the rescue of lady-in-distress Eleanor Roosevelt, and must match wits with a right-wing fanatic who is scheming to overthrow the U.S. Government. #309 $3.95

JOSEPH KOENIG
FLOATER
Florida Everglades sheriff Buck White matches wits with a Miami murder-and-larceny team who just may have hidden his ex-wife's corpse in a remote bayou. #521 $3.50

ELMORE LEONARD
THE HUNTED
Long out of print, this 1974 novel by the author of *Glitz* details the attempts of a man to escape killers from his past. #401 $3.95

MR. MAJESTYK
Sometimes bad guys can push a good man too far, and when that good guy is a Special Forces veteran, everyone had better duck. #402 $3.95

THE BIG BOUNCE
Suspense and black comedy are cleverly combined in this tale of a dangerous drifter's affair with a beautiful woman out for kicks. #403 $3.95

ELSA LEWIN
I, ANNA
A recently divorced woman commits murder to avenge her degradation at the hands of a sleazy lothario. #522 $3.50

THOMAS MAXWELL
KISS ME ONCE
An epic *roman noir* which explores the romantic but seamy underworld of New York during the WWII years. When the good guys are off fighting in Europe, the bad guys run amok in America. #523 $3.95

THE CURSE OF THE PHAROAHS
Amelia and Radcliffe Emerson head for Egypt to excavate a cursed tomb but must confront the burial ground's evil history before it claims them both.   #210 $3.95

THE SEVENTH SINNER
Murder in an ancient subterranean Roman temple sparks Jacqueline Kirby's first recorded case.   #411 $3.95

THE MURDERS OF RICHARD III
Death by archaic means haunts the costumed weekend get-together of a group of eccentric Ricardians.   #412 $3.95

ANTHONY PRICE
THE LABYRINTH MAKERS
Dr. David Audley does his job too well in his first documented case, embarrassing British Intelligence, the CIA, and the KGB in one swoop.
                                                              #404 $3.95

THE ALAMUT AMBUSH
Alamut, in Northern Persia, is considered by many to be the original home of terrorism. Audley moves to the Mideast to put the cap on an explosive threat.   #405 $3.95

COLONEL BUTLER'S WOLF
The Soviets are recruiting spies from among Oxford's best and brightest; it's up to Dr. Audley to identify the Russian wolf in don's clothing.
                                                              #527 $3.95

OCTOBER MEN
Dr. Audley's "holiday" in Rome stirs up old Intelligence feuds and echoes of partisan warfare during World War II—and leads him into new danger.   #529 $3.95

OTHER PATHS TO GLORY
What can a World War I battlefield in France have in common with a deadly secret of the present? A modern assault on Bouillet Wood leads to the answers.   #530 $3.95

SION CROSSING
What does the chairman of a new NATO-like committee have to do with the American Civil War? Audley travels to Georgia in this espionage thriller.   #406 $3.95

HERE BE MONSTERS
The assassination of an American veteran forces Dr. David Audley into a confrontation with undercover KGB agents.   #528 $3.95

BILL PRONZINI AND JOHN LUTZ
THE EYE
A lunatic watches over the residents of West 98th Street with a powerful telescope. When his "children" displease him, he is swift to mete out deadly punishment.   #408 $3.95

PATRICK RUELL
RED CHRISTMAS
Murderers and political terrorists come down the chimney during an old-fashioned Dickensian Christmas at a British country inn.
#531 $3.50

DEATH TAKES THE LOW ROAD
William Hazlitt, a universtiy administrator who moonlights as a Soviet mole, is on the run from both Russian and British agents who want him to assassinate an African general.
#532 $3.50

DELL SHANNON
CASE PENDING
In the first novel in the best-selling series, Lt. Luis Mendoza must solve a series of horrifying Los Angeles mutilation murders.
#211 $3.95

THE ACE OF SPADES
When the police find an overdosed junkie, they're ready to write off the case—until the autopsy reveals that this junkie *wasn't* a junkie.
#212 $3.95

EXTRA KILL
In "The Temple of Mystic Truth," Mendoza discovers idol worship, pornography, murder, and the clue to the death of a Los Angeles patrolman.
#213 $3.95

KNAVE OF HEARTS
Mendoza must clear the name of the L.A.P.D. when it's discovered that an innocent man has been executed and the real killer is still on the loose.
#214 $3.95

DEATH OF A BUSYBODY
When the West Coast's most industrious gossip and meddler turns up dead in a freight yard, Mendoza must work without clues to find the killer of a woman who had offended nearly everyone in Los Angeles.
#315 $3.95

DOUBLE BLUFF
Mendoza goes against the evidence to dissect what looks like an air-tight case against suspected wife-killer Francis Ingram—a man the lieutenant insists is too nice to be a murderer.
#316 $3.95

MARK OF MURDER
Mendoza investigates the near-fatal attack on an old friend as well as trying to track down an insane serial killer.
#417 $3.95

ROOT OF ALL EVIL
The murder of a "nice" girl leads Mendoza to team up with the FBI in the search for her not-so-nice boyfriend—a Soviet agent.
#418 $3.95

JULIE SMITH
TRUE-LIFE ADVENTURE
Paul McDonald earned a meager living ghosting reports for a San Francisco private eye until the gumshoe turned up dead . . . now the killers are after him.   #407 $3.95

TOURIST TRAP
A lunatic is out to destroy San Francisco's tourism industry; can feisty lawyer/sleuth Rebecca Schwartz stop him while clearing an innocent man of a murder charge?   #533 $3.95

ROSS H. SPENCER
THE MISSING BISHOP
Chicago P.I. Buzz Deckard has a missing person to find. Unfortunately his client has disappeared as well, and no one else seems to be who or what they claim.   #416 $3.50

MONASTERY NIGHTMARE
Chicago P.I. Luke Lassiter tries his hand at writing novels, and encounters murder in an abandoned monastery.   #534 $3.50

REX STOUT
UNDER THE ANDES
A long-lost 1914 fantasy novel from the creator of the immortal Nero Wolfe series. "The most exciting yarn we have read since *Tarzan of the Apes.*"—*All-Story Magazine*.   #419 $3.50

ROSS THOMAS
CAST A YELLOW SHADOW
McCorkle's wife is kidnapped by agents of the South African government. The ransom—his cohort Padillo must assassinate their prime minister.   #535 $3.95

THE SINGAPORE WINK
Ex-Hollywood stunt man Ed Cauthorne is offered $25,000 to search for colleague Angelo Sacchetti—a man he thought he'd killed in Singapore two years earlier.   #536 $3.95

THE FOOLS IN TOWN ARE ON OUR SIDE
Lucifer Dye, just resigned from a top secret U.S. Intelligence post, accepts a princely fee to undertake the corruption of an entire American city.   #537 $3.95

JIM THOMPSON
THE KILL-OFF
Luanne Devore was loathed by everyone in her small New England town. Her plots and designs threatened to destroy them—unless they destroyed her first.   #538 $3.95

DONALD E. WESTLAKE
THE HOT ROCK
The unlucky master thief John Dortmunder debuts in this spectacular caper novel. How many times do you have to steal an emerald to make sure it *stays* stolen? #539 $3.95

BANK SHOT
Dortmunder and company return. A bank is temporarily housed in a trailer, so why not just hook it up and make off with the whole shebang? Too bad nothing is ever that simple. #540 $3.95

THE BUSY BODY
Aloysius Engel is a gangster, the Big Man's right hand. So when he's ordered to dig a suit loaded with drugs out of a fresh grave, how come the corpse it's wrapped around won't lie still? #541 $3.95

THE SPY IN THE OINTMENT
Pacifist agitator J. Eugene Raxford is mistakenly listed as a terrorist by the FBI, which leads to his enforced recruitment to a group bent on world domination. Will very good Good triumph over absolutely villainous Evil? #542 $3.95

GOD SAVE THE MARK
Fred Fitch is the sucker's sucker—con men line up to bilk him. But when he inherits $300,000 from a murdered uncle, he finds it necessary to dodge killers as well as hustlers. #543 $3.95

TERI WHITE
TIGHTROPE
This second novel featuring L.A. cops Blue Maguire and Spaceman Kowalski takes them into the nooks and crannies of the city's Little Saigon. #544 $3.95

COLLIN WILCOX
VICTIMS
Lt. Frank Hastings investigates the murder of a police colleague in the home of a powerful—and nasty—San Francisco attorney. #413 $3.95

NIGHT GAMES
Lt. Frank Hastings of the San Francisco Police returns to investigate the at-home death of an unfaithful husband—whose affairs have led to his murder. #545 $3.95

DAVID WILLIAMS' "MARK TREASURE" SERIES
UNHOLY WRIT
London financier Mark Treasure helps a friend reaquire some property. He stays to unravel the mystery when a Shakespeare manuscript is discovered and foul murder done.   #112 $3.95

TREASURE BY DEGREES
Mark Treasure discovers there's nothing funny about a board game called "Funny Farms." When he becomes involved in the takeover struggle for a small university, he also finds there's nothing funny about murder.   #113 $3.95

■ ■